Love
WITHOUT
CONTROL

THE BOUVIER FAMILY SAGA

book 4

Cover Design by KB Barrett Designs

Editing and proofreading by **Chrisandra's Corrections**

This is a work of fiction. Names, characters, businesses and locations are either products of the writer's imagination or used in a fictitious manner. Any resemblance to actual persons, living or dead, is purely coincidental.

⚠ **TW: Missing Person, Human Trafficking, Some scenes of violence**

CONTENTS

Author's Note

There are some dark themes in this book, including human trafficking. Most families in real life don't get a happy ending like Evie's family did, and that absolutely kills me. I've cried more while writing this book than any of my others, and my heart goes out to all the victims, survivors, and their families.

If you or anyone you know is a victim of trafficking, the National Human Trafficking Hotline can help. There is also plenty of information there so you can better educate yourself about this international crisis. Here is their contact information:

Website: https://humantraffickinghotline.org/en

Phone Number: 1-888-373-7888

Text* 233733

If you'd like to donate to causes related to trafficking, here is an article I found on the subject: https://theexodusroad.com/trustworthy-human-trafficking-nonprofits/

I've provided this link for informational purposes only. Please do your research to determine which organizations align with your goals to help.

PROLOGUE

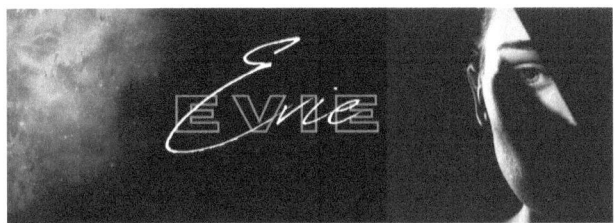

I WALK TOWARD THE man I haven't seen in years, my heart hammering in my chest. My brother, Monty Bouvier.

God, he's gotten big. Which is a silly thought because he's a grown-ass man now, and the last time I saw him in person, he was only seventeen.

He stares at me with confusion on his face, and I see the moment he recognizes me. We simultaneously break into a run, our arms entwining around each other when our bodies crash together. He's so strong now, lifting me from my feet with ease as my legs wrap around his waist.

Tears. Nothing exists except for the tears of sorrow and regret that stream down my face and soak his shirt. I can feel his own grief dripping down my neck.

We say nothing for the longest time, aside from murmuring each other's names. His comes out as a question each time, as if to assure himself that it's really me.

"Evie?"

"Monty."

"Evie?"

We go back and forth like that until he finally pulls his head from my neck and searches my face. His blue eyes mirror my own, blue and extremely wet.

"It's you." His tone is awestruck and raspy as he touches my face and swipes at my tears. "It's really you." My brother's voice is so damn deep now, but there are cracks between each word that I know match the cracks in his heart.

Because of me.

"It's really me," I promise him.

Monty shakes his head back and forth, his expression a jumble of wonder and confusion as he sets me down.

"Where have you been all this time? What the hell happened to you, Evie?"

Well, here the fuck we go.

I heave out a long breath and spit it out. "I was kidnapped."

My brother's expression transforms into one of rage, of the protective big brother, even though he's a year younger than me. "By whom?" he grits out.

I glance over my shoulder at the man standing nervously near a tree about twenty yards away, his face a mask of apprehension as our eyes meet.

Dear god, Monty is going to kill him.

But I can't let that happen. Because while Dane is the man who took me away from my family, the man who was my captor...

He is also the man I love.

CHAPTER 1

AGE 18

"I am not banging the dude with the mullet." The proclamation was punctuated by the slap of my hand on the shiny wooden table.

"But did you see the size of his bulge?" my friend Holly Draper asked, her hazel eyes rounder than usual. "Good grief! He's like a one-man meat packing plant. You know how they say mullets are business in the front and party in the back? Well, this dude's front is screaming party to me. A *big* party."

I laughed, along with my other four friends, at Holly's antics. We'd just finished eating dinner at the casual beachside restaurant at our resort in Mexico, and now we were relaxing with our second round of margaritas. *Or was it our third?*

Madalynn Papadopoulos, a Greek goddess in human form, dabbed her perfect lips. "I agree. The damn thing stared right at me like a one-eyed monster every time he walked by us on the beach today. But the man only had eyes for you, Evie Bouvier."

Her twin, Emersyn, who wasn't quite as well-groomed as Mady, shook her head. "I disagree. No peen is worth that hairdo."

"Let's vote on it," Holly said, her pearly white grin a sharp contrast to her dark skin.

"No!" I shrieked. "My love life is not up for votes. This is not a bitch-oc-racy."

My best friend, Juliette McNamara, giggled beside me. "Evie's right. It's her choice, and she chooses not to run her fingers through the party in the back."

Madalynn and Holly booed good-naturedly while the other member of our party, Arya Beck, shook her head, straight red hair bouncing in the slight breeze coming off the ocean.

"I think his mustache has herpes," she declared. "Avoid herp 'stache at all costs, Evie."

I hooted with laughter, so happy I'd come on this Spring Break trip with my college friends. I'd gone to Texas last fall, not knowing a soul except for Juliette. She and I met as kids when we were assigned to be roommates at a summer camp in Arkansas. As soon as I'd arrived, Juliette had unashamedly thrown her arms around me and declared that we were going to be besties.

And she wasn't wrong. I freaking adored Juliette McNamara. She was funny, sweet, and a complete dingbat. Juli was an English lit major who could tell you anything you wanted to know about practically any book ever written, but when it came to street smarts, she was severely lack-ing. Which only made her more endearing. The woman was completely gullible; she'd literally been named *Most Likely to Buy an Ice Bridge at the Equator* in her high school yearbook. I'd seen the proof with my own two eyes.

Stirring the last dregs of my frozen margarita, I sucked down the con-tents. "I didn't come here for random hookups. I came here to spend time with all of you."

"I can do both," Madalynn announced with a flip of her long raven locks. "I'm talented like that."

"Then *you* hook up with mullet guy," Emersyn shot back, and then added with faux sweetness, "and let me know if you want me to go to the clinic with you when you're done."

Mady eyed her sister with a glare. "Great, I think the clinic is right beside the salon. Maybe they can wrangle those caterpillars you call eyebrows into submission."

Emersyn responded with a waggling middle finger in her twin's face. These two... they loved each other, but they fought like... well, like sisters.

"So what are we doing tonight?" Arya asked, breaking the sibling stand-off.

Holly's face lit up and she brushed a hand over her short, spiky hairdo. "Oooh, there's this club in town that's supposed to be hot as hell."

My shoulders slumped. "I can't. I promised my brother I wouldn't leave the resort."

"Awww, please, Evie? It will be so much fun!"

"I know, and I don't care if you all go. I just swore to Monty that I would stay on the grounds. He worries about me."

"How is your younger brother?" Madalynn asked, wiggling her perfectly plucked eyebrows.

"Still madly in love with Kassie," I told her pointedly.

Her smile turned catlike. "And what about Auburn? Is he in love with anyone?"

Scoffing, I shook my head. "I'd be surprised if my big bro ever fell in love."

She twisted a finger around one strand of hair. "He needs a good Greek girl."

"Too bad you've never been a good girl a day in your life," her sister retorted, and we all laughed.

Mady glared at her twin before tossing that piece of hair over her tanned shoulder. "That may be true, but I'm a very, *very* good girl at night."

"Ewww! That's my brother," I whined.

I was no stranger to women panting after my brothers. Objectively, they were very good looking with their blue eyes that matched my own and hair that was a few shades darker than mine. Auburn was five years older than me, and Monty was a year younger. I idolized both my brothers, but I was much closer to Mont.

"What are you doing for your birthday this year?" Arya asked me.

"I'll fly home the weekend before and spend it with my family," I told her. "Monty and I share a birthday, and I don't really want him to be alone this year."

"Because his girlfriend just had a miscarriage?" Emersyn asked, with a sad downturn of her lips.

"Yeah, and then Kassie's been ghosting him. I love her to pieces, and I know it's different because she's the one who was actually carrying the baby, but I'm not sure she realizes how hard Monty is taking this. He was so excited about being a dad."

Madalynn shook her head. "That's so sad for him. He seems really sweet. There aren't many teenagers who are happy they knocked up their girlfriend."

"Yeah, it was a shock for them both, but from day one, he supported her. He never missed a doctor's appointment and always made sure she had every single thing she was craving." I handed my debit card over to the waitress to take care of everyone's meal tonight when she brought the black folio. "I'm sure Kassie will get in touch with him soon. Those two are end game."

"Maybe she'll come back for his birthday. Speaking of that, you're the last one of our group turning nineteen," Juliette commented. She, Holly, and the twins had all turned nineteen during the school year, and Arya was already twenty.

"Yep, I'm the baby of our group," I laughed, "and my brothers treat me like I'm the baby of the family even though I'm the middle child."

"Is your father sending his plane for you?" Mady asked, as if that was the most normal thing in the world. And it was for my family and the Papadopouloses. Not so much for Holly and Juliette, whose families were firmly middle class, or Arya, a scholarship pre-med student who was from a low-income family. Her father wasn't around, and her mother had... issues.

"He is," I confirmed. "And I can't wait to see my family again."

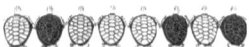

"You didn't have to stay behind with me," I told Juliette as we stepped into the elevator later that evening. "You could have gone to that club with the other girls."

"Nah," she said, pushing the button for the third floor. "I've actually been working on something, and I wanted you to see. Will you come to my room?"

"Of course. What is it?"

She bit her bottom lip, showing a bit of nerves as the car rose. "I've been writing a book."

"No way!" I exclaimed, my eyes popping wide. "What kind of book?"

She scrunched her adorable nose. "It's a romance novel, and I think I love it. I still want to become a librarian, but... I don't know... I have all these words and stories inside me that are dying to get out."

"You can do both," I assured her. "And there's nothing wrong with romance novels. There's a huge market for it, and the genre only seems to be growing."

She unlocked the door to the room she shared with Arya and led me inside before pulling out her computer. Thirty minutes later, I blinked in awe at the screen.

"Juli, this is awesome! And I can't believe you named your main character Evie."

"You don't mind?" she asked, her pretty eyes intent on mine.

"Heck no. In fact, I want to be Book Evie. She's certainly getting more action than me."

Juliette laughed. "Okay, but let me know if you want me to change the name. I can do that easily."

"Don't you dare," I said, leaning over and giving her a big hug. "I'm honored. I know it was only fifteen chapters, but what you've written so far is fantastic. I can't wait to read what happens next. Are you going to publish it?"

"I'm looking for an editor. I joined some Facebook groups for romance authors, and the ladies there are so nice. Very willing to give suggestions to aspiring authors. There's one author named AK Landow who is amazing. Her books are so funny and hot." The smile widened on her beautiful face. "She reminds me a lot of you. She's super sweet but also so fucking sarcastic. She's really helped me a lot."

"That's so cool that she's willing to help."

"I know," Juli said, her aqua-blue eyes wide. "We even talk on the phone sometimes. We had an hour-long conversation the other day about whether or not lube is necessary for anal sex."

I tried not to scrunch up my nose. "I'm voting yes on that." Though I was by no means an expert since I'd never actually done that particular act. "I'm really proud of you, Juli, and I want to buy the first copy when you publish it."

"*If* I publish it," she insisted.

"*When* you publish it," I insisted harder. "Also, where can I find a Colton in real life?"

"If I figure it out, I'll let you know while I'm trying to find out if he has a brother or something for me." Juli reached out and squeezed my bicep. "You deserve a good man, Evie. You haven't even seemed interested in anyone else since you broke up with Marty McFly."

That's what she called my ex-boyfriend, Marty, since we broke up a couple months ago. "You know me. I'm a prude."

"You're not a prude," Juliette said firmly. "You're selective about who you share your body with, and that's okay. Better than okay. The way Mady and Holly are with guys... that's fine for them, but it wouldn't work for you."

I nodded. I'd only had sex with two guys in my life. The first was my high school boyfriend, and the other was Marty, who I met at a party a few weeks after starting college. Our relationship had been going strong. Or so I'd thought until I overheard him telling a friend he was only with me because of my family.

Marty was majoring in fashion merchandising, and my family owned one of the biggest fashion companies in the United States. Bouvier clothing had been worn on every newsworthy red carpet for the past few decades, and apparently, Marty wanted a piece of the Bouvier pie.

Juliette wrapped her long blonde hair into a messy knot on top of her head. "You'll find a man who's worthy of you when it's your time, Evie. Marty was a fucking prick, and he can go suck a big fat donkey cock."

I laughed at that. My bestie had the face of an angel, with delicate features and wide crystal aqua eyes. That mouth of hers though... It was comical hearing those words come from her sweet face in that melodic voice of hers.

"How are things going with you and Bryan?" I asked, leaning forward and lowering my voice as my eyes darted toward her laptop. "And was that hot-as-sin sex scene based on actual experience with him?"

She laughed. "Oh hell no. Bry has a big dick, but he's still learning how to use it effectively. It's just kind of in-out-in-out procedure without any real finesse at this point. We'll get there though."

"He's only twenty-one. Plenty of time to let his sexual prowess mature." I lifted my arms over my head in a long stretch before cautiously saying, "He's got a lot of maturing to do in several areas."

"No doubt. His parents did everything for him growing up. I'm convinced he would have died by now if he didn't have good roommates when he moved off to college. The other day, he told me his dad informed him it was time for an oil change, but he didn't know where to go or what to do." She rolled her eyes with a dramatic flair. "I, on the other hand, learned to change the oil in a car when I was twelve in my dad's shop."

I snickered. "You're like Marisa Tomei in *My Cousin Vinny*."

"Oh my god, she was such a boss biotch in that movie. I love her!"

"Me too," I said, stifling a yawn. "I think I'm going to hit the sack."

"What are we doing tomorrow?" Juli asked, taking my seat in front of her laptop when I stood.

"Beach day, and then the resort is hosting the bonfire and beach party tomorrow night."

"Oooh, that's going to be so much fun. I think I'm going to bang out another chapter before bed."

"Will Book Evie be doing any banging?" I asked, wiggling my eyebrows at her.

"Oh girl, I'm gonna do you right. Book Evie is about to get bent over every flat surface in that restaurant."

I laughed and headed toward the door to go up to my room on the seventh floor. "I can't wait to live vicariously through my fictional namesake. See you tomorrow, Jules."

She gave me a distracted wave as she trained her eyes on the screen in front of her, already lost in her writing process.

CHAPTER 2

"WHY WAS EMERSYN SO grumpy today?" Juliette asked me in my room the next evening as we got ready for the beach party.

I fingered through the beach waves in my caramel hair before pinning a purple flower clip over one ear. "She didn't get any sleep. Mady brought some dude back to the room, and he apparently made rhinoceros noises while fucking."

My friend burst into laughter while matching my hairstyle with a light-blue flower in her blonde hair. "I can see where that would be distracting."

"She called me about three in the morning and asked if she could come sleep in my room. I told her of course."

The Papadopoulos twins shared a double room on the sixth floor, Juli and Arya's was on the third, and Holly and I both had single rooms on the seventh. I wouldn't have minded sharing with Holly, but I think she'd wanted her privacy. Probably so she could bring her own rhino man to her room without disturbing me. Very thoughtful of her, in my opinion.

"That was nice of you," Juli said, straightening the cups of her sky-blue bikini top. "These sarongs and swimsuits are hot as hell. Tell your dad thank you."

"He said to send pics of us wearing them for the company's Facebook page. *Bouvier* has only recently started making swimwear, and they're marketing them toward people our age."

"Well, let's get pics before we get all glassy-eyed. Wouldn't be good for Paul Bouvier's daughter to look like she's snockered in the posts."

"Agreed. Because I plan to drink all the margaritas tonight."

"This one or this one?" I asked Juliette, handing her my phone.

"The first one," she replied with a firm nod of her head. "Mady's eyes are half closed in the second one. Also, your phone looks like something out of *The Jetsons*. I can't believe how clear these photos are."

"It's called an iPhone," I informed her. "It's made by Apple."

"I've heard of them, but they're way out of my price range. And you can just send that pic to your dad with your phone?" Her voice was incredulous.

"Yep, by email or text message."

I smiled at the picture of the six of us. We looked like a rainbow. Juli and I were in the middle with our lilac and sky-blue bikinis with matching sarongs. The twins were to the right of me in red and orange, and Arya and Holly sported yellow and lime-green on the other side of Juliette. The sun had already set, but our faces were lit by the flames of the big bonfire on the sandy beach.

I was the shortest of the group, a fact that was even more apparent when I stood next to my best friend, who was statuesque. Arya was the same height as Juli, but she had smaller boobs and hips. The Papadopoulos sisters, on the other hand, had enviable curves for days, while Holly looked like a badass motorcycle chick with her spiky hair and tight muscles beneath her dark skin.

After shooting off the picture to my dad, I stuck my phone in my bikini top and joined the ongoing party.

The deejay began playing "Hips Don't Lie" by Shakira, and our little group hit the dance floor, which was actually just a flat area of sand set about thirty feet from the shoreline. There was much bouncing and booty shaking as one song bled into another.

"I'm parched," Arya yelled over the music five songs later. "Let's get some drinks."

The half dozen of us skirted around the deejay booth that was on a raised platform near the stairway leading to the resort.

"Hey, you ladies need some drinks?" a man asked. He was holding a tray of plastic cups and held it out to us.

"Oooh, I want the pink one," Juliette said, reaching for the beverage, but I grabbed her wrist to stop her.

"No thanks. We're going to the bar," I told the guy. He was short and stocky with sandy-brown hair, and his lips turned down when we strolled past him.

"Why are we going all the way to the bar when he had drinks *right there?*" my best friend asked, peeking over her shoulder as I dragged her away.

"He could have put something in them," Emersyn informed her.

"Right, and he was wearing a yellow polo like the staff here, but it didn't have the resort's logo on it," I added. "That seemed shady to me."

"You mean, like, he may have put drugs in the drinks or something?" Juli asked, her guileless aqua eyes rounding. "I didn't know that was really a thing."

"Definitely a thing. Don't ever take a drink from anyone except a bartender." I was going to have to keep an eye on my sweet friend. She'd grown up in a small town in Texas, while I'd grown up partying in New York City, so I was aware of the dangers. I would never forgive myself if something happened to her.

"What can I get you ladies?" the cute bartender asked as we approached the tiki hut that was strung with chili-pepper lights.

I leaned over the bar. "First of all, there's a guy on the other side of the deejay booth trying to give drinks to girls as they pass. He's not wearing the staff shirt with the logo we were told to watch for."

The man squinted into the distance before pulling a walkie-talkie from his hip and speaking into it. "I've alerted security," he told me, hooking the device back on his hip. "Thanks for letting us know."

"No prob. Can we get a round of margaritas?"

We were having so much fun. We'd each had three frosty margaritas, and our entire group had let loose on the makeshift dance floor. The normally reserved Arya had her sarong tied around her head like a scarf, moving her body sinuously as we danced to a cool mashup of "Promiscuous" by Nelly Furtado and "SexyBack" by Justin Timberlake.

A pair of warm hands encircled my waist, and I spun to find a dark-haired guy with a sexy grin and no shirt. "Hey, gorgeous. What's your name?" he asked with a slight Spanish accent. He had a snake tattoo winding down one bicep.

"Evie," I told him, draping my forearms over his shoulders.

"Evie what?"

"Business."

His dark eyebrows rose. "Your name is Evie Business?"

"Yep. My middle name is Nunya."

The man threw back his head and laughed. "Well, it's nice to meet you, Evie Nunya Business. I'm Felipe."

We danced to the rest of the song, and then I backed away, throwing him a friendly wave as I made my way over to my friends. Everyone was covered with a fine sheen of sweat from the heat of the night and the nearby fire, and Mady was holding her mass of dark locks on top of her head.

"That guy was cute," she commented.

"Yeah, he was," I told her. "I'm going to the bar to get a bottle of water. Anyone else want one?"

Everyone raised their hands, and Holly decided to walk with me. "You having fun?" she asked me once we passed the stacks of speakers and the noise level subsided a bit.

"A blast. How about you?"

"Amazing trip. I've seen so much wildlife here. I was hoping to see some turtles nesting though."

"Turtles don't nest here till May, and it usually runs through October," I said, and she shook her head.

"I'm the one majoring in wildlife & fisheries. How the hell do you know more about turtle nesting than I do?" she questioned and then waved her hand. "Never mind. I forgot you're the trivia queen of our group."

"I'm full of useless facts," I agreed with a laugh. "Not to mention, I'm a little obsessed with animals, especially turtles. Plus, you're just a freshman. I'm sure you'll be able to blow my knowledge out of the water once you get into your higher-level classes. I think it's really cool that you want to be a game warden. I don't think I've ever met a female game warden."

"There are quite a few women that work for Texas Parks and Wildlife. Most of them are biologists and/or conservationists though."

"And you're double majoring, right?"

"Yep, also doing criminal justice. That's what my dad did."

"I'm kinda following in my father's footsteps too, though I want to be more on the marketing side of our family's business."

We approached the bar, and a different bartender slid down to wait on us. "Six bottled waters, please," Holly told him and he placed them in a small bag so we could more easily carry them.

Once Holly and I returned to our group, we all downed our waters before joining the dancing crowd once again. I giggled my way through a not-so-great salsa with a guy named Billy, who had the most adorable British accent, and then joined Juliette and Emersyn for a head-banging rendition of an old Ratt song.

"One more margarita before the bar closes!" Madalynn announced, and five minutes later, I was guzzling the tangy beverage to soothe my dry throat. I had never yelled and laughed so much in my life.

"I can't wait for karaoke tomorrow night," Juliette said, licking some grainy salt from the rim of her plastic cup.

"I can't sing worth a shit, but horrible karaoke is the best," I replied with a laugh.

"Eviiiiiiiie!" I turned at my name to find Felipe jogging toward me with a big grin on his face. "Hey, girl. You're mine for the last dance," he insisted, and I drained the rest of my glass, tossing it into a trash can as he grabbed my free hand and dragged me toward the dance area.

The booming beat faded away and morphed into a slower song, "Be Without You" by Mary J. Blige, and Felipe pulled me against his hard body. He really was handsome.

"This has been so much fun. They should do beach parties every night," I proclaimed.

He nodded his agreement, moving our bodies together to the sultry music. "They should. You're American?"

"Yes, what about you?"

"I'm Mexican. I've been to Texas a few times though. Is that where you're from?"

While I was gloriously tipsy, I wasn't drunk enough to give away too much information. "I've been there too," was all I allowed.

Felipe brushed his lips across my cheek before whispering in my ear. "You are so beautiful, Evie."

"Thank you," I replied as our bodies swayed to the music.

"I'd love to spend more time with you. Can I come back to your room?"

I internally startled at his bold question, but I guessed it wasn't that bizarre. People hooked up all the time at these vacation resorts, though that wasn't me.

"That wouldn't be a good idea. I have a roommate," I lied.

"Maybe I could come back tomorrow night and we could take a moonlight swim. Or are you leaving tomorrow?"

"No, we'll be here till Sunday."

He nuzzled at my ear again. "Hmmm, that gives us two more nights together then."

Felipe was being awfully presumptuous. He was cute though. Maybe it wouldn't hurt to hang out with a good-looking guy for a couple nights.

"We could meet up tomorrow night after karaoke. My friends may already have plans for Saturday though," I told him, not wanting to over-commit. I'd see how things went tomorrow.

"I look forward to it," he said, his accent thick in my ear. Then he spun me under his arm before pulling me back against him. His body was warm and firm, the muscles bunching beneath darkly tanned skin. "I'll meet you by the staircase leading to the beach at ten."

"Sounds good," I told him, pressing a kiss to his cheek as the song ended. "See you then, Felipe."

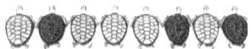

"Well, someone was getting cozy with the hunk," Madalynn teased as we entered the elevator at the resort.

"Yeah, he seemed nice," I said.

The elevator stopped on the third floor, and Juliette and Arya disembarked, calling that they would see us at breakfast. More passengers got off on the fourth and fifth floor and the Papadopoulos twins on the sixth, leaving only me and Holly to ride to the seventh.

"I hate that we're not all on the same floor," I lamented as we walked down the hallway toward our rooms.

"I know. Arya requested it, but the resort said they were already almost fully booked. I guess when you get free rooms, you take what they have left."

Arya had won the vacation package from some radio call-in contest, and it included airfare and three rooms. Since Holly had wanted her own room, she'd paid extra for it.

"I'm going to grab my ice bucket and have a big glass of water before bed," I said when we neared Holly's room.

She paused in the act of inserting her card in the little slot. "Want me to walk with you?"

"No, silly. I'm just right there," I told her, pointing to my room on the opposite side of the corridor and three doors down. "And the ice machine is across the hall from me."

"Okay," she agreed, quickly hugging me before opening her door. "I feel gross, so I think I'll take a shower before hitting the sack."

"See you at breakfast. I'm looking forward to the fruit bar again. That pineapple was so sweet this morning."

"Me too. Bye, Evie."

"Bye," I said, skipping backward down the hallway until her door closed. When I reached my room, I pulled the key card from my bikini top and froze. "Shit, where's my phone?"

I frisked myself like an idiot, though it obviously wasn't in the tiny bit of clothing I was wearing. "Noooo, my dad is going to kill me," I groaned, slumping against the wall. That phone had cost around six hundred dollars, and while that wasn't a lot to someone with as much money as Paul Bouvier had, he was not a man who appreciated wastefulness.

"Shit, shit, shit," I grumbled, pushing away from the wall and opening the stairwell door. I'd just go look for it, and if I didn't find it, I would buy another one myself. I had money now, thanks to the trust fund I'd gotten from my grandparents when I turned eighteen last year.

Still, I wasn't sure if I'd be able to keep my same number on a replacement phone, and then I'd have to admit to my dad that I'd lost mine. I really needed to find it. Jogging down the stairs, I pushed open the door at the bottom, trying to get my bearings. This door didn't lead to the well-lit lobby, instead exiting onto a darkened concrete patio.

Pausing for a moment, I inhaled a deep breath and shook my head. "You're fine, Evie. You're almost nineteen years old. No need to be afraid of the dark."

I skirted around the corner, relieved when I saw the path leading to the beach a few feet away. It had been lit with tiki torches ten minutes ago, but they had all been extinguished, leaving me only the light of the moon to navigate by. No one else seemed to be around.

My eyes scanned the ground as I retraced our steps. Maybe the phone had fallen out while we were dancing. As I passed a copse of palm trees on my right, I noticed the bonfire was burning low down on the beach. That would probably give me enough light to search when I got down there.

Trotting down the stairs, I let out a little shriek when a dark figure appeared in front of me. "Evie?"

"Oh my god," I breathed, patting my chest over my rapidly beating heart. "Felipe, you scared me to death."

"What are you doing out here?" he asked, taking my hand and squeezing it.

"I lost my phone, so I came back to look for it."

"What does it look like?"

"Um..." I held up my hand in the approximate size of the device. "About this big, silver and black."

Felipe's hand reached into his shorts and pulled out an iPhone, his dark brows rising. "Is this it?"

"Yes!" I squealed, reaching for it when he held it out. "Where did you find it?"

"Near the bar. I was about to take it to the front desk."

"Thank you, thank you, thank you," I gushed, giving him a hug. "I was so worried."

"No problemo," he said easily. "I'm glad I found it. It gave me an excuse to see you again." Felipe took my hand and linked his fingers with mine as he guided me back up the stairs.

"What are you doing?"

"Walking you back to the resort to make sure you get there safely."

"Oh, you don't have to do that," I assured him, but in reality, I was glad for the company. It was super dark out here.

When we reached the main walkway, Felipe pulled me to a stop beside the palm trees. "I want to. I like you a lot, Evie."

"I like you too, but I really need to get to—" I stopped when his brown eyes flashed to something behind me. "What are you—"

Something else halted my words that time. A damp rag over my mouth and nose.

"No!" I screamed, but the sound was muffled, and in the next instant, a large arm wrapped around my waist from behind, binding me to a big, flabby body. My eyes met Felipe's, begging him to do something, to punch whoever was holding me, to save me.

But he didn't.

A slow smile crept across his lips, and the realization hit me like a ton of bricks. *Fuck*, I thought as I inhaled the sickly sweet scent of what I assumed was chloroform on the rag. My mind went crazy, knowing I needed to get out of this before I lost consciousness. Managing to lift both my legs and kick out, I felt a sense of satisfaction when one of my bare feet made contact with Felipe's crotch.

"Chingados!" he cursed, doubling over as I flailed my entire body in an attempt to get loose.

The man holding me chuckled. "Ella es una salvaje. Agarra sus piernas."

I'd taken several languages in junior high and high school. My French was excellent, my Italian good, and my Spanish passable. But I knew he'd just called me a wild one and told Felipe to grab my legs.

A wild one? Buddy, you have no fucking idea.

One of my arms was pinned by his thick arm, but he couldn't quite reach the other one, so I used it, reaching up to punch and scratch every inch of his head I could manage. Meanwhile, my legs continued to kick as Felipe—if that was even his name—struggled to grab them.

Both men cursed and grunted, working to contain my wriggling body and one thrashing arm. I kept screaming, hoping someone—*anyone*—would hear me, but all that was audible was a series of muted squawks. I tried elbowing flabby boy in the gut, but it didn't seem to faze him, so I reached up and gathered his hair in my hand, feeling a chunk of coarse strands pull free when I yanked with all my might.

"Puta de mierda," he spit out, tightening his arm around my middle until I was afraid he'd crack my ribs.

After Felipe received a kick to the face—courtesy of my left foot—he finally managed to wrangle my ankles beneath his arms, holding them so tightly against his body it hurt. Despite my fighting, the hand over my mouth and nose was unyielding, and all I could smell was the chemical on that rag.

This is not good. Not good at all.

My body was weakening, but my resolve wasn't, and I knew I needed to try and stay awake to fight them off. I was in another country, and god only knew what their plans were. I needed to get away, to get help, to...

I attempted to jerk my head back and headbutt the man holding me, but my neck felt like it was made of marshmallows, soft and squishy, so the movement was more of a sluggish loll. Darkness began to settle over my struggling body and frantic mind, weighing me down even as I began floating.

The words the two men spoke sounded soupy and thick to my ears, but I made out Felipe's directive. "Lleva a la perra al barco." *Get the bitch to the boat.*

No. Dear god, please. No.

If they took me away from here, no one would know how to find me. Images flickered through the sludge of my brain... Juliette... my other friends... Auburn... Dad... Monty.

Someone please help me. Don't let them take me.

That was my final thought before the darkness swallowed me whole.

CHAPTER 3

THE ENGINE OF MY black Porsche Carrera GT roared as I wheeled around the corner on a darkened, narrow road just north of New York City. I was headed to my father's house since I'd been *summoned*, which irked the fuck out of me.

I absolutely hated my father, Luca Cappitani. The man was disgusting, but he was also very powerful, the underboss of one of the most powerful crime families in the city. So when he said to come to his house, I dutifully—though reluctantly—complied.

"Identification, please," the guard demanded when I wheeled up to the gate outside my father's estate.

"For fuck's sake, Cesare. This is my father's house," I complained, though I reached into my back pocket for my wallet anyway, flopping it open to reveal my driver's license. "And you just saw me here a few weeks ago."

"I do as I'm told," he said, inspecting my license like I was a goddamn criminal here to rob the place, his eyes darting from the card to me several times before nodding his approval. "Have a nice day, Mr. Cappitani."

"Fuck off," I muttered, squealing my tires as I peeled out up the curved, concrete driveway. At the top of the hill sat my father's home, or the Pervert Palace, as I liked to call it. But never to his face, of course. I enjoyed having my head attached to my body.

Wheeling up in front of the mansion, I parked and slid smoothly out of the sleek vehicle before climbing the stairs to the porch. At my knock, the door swung open, and Sebastian, my father's butler, gave me a tight smile.

"Master Damiano. Your father is waiting for you in his study," he intoned formally.

"Thanks, Sebby," I said, knowing the nickname annoyed him but not giving a ripe shit. Crossing the fancy gold marble floor of the foyer, I hung a right to take the dim hallway that ended in a set of wooden double doors. As soon as I lifted my fist to knock, my father yelled at me to come in, and I glanced up to see a camera above the door.

Well, that's new. The fucker got more and more paranoid by the day, especially since he would be taking over as Don of the family once my great-uncle Leo retired or died. I wouldn't put it past my father to have his uncle taken out. He was a power-seeking, ruthless bastard.

I actually liked Uncle Leo. Yeah, he was a criminal, involved in all kinds of shady shit, but we all were in this business. Leo was tough but fair, and he'd always been good to me.

Entering the massive room covered in velvet-patterned green wallpaper, I strolled unhurriedly across the dark, wide-planked floor before taking the seat beside my brother. My father leaned back in his chair and looked at us over his massive desk. Seriously, you could park a fucking Buick on that thing.

"Damiano, aren't you going to say hello to your brother?" he cajoled.

I didn't even spare my sibling a glance. "No. Fuck him."

Our father attempted a scowl but not before we caught his furtive smirk. He loved this shit. After all, he's the one who pitted us against each other all those years ago.

"Now, now. Play nice. Fiero is your brother," he said in a false tone of placation.

"Can we get this meeting started, please?" I asked, flicking my eyes toward Fiero. "The stench in here is ungodly."

Luca chuckled and shook his head. "Okay. I need help with some business and, ah, personal matters this week. I'm flying to Las Vegas for a meeting I can't miss. Fiero, you will go with me on the jet."

"Okay," my brother replied simply.

Our father turned to me. "Your task is a personal favor to me. Since I can't miss this meeting, I need you to go to New Orleans and pick up an... item I have acquired. You'll take the helicopter."

I nodded slowly, trying not to let him see my excitement. New Orleans was a fun city, and I hadn't been in a couple years. Lots of amusing trouble I could get into there. "Fine," I told him, maintaining my surly attitude. "What will I be picking up?"

Hell, it could be anything. Guns. Money. Or...

"It's not drugs is it?" I asked, my stomach coiling like a rope.

My father's face reddened, as if he were about to explode with rage. "No, for fuck's sake. I'm aware of your issues, which I'm getting sick of, by the way. You need to stop being such a goddamn pussy about that." I easily could have killed him without a second of remorse. He sat back and smiled smugly, lowering his voice. "I'm acquiring a new... friend."

A woman.

"What happened to Maryanne?" I asked, hiding my disgust by pulling out my knife and flicking it open to casually clean beneath my fingernails with the tip.

"I gifted her to one of the capos." *God, he's such a fucking pig.* "Then there was Pepper after Maryanne. I don't think you ever met her since you never come to visit me."

"Pepper?" I asked, and my father shrugged.

"Not sure of her real name. That's what I called her because she had a spicy pussy." My fingers tightened around the handle of the knife, and Fiero's knee pressed subtly against mine. A warning. "My pretty Pepper met with an unfortunate accident yesterday, and I need a replacement."

One flick of my wrist, and I could have my blade embedded in his throat. Watch him bleed out like the pig he was. Beside me, Fiero spread his legs, bumping my knee with his once again. Another warning.

But our father didn't notice because he had risen and was twisting the dial on his standing safe in the corner. With some effort, he pulled out three black duffel bags that looked heavy.

"You'll need to take these with you. The folks in New Orleans only deal in cash."

Cash? He was *buying* a woman? Fuck almighty!

Fiero and I were both silent as Father closed the safe and left the bags on the floor before going back behind his desk. "Come around here. I need you to take a look at the friend I've selected. I don't want those fuckers to try the old bait and switch with me."

Friend. That word irked me more than anything. *He's buying a fucking person!* And I was a hundred percent sure she wouldn't want to be *friends* with Luca Cappitani.

Rounding the desk, I stood behind my father's chair as he sat and wiggled the mouse to turn on his desktop computer. His fingers clacked across the keys, bringing up a black-screened website with Goods & Services, Incorporated written across the center in a bold white script. *Well, that's vague.*

"Both of you, turn around while I put in my password," Luca snapped, and we did. After a few keystrokes, he muttered, "Okay, you can look now."

I did and wished I hadn't. My father leaned back in his chair and stroked a finger over his lips as we watched the video on the screen. It was surprisingly clear.

"My girl is number five," he said, almost dazedly.

The camera stalled on a raven-haired Latino woman with the number one on a white sheet of paper duct taped to her chest. She was standing against a wall wearing a tank top and shorts, and her eyes looked hazy as she glanced to her right and then back at the camera. It was obvious she was being coached because she pushed a tremulous smile across her lips.

The view moved to the woman on her left, number two, a blonde who repeated the rightward glance and forced smile. Three was another blonde, and tears dripped down her face as she attempted to push the corners of her lips upward. She looked so afraid, and rightly so.

Woman number four was obviously still affected by whatever drug they'd given her because she swayed as she looked at the ground, her red hair draping across her face. There was no sound on the video, but someone must have snapped at her because her head rose, one hand swiping the damp strands from her face.

I glanced at Fiero, whose lip was curled up into a grimace of revulsion. I'm sure mine looked the same.

"Here she is," Luca said, his words almost coming out in pants as he palmed his crotch. I wondered how difficult it would be to cut off his dick with the letter opener on the corner of the desk.

My eyes slowly returned to the screen and then widened in shock. The caramel-haired beauty also had a number taped to her chest, which was exposed by the light-purple swimsuit she was wearing. She was gorgeous, but the most striking thing about her was the resolute glare in her bright blue eyes.

She didn't smile at all, her lips instead forming a defiant sneer that only made her more beautiful. Bruises dotted her arms and legs—which made me want to hurt whoever had dared to touch her—and when she lifted both hands, I noticed she was the only woman who was bound with thick layers of duct tape around her wrists.

Her blue eyes narrowed toward whoever was speaking off camera and then rolled back to stare out at me. Or it felt like she was looking directly at me... into my fucking soul. Then she bared her teeth in the meanest smile I'd ever seen on such a pretty face at the same time she lifted both middle fingers.

I barked out a laugh—though there was absolutely nothing funny about this situation—but her sheer bravery was captivating. She had to be scared to death, and yet she'd just given a big *fuck you* to whomever was watching. I was weirdly proud of her.

"Worth every penny of the seven million I'm paying for her," Luca muttered. "She's going to be fun to break."

Over my cold, dead body. I wasn't sure where that thought came from, besides being outraged at the treatment of these women like any decent human would be. Not that I was entirely decent. Not even close, but I did have a tiny bit of humanity left in my dark heart.

But this was something greater than mere humanity. It was *her.* Number five. Fuck, I didn't even know her name, but I knew she was something special.

Luca continued, unaware that my hands were reaching for his neck, prepared to strangle him from behind. "Tits are kinda small, but I'll get her some implants."

You sick, motherfucking prick...

I was an inch from taking my father's life when I was yanked backward by the neck of my dark-gray dress shirt. "Okay," Fiero said, "you've seen who he wants. Now get going. I'm tired of fucking looking at you." He shoved me toward the bags on the floor, his brown eyes flashing like a caution flag as he followed me.

Pulling myself from the spell the feisty woman had put me under, I stomped toward the duffels and picked one up. "Make yourself useful and carry one of these to my car," I demanded, shoving it at him. It weighed around fifty pounds.

I picked up the other two as my brother muttered, "Whatever will get you out of here sooner."

Almost to the door, I paused when my father called my name. "Damiano." I glanced over my shoulder to find his smug-as-hell smile. "Don't fuck her. I want her fresh when I get home from Nevada."

The only thing that saved his life was a hard push in the back from my brother. "Jesus. Move already. I've got shit to do."

Every nerve ending in my body was being seared by a fury like I'd never known, but I pushed it way down deep before stopping beside a framed photograph in the foyer. Dropping one of the bags, I kissed my first two fingers and pressed them against the faces of my mother and sister. When I was done, Fiero did the same.

Then I picked up the dropped duffel and walked out the front door, which was being held by Sebastian, with my brother on my heels. Popping open the trunk, I shifted my eyes to find Fiero looking warily at me.

"You all right?" he muttered under his breath.

"He's buying a fucking human," I hissed.

"I'll talk to Leo," he whispered, making a show of shoving me aside when a guard approached, armed with a semi-automatic rifle as he made his rounds. "Jesus, let me do it. You can't fucking do anything right." That was said in a louder voice for the benefit of the guard.

The big dude chuckled. "You two try not to kill each other in the driveway. The gardener's going to be pissed if he has to break out the power washer to clean up the stains."

"I'll make sure to shove Fiero into the grass before I blow his brains out," I commented, earning me another laugh from the man as he sauntered around the corner of the house.

My brother and I had to put on this show of hatred for each other, although, in actuality, he was the only person in the world I gave a shit about. However, we couldn't let our father know that. In his mind, any loyalty shown to anyone but him was a betrayal.

Once the guard was gone, Fiero shoved his bag of money into the trunk. "You need to keep your cool, Dame. I saw you almost lose it in there."

"That was a goddamn trafficking site. Has he done this before?"

My brother shook his head. "Not that I know of. He usually picks up a girl in the club and then takes her home and keeps her. Leo's not going to be happy when he finds out."

I nodded, wedging one of my duffels into the trunk. "He's done his best to keep any kind of human trafficking out of our business." Picking up the other bag, I realized it wasn't going to fit into the tiny trunk of the Porsche and went around to the passenger side, sticking the final bag of money onto the seat.

"I'll talk to Leo and try to take care of this."

"Thanks, Fi," I said quietly, glancing around to make sure no one was looking. We couldn't even risk a fist bump or handshake of solidarity because there were cameras everywhere outside our father's estate. "Stay safe, brother."

"You too," he said, giving me a solemn nod.

As I climbed in my car and drove away, the stunning blue eyes of the woman my father was purchasing floated through my mind, and I hoped Leo could get Luca Cappitani in check. Because there was no way I was handing that fierce angel over to be abused by the man I despised.

No way in hell.

Chapter 4

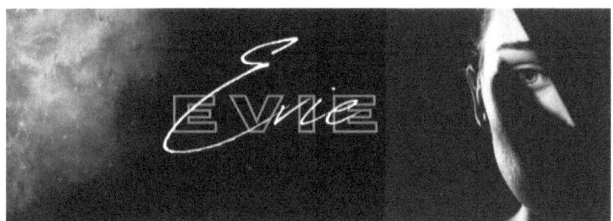

Smile pretty for your new owner.

These fucking assholes.

I'd earned a backhand to the face for my double middle finger stunt when they were done filming me, and my cheek still stung. But hell. I'd never been more pissed off in my life. Or afraid.

I never knew this about myself before, but apparently fear made me stupid.

When I woke up after being taken in Cancún, I was in some kind of warehouse, fairly certain I was still near the Gulf of Mexico, if the warmth and the smell of salty air was any indication. Felipe and flabby guy, who I learned was named Ethan, had been joined by five other men with big guns who strolled around inside the warehouse. Despite their well-armed status, I had tried to run as soon as my legs were able to work again, and after that, they'd taped my wrists together and put handcuffs around my ankles.

There were four other women being held here, and the one beside me didn't seem to be handling the chloroform—or whatever drug they'd used to take us—well. She'd thrown up twice already.

When they started filming us one by one, I thought it was for some ransom thing they were pulling—trying to get money from our families—but when Felipe had instructed me to smile for my new *owner*, that's when realization set in like a ton of bricks. This was no kidnapping for ransom; I was being trafficked.

After the filming, we were allowed to sit on the floor, and they passed out lukewarm bottles of water and granola bars. I ate and drank ravenously, knowing I would need my strength if I was to escape.

"Okay, beautiful ladies," Ethan crooned, "it's time to move to the next location."

They're moving us? Maybe this would be a good time to try and get away again.

The only problem with that ill-advised plan? Having your ankles cuffed together is not conducive to running, and I only ended up with scraped knees and hands for my efforts when I fell on the concrete outside.

One of the guards pulled me up by my hair and roughly led me to a large cargo truck in the parking lot, my feet shuffling to try and keep up. When I inched my way up the ramp and into the back, my scraped knees almost gave way as Felipe pushed aside a panel on the inside of the truck, revealing a dauntingly narrow hidden compartment.

My heart slammed against my ribs, and I fought back tears. I hadn't cried in front of these assholes yet, and I wasn't going to start now. But I wanted to because it was obvious they were going to put us in that tiny space. It was at least a hundred and ten degrees in the back of this truck and closing us up in that narrow area would only make it worse.

I noticed five sets of chains bolted into the wall, and that's when I knew with certainty...

Even if I managed to survive this journey, I was never going to see my family again.

CHAPTER 5

"AND THEN THE ALIENS fed me Cheez-Its before dropping me back on Earth," Rodrigo said.

"Umhmm, that's nice," I murmured before what he said registered. I snapped my head toward him. "Wait, what?"

My longtime friend and confidant chuckled as he piloted the helicopter through the dark Louisiana sky. "Just seeing if you were paying attention. You weren't, by the way."

"Damn. Did I miss the part where you got an anal probe?" I asked, amusement pulling me from my thoughts.

"I declined that particular procedure," he quipped, maneuvering the control wheel to bank us slightly to the south. "You want to tell me what's going on that's got you so distracted?"

A puff of breath left me on a sigh. "I'm just not thrilled about this... *assignment*." That last word curled into a sneer.

Rodrigo's eyes darted toward the back where a plastic bag of chains, straps, handcuffs, and tape sat on an empty seat. "Who are we picking up?"

"A girl." But she was more than a girl. She may be young, but she was a woman. A feisty woman that had fascinated me with a set of blue eyes and rebellious middle fingers. "He bought her."

His head jerked back, and his mouth turned down in disgust. "Dear god. What the fuck?"

"Fi is going to talk to Leo and see if he'll set Luca straight on this. He's the only one who can control him. Hopefully, by the time I've gotten her, our directive will have changed and we can get her back to her family."

Rod shook his head. "I need to fucking retire from this shit."

"You should. Spend some time with that new granddaughter of yours."

The man's eyes lit up like the Fourth of July in the dim light of the cockpit. "She's such an angel. I'm her favorite person, you know."

"I have no doubt, Rod. Tell me more about her." *And distract me from the task that lies ahead of me tonight.*

After a couple refueling stops, we landed at a private airstrip north of New Orleans, and I stepped out of the chopper and into the muggy night air, my ears still buzzing from the noise.

"Damiano, my boy!"

I did my best not to roll my eyes. Guido Conte—or *cunty*, as I liked to call him—was twenty-seven years old, only two years older than me, but he always insisted on calling me *my boy* like he was my grandpa or some shit. In a pale-blue velvety tracksuit, an overextended belly, and gold chains around his neck, he looked every bit the low-level mobster he was.

"Guido," I greeted shortly. I hated this fucker.

He began unloading the bags from the helicopter and placing them in the black sedan that was waiting on the tarmac for me. "I'm putting the money bags in the trunk. Where do you want this?" he asked, holding up the bag of restraints.

"Toss them in the trunk too. I won't need them." *Hopefully.*

He eyed me curiously before doing as I asked. "I put the address to the location in the GPS, as well as the address where you'll be staying tonight. It's a safe house we keep here."

"I thought we were flying back tonight," I protested.

"Naw, Luca wants Rodrigo to get some sleep. Otherwise, he'll be over on his flight hours, according to the FAA. You'll leave in the morning."

My father would buy an actual human being, but god forbid he break Federal Aviation Administration rules. *Mafia morals.*

Grabbing my leather Nike go-bag from the helicopter, I placed it in the backseat of the sedan. I never went on an assignment without it.

"Fine. What time are we leaving in the morning?"

"Eight sharp." Then he cast a leering grin my way. "Don't have too much fun with the new... *acquisition* and oversleep."

My fingers twitched, wanting to reach for the pistol hidden beneath my finely cut gray suit. I may be a lot of things—most of them bad—but a fucking rapist wasn't one of them.

"I'll be here."

"One more thing," Guido said, handing me the keys to the car. "Your father said to leave the money locked in the car while you go inside the house and inspect the merchandise. This is the first time he's working with these guys, and he doesn't trust them."

"Never trust a criminal," I quipped, feigning nonchalance, though I felt that twinge to reach for my weapon again at his mention of *the merchandise.*

The drive to the destination was short, and I paused the vehicle in front of the huge house, a white building with a hipped roof. Dual galleries—a type of porch or balcony—rested one above the other, the top being held up by white columns. In the classic architecture of an older New Orleans home, intricate balusters framed the top balcony.

It looked nondescript, a typical house on the corner of a seemingly quiet neighborhood. Per my instructions, I pulled around to the back and punched in a number on the keypad that was positioned in front of a tall, wrought iron gate. It slid aside, and I pulled in, finding a single guard in front of the wooden door around back.

Leaving the money in the car, I locked it and approached.

"Name?" the word was a mere grunt from the burly guard, who was holding a semi-automatic weapon in his large hands.

"Cappitani."

"Identification." I whipped it out and he inspected it before nodding. "You're the last one to arrive. All the others have picked up their merchandise already."

There was that word again. *Merchandise.* Jesus, what the fuck was wrong with these people?

Without a word, I reached for the doorknob, but he stopped me with an arm across the door.

"I need your weapon before you go in," he informed me, nodding toward an empty wooden box on a small table beside him.

I pulled my Beretta from my shoulder holster and placed it inside, and as I was about to reach for the pistol tucked into the back of my pants, the guard moved his arm and pushed open the door. *Huh? Did he honestly think I only carried one piece? Dumb fuck.*

Covering my movement by pretending to straighten my suit jacket, I rolled with it, stepping inside with the silenced 9mm still concealed at my lower back. "Go down the hallway, through the living room, and to the hall on the other side. Last door on the right," he instructed, closing the door behind me.

The hallway was narrow and dim, lit only by brass sconces every few feet that emitted a dull, yellow glow that revealed a faded floral wallpaper. My eyes swept everything, noting that the doors on either side of the corridor were open and the rooms beyond them empty.

I passed a kitchen on the right and noticed the small wooden table littered with beer and liquor bottles, but there were no people present. Making my way down the hall on the other side of the living room, I slowly approached the last door on the right, which was slightly open. With my back pressed against the wall, I peeked through the small crack and saw two men sitting on a mattress on the floor, both scrolling on their phones.

I didn't see the girl, but I could hear her. "Helloooo? I said I need some water."

"No," the man on the left side said without even looking up. "If I give you water, you'll need to pee, and I'm not going through that shit again."

The speaker was blond and chunky, while the other man was more well-built and appeared to be Latino. A pistol sat on a weathered night-stand beside chunky.

"Awww, I'm sorry," the female voice said mockingly. "Did I hurt your teeny-tiny little balls? I should get some kind of award for actually finding them with my knee."

The man glared toward the corner of the room not visible to me. "Shut the fuck up, Evie."

Evie. Her name is Evie. I liked it.

"I will not shut the fuck up until you bring me some water, Ethan. It's been, like, eight hours since I've had anything to drink. I'm going to get a kidney infection."

"I. Don't. Care," he gritted out.

"What kind of name is Ethan for a kidnapper anyway?" Evie taunted. "Sounds like you should be the third-string quarterback at a prep school."

I could hear his teeth grinding from out here, and I smiled to myself. She knew how to push his buttons. Probably not the smartest idea, but I liked it nonetheless. "I'll have you know, I was second-string."

"Ohhh, very impressive. If I wasn't fucking handcuffed, I'd give you a round of applause," the smartass—who I was liking more and more by the second—shot back. "And you can forget the five-star review on Yelp! for this kidnapping. In fact, I'd like to speak to your manager."

My hand covered my mouth because I was finding it difficult not to laugh.

The Latino man nudged Ethan. "Shut her up. I'm tired of listening to her shit."

The blond stood, picked up a dirty rag from the nightstand, and rounded the bed.

Nope. Not gonna happen.

I pushed open the door and the hinges squeaked, drawing the attention of the two idiots. The dark-haired one stood from the mattress and stuck his phone in the pocket of his cargo shorts.

"Hey, uh, you here to pick up number five?"

I nodded curtly, and then my gaze found her. Not number five. *Evie.* She was sitting with her ankles chained to the legs of a metal chair and her hands bound behind her. The dress she'd obviously been forced to wear was black and slinky, barely covering her toned thighs. My temper flared when I saw her face.

"She's been marked," I snapped.

Ethan pulled at the back of his neck, obviously uncomfortable. "This one gave us a lot of trouble."

Good.

"Unchain her and then leave the room," I commanded, bringing my attention back to the woman. She eyed me warily but didn't speak.

"Felipe, uncuff her," Ethan ordered before turning to me. "You can use the bed, but we need to get paid first before you can fuck her. Want us to get the money from your car?"

I leveled him with a glare so fiery, I was surprised he didn't burst into flames. "No. You're not seeing a dime until I talk to her."

"Talk?" he asked like he didn't know what that word meant.

"Out," I barked in response, my tone steely and unrelenting.

Felipe stood and backed away quickly, probably to avoid Evie's now unchained feet. "Watch your cojones, dude." His fingers brushed across a set of scratch marks on the side of his neck that matched the ones I'd seen on the other guy's face. I wondered if Evie had left them there. I hoped so. "Chick is loco. Don't say we didn't warn you."

The duo left, and I cautiously approached the woman in the chair, who was looking up at me with apprehensive eyes. "I'm not going to hurt you," I said quietly, and her eyebrows squished together, forming a soft pad between them. "Can you stand?"

Evie nodded, and I took both of her hands to help her up. She wobbled on the ridiculously high heels on her feet. They were stilettos and at least six inches. Even with them, she was a tiny thing, and I had to look down at her as I voiced my greatest concern at that moment.

"Did they..." I inhaled a deep breath. "Did they sexually assault you?"

I released the air from my lungs when she shook in the negative and said, "No, they kept threatening to, but I think it's against the rules or something. I heard them talking about it in the hallway."

My thumb brushed ever so gently across the bruise blooming on her right cheek. "Who did this to you?"

She swallowed. "Felipe."

"And this?" I dropped my thumb to just below her lower lip, where a split in the rosy flesh was crusted with blood. My voice was quiet, belying the fury sizzling in my veins.

"That was courtesy of Ethan the fatass."

I nodded, silent for a moment as my mind processed my next move. With this woman standing in front of me, beautiful even though she was battered and bravely afraid, I knew I couldn't hand her over to my father, no matter what Leo decided. I think I knew that from the second I saw her in the video, but the knowledge of that fact was stark in the reality of seeing her in person. Of holding her small hands in mine.

"Take off your shoes, Evie."

Her chin trembled, but she stopped it with an audible click of her teeth clenching together, blue eyes flitting nervously to the bed.

"But... I thought they said..." She couldn't quite manage the quiver of fear in her voice.

"I'm not going to rape you, Evie. Never. I need you to be able to run."

That soft pad of flesh appeared between her eyebrows again. "Why?"

"Because I'm about to fuck some shit up."

Chapter 6

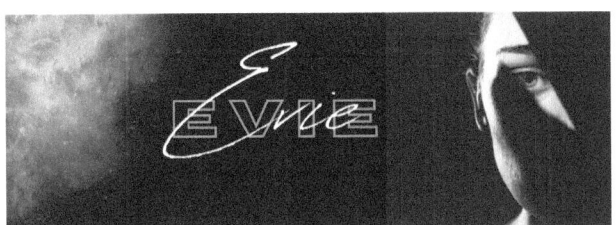

Because I'm about to fuck some shit up.

I wasn't sure why, but those words calmed me just a bit. They probably shouldn't have. *Fuck some shit up.* What did that even mean?

I was fully aware that this man was likely the one who had *purchased* me—*and how messed up is that?*—but I wasn't afraid of him. That was likely stupid on my part because he looked dangerous.

Dark hair swept back from his forehead to reveal brown eyes and high cheekbones. He was model pretty with a perfectly proportioned face—other than his nose, which was slightly crooked from being broken. Tattoos peeked out from beneath the white cuffs of his shirtsleeves.

Everything about him screamed danger, including the... *oh shit.*

The man pulled a black gun with a long tube on the barrel from behind him, and I knew from all the action movies I'd watched with Monty that the tube thing was a silencer. I took a step back, unsure of where the hell I thought I was going to run, but he gave me a sharp shake of his head.

"I'm going to get you out of here and back to your family."

When he whispered those words, realization sunk in, and my knees almost buckled in relief. This guy didn't buy me; he was here to rescue me! He was probably an undercover agent with the FBI. Or was it the CIA? Whoever the hell it was that handled international incidents.

Holding my hand with his free one, he nodded toward my shoes in a silent reminder. I slipped them off, making me have to crane my neck to look up at him. This guy was super tall, and I knew the gray pinstriped suit he wore must be custom made. I'd grown up in the fashion industry, after all, and I knew suits.

"What do I call you?" I asked in a quiet voice.

After a brief hesitation, he said, "Damiano."

"Okay, Agent Damiano. What's the plan?"

His chin jerked back, and a slight smile curled his lips upward, revealing a flash of white teeth. "Just stay behind me and run when I tell you to."

"And then what?"

"Fuck if I know," he muttered, moving to stand between me and the door as he called, "We're done in here." His right hand, the one holding the gun, was hidden behind his thigh.

Prick one and prick two reentered the room, and Ethan rubbed his hands together like a greedy pig. "I'm assuming everything is satisfactory? Ready to make the transaction?"

"Actually, no. My property has been damaged, and I want a discount."

Property? Ah, hell naw! I was about to lift my leg to knee him in the ass when his left hand reached back and found mine, giving it a gentle squeeze of warning. So I kept my mouth shut and my knee down. For now.

"There are no fucking discounts," Felipe snapped. "You agreed to seven million, and you're not leaving here with the girl unless you pay every penny."

Seven million? As in *dollars?* The implications of why someone would pay that kind of money was daunting. And scary as hell.

Agent Damiano let out a low chuckle. "I wasn't thinking of monetary compensation. I had... something else in mind."

"Yeah, what's that?" Ethan sneered. God, I hated the sound of his whiny voice.

The agent tilted his dark head a bit to the right. "Your lives aren't worth much to me, but I guess they'll have to do." I was aware of his right arm swinging up and then a muffled *pew pew* sound, followed by two thunks.

What the actual hell? Did he just...

Peering around him, I saw that my suspicion was confirmed. He'd shot Felipe and Ethan. Like, *shot them! Dead!*

"Y-you... they're..." I stammered. I wasn't sad that they were dead. They were both horrible people who had been nothing but cruel to me, but I was shocked to my core.

"Dead, yeah," he grunted, pulling me across the room by my hand. It only took a couple strides because the space was minuscule. Damiano paused and looked down at my bare feet only inches from the blood that was pooling and spreading from the bodies. "Don't look at them. Just close your eyes."

I did and then almost screamed when my feet left the floor, but I managed to clamp my lips together to contain it. The man had just casually tossed me over his shoulder and was carrying me. My body bumped against his as he moved swiftly, and a few seconds later, I was back on my feet in the threadbare living room I'd passed through hours earlier.

"Stay behind me," Agent Damiano ordered, and I gladly complied. After all, he was a trained professional. I had to jog to keep up with his long strides as we passed through the other hallway, and then we stepped through an open door. The room was set up like the one I'd been kept in, with only a mattress on the floor and a nightstand, and I wondered if one of the other women had been kept here.

"What are we doing?" I hissed quietly.

Damiano leaned forward, his lips to my ear. "Stay in here while I take care of the guard."

I was pretty sure I knew what he meant by *take care of the guard*, but I didn't want to think too much about that. Freedom was within my grasp, close enough I could smell it. Or maybe that was my body odor since they hadn't allowed me to shower since I'd been taken. Was that yesterday? The day before? The timeline was fuzzy in my head.

He backed out of the room, closing the door silently behind him, and I rubbed my hands up and down my bare arms, suddenly chilled now that I was alone. Muffled voices carried from the back door.

"You need help getting the money out of your car?" *That must be the guard.*

"Actually, Ethan asked me to come get you. He said he needs to talk to you about something."

Lumbering footsteps plodded against the floor outside the room I was standing in. "Huh. What's he need?"

"Not sure. He's in this room."

I had a moment of panic, thinking he was going to bring the guard in here, but I calmed once I heard them enter the room across the hall from me. Though I knew it was coming, I startled at the muffled gunshot and the subsequent sound of the guard's heavy body hitting the floor.

Jesus, how is this my life? It was like I was in a movie. Kidnappings and shootings and big, dark strangers coming to the rescue.

My breath stalled in my lungs when the door opened, suddenly afraid Damiano was the one who'd been shot and the guard was coming for me. But it was the agent in question who opened the door and gestured for me to follow him. He'd thankfully closed the door across the hall so I didn't have to see yet another dead body tonight. Nope. I'd seen enough corpses in the past ten minutes to last me a lifetime.

"Come on, Evie. It's safe now."

Safe. It was a single syllable, but after what I'd been through, it was the most profound word I think I'd ever heard in my life. My throat burned with so many emotions as we exited the house into the muggy night. *Free. I'm free.* And that was synonymous with *safe* in my mind.

I gritted away the tears threatening to spill down my face and limped toward the black sedan parked behind the house. Both of my knees were skinned from my fall when I'd stupidly tried to run with my legs shackled, but the left one seemed to have taken the brunt of the impact. It hurt like hell.

Damiano opened the passenger door for me, his eyes darting around before he went back to the porch and retrieved something from the wooden box there. Another gun.

"You're awfully shooty," I told him when he slid into the driver's seat, and he glanced over at me in bemusement.

"I'm *shooty*?"

God, what am I saying? This man just rescued me from the most horrible fate I could have imagined, and all I could come up with was: *You're awfully shooty?*

I hastily corrected myself. "Not that I'm complaining. At all. I'm just not used to..." My voice shook, and I pressed my lips together to try and get myself under control. "Thank you," I whispered, meeting his brown eyes in the darkness.

"Don't thank me," he said gruffly, turning away and starting the vehicle. "You were limping. Do you need a doctor?"

"N-no. Just some scrapes." The reality of being free was starting to sink in, and my hands began to shake, so I stuffed them beneath my thighs. "Can I use your phone to call my family?"

He glanced over at me before circling the car around and pulling up to an iron gate. "Not tonight. We have to get to the safe house."

I tried to cover my disappointment. All I wanted was to talk to my dad and my brothers. Hell, I'd even like to speak to my bitchy mother at this point. Anyone from home. My nerves settled at yet another four letter word: *home*.

Safe. Free.

Home.

My eyes darted around as we pulled out onto a quiet street. "Where are we? Not still in Cancún, right?" We'd driven for a long time, me and the other girls practically suffocating in the narrow space in the back of that truck. Just the thought of it almost gave me a panic attack.

Damiano's full lips pulled up on one side. "No, New Orleans."

More relief flooded my veins. I was back in the United States. "Is it okay if I open the window? I want to breathe the outside air."

"Of course," he said, and I pressed the button to lower my window a few inches, closing my eyes and taking in the scent of freedom. And something sweet. Probably beignets. My stomach growled in response.

A few minutes later, I opened my eyes when I felt the car slow and turn. We were in the parking lot of a fast-food burger place. My stomach came to life once again, making a noise like an angry bear.

"Burger and fries okay?" the man beside me asked, and I'd never felt more grateful. I seriously could have kissed him just then.

"Yes, please." I gestured at my very skimpy dress. "I obviously don't have any cash on me."

He shook his head as he pulled up to the speaker and rolled down his window. "Don't worry about that. What do you want to drink?"

"Dr Pepper." Juliette was a fiend for that soda, and she'd gotten me hooked on it when I moved to Texas. "Actually, I probably need to drink some water instead. I haven't had any in... I don't know... a long time."

"Can I take your order?" a tinny voice said from the speaker.

Damiano leaned to his left. "I want the burger combo with a Dr Pepper and also two glasses of ice water."

Five minutes later, I had inhaled one glass of water and started on the hamburger. I didn't give a damn about manners, ravenously eating like I'd never seen food before.

"Drink your other glass of water, and then you can have the soda," Damiano informed me.

I glanced at the cup between his thighs. "I thought that was for you."

"Nope, all for you."

By the time we pulled onto a gravel driveway, I had scarfed down all the food and was sipping on the Dr Pepper. The sugary soda tasted so damn good on my tongue.

The frame house wasn't big, but it wasn't small either, the nondescript gray exterior a bit weathered. A garage door lifted, and when Damiano pulled the sedan inside the bay, I saw a man standing beside the door that led into the house.

The garage door closed behind us, and my stomach turned over at the sense of being trapped.

"Who is that?" I breathed around the bile in my throat, cramming the soda cup into the drink holder so I could clasp my hands into tight fists in my lap.

"That's Rodrigo."

The man appeared to be in his sixties or seventies, and in the muted glow of the overhead light, I could see a jagged scar that bisected one eyebrow before snaking upward and into his hairline.

Rodrigo. The name meant nothing to me, but I figured he was another agent. As soon as Damiano rolled up my window, panic seized around my heart. I needed to be out of this vehicle. Now.

Scrambling for the door handle, I jumped from the car so quickly, I stumbled. Strong hands caught me, and I gazed up into a pair of hazel eyes. Despite his scar, Rodrigo's face was kind, and I swallowed hard.

"Sorry," I muttered, embarrassed. "I don't like to be closed up."

"It's okay," the older man said. "Let's get you inside. The house is spacious."

He was right. Entering through the door into a tidy kitchen, I noticed the open floor plan that bled into a small dining nook and then a living room. There was no television there, only a couch that had seen better days and an end table.

"Thank you, Agent Rodrigo," I said, and a bemused smile turned the corners of his lips up, revealing a set of slightly crooked teeth.

"No problem. I've set you up in the middle bedroom."

Damiano had followed us into the house, and he handed over the car keys to Rodrigo. "Let's get Evie settled, and then I need you to run an errand for me."

The man pocketed the key ring and nodded.

My bedroom was painted in a soft taupe, and a double bed rested in the center of the far wall. The bedcovers were a simple white and looked like something you'd see at a Hampton Inn or something.

"You have your own bathroom," Rodrigo said, standing just inside the room and gesturing toward a wood paneled door.

Bathroom? Yes, please.

"I-I need a shower," I stammered as the events of the past few days began weighing on me. I'd put on a brave face for as long as I could, but *fuck*. I was exhausted, and my nerves were frayed like an old rope.

Damiano's hard face seemed to have relaxed slightly now that we were at the safe house, and he stepped forward and gently squeezed my upper arm.

"Take your time. I'm going to talk to Rod for a few minutes. I'll be out here if you need anything."

"Thank you," I barely managed to say through the swelling in my throat. I wished I could think of something else to say. I owed this man way more than a simple thank you.

"I'll leave the door cracked," Damiano said, stepping into the hallway and pulling the knob until there was only a slit between the door and the frame. "You're safe, okay?"

Those two small kindnesses—leaving the door slightly open and reminding me I was out of danger—almost broke me, but I managed to get a hold on it, my fingers pinching the extremely short hem of the slinky dress they'd made me wear. Slipping into the bathroom, I stripped the horrible garment off and threw it to the floor with force.

Fuck you, dress. And fuck you, Ethan and Felipe. Rot in hell.

I should probably feel bad about being glad they were dead, but I hadn't asked for any of this... being taken, held captive, and sold. So no, I didn't feel any remorse at the way they'd met their end.

Looking into the mirror over the white sink, I saw a woman who was bruised, scraped, and afraid, but she was also alive.

As soon as I turned on the shower to warm, my eyes let loose everything I'd been holding back, mimicking the spray from the shower head. Tears poured down my cheeks until I could barely see the towel rack beside the tub. Through the blur of my emotions, I located a dark-blue washcloth and stepped in beneath the hot water.

Oh my god. I've never been so happy for the gift of warm water.

With my hands pressed against the white fiberglass wall, my chest heaved with silent sobs as I watched the blood and grime slide from my body, become diluted, and make its way down the drain. I'd never felt more gross in my life.

The hot water stung the scrapes on my legs and hands, but that pain was a mere blip compared to the ache pulsing inside my heart. Rotating in a circle, I let the water wash over me before tilting my head back and wetting my hair as I cried to my heart's content.

There was a small bottle of shampoo on the lip of the tub, and as soon as I got my hair lathered and rinsed, the food I'd eaten a few minutes ago revolted in my stomach. Slapping my hand over my mouth, I scampered out, naked and dripping, and dropped to my knees in front of the toilet.

Probably ate too fast after having virtually nothing for god knows how long, I thought as I emptied my guts into the porcelain bowl. When I was done, I pushed to my feet, suddenly more tired than I'd ever been in my life, and made my way back to the shower.

I used the rest of the shampoo and washed my hair again before applying conditioner and rinsing. Then I opened the small bar of soap, which looked like it was from a hotel, and went to work on my body with the washcloth, taking care around my injuries. I washed myself again and again until the soap was nothing but a slippery nub.

Lifting my face to the water, I let it wash away the rest of my tears, my hands clasped together beneath my chin in some kind of silent prayer of gratitude. *I'm going to see my family tomorrow.*

I wasn't sure how long I'd been in the shower, but it was a long time, and my bones ached with weariness when I finally stepped out and dried myself. My gaze flitted to the tiny black dress on the floor, and I decided I'd rather run around naked for the rest of my life than put on that vile piece of clothing ever again. It had barely covered my boobs and crotch.

There were plenty of towels in here, so I wrapped one around my wet hair and then grabbed a dry one to loop around my torso. I would just sleep in that tonight.

To my surprise, when I trudged into the bedroom, I found a baby-pink floral pajama set with the tags still on it and a pack of cotton panties sitting on the bed. My hand lifted to my heart as I stared at these simple but thoughtful gifts.

My scrubbed skin practically sighed with relief when I slipped into the soft clothing. Limping to the door, I stuck my head out and saw Damiano in the living room. He quickly strode toward me, holding several Walmart bags.

"Hey, I see you found the pajamas."

"Yes, thank you," I told him, again wishing I could come up with better words to express myself, but I was just so fucking tired.

"I had Rodrigo get you a toothbrush and some medicine too," he said, and I stepped back to let him inside the room. He rummaged around and produced a travel-sized toothbrush and toothpaste as well as a hairbrush.

I kissed the toothbrush with a series of *mwah* noises, and Damiano laughed. "I figured you'd like that. Go do what you need to do. I'll wait out here."

Using way too much toothpaste, I scrubbed my teeth and mouth thoroughly in the bathroom before brushing out my hair and leaving the damp strands loose around my shoulders. When I exited back into the bedroom, the agent gestured for me to sit on the bed.

I did, and he kneeled in front of me, inspecting the wounds on my hands and knees. "How did this happen?" he asked, glancing up at me with his coffee-colored eyes. I liked his voice. It was deep and rumbly but somehow soothing.

"I fell when I tried to run. FYI, it's not a good idea to run while your legs are shackled together."

His lips smirked up on one side. "I'll try to remember that for future reference."

Over the next ten minutes, he meticulously cleaned and treated my scrapes with hydrogen peroxide and antibiotic ointment before bandaging them. He even applied a thick layer of the salve to the raw spot that was left by the duct tape they'd used to attach the number five to my chest. Somehow, that ranked near the top of the most humiliating things I'd endured since being taken.

Damiano's hands were large and rough, but he was so damned gentle as he took care of me. I'd suffered nothing but abuse for days, so this care brought on the threat of a new wave of tears, but I clamped my eyelids shut to contain them.

I'd thought I was done with crying, but this big man on his knees, treating me with such tenderness, almost undid me. His lips tightened when he noted the raw skin around my ankles and wrists from the restraints.

"This is arnica," he told me, smoothing a different ointment around my bruised and scraped joints and then over the marks on my arms and legs that had been left by Felipe and Ethan's harsh fingers. "It should help with any pain and inflammation."

"It was really thoughtful of you to get all this. Can I thank Rodrigo too?"

"He's already in bed, but you can tell him in the morning. He needs to get some sleep because he'll be flying the helicopter tomorrow."

"Are you taking me to New York to my family?" I asked, and he glanced up at me with a furrowed brow.

His reply seemed distant and laden with something I couldn't quite define. "New York? Yeah, I'll get you to New York." With his eyes still on mine, he cupped my chin with one hand, angling my face to the side so he could see my cheek. "Swear to god, if those fuckers weren't already dead, I'd kill them for marking you like this."

The words were muttered but no less fierce as he smoothed the arnica over the bruise from the backhand I'd taken to the face. I wasn't sure why he was acting like Ethan and Felipe had hurt him personally, but maybe it was just his nature. Protectiveness as a result of his job.

With tender pressure, Damiano tilted my head until I was facing him again, and his eyes dropped to my mouth. "I'm sorry they hurt you," he murmured, smoothing some of the arnica over the split in my bottom lip.

"It could have been worse," I whispered, and his gaze locked with mine.

"Yeah, it could have been." A muscle clenched in his jaw as we stared at each other in what felt like a very intimate moment. Then he dragged his eyes away and reached for another of the bags, pulling out a cool bottle of water and some ibuprofen. "Take these," he said, spilling four of the tablets into my palm.

The bandages made me clumsy, and Damiano caught the pills I dropped before they hit the floor. To my surprise, he held two of them to my lips with his long fingers, and I took a drink of the water to swallow them before he repeated it with the other two.

"Thank you," I told him. "I feel like I keep saying that, and I know it doesn't come close to being enough. I'm just too tired to think of anything else."

"It's okay, Evie. Why don't you get some sleep now?"

I nodded. "I need it. I don't remember the last time I slept." I attempted a small smile, but I could feel that it was weak.

Damiano took the bottle of water from me and placed it on the small table beside the bed before pulling back the covers for me. I slid my legs beneath the cool sheets and rested my head on the pillow.

The man stood and pulled the covers up over my body. "My room is next door if you need me. Is there anything else I can get you right now?"

My tired mind could think of only one thing. It was probably wholly inappropriate, but fuck it. Sitting up, I held my arms wide. Damiano didn't even hesitate. He sat on the edge of the bed and allowed me to hug him, his large hands finding my back in a soothing up and down movement.

A sigh escaped me at the comfort a simple hug brought me, but I couldn't muster up any words. So I clung to this man. This stranger. My savior.

Damiano's deep voice rumbled his chest and vibrated low in my ear. "Do I need to pull a chair in here and stay with you?"

Yes!

But I couldn't ask him to do that. He needed to sleep too, so I shook my head and reluctantly pulled back. "No, it's fine."

With one hand on the back of my head and one pressing against the center of my chest, he guided me down until I was once again resting on the pillow. "I'll stay till you get to sleep."

My eyes closed instantly, and I felt fingers brushing the hair from my face as my exhausted body finally relaxed. And then... I slept.

CHAPTER 7

LOOKING DOWN AT THE woman in the bed, I wondered why the hell I was running my fingers through her damp hair. I was pretty sure I'd never done that before.

Pulling a woman's hair while fucking her from behind? Yeah, I'd definitely done that. And thoroughly enjoyed it. But somehow not as much as I enjoyed stroking Evie's hair with a tenderness I didn't think myself capable of.

What the hell is it about this chick? Shit, I didn't even know her, but for some reason, she'd gotten under my skin with her boldness, her tenacity. I... admired her.

Now fully asleep, Evie's face had relaxed into pure softness, making her look like an angel. But I knew beneath that sweet, pretty face lay a fierceness that drew me in. She was an angel all right, but one forged from fire and ice.

I mean, I should be pissed at her because she was going to totally upend my life. Once I returned her to New York, I was going to have to go on the run because there was no way Luca Cappitani was going to let this shit go. Stealing his new "toy" and his money? Nope. I was a dead man.

It was March now, and I probably wouldn't make it to the end of the year before he found me and killed me in the most heinous way imaginable.

Probably tortured for days by his men before he personally decapitated me. That was Luca's specialty.

There would be no reprieve for me because I was his son. No, that would only make the betrayal more malignant in his eyes.

Nevertheless, I planned to give Evie the seven million dollars. Poor kid deserved it after what she'd been through. She could use the money to go to school or buy a house or whatever. She would always have mental scars from the past few days, but hopefully, the money would change her life for the better and allow her the financial freedom to move past this in the best way she could.

But first, I needed to get her back to New York, the last damn place I wanted to go. Why couldn't she be from Kansas or Oregon or fucking anywhere else but where my father lived? Luckily, he'd still be in Las Vegas and not waiting at the airfield for us when we arrived. I'd get Evie to a safe place and then haul ass to... *somewhere*. And then I'd bide my time until he came for me.

I'd never held any notion that I'd live a long and happy life. Fiero played his part well as the eldest son, but I was a bit more rebellious. And as the youngest child, I was pretty much expendable in my father's eyes.

Rising from the bed without jostling Evie, I stared down at her for a long moment. Hopefully Luca would never find her again because, if he did, there would be hell to pay for daring to escape him. Maybe I could talk her into taking the money and relocating somewhere outside the city with her family.

I made sure to leave her door cracked a little when I left and went to my room. Stripping off my suit, I took a shower and climbed into bed for what I hoped would be a good night's sleep.

Because come tomorrow, I was going to need my wits about me.

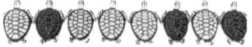

"Can I call my family now?" Evie asked from the backseat as we drove back to the airstrip in New Orleans. She'd insisted on sitting back there so Rodrigo could sit in the front. I had the impression it was because he was older, which gave me a chuckle. Rod may not be a spring chicken anymore, but he was about the toughest old bird I'd ever met.

"We can't do that right now, but you'll be with them soon." My eyes caught the droop of her lips in the rearview mirror, and I hated that. So I opened my mouth and told a big, fat lie. "They'll be waiting for you when we land."

That was one hundred percent *not* going to happen. I was still working out the logistics in my mind, but I needed to stall her for at least an hour after we landed in New York to give myself time to get away. And I needed to fabricate some kind of story that wouldn't implicate Rodrigo. Fuck.

Evie mentioned her dad and brothers, so I was positive they'd show up with law enforcement if they knew she was being brought back to New York, and that wouldn't bode well for me. I could probably talk my way out of prison since I'd rescued her from the traffickers, but jail time was not my biggest concern. Luca Cappitani was the more dangerous threat.

Nope. I needed to be long gone before her family was called and dragged the cops into it.

To quell any more questions from Evie, I turned on the radio and tuned in to a classic rock station. Bon Jovi's "Livin' on a Prayer" bled from the speakers, and the irony of that particular song wasn't lost on me. *How apropos.*

Evie's head appeared between the front seats. "Did you know Frank Sinatra was Jon Bon Jovi's great-uncle?" she asked.

Rod and I glanced at each other before shaking our heads. "I never heard that," he said.

"Yep, on his father's side. If you look at their eyes and the shape of their faces, you can see the resemblance. Jon used to keep a picture of Frank backstage at all his shows."

"How'd you know that?" I asked, and she shrugged as she sat back.

"I know lots of things. My brother Monty calls me a font of useless drivel." She smiled fondly, and I liked seeing it on her face. "I can't wait to see him. I'm closest to him because we share a birthday."

"Twins?" Rod asked.

"No, I'm a year older than him, but he's a lot taller so he thinks he's the boss of me."

"How old are you, Evie?"

"I'm turning nineteen this month, so Monty will be eighteen." Her voice turned wistful. "I'm so happy we'll be able to spend the day together."

"You'll see him soon," I promised.

"I miss my other brother and my dad too. Heck, I'll even be glad to see my mother." I sensed the tension in that last sentence but didn't have time to ask any questions because we were pulling up to the hangar.

Putting the sedan in park, I swiveled around to face her. "Look, Evie. I need you to do something for me."

"Anything," she agreed with an up and down bob of her head. She looked so much better today. Still bruised and with a cut lip, but there was a brightness in her eyes that was missing yesterday.

"There's a guy here, and I need you to pretend to be my prisoner when we're around him."

"Why?" she asked, her eyebrows furrowing in confusion before rising. "Ohhh, he's not part of the operation or whatever you call it?"

I ignored Rodrigo's smirk of amusement at Evie still thinking we were Feds. "Right. He's definitely not part of the operation," I answered. "We're going to have to stop a couple times to refuel the helicopter, but we'll have you home really soon. Just play your part until we're in the air."

"So don't try to kick or scratch you?" she asked, one side of her lips tipping up, and I chuckled.

"Exactly. Try and control your wildcat instincts."

"Okay, anything else?"

"Just... don't talk to anyone but me, okay? And only if I speak directly to you." Her lips pinched together in disapproval, but I couldn't worry about that right now. We needed to get past Guido without arousing suspicion. *And speak of the devil...*

Guido strolled out of the cream-colored metal hangar sporting about five more gold chains than he needed to wear. "That's the guy I need you to avoid talking to," I whispered fervently, my eyes flitting between Evie in the rearview mirror and the idiot in the purple track suit.

"Jesus, is that velour?" Evie asked, her nose scrunching up. "I didn't even know they still made that stuff."

Rodrigo covered his laugh with a cough as Evie continued. "Just to clarify, I'm not allowed to call that guy Flava Flav?"

"No," I replied wryly, "but you can say it in your head."

"Like you could stop me," she muttered under her breath as Guido approached the car.

Opening my door, I stepped out, and the prick slapped me on the shoulder. "Damiano, my boy. Everything go okay last night?"

"Fine." *If you consider taking out everyone in the house and then planning to completely screw over my father as fine.*

Guido nodded, his smug smile irritating me as he clapped his hands together. "Great. Let's get you on the road. Or in the air, I guess," he said, and something about his subsequent laugh seemed tinged with nervousness. *What the fuck is that about?*

Rodrigo appeared beside me and nodded curtly at the other man. "Morning. I'm just gonna check on the helicopter."

Guido's head bounced up and down on his thick neck. "Oh, don't you worry about that. I've got it all ready for you. Fuel, flight plan. Everything's good to go." The incessant nodding was making me dizzy, and I walked to the back of the car and popped open the trunk.

"Rod, you wanna help me with these bags?" I asked, shooting him a look.

"Yeah, I gotcha."

He took two of the heavy duffels containing the money I was supposed to have handed over last night, and Guido frowned. "What's in those?"

Rodrigo leveled him with a no-nonsense glare. "Necessities we had to pick up, which are none of your business."

Guido followed him inside the hangar, but I didn't need to worry about him snooping through the bags. Rod could handle that punk. Once they were out of earshot, I opened the back door and helped Evie out. She was dressed in more of the clothes I'd had Rodrigo pick up from Walmart last night, including denim shorts, an army-green T-shirt, and brown sandals. She looked younger than her eighteen-almost-nineteen years.

"Let's go. Be good," I told her in a low voice, reaching for her bag—another Walmart purchase. It was cheap, floral, and contained Evie's toiletries and another change of clothes, and I looped the strap over my shoulder.

Gripping Evie's hand with my free one, I led her to the hangar. Guido immediately gave her a slow once-over with his beady black gaze, and my blood began to boil.

"Keep your fucking eyes to yourself unless you want them removed with a rusty spoon," I growled, and the prick immediately looked away. I turned to Evie and pointed to one of the seats in the chopper. "Sit there and don't give me any shit. Understood?"

Her eyes were downcast, but she raised them to mine and said demurely, "Yes, sir."

Fuck me. My suit pants stretched around my swelling cock at those words. And at the sight of her tight ass in those shorts as she climbed into the helicopter. *Cut it out, Cappitani. This is not the time nor the place. And certainly not the woman you need to be lusting after. A woman you will never see again after today.*

That thought brought to the forefront an emotion I couldn't quite define, but I was pretty sure it was akin to sadness. Shit, I liked this chick. She was funny, brave, and spunky as fuck. *And goddamn gorgeous even beneath the bruises.*

Rodrigo was in the chopper, doing whatever pre-flight checks he always did. "What's the deal with this flight plan?" he called to Guido, who was standing just inside the hangar. "It's got us going southeast over the Gulf of Mexico instead of straight to the northeast."

"Dunno. Luca sent it. Said he wanted you to stay just off the coast for a bit and then refuel in Florida." He shrugged, his hands jiggling in the pockets of his pants. "I just do what I'm told, and I was told to make sure you leave on time, soooo..."

He let the word linger, and I rolled my eyes, taking my time walking back to the car to retrieve the final money duffel and my own leather bag. Just to piss him off.

A chirping sound came from my bag and I frowned, unzipping it enough to pull out my burner phone. Fiero was the only one who had that number. Flipping it open, I saw a text in all caps, and my blood ran cold.

[unknown]: DO NOT GET ON THAT HELICOPTER!

CHAPTER 8

WHAT THE ACTUAL FUCK?

My brother and I never used names on these messages in case someone found our burner cells, but I checked the number, and it was definitely Fiero's secret phone. I texted him back.

> **Me: Can I call you?**

> **[unknown]: I'm not alone. I'll call you when I can. Whatever you do, don't get on there.**

> **Me: Why?**

I stared at my phone, waiting for a response, but one never came. He must be with our father or one of his goons. Stuffing the phone into the front pocket of my suit pants, I fisted the bags and walked back to the hangar, my nerves on high alert.

Why the hell didn't my brother want me on this chopper? With sharp eyes, I took in everything as I secured the bags, furtively darting my gaze from the back to the front of the interior.

Wait. Is that...

Moving forward and crouching beside Rodrigo, I hissed, "I need Guido to disappear for a few minutes."

Without a single question, he flicked one more knob, unbuckled himself, and climbed out. "Guido, I need to hit the pisser before we lift off," he called to the man standing in the hangar opening.

"Fuck's sake. You're throwing the schedule off, old man," he groused, lifting a stubby finger to point. "It's back there."

Rod craned his neck and squinted. "Where?"

"That door back there," Guido sighed, waggling his finger at the very clearly marked restroom door.

"Which one? There're two doors."

"Can you even see good enough to fly this damn thing?" The punk's eyes rolled to the top of his head. "Fuck it. I'll show you."

As soon as they were walking away, I dropped to my back and slid my head beneath the pilot's seat. *Motherfucker.*

Pieces started falling into place. Guido's nervous demeanor. His insistence that we leave immediately. But who was behind it? I was pretty sure I knew, but I needed confirmation.

"What are you doing? You're going to get your suit all dirty." Evie's quiet voice penetrated my thoughts, and my heart rate kicked into overdrive as the implications of what I'd just seen sank into my bones.

"Come here," I told her. I hated to scare her after everything she'd been through, but I needed her to see this for herself. Because everything I had planned was about to change.

After a brief hesitation, she lowered herself to the floor beside me, and I pointed at the underside of the seat.

That little soft spot appeared between her eyes for a long moment before she angled her gaze toward me. "Is that..."

"An explosive device," I confirmed, and her blue eyes rounded. "In exactly," I checked the timer, "ninety-eight minutes, this helicopter will explode."

"Oh my god. What... who... I-I don't understand." She scrambled to her feet, her hands flapping like wounded birds, and I followed her.

"Listen to me, Evie." I gripped her pretty face with both hands, my voice hard and forceful. "I need you to run to the car before Guido gets back. Stay there, and do not get out, no matter what. Do you understand?"

"Flava fucking Flav was going to blow us up?" she screeched, and I shushed her.

"Keep your voice down and go. Now. Stay to the right, and the helicopter will block you from his view."

Her eyes circuited back and forth between mine three times before she nodded. I helped her from the helicopter and watched as she darted to the car, my lungs finally deflating once she was safely inside.

Then I brushed off my rear and pulled the suppressed gun from the back of my pants before straightening my suit jacket. Keeping the weapon slightly behind me, I strolled to the back of the hangar.

"What's the hold up?"

Guido's ugly face scrunched in annoyance. "He said he ate something bad. Fucking ridiculous."

I whipped the gun out and placed it against his forehead. "Who?"

"Wh-who wh-what?" he stammered, though he knew exactly what I was asking.

Keeping my eyes trained intently on him, I didn't let on that Rodrigo was now standing directly behind him. "Who told you to put the explosive device on the chopper?"

"Me? I wouldn't... I don't know what you're talking about." A droplet of sweat dripped from his dark hair and slid down his temple.

I noticed his hand slowly inching toward his jacket pocket, and I pretended not to notice. "Was it Luca?"

I could read the answer in the fearful gleam of Guido's eyes, but I wanted to hear it anyway. His hand finally reached into his pocket, and I tried not to smile.

"Looking for this?" Rodrigo asked, walking around Guido and dangling the idiot's gun by two fingers. Rod was a slick motherfucker, I'd give him that. He tapped a button on the wall, and the hangar doors began to close.

The man with my gun barrel still pressed against his head began babbling as tears poured down his face. "I-I didn't want to. I swear, I didn't. I like you, Damiano. You know how Luca is though. He'd kill me with a snap of his fingers."

"Why does he want me dead?" I asked, my voice cold even as I burned with hurt inside. I knew my father didn't give a shit about anyone except himself, but hearing the actual words... Yeah, not a great feeling.

"Don't know. H-he called me in the middle of the night and said he found out something, and this was the only way to fix it. He was fucking crazy. Sent me a flight plan and told me to set up the device so it would blow up over the water. Then called again a little while ago to make sure I'd done it. That's all I know."

"That's why this asshole was so anxious for us to leave," Rodrigo noted, meeting my gaze. "The timing."

"I'm sorry," Guido blubbered. "Please don't—"

Blood sprayed from the back of his head as my bullet shut him the fuck up. Permanently.

Rodrigo stared down at the body. "How long till it blows?"

"About an hour and a half."

"Where's Evie, and does she know?"

"Yes, I showed it to her and then had her go get in the car."

"Fuck, you've gotten yourself into a goddamn pickle, son." His worried brown eyes rose to mine.

"No shit."

"Let's go check on the girl while I think this through," he said, pushing the button for a couple seconds to open the doors a crack. "Do you think Luca found out about what happened at the house last night?"

We walked swiftly across the concrete floor. "No clue. I made sure to shoot the guard inside the house because, even in New Orleans, a dead body on the back porch would draw alarms."

"What made you think to check the bird out?"

"Got a tip."

Rod nodded, knowing without me telling him that it had come from my brother. He opened the back door to the car, and I was relieved to see Evie sitting there, her thumbnail in her mouth.

"Why the hell is there a bomb on that helicopter?" she demanded to know.

"We're still trying to figure that out," Rodrigo told her in a soft tone. "We'll make sure to get you out of here and safe before it goes off."

Her crystal-blue eyes jerked back and forth between us, and then she nodded. "Okay, what then?"

I don't have the first fucking clue.

"Rodrigo's working on a plan," I told her, my hand going to my pocket when I felt the phone vibrate with a call. "He'll stay in here with you while I take this. Might be more information."

My finger pushed the button to answer as I heard Rod climb into the car and shut the door. "Yeah."

"Jesus fucking Christ. This is a nightmare, bro. Do you have any idea who that girl is?" My brother sounded as frantic as I felt on the inside.

I strode to the hangar, leaning my shoulders back against the metal wall and keeping an eye on the car. "Her name is Evie."

"Yeah, Evie, which is short for Evelyn."

"Okaaaay?" I drew out.

"Evelyn 'Evie' Bouvier is the only daughter of Paul Bouvier."

My blood stopped flowing through my veins so abruptly, my knees went weak. "The fashion guy?"

"That one. He's a goddamn billionaire, one of the most well-known people in New York. Hell, the whole damn country. They've brought in the Feds, and the media is all over it. Have you even turned on the news?"

I shook my head, even though he couldn't see it. "No. I haven't exactly had time."

"Luca saw a press conference last night. I was out, but one of the guards called and told me to get back to the suite because our dear father was on a rampage."

Fucking hell. Press conferences and a famous family shoved this situation directly into a high-profile nightmare, something Luca Cappitani did his best to avoid.

"What happened?"

"I came back to the hotel, and he was losing his shit. Tore the entire room apart. He swore he would do whatever he had to do to keep this from coming back on him."

"So he was going to get rid of the evidence," I added flatly.

"Yeah, I overheard him on the phone with Guido this morning, asking if he'd planted *it* in the chopper and if he had the timing right. He said he wanted it to blow up off the coast. That's when I figured out what he was planning. Did you find it?"

"Yep, under one of the seats. It's on a timer."

"Shit, bro. This is not good. You're not safe and neither is Evelyn Bouvier. You need to get the fuck away from her because he'll be coming for her once that chopper explodes while still on the ground and he realizes she's still alive."

The thought of leaving her to fend for herself against the most brutal man I knew turned my stomach. "I'll talk to Rodrigo and let you know the plan."

"Okay, brother. Stay safe."

"I'll try. I wouldn't be if you weren't looking out for me." My voice clogged with emotion. "Thank you."

"You'd do the same for me." His own tone was slightly husky. "Later, Dame."

"Later, Fi."

My temples throbbed as I replaced my phone in my pocket. This already horrible situation just took a hard right turn onto shitshow road. I'd thought my father would be after me and me alone when I didn't show up with his *prize*. I thought he'd never know who the hell the girl even was. But now he did know.

And Evie Bouvier was in grave danger.

Steeling my spine, I walked over to the car and plastered a fake-ass smile on my face for Evie's benefit before opening the door. "We'll be leaving in a few minutes," I told her. "Just need to talk to Rodrigo for a second."

She frowned but bobbed her head in a nod, fingers twisting nervously at the fabric of her shirt. Hell, I didn't blame her. There was literally a ticking time bomb less than fifty yards away.

"What is it?" Rod asked when he was out of the car and we'd walked out of hearing distance. As I explained who Evie was and my father's extreme response to it, his haggard face grew more grim by the second. "Fuck. This is bad, Damiano. He's never going to let up as long as she's alive."

"I know." Not much more I could add to that.

"I've been thinking about what to do, and well... it's pretty fucking extreme, but with what you just told me, I think it's our only option."

"Hit me with it."

"Luca has to believe we're all dead. That we blew up in the helicopter over the Gulf of Mexico."

Those words sank like a sack of stones in my gut. "I'm not going to be able to get Evie back to her family, am I?"

"No, son, you're not. All of us have to go underground."

I screwed up my face and scruffed a hand through my hair. "How the hell are we going to fake a helicopter explosion?"

Rodrigo's lips tipped up on one side. "I'm going to fly it out over the Gulf and..."

"No, absolutely not," I hissed fiercely.

He placed a calming hand on my upper arm. "Let me finish. You know I always keep parachutes in the chopper. I'll take her up, set the course, and then jump out well before time for it to go boom. I have a friend that can pick me up in a boat if I give him the coordinates."

My eyebrows rammed together. "Who the fuck are you? James Bond?"

Rod let out a humorless chuckle. "Something like that. Luca will have someone tracking the helicopter, and when he sees it disappear from radar, he'll think his plan worked and that we're all dead."

"What about Guido and the bodies in the house from last night?"

"I'll handle all that. I've got someone I can call to take care of it. She likes to call herself a cleanup artist."

I didn't bat an eye that this person was a female. Nothing at all could surprise me today. "Okay, let me give you one of the money bags."

"Don't need a whole bag. I'll just take enough to leave here for the cleaner to do the jobs and then be on my way. Time's a tickin'."

"And some extra for yourself," I insisted. "Where will you go?"

"Don't worry about me. Just worry about you and Evie."

"I don't even know where we're going to go," I muttered, jacking up my hair with my hand again.

"Gotcha covered on that. Do you remember my cousin, Rocco?"

I scanned the recesses of my brain. "Yeah, I do. He worked for Luca and then disappeared about... what... six or seven years ago? I thought he was dead."

"Eight," he corrected. "And that's what he wanted everyone to think. He got word that Luca was about to have him taken out over some shit that went down, so he made himself disappear. Rocco and his wife live just north of Jacksonville." He handed me a card with a Florida address, no name, and I pocketed it.

"You think he can help us?"

Rodrigo's face turned grave. "He's the only one who can. I'll call and tell him to expect you."

I shook my head in wonder. "You're not going to have enough time to do all this shit, Rod."

"Three quick phone calls and stashing some money behind the toilet in the bathroom for the cleaner," he said, jerking a thumb toward the hangar. "I'll be lifting off in ten minutes." He handed me a set of keys.

"What are these?"

He gave me a broad grin. "I palmed them from Guido at the same time I took his gun. We need his car to be gone from here so we don't arouse suspicion, so you and Evie will leave in that." He pointed to a tricked-out, sky-blue Cadillac around the corner of the metal building.

"Jesus, that's not conspicuous at all," I retorted, letting the sarcasm seep into my tone.

"Yeah, but we can't leave it here. Guido's address should be in the GPS, so park the car at his house and take one of his other ones. Then get to Florida."

"Okay, what else?"

"I need your regular cell phone, the one your father knows about. We can't have that pinging if he has a tracker on it, which he probably does. It's got to go up in the helicopter with me."

Taking out my cell, I handed it over. "Thank you, Rodrigo." Now I knew what Evie meant last night when she said that phrase didn't seem like enough. This man was going to have to go underground to protect me. He'd likely never see his daughter, granddaughter, or anyone else in his family for a very long time.

"No need for thanks," he said, looking at me with damp eyes.

I wasn't a hugger by nature. Pretty sure I hadn't hugged another adult since before my mother died—until Evie last night. But I reached for

Rodrigo and wrapped my arms tightly around him. He looked like he needed it.

"Thank you anyway. You don't have to do this, you know."

He squeezed me so hard I could barely breathe, but it felt... good. "I'd do anything for you. I never had a son, but I always felt like you and your brother were mine."

So many emotions welled up in my chest. Sadness. Fear. Affection.

"Anything else I can do for you, Rod?" I choked out.

To my surprise, he pulled back, grabbed my face in his wrinkled hands, and kissed me hard on the forehead before whispering, "Live, Damiano. Just live."

CHAPTER 9

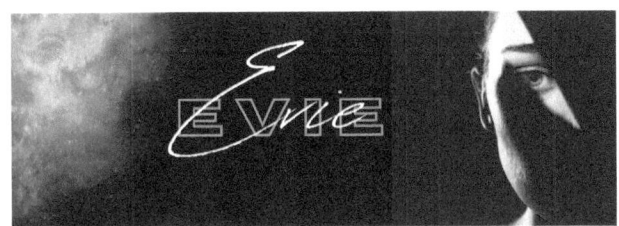

I WATCHED THROUGH THE window as the two men embraced. It looked like a goodbye type of hug. But why would they be saying goodbye? Weren't agents supposed to travel in pairs?

Unless...

The door to the car swung open, and Rodrigo extended his hand for me. Taking it, I stepped out of the vehicle. With his hands braced on my shoulders, his eyes commanded my attention.

"Evie, it was a pleasure getting to meet you."

My stomach clenched. "You're not coming with us?"

"No, I've got to... take care of some things, but Damiano will keep an eye on you."

For some reason, it made me sad that we were parting ways, which was bizarre because I'd only met the man last night. But he'd been nothing but kind to me. Hell, he'd bought me underwear. If that didn't forge a bond between two people, I wasn't sure what did.

"What's happening?" I asked.

"Damiano will explain everything to you. Can you do something for me?"

I nodded, and he gave me a sad little smile. "Take care of my boy for me. Down deep beneath all that he is, he's got a good heart. Just remember that and show him some grace, okay?"

"O-okay," I stammered, still not sure what the heck was going on. Especially when I saw that Damiano was heading into the hangar. Panic—a sense I was becoming way too familiar with—set in. "Why is he going in there? We're not taking the bomb chopper, are we?"

Rodrigo chuckled and placed a hand between my shoulder blades, guiding me to the side of the hangar. "Nope, you're just switching vehicles."

My eyeballs almost popped out of my head when I saw where he was leading me. A sky-blue Cadillac sedan almost blinded me with its glittery exterior. The alloy wheels were huge and shiny, and a chrome grill took up the entire front of the car. A figurine of a naked woman dangled from the rearview mirror.

"Let me guess," I deadpanned. "That's Flava Flav's car."

"Well, it was."

"Was?" A sigh huffed from my lungs. "Damiano got shooty again, didn't he?"

Rodrigo chuckled. "I like you, Evie. You're refreshing as hell."

"Don't worry about me. I've got it," Damiano grumbled, walking by with his hands full of bags.

The older man winked at me. "Get in the car, and I'll help him."

As the guys walked back inside, I opened the Caddy's car door and almost passed out from the stench of way too much Axe Body Spray. It floated out like some kind of fog I was convinced would either burn off my skin or give me hallucinations if I didn't let it air out a bit.

"Jesus, Flav. Subtlety was not your strong suit."

A minute later, they had the car loaded and Damiano and I were climbing inside. He coughed, rolling down the windows after cranking it. Then he yanked the naked woman figure from the mirror and tossed it in the back before searching for something in the GPS device.

"Where are we going?"

"We're dropping this car off at Guido's house." His eyes swung from side to side as he drove across the tarmac.

"Why?"

"So no one knows he didn't leave here."

"Why does that matter?"

"You ask a lot of questions."

I widened my eyes incredulously. "Well, excuse me. I've been drugged, kidnapped, sold, hit, stuck in the back of a truck for hours, hit again, forced to wear a hooker dress, rescued, seen corpses, taken to a safe house, almost blown up in a helicopter, and now I'm riding in a pimpmobile. Pardon the hell out of me if I have questions."

My voice had risen almost to a yell by the end, and as my chest heaved with frustration, Damiano turned the car onto a surface street and sighed. "You're right. It's a long story, so let's talk after we switch cars. The house is only a few minutes away."

I acquiesced and stayed silent until we arrived at the ramshackle house with a charcoal-gray Ford Explorer parked in front. Damiano parked the pimp car, used a key from the keyring to get inside the house, and came back a few minutes later with another set of car keys.

I looked around, but no one was paying us any attention. This seemed to be the kind of neighborhood where no one asked questions.

After transferring everything to the SUV, we got in and headed out. I lasted all of two minutes before asking, "Is Rodrigo your dad or your uncle or something?"

Damiano's lips pressed together. "I wish he was my father, but no, we're not related."

"You're not an FBI agent, are you?"

"No."

"CIA?"

"No."

Pressing my fingertips into my eyeballs, I puffed out a long exhale. "Are you some kind of vigilante?"

His lips twitched slightly. "I guess you could call me that."

I did one of those closed-mouth quiet screams as Damiano took the onramp onto Interstate-10, heading east. "You know, it wouldn't kill you to say more than a few words at a time. Perhaps you could spill what you know without me having to drag it out of you."

A muscle clenched and released a few times in his jaw. "You're right." He drummed his thumbs on the steering wheel before glancing over at me. "Have you ever heard the name Luca Cappitani?"

My eyes drifted up to stare at the top of the windshield as I tried to place the name. My mind brought up the picture of a man with a receding hairline, jowls, and a protruding belly. "Isn't that some Mafia dude in New York?"

A vein throbbed in his temple. "Yes, he's the one who tried to buy you."

My stomach roiled with nausea, and I croaked out, "Why would he do that?"

Damiano shot his chocolate-brown eyes in my direction again. "Why do you think?" His teeth worked over his bottom lip, back and forth a few times before he spoke again. "He doesn't treat his woman well, Evie. He keeps them drugged and..."

"And what?"

"He uses them whenever he wants. He has a medicine cabinet full of Viagra if you're not catching my drift." *Shit.* "When he's done with them, he passes them on to one of the men under him in the organization. Or worse."

Worse?

I covered my mouth with my hand. "And how do you know all this?" The words were muffled, but I knew he could hear them because his knuckles turned white on the steering wheel.

"Because I was sent to pick you up for him." There was a long pause before he said, "Because Luca is my father."

I'd experienced the most horrific fear imaginable over the past few days, and I thought the worst was over. But I was dead wrong. It slammed back into me with a vengeance as I realized what he'd just said.

"Are you taking me to him?" I asked, a tear slipping down my right cheek. Swiping it away angrily, I turned my face fully toward the man who was maneuvering through traffic, a stoic expression on his face.

"I am not," he replied through gritted teeth.

"Are you in the Mafia too?"

"I was but not anymore."

"Since when?" I asked, pretty sure I already knew the answer.

"Since I saw the woman I was supposed to be picking up on that video. A little wildcat with fire in her blue eyes and a big *fuck you* written on her face." Damiano slowed and then stopped the car as traffic stalled on the freeway, swiveling his head to meet my unrelenting gaze. "Till I saw you, Evie."

I was completely lost for words. My mind couldn't process all this new information. *Damiano is a Mafia man who saved me from the even worse Mafia man, and now he's not in the Mafia anymore.*

"I don't understand what that means," I told him, my voice shakier than I wanted it to be.

"That makes two of us," he muttered. "I can't explain it, Evie. I saw that video, and you were vulnerable but so fucking strong at the same time. Luca said he was going to have fun breaking you, and I almost killed him on the spot." His right hand left the steering wheel and reached toward me before he pulled it back and let it fall into his lap, but his eyes remained on mine. "I couldn't bear to think of him breaking your spirit."

"Wow. Okay. That's... a lot." I smoothed my index finger absently over the cut in my lip. "What happens now?"

A car horn beeped, and Damiano pulled his head around to find that traffic had started moving again. Placing both hands on the wheel, he drove without speaking for about a mile before I repeated myself.

"Damiano, what happens now?"

He sucked in a breath through his nose. "We have to go into hiding." The air pushed from his nostrils so forcefully, they flared. "If he finds us, we're both dead."

"My family can hide us," I said quickly, not thinking too much about the fact that I'd used the word *us* instead of *me*. That should go over well. *Hey, Dad and Mother. This is Damiano. He's a stone-cold killer, and he'll be staying with us while his psycho father looks for us.* "They have money and—"

I cut myself off at the sharp shake of his head. "We have to go deeper than that. And besides, if you arrive back at your family's house, law enforcement will know, and then Luca will inevitably find out. He has spies everywhere, including in the Feds and local police."

"So we're going into the Witness Protection Program?"

The shake of his head made my heart sink even further. "Have you ever wondered why my father is a notorious gangster and yet he's never spent a day in jail?"

"Weirdly enough, I've never given that much thought," I shot back.

Damiano ignored my sarcasm. "Fourteen people who were going to testify against my father have gone into WITSEC over the years." A muscle twitched beneath his eye. "Guess how many survived."

A sharp pinch formed over my chest and deepened into my heart. From the firm set of his jaw, I knew the answer. "I'm guessing none."

"Correct. If he can't find them, he draws them out of hiding by going after their families or loved ones. The only way you and your family will be safe is if... if he thinks you're dead."

A cold dread seeped over me, bringing with it an involuntary shudder, and I rubbed my hands up and down my arms. "He's the one behind the helicopter, isn't he?" My heart went out to Damiano when he nodded. "But he knew you were going to be on there too. His own son."

Bitterness curled the corner of his mouth upward and wrapped around his words. "Yeah. He's a fucking peach of a father, isn't he?"

I reached out and laid my hand on his forearm. "I'm sorry, Damiano. My mother is a cold-hearted bitch, but I think your father has her beat for the suck-ass parent of the year award."

"Fuhgeddaboudit," he drawled, feigning indifference with a shrug of one shoulder. "Rodrigo is taking care of the chopper situation. It will blow up off the coast just like Luca expects it to. That way, he won't be looking for us as long as there's no reason for him to suspect we're still alive."

"Why the hell does he want me dead so badly?" I fumed.

Damiano turned on his blinker and merged into the center lane as traffic began to thin out and speed up. "He saw a press conference with your family last night, and that's when he realized who you were. Then the paranoid sonofabitch freaked out because your disappearance is high profile and the extra media attention turned up the heat. He decided the only way to keep anything from being traced back to him was to make sure you were... out of the picture."

At the mention of my family, my chest swelled with an ache so profound, I was afraid my ribs would crack. "I need to call them and tell them I'm okay. I'm sure they're worried sick. Can I use your phone?"

"I don't think that's a good idea," he hedged.

"Well, I think it's a great idea," I argued. "I can't just let them wonder where the hell I am. I'll tell them not to say anything to anyone."

"Not good enough."

My cheeks flared with red anger. "If I explain it to them..."

"Listen to me, Evie. If you were my sister and you were missing but suddenly called and told me you were fine and not to worry, you know what I'd do? I'd burn up the goddamn world getting to you."

I stayed silent because that's exactly what my family would do.

"If they were to tell anyone from the media or the FBI or even a friend, and it got back to my father, you'd be dead before you knew what was happening. In fact, the Feds undoubtedly have your family's phones monitored. Luca is ruthless and powerful, and he will stop at nothing to save his own skin. Including blowing up a helicopter with his own fucking son in it," he shouted, slamming his fist against his chest. Damiano took a few heaving breaths and then his voice softened marginally. "Wouldn't your family rather you be safe and they be unaware of it than to know for sure that you're dead?"

I pressed the heel of my hand against my forehead. "It's so cruel to leave them wondering though."

"Then let's turn it around. If Luca got even an inkling that you were still alive, he'd do everything in his power to find you, including using your family. How would you feel if you turned on the news one day and saw a story about your mother opening a package and finding one of your brothers' heads in it? How would you feel if you knew you could have prevented that by going underground?"

Gasping, I covered my face with both hands, the unimaginable vision of Monty or Auburn... No. It was too fucking much, and tears leaked from beneath my hands to drip from my jaw.

"Don't say shit like that," I wheezed as my chest contracted in on itself. "You're scaring me."

A hand brushed down my arm so softly I could have imagined it. "I'm sorry, Evie, but you need to be scared. You need to take this seriously because that's exactly my father's M.O."

I tilted my head against the slightly open window, letting the breeze dry my tears into a fine crust on my face. "I hate you for this, Damiano. I'll always hate you for this."

The interior of the vehicle was silent for a long while before I heard, "If that's what you need to do, Evie, then fine. At least you'll be alive to remind me how much you hate me every day."

CHAPTER 10

THE NEXT FOUR HOURS of the drive were made in relative silence, other than the radio. The only words I spoke were along the lines of *what do you want for lunch* and *do you need to go to the bathroom*. And Evie answered with as few syllables as possible each time.

My nerves were at a sky-high level when we stopped for a bathroom break somewhere in Mississippi. I was so afraid she was going to go rogue inside the store and scream at the top of her lungs that she was Evie Bouvier and she'd been kidnapped.

But she didn't. She dutifully tucked her hair beneath the ball cap and put on the sunglasses I'd grabbed from a convenience store when I'd stopped to gas up.

Rolling my shoulders to try and get rid of the kinks, I looked over at Evie. She was napping, but at my gaze, she popped her eyes open and blinked sleepily a few times before stretching her arms over her head and yawning.

"Where are we?"

It was the first time she'd initiated any conversation since she told me she hated me. I wasn't usually a man who gave a ripping fuck what anyone thought of me, but I'd be lying if I said hearing those words from Evie didn't bother me just a little bit.

"We're in Florida."

She rubbed at her eyes with her fingertips. "I didn't even think to ask where we were going. I was a little overwhelmed with everything else."

"Understandable," I said, tilting my head back and forth. "We're headed to Rodrigo's cousin's place north of Jacksonville."

"Where is Rodrigo?"

My heart thumped mightily a few times, and I inhaled a long breath to quell it. "I'm not sure. I gave him my regular phone to take up in the chopper with him and forgot to put his number in my spare phone." *Stupid. I've been worried about the old guy for hours.*

Evie held up a hand, her voice rising an octave. "Wait. He went up in the helicopter? The one with…"

"He had a parachute, Evie. I'm sure he's fine. We'll find out once we get to his cousin Rocco's house."

She relaxed back into her seat a bit. "Okay. How long is all this going to last? The running thing?"

"I'm not sure," I replied, and she eyed me skeptically. "I'm trying to be as honest as I can, Evie. I just don't know. Rocco disappeared a long time ago to escape from my father. I didn't even know he was alive until Rodrigo told me earlier today. Rod thinks his cousin can help us disappear since he did it so effectively."

Her eyes closed and her face squished into a grimace of resignation. "All right. This is all way out of my league, so I'm trusting you on this. You haven't hurt me yet." She blinked over at me, a rare vulnerability slipping into her voice. "Are you going to?"

"No, Evie. I will never hurt you, though I can't promise not to piss you off from time to time."

The sigh she emitted seemed to be never ending. "Okay, I guess that's the best I can ask for at this point." She straightened in her seat and stared out the front windshield. "But I still hate you."

"Fair enough," I told her, trying not to smile. *Stubborn little wildcat.*

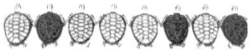

Pulling the SUV onto the driveway, I was surprised at the lack of security measures. There was no gate, no guard, nothing. Just a long, winding seashell drive that led to the pretty little home that was partly visible from the road.

"This looks nice," Evie said, leaning forward to peer at the white wood house with black shutters and colorful flower boxes. *Nice* was a perfect description for it, large enough to be comfortable but small enough to be cozy.

I didn't recognize the man who stepped onto the porch and lifted one thick hand in greeting. He was wearing camouflage cargo pants and a black tank top. "Stay in here and let me check it out. We may be at the wrong address," I told Evie as I pushed open the door.

"Hey, I'm not sure I'm at the right place," I called, but when a deep chuckle met my ears, my steps faltered. Squinting against the late afternoon sun, recognition sparked in my brain at the familiar sound.

I'll be damned. Rocco?

Rocco Scordato looked different from the last time I'd seen him. A lot different. Most noticeably, he'd put on about forty pounds. He definitely wasn't fat, but gone was the rail thin man I'd known when I was a teen. He was also bald now and sported a black beard with a smattering of gray, making him look more like a rugged biker than a slick mafioso.

"You're at the right place," he said, crossing the dark-green manicured lawn to slap me on the bicep. "Come on inside. My wife's got an early dinner ready."

"I... okay. Sorry about that. I didn't recognize you at first."

"And that's the whole point," he pointed out with a wry lift of one bushy eyebrow. "Do you have suitcases?"

Stepping closer, I lowered my voice. "I have three duffels full of cash."

He jerked his chin up and down. "Definitely want to bring those in then. This is a nice neighborhood, but you never know. I was talking about your personal things though. My cousin said you had a lady friend with you, so we made up both guest rooms. I wasn't sure if you'd be sharing or not."

"That's gonna be a no on the sharing," I told him, figuring I could confidently speak on Evie's behalf. *Though I certainly wouldn't mind...* "We don't have much in the way of personal belongings. We kinda left in a rush. Are we, uh, staying here?"

"Of course," he boomed. "My cousin was in a hurry so he didn't give me much information, just that you and your friend needed help. Come inside, and you can tell me everything."

"All right," I said, walking around to the passenger's side. "Let me get E—"

"No names until we're inside," Rocco broke in, his voice sharp as a dagger as his eyes darted around the well-kept yard.

"Right." I held open the car door for Evie as she emerged without her sunglasses and cap.

When I turned back to Rocco, his eyes were trained on her and as wide as dinner plates. "Holy fucking shit," he muttered, apparently recognizing her, probably from the news coverage. "Whew, you do need our help, son. Get her in the house quickly, and I'll unload the car."

Tossing him the keys, I led Evie across the lawn and up the two wooden steps. Before I could knock, the door swung open to reveal a beautiful woman with a full figure and a broad smile. Her curly brown hair was pulled up in a ponytail, and green eyes gleamed from her mocha-skinned face.

"Come on in. I'm Jamie." She said with a slight Jamaican accent, sweeping an elegant hand toward the living room, which was decorated in gray and red.

"Thanks for having us," I told her, unsure if I was supposed to give this woman our names. Her eyes were trained on Evie, and I saw the flicker of recognition there, but she brushed it off with a shake of her head and stepped toward the other woman.

"Look at you, sweetheart," she crooned softly, drifting her fingertips beneath the bruise on Evie's cheek. "Who the hell did this to you?" Her eyes darted accusingly toward me, but Evie shook her head.

"It wasn't him. It was the... the people who took me."

Jamie nodded, her lips pressed into a sad smile. "All right, sweetie. Let's get you settled and you can tell us more."

"Thank you," Evie replied.

Rocco lumbered in then, a duffel in each hand and Evie's flowery bag slung over a thick shoulder. Jamie's eyebrows shot up. "Well, I think floral is your color, honey."

He dropped the bags and glared at her without an ounce of ire. "You got a smart mouth, woman."

"And that's why you married me," she said with a wink before turning her attention back to us. "Follow me."

Evie and I trailed her across the living room and down a hallway. "You don't have to put us up," I told her. "We could have stayed at a hotel or something."

"Nah, we have a lot of work to do, and it's easier and safer if we're all under the same roof," she said before opening a door on the right. "Evie, this can be your room. It's more girly than the other one."

"It's beautiful," Evie said, entering and looking around at the soft pink wallpaper and white bed. Gauzy white curtains draped over the two multi-paned windows.

"There's a bathroom here," Jamie said, sliding open a white barn door. "It connects to the other bedroom, so you two will have to share."

We walked through and into the other bedroom, which was done in shades of blue. "This is great. Thank you," I told her and received a warm smile in response.

Retrieving our bags from the living room, I dropped Evie's off in her room. "There's one more change of clothes in here. I'll see about getting you some more things, if you'll make me a list. Like the kind of hair stuff you like or... I don't know... whatever else girls need."

She almost smiled at me but not quite. "Thanks. I think I'd like to take a shower, if that's okay."

"Of course. I'll close my door so you'll have some privacy."

I found my way to the kitchen where I found the couple working side by side at the counter. "Rocco," I started.

"Robert," he corrected. "That's my name now."

"Oh, gotcha. Have you talked to Rodrigo lately? I don't have any way to contact him, and I've been worried."

"I heard from him a couple hours ago, just briefly. He's fine and holed up near the coast of Mississippi. Don't worry about him."

Relief flooded me, and I let out a long breath. "Okay, good. Evie is in the shower. I need to get her some more clothes and stuff at some point."

"I can run to Target later," Jamie said, glancing toward the hallway where our bedrooms were located and lowering her voice. "Tell us what's going on and why the hell you have a missing fashion heiress on the run with you."

I filled them in while they stacked warm sandwiches on a platter, Jamie stopping a couple times during my story to press a hand over her chest. "Oh, that poor girl. And you. Dear god, your father is just as horrible as Robert told me."

"You don't know the half of it," I muttered.

"And how does Evie feel about being kidnapped, rescued, and then kidnapped again," he asked.

"I didn't kidnap her," I snapped out, scowling at Rocco, er, Robert. "I explained the consequences and she said she'd go along with it." Then I rolled my eyes and added, "Reluctantly, okay? She's not thrilled about this."

"I imagine not," Jamie said. "Well, we'll do our best to make it as... comfortable as possible for her."

We cut off our conversation when we heard footsteps coming down the hallway, and Robert picked up the tray of food while Jamie and I carried the drinks and chips into the sunny dining room.

"Can I ask you a question?" Evie asked, biting off the point of her honey ham and swiss cheese sandwich.

"Sure. Anything," Jamie told her.

"How did you two get together?"

Robert chuckled and leaned forward on his forearms, looking ready to roll. "I'm glad you asked. This is a great story."

Jamie held up her palm to him. "Let me tell it. I do it better."

"You do not," he argued. "I'm an excellent storyteller."

She scoffed. "Whatever. You have no flair... no pizzazz!" Jamie emphasized her claim with spread fingers and shaking hands.

"We don't need jazz hands to explain our story, Jamie honey."

The woman cocked her head and pursed her lips. "We do, if we don't want it to be boring."

He chuckled. "The way we met is anything but boring, honeybunch." His large hand made a sweeping gesture to the woman beside him. "By all means..."

"Thank you," she retorted smartly before turning her attention to Evie, who was seated on a cream, padded chair beside me. "You see, it was a dark and stormy evening in mid-July." Her husband gave a *here we go* roll of his eyes, and she elbowed him for his insolence. "The moon was hidden behind a bank of clouds, leaving all corners of Florida bathed in darkness."

"Dramatic woman," Robert mumbled, and Jamie flipped him her middle finger.

"Anywayyyyy, I was at my office late, working on some charts."

"They don't even know what you do," her husband pointed out.

"I was getting to that." She shot him a side eye and stole one of his sour cream and onion chips as punishment. After crunching it loudly in his ear, she explained to us, "I'm a reconstructive and cosmetic surgeon."

"The best damn plastic surgeon in Florida," Robert said, beaming at his wife.

Jamie's hand reached up and stroked his beard with a familiarity and affection that told me she did this often. He was practically purring like a fucking kitten at her attention.

"Thanks, babe. Anyway, like I was saying, I was working late on that dreary night when a man suddenly appeared inside my office, all wet and menacing looking." She smacked her hand against the table. "He had the damn audacity to wave a gun around and insist that I perform surgery on him to change his appearance."

Beside me, Evie widened her eyes in horror. "What did you do?"

Jamie bobbed her eyebrows up and down. "I reached in my desk drawer and pulled out my own gun. Clicked off the safety and pointed it directly at his head."

"Such a badass move," Robert said, kissing her temple.

"You still didn't leave," she reminded him, casting a fond look up at his furry face before returning her attention to us. "The jackass made himself at home in the chair across from my desk—with my gun still trained on him, mind you—and spilled his guts. He'd been in the Mafia in New York but wanted to go straight. He begged me to help him because some asshole named Luca Cappitani was after him." She cast a chagrined smile at me.

"Sounds familiar," I said dryly. "What happened next?" I was fully invested in this story now.

"I told him to place his gun carefully in my desk drawer, and then we'd talk. To my surprise, he did."

"May I add something, oh, great storyteller?" Robert asked his wife, and Evie giggled at their antics.

"Please do," Jamie said solicitously.

He gave her another temple kiss before speaking to Evie and me again. "I'd been watching this beautiful lady for a few days and was already half in love with her."

"Stalker," Jamie said around a fake cough, and we all laughed.

"I mean, she was an older woman…"

"Three years, Robert," his wife scolded, holding up that many fingers for emphasis. "I'm only *three years* older than you."

He ignored her and continued. "But she was the most beautiful woman I'd ever seen. And so fucking smart. She sat there that night and listened to me." His voice turned quieter. "Her brother had been killed by the Shower Gang in Jamaica, which is kinda like our Mafia here, so she took pity on me since I wanted to get out of that life. She agreed to help me."

Evie reached across the table and squeezed the other woman's hand. "I'm so sorry about your brother, Jamie."

"Thank you. I told Robert—well, Rocco back then—if he was serious about cleaning up his life, I would do what I could. Instead of radical reconstructive surgery, I suggested he shave his head and grow a full beard. Facial hair on a man can completely change their look. He had a very prominent brow line, so I did do surgery to reduce that."

"Cro-Magnon head, I believe were her exact words," Robert added, and I snickered. "As soon as I was healed, she sent me away and told me not to come back until I had my shit straight. So I went to school and became a coiffure artisan."

A… what?

"He's a hairstylist," Jamie informed us dryly.

My chin pulled back in surprise as I looked at the smug face of Robert. "*You* are a hairstylist?"

"Don't sound so shocked," he said with a grin, twiddling his large fingers at me. "These hands can work hair magic. That's my day job, of course. By night, I'm a covert computer and technology guru."

At my questioning gaze, Jamie huffed out an explanation with a roll of her eyes. "Hacker."

"Covert computer and technology guru," Robert insisted. "I know I said I was going straight but..." He shrugged his big shoulders. "Instead of using my computer skills to launder money for the mob, I now use it to help people who need me."

"What kinds of people?" Evie asked, speaking for the first time in a while.

Jamie gave her a soft smile. "We work with a lot of abused women or people who need to disappear like Robert did. People who are searching for a better life."

Evie nodded once and dropped her chin to her chest. I could hear her breathing pick up, and then she stood abruptly, mumbled, "Excuse me," and hightailed it down the hallway, presumably to her room.

Starting to push from my chair, I said, "I'll go check on her."

Jamie rose gracefully and motioned for me to sit back down. "Let me."

Exhaling a long breath, I sank back down and rested my elbows on the table, sinking my fingers into my dark hair.

"You all right, man?"

I lifted my weary head, clasping my hands at the back of my neck. "I'm trying like hell to save her, but all I'm really doing is hurting her."

Robert was silent for a long moment, staring down at his empty plate before lifting his concerned gaze to mine. "I know, Damiano. But sometimes those things are not mutually exclusive."

CHAPTER 11

I CLOSED THE BEDROOM door behind me and leaned my back against it, eyes closed and breaths labored. *Fuck. Fuck, fuck, fuck.*

My body jolted when a soft knock reverberated through the wood of the door and into my right shoulder. With a shaky voice, I called, "Yeah?"

"Evie, may I come in?"

Jamie. Hell, this was her house. How could I tell her she couldn't come in? Scrubbing my hands up and down my face, I stepped away from the door. "Of course."

I heard the swish of the door opening and then felt a slight touch between my shoulder blades. "Tell me what happened, honey. Did I say something to upset you?"

With a jaw made of steel, I turned with a forced smile on my face. "It wasn't you. And I'm sorry I ran off like that. It was rude of me."

Her pretty lips slid into a crooked smile. "Don't bullshit me, Evie. Tell me." Her voice left no room for argument, and for some inexplicable reason, I trusted this woman. Wanted to talk to her. Jamie was brash and funny, but at the same time, she was gentle and caring.

Running the fingers of one hand through my still damp hair, I let out an exhale that felt like it had been roosting in my lungs for days.

"You said you help people who are searching for a better life but..." My fingers gripped thick locks of hair, tightening until I could feel the tug against my scalp. The slight pinch seemed to give me that last ounce of strength I needed to continue. "I already have a good life. *Had* a good life, I guess, since everything is all fucked up now."

Deflating like a popped balloon, I sank into a crouch, palms pressed to my face. "I want my life back."

Jamie didn't say anything, but I sensed movement and peeked through my fingers to see her sitting at my level, cross-legged in front of me. She gestured for me to do the same.

"Sit, honey. Trust me, your knees will thank you once you reach my age."

At first glance, I'd thought Jamie was in her forties, but on closer inspection, the tiny lines around her eyes and the hints of gray snaking through her dark hair told me that was probably an underestimation. I sat, mimicking her position and clasping my hands in my lap.

"Evie, marrying a former mobster and secretly helping people go underground was not in my life plan."

The blunt statement and sarcastic undertones in her voice made me smile. "I imagine not."

"I was married once before, in my twenties, but when we found out I couldn't have children, he left me. I was resigned to being alone, focusing on my career. Don't get me wrong, I wasn't some recluse with no friends. I had an active social life and a fulfilling job."

I stayed silent, letting her speak as she leaned back with her palms against the floor. "At least I thought I was fulfilled until that big oaf busted into my office that night. But Robert and the job we do now were like the puzzle pieces I didn't know were missing." Jamie smiled at me. "What I'm trying to say with all my rambling is that life doesn't always go the way we expect it to. There are bumps and twists and turns that move us in a different direction. And I know, sweetie, I know you're in a horrible situation, and I hate that for you, but your focus right now needs to be on surviving."

With my fingernail, I flicked at the edge of the bandage on my right knee. "I know people have it a lot worse than me but—"

"No," Jamie cut in with a shake of her head, "don't compare your situation to others'. What you've been through is horrific, and you're allowed to have all the feelings about that."

"I hate Damiano," I admitted. "I hate him for deceiving me, for being a criminal, even for being related to Luca Cappitani, though I know that last one's not his fault."

Jamie was quiet for a beat. "Did you have a good father growing up?"

A little surprised by the change in direction, I bobbed my head up and down. "The absolute best." My heart squeezed behind my breastbone. I missed my dad so much.

"I did too, but Damiano didn't. He grew up a criminal because that's what he learned from a very young age. His father is..." She shook her head and pressed her lips together. "He's a very bad man."

"As bad as Damiano said?"

Her face was solemn. "Probably worse. From what my husband told me, the way Luca treats women is absolutely disgusting. I know what you're going through now seems bad, but you're lucky Damiano didn't deliver you to him."

I stared at my knee, watching my thumb smooth down the corner of the bandage I'd been picking at. "I know, and I am grateful for that, but he lied to me. He said he was taking me to my family. He let me believe he was some kind of agent that had come to rescue me."

"Definitely an asshole move. Are you afraid of Damiano?"

My mind played through all the memories I had of the man in the short time I'd known him. "I probably should be, but no. He's actually been very kind to me."

"Would you prefer to go on the run by yourself? Because we can make that happen."

I was surprised at my instantaneous response to the question, at the fear provoked by the thought of being alone out in the world, not knowing a soul. Even being with Damiano would be better than that.

"No. I know he's a criminal, but I somehow feel kind of safe with him. I don't think he'd let anyone hurt me."

"I'm inclined to agree," Jamie said thoughtfully. "Sometimes a person from the wrong side of the law is the best person to protect you from others on that same side."

"So what happens now?"

"Robert and I will talk it out and come up with a plan. We can go over it with you and Damiano tomorrow." Her lips curved into a small smile. "You actually picked a good time to get kidnapped. Robert and I are on vacation from our jobs right now."

My brow creased. "I'm so sorry to interrupt your vacation."

She waved a hand at me. "No worries. We weren't going anywhere, just having a bit of a staycation at home." Standing, she held out a hand toward me. I took it and let her help me to my feet.

"Thank you for checking on me. I just have all these emotions I don't know how to handle."

"It's okay, honey. I'm sure all this is unprecedented in your life."

That made me chuckle. "Truth. I've never been kidnapped, sold to a mobster, and then almost blown to smithereens before." I sighed. "I just feel like I don't have any control over my own life anymore."

Jamie surprised me with her next words, honest ones, not *blowing smoke up my ass* ones. "You really don't for the most part. You can only control what you can control, Evie."

"Which is pretty much nothing right now."

Her head tilted to the side in thought. "You can pick your new name."

"My new... oh, right. I can't exactly go around calling myself Evie Bouvier."

"Nope, you can't. Robert and I have found that most people find it easier to adjust if they use the same first initial, but that's not a hard and fast rule. If you want to call yourself Marjorie, Queen of the Fairies, go for it."

I allowed my lips to lift a bit at the corners, even though the thought of changing my name made me feel a little queasy. "That does have a nice ring to it."

"And you have some say about where you'll live. Do you prefer a coastal, mountain, or desert setting? Or maybe on a farm in middle America?"

"I loved living in New York, but when my dad would ask us where we wanted to go on vacation, I always voted for the beach. It's my favorite place to go."

She nodded thoughtfully. "I think we can make that work." Pulling out her phone, she tapped her thumb against the screen a couple times. "I'm about to run to Target to get you and Damiano a few essentials. What do you need?"

"It's okay. I don't need—"

"Favorite body wash?" Jamie asked, ignoring my protest. Resigned, I rattled off the name and answered the other questions she asked regarding my sizes and other products. Her green eyes sparkled when she looked up at me. "See? You do have control over a few things. I turn into a total grump when I don't have my favorite smells around me."

A smidgen of the frustration inside me dissipated. The thought of having my honey and vanilla body wash—hell, even my fruity shampoo—was somehow comforting.

Jamie was right when she said all I can control is what I can control. And all I could control right now were tiny things like my preferred bath products. But for tonight, that would have to be enough.

CHAPTER 12

I WOKE UP THE next morning, determined to keep a positive attitude about all the unwanted changes in my life. Robert and Jamie had welcomed us into their home and were trying to help us, so I put a smile on my face when I entered the dining room wearing frayed jean shorts and a blousy lilac top, one of the outfits Jamie had purchased last night.

"That looks cute on you," she said, looking up as she laid a platter of bacon on the table where Damiano and Robert were sitting.

"It's my favorite color," I admitted. "My dad always buys me lilacs on my birthday." *Don't think about your birthday, Evie. Or your dad. Or your brothers. Or pretty much anything.* So I pushed the thoughts away and took a seat.

"I know you're probably used to wearing the Bouvier brand, but all the boutiques were closed by the time I went shopping last night."

"I do, but I shop at regular stores as well. Everything you bought is perfect. Thank you."

"Okay," she said, sliding onto the chair beside her husband. "We've got a lot to do regarding appearances. Why don't we talk about that over breakfast?"

"Are you going to reconstruct my face? If so, I'd like to look like Angelina Jolie," I teased, drawing chuckles from around the table.

Jamie shook her head. "I'm not going to change anything about the structure of your face, Evie. Your eyes though, they're your most striking feature, so we'll start there. Have you ever worn contact lenses?"

"No."

"Okay, I'll teach you. We have a supply of colored ones here. I think brown would be best, if that's okay."

I appreciated her asking for my input, attempting to give me a semblance of the control I craved over my own damn life. "That will be fine."

Robert inspected me as he nibbled on a slice of bacon. "Your look is very classic, Evie. I was thinking we should go a bit edgier with your hair. Shorter and darker. I could even add a lilac streak, if you want."

Suppressing the grimace I felt at the thought of cutting my hair, I forced a smile onto my face. "That sounds... great."

Jamie rubbed a palm over her husband's bald head. "Don't let the lack of hair fool you. Robert really is good at finding the best styles for people."

"Do I have to become a cue ball too?" Damiano asked flatly.

Robert grinned at him. "Exactly the opposite. We're going to let your hair grow out."

"The broken nose though," Jamie said, circling her fork with a bite of pancake on the end. "Will you let me fix that, Damiano? I think it could change your entire look. Add in the long hair and a beard, and you'll be virtually unrecognizable."

His finger swooped along the crook in his nose. Despite that, he was a very handsome man with his dark hair, olive skin, and cheek bones that would make a model weep. And those lips... gahhh! I mentally scolded myself for noticing.

"If you think it will help, do it," Damiano replied. "But won't there be hospital records and staff to worry about?"

"It's an outpatient procedure, so we can do it at my office after hours," Jamie informed him. "My surgical nurse is a woman we helped who was in an abusive relationship. Robert and I paid for her to go to nursing school, and she's become a vital part of our team. Very trustworthy."

"How many people have you helped?" I asked before forking a bite of fluffy pancake into my mouth.

Jamie hummed, rolling her eyes to the ceiling. "Not sure of the exact number, but it's a few people per year. We're very selective, which is out of necessity. We only take people who are referred by someone we trust. Like Rodrigo."

"Have you heard from him today?" Damiano asked, worry etching lines into his forehead. He really seemed to care about the older man.

Robert gave him a thumbs up. "He texted this morning with the one-word code we use to let me know he's safe." A smug smile inched across his lips. "We probably won't hear from him for a while. He's shacked up with that cleaning woman."

"A maid?" I asked, and Robert chortled.

"No, she cleans up... *messes* other people leave behind."

Oh. I got the message. "What's the code?"

I realized that was none of my business as soon as I asked it, but he answered anyway. "Tiramisù, but we change it every few months."

For some reason, that gave me the giggles. "I love tiramisù. There's a place in New York my father takes me every year for my birthday that has the best I've ever had."

Robert pointed a thick finger at the man beside me. "Then you've never had Damiano's. I could eat an entire pan of his without blinking an eye."

"Which would be fine if I was a cardiologist," Jamie said dryly.

I was still trying to process the fact that the killer beside me could even find his way to the kitchen, much less make tiramisù.

Robert leaned back in his chair, eyes to the ceiling as if reminiscing. "I think it was about ten years ago when me and Rodrigo found you working away in the kitchen, Dame. You couldn't have been more than fifteen, but you were whipping and stirring like a pro."

"My mama taught me everything I know," Damiano said quietly, and Robert gave him a sad smile. I wondered what that was all about.

"I just thought your cannoli were a dream until you served us your tiramisù. Mmm, so decadent." His eyes closed and his mouth gaped open.

"Would you cool it?" Jamie asked. "They don't want to see what your O-face looks like."

"Agreed," grunted Damiano, his nose crunched up.

Jamie continued, "Okay, backstories. We decided it would be best to say you're both only children and that your parents are no longer living. That way there won't be any questions about your families."

We nodded as Robert took over. "Jamie and I have a beach house in the Keys, so you can stay down there as a newlywed couple."

"No!" I practically shouted, leaping from my chair and jerking my thumb in Damiano's direction. "I am *not* marrying him."

"On paper only," Jamie said in a soothing voice. "There are two bed-rooms in the house."

"I have to *live with him*?" I was pretty sure my eyeballs were about to spring from my head and onto the table.

"Honey, what did you think was going to happen?"

My brain scrambled for an answer. "I don't know. I guess I thought we'd live on the same street or something." *Okay, I admit. That sounded a bit lame.*

"Evie, there's safety in numbers. And anyone looking for you won't be looking for a married couple. It's really the best cover."

I crossed my arms over my chest and turned my back on them, pacing a few steps away. What they said made sense, but I didn't like this. Not at all. But I was scared, and truth be told, I didn't want to be alone. After a few minutes of silence where I massaged the tightness in my temples, I finally turned back around and leveled everyone at the table with a glare.

"If we do this, I have some rules."

Damiano's lips tipped up on one side, like I was fucking amusing him. "By all means, tell us your rules."

"I'm not living with some Mafia thug," I announced.

"Well, I'm obviously not with the family anymore," Damiano pointed out, and I narrowed my eyes at him.

"That means no whacking anyone."

Giving me a curt nod, he said, "Fine."

"Also, no drugs."

His jaw clenched, and his voice was firm and quiet. "I don't do drugs. Ever."

Walking up to him, I poked him in the chest. "And you better not leave your dirty socks in the living room."

As I whirled around and stomped from the room, I heard Damiano mumble, "We've only been married ten seconds, and she's already nagging."

I made a sound of annoyance in the back of my throat and tried to talk myself down. Otherwise, I'd be the one doing the whacking.

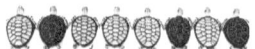

"Okay, try one more time."

"It's so big," I complained.

Jamie chuckled. "Evie, it's fourteen millimeters in diameter."

I stared down at the contact lens on my fingertip. "Are you sure? It seems like it's bigger than a dinner plate."

"I assure you, it's not."

The bathroom I shared with Damiano had a knee space, and I was seated on the small, padded chair with a stand mirror in front of me. "Okay, I'm trying again."

Holding my eyelid with the fingers of my other hand, I edged the contact lens toward my cornea. It seemed to triple in size the closer it got, and I let out a whimpered, "Shit," before pulling my hand back. "Sorry, Jamie."

A dark presence seemed to invade the space a second before I heard a deep voice ask, "What's going on?"

"Evie's just having trouble getting her contacts in," Jamie explained to Damiano, and my face flushed with embarrassment. Why the hell was this so hard? Millions of people wore contact lenses every day.

"Turn around," he demanded, and my stupid body did what he asked without my permission. Taking the lens from me, he rinsed it off with the small bottle of solution sitting on the counter before arranging the devilish piece of silicone hydrogel on his index finger. "Open wide, Evie."

"What the hell do you think you're doing?"

In answer, he placed a large hand on top of my head and tilted my chin up. "Putting this in for you. My brother started wearing contacts when he was sixteen, and he acted like a little pussy." Then he added with a smirk, "Just like you."

My eyelids popped open wide in shock and anger, but before I could come up with a snarky retort, he stuck the lens in my eye.

"Aghhhh!" I shrieked, his low laughter providing a background to my distress. "You... you..."

"How does it feel?" he asked, completely unaffected by my irritation. I blinked rapidly about a thousand times, surprised when it felt... normal.

"It's okay," I admitted reluctantly.

He pointed at the white case sitting on the counter. "Now do the other one, or I'm going to do it for you." His smugness pissed me off, and I swiveled around, completely motivated by stubbornness now.

I got the lens on my cornea on the second try.

"Good girl," he said, stroking a hand over the top of my head before strolling casually back into his bedroom.

His touch and parting words roused an unwelcome feeling in my throat, but I swallowed it down and mumbled, "Asshole," as I looked over at Jamie. She was covering her mouth with her fist, but I could see the smile hiding behind it.

"They look good. What do you think?" she asked, gesturing to the mirror.

At first glance, I was startled. The blue eyes I'd seen in the mirror for over eighteen years were gone, replaced by brown ones. Tilting my head from side to side, I said, "I don't hate them. They look very natural. It's just different."

"That's the point," she said, patting me on the shoulder. "Now let's get Robert to work his magic on your hair."

"Can we talk about the money?" Robert asked as his hands worked in my hair.

"What money?" I asked, purposely not looking at the strands of my caramel hair falling to the floor.

"Uh, the almost seven million in cash that's currently sitting in there," he replied, tilting his head toward the house. We were in the small building behind his house that he used as a makeshift salon.

"Oh, well, I don't really know much about it besides the fact that asshole Luca was going to buy me with it."

"Yeah, but since it's yours now, I was—"

"It's not mine," I argued, and Robert's hand stilled before he set his scissors down and rested his hands on his knees, bringing himself to my eye level.

"Damiano said he was giving it to you." I stared blankly at him, and his eyebrows pressed together in confusion. "He said he planned to give the cash to you when he dropped you off with your family. He didn't tell you that?"

My heart rose up into my throat. *What the hell?*

"No," I told him, swallowing hard to try and clear my windpipe. "Why?"

"He thought you and your family could use it." A chagrined smile quirked his mouth up on one side. "Of course, at the time, he didn't realize who you were and that you probably have more cash than that in your couch cushions."

"W-why wouldn't he just give it back to his father when he went back home?"

Robert shook his head, looking slightly amused. "He wasn't going back, Evie. He was going to take you home and then scram."

"Scram?"

He sighed and stood upright, bracketing his jaw with his hand before stroking downward. "If Luca Cappitani gives you an order, you do it or else. You get what I'm saying?"

My mind worked to keep up, to put all the pieces together. "Damiano was going to let me go, but then, if he went home without his father's *purchase*, he would be dead meat."

"Now you're getting it," he said, picking up the scissors again, holding a piece of my hair between two fingers and snipping off the ends. "And don't even ask me why because I can't give you the answer to that. All I know is that once Luca found out who you were, everything changed. Damiano knew you—and every member of your family—would become a target."

As Robert finished the haircut, I was silent, processing everything I knew, but it still didn't make sense. Damiano didn't even know me. Why the hell would he care if I was a target? Why the hell would he protect me when I'm sure it would have been simpler for him to disappear without me in tow?

When Robert started brushing the dark-brown color onto my hair with a black, long-handled brush, I spoke again.

"This thing you and Jamie do... do you have a success rate?"

When he was silent, I lifted my eyes to find his jaw clenched. Finally, he said, "Almost perfect. Only one loss." His voice took on a hint of anger. "He didn't follow our directions."

"What did he do?"

Robert's eyes dropped to mine, boring into them like he was imparting something very important. "We told him no contact with anyone in his old life, but he didn't listen. He called his mistress, and, of course, the Bratva had her phone tapped. That's how they found him."

His lips pressed hard together as his hands continued their work.

"Why were you asking about the money earlier?"

"Oh, yeah. That. You're not going to have to worry about rent or anything, but I was wondering if you minded using that money for yours and Damiano's living expenses."

"Like I said, it's not mine, so I don't care," I replied. "How long until Luca forgets about me so I can go home?"

"That asshole has a very long memory, Evie. There was one guy who wronged him and then disappeared. Luca found him nine years later and decapitated him in front of his wife and kids."

Bile rose in my throat, and it took great effort to swallow it down. "So if he's not going to forget about me, what's the end game?"

"Someone has to take out Luca. No one under him has the balls to do it, so it has to come from the top. From Leo, the Don. The only problem is, Leo is Luca's uncle, and he's always been reluctant to kill a member of his own family."

"How noble of him," I said sarcastically, sliding my hands beneath my thighs. I thought maybe we were going into hiding for a couple months or something, but any hope of seeing my family anytime soon was beginning to fade.

"Damiano's brother is talking to Leo, but there's no guarantee it will work. He has to be cautious though so Luca doesn't find out. We need to keep Fiero in place because he's the only one we can trust within the family." Robert pressed a finger against the back of my head. "Tilt forward."

I did, feeling air against the back of my neck. Though with all this new information, some missing hair seemed a lot less important.

Once the color was done processing, Robert sat me in another chair and leaned my head back into the single shampoo bowl along one wall of the metal building.

"Oh my god, that feels good," I sighed as his fingers scrubbed and massaged my scalp.

He looked down at me and smiled. "Jamie says the same thing. She loves when I wash her hair."

This big man's face took on the consistency of a melting marshmallow when he spoke of his wife. "You are the cutest couple," I commented.

"You and Damiano will be too."

I jerked upright, splashing water and shampoo all over. "We are *not* a couple," I gritted out, and Robert's eyebrows lifted high on his forehead as he eased me back down.

"Okay, killer. Calm down. All I meant was that you two will look good together. Should be easy enough to make people believe you're really newlyweds."

Even the thought of that rankled me. "Except for the fact that I don't like him."

"I'm aware," he said with a chuckle. "But you're going to have to show off your acting skills and pretend when you're out in public."

My nose crinkled because I knew he was right. "I'll start working on my Oscar award acceptance speech," I grumbled.

Robert laughed. "Good. Though no one says you have to act nice when you're not in front of others." His grin turned positively wicked. "In fact, when you're in private, I think you need to give Damiano hell every chance you get."

With an upward curve of my lips, I assured him, "Oh, that, Robert... *that* I can do."

CHAPTER 13

WHILE ROBERT AND EVIE were out back in the salon, Jamie was working with me to tone down what she called my "thick New Yawk accent."

"You're doing well," she said. "Just remember, they speak a little slower down here in the south so let your words dawdle a bit more on your tongue instead of talking ninety miles an hour."

"And you're sure I can't say *fuhgeddaboudit?*" I teased, and she laughed.

"Absolutely not." Her head tilted toward the back door when we heard it open. Two sets of footsteps—one heavy and one light—made their way toward the living room. "I guess they're done. I'm excited to see what Evie looks like." I was too. They'd been back there for hours.

Robert walked into the room and swept his arm out as he stepped to the side. "Ladies and gentlemen—or Damiano—I present to you... Eden."

My eyes narrowed into a squint. I almost darted my gaze around to look for Evie until I realized she was standing right there. "Evie?" I asked, and her eyes met mine.

"Eden," she corrected. "That's the name I chose."

"I get it," Jamie said, standing and striding a circle around her. "Evie... Eve... the Garden of Eden."

"Yes, is that dumb?"

"Not at all. I love it. And this look! Whew, girlfriend!" She did that Z-snap thing girls do. "You are one hot tamale, Eden."

Meanwhile, I was simply gawking like I'd never seen a woman before.

Gone was the pretty girl next door, and in her place stood a goddamn vixen. Her hair was short, dark, and messy, a thin streak of lilac on one side of the fringe that draped over her forehead.

Her eyes, now brown due to the contact lenses, looked rounder somehow with the new hairstyle. They softened the edgy visage just enough to compel a man to want to treat her like a princess while bending her over any nearby flat surface.

She. Is. Stunning.

Her eyes found me, and her teeth sank into her bottom lip almost shyly. "What do you think?"

She was seeking my approval, and she damn well had it. When I opened my mouth, my tongue forgot how to form actual words, and I ended up mumbling a bunch of vowel sounds. "Uhhh, I, ahhhh." Clearing my throat, I said, "It's fine."

Her gaze fell to the floor, and I knew instantly that I had fucked up. She was enduring all these changes, and all I came up with was *it's fine?*

Before I could rectify the situation, the doorbell rang. "That's probably the pizza," Jamie said, checking something on her phone before heading for the door.

"Why don't you have more security here?" I asked Robert. "Like gates or cameras."

"We have cameras. You just can't see them," he replied. "That was what Jamie was checking on her phone. One of the tricks of staying under the radar is not holing yourself up in a fortress. Shit like that makes people suspicious. To the outside world, we're just a normal couple in a normal house."

I nodded. That made sense.

We settled at the dining table for dinner with three different pizzas laid out in front of us. "I've been informed by my husband that the pizza in

Florida is subpar when compared with New York pies, but this is the closest he's found," Jamie said, reaching for a slice of pepperoni.

"It's tolerable," he grunted, taking three pieces that were fully loaded. I did the same. Evie—no, *Eden*—snagged a slice of what looked like meat lovers.

"So, we have Eden's new name. Now we just need to come up with something for Damiano. Have you thought about any D names you like?" Jamie asked, turning her green eyes on me.

"Not really. I'm open to suggestions," I told her, taking a large bite. It wasn't like home, but it was decent.

"I have some suggestions," Eden piped up. "What about Dillweed?"

I choked on the bite I'd just swallowed, pounding my chest with my fist as my eyes watered. Once I recovered, I turned my face slowly toward her. "Dillweed?" The little wildcat had the audacity to smile at me.

"You don't like that one?" she asked sweetly, batting her eyelashes at me. "What about Dickhead, Demon, or Dracula?"

"No, no, and no," I snapped.

"Oooh, maybe something more subtle like Draco. I think you'd definitely be in Slytherin."

"She's got a point," Robert said, sounding more amused than he had a right to be. "You're definitely a Slytherin kind of guy." Then he winked at Eden, a conspiratorial little gesture.

"Negative on Draco," I said, gritting my teeth, but it was mostly to keep myself from smiling.

"If you don't want to go with one of my D names, I have some great ones that start with F. Like Fu—"

"What about Dane?" Jamie suggested, apparently the only helpful one at this fucking table.

"Dane... Dane..." I rolled the name from my mouth a few times. "That's cool, Jamie. I like it."

Eden made a tsking sound and shook her head, like I was missing some grand opportunity to be called Dracula.

Later, when it was time for bed, I knocked on the bathroom door that led to her room. I could practically hear her eyes rolling through the white wood. "What?"

"Can I come in?"

"If you must," she sighed.

Sliding the door to the side, I entered to find her dressed in silky sleep shorts with a matching top in a yellow the color of butter. Tiny white flowers dotted the shiny material, and Eden suddenly looked very young.

"I'm sorry I said you looked fine earlier. You look much better than fine."

She scoffed and turned her back to me, exposing the bare nape of her neck. I was dying to sink my teeth into the flesh there. *Nope. Too young for you, remember? Not even nineteen. Does that ring a bell?*

"I wasn't fishing for compliments, Dami—Dane," she sniffed, busying her hands by folding clothes and placing them into the top drawer. "It was a lot of change for me, and I guess I was... apprehensive."

"You needed my approval, and I flubbed it."

Eden whirled around, eyes narrow. "I don't need your approval."

With my hands in my pockets, I covered the space between us in a few slow strides, my attention never wavering from her. "Well, you have it anyway."

She dropped her attention to the piece of clothing in her hands, folding and refolding it. "Since you're the one that's going to have to look at me every day for the foreseeable future, I guess that's good."

"Eden." When she didn't look up, I took the garment from her to stop her fidgeting and placed two fingers beneath her chin, lifting until our eyes locked. I willed my mouth to do what the fuck it was supposed to this time.

"The reason I fumbled around with my words earlier was because you stole my breath. I feel like the luckiest man in the world to call you my wife, Eden. You are beautiful."

The most mesmerizing shade of pink colored her cheeks, and I could tell she was fighting a smile. "*Fake* wife."

We'll just see about that.

I took in every inch of her face, taking my sweet time as I memorized her. "You got your nose pierced," I commented, noticing the tiny purple rhinestone nestled in the curve of her right nostril.

"Yes," she said, lightly touching it with the pad of one finger. "I've always wanted one, but my mother would never let me."

"Seriously, you look like a damn rock star."

Eden looked up at me from beneath her dark lashes, a hint of a smile teasing her lips. "Thanks, Dillweed."

"Christ, I think I prefer Dracula," I muttered before pivoting to hide my amusement and walking back toward the bathroom. "See you tomorrow, Eden."

"I could get you a cape if you want to be Dracula," I heard her say from behind me. "Then you could swoop around the house like the Prince of Darkness."

"Ozzy Osbourne is the Prince of Darkness, not Dracula." The sound of her laughter followed my retort.

It wasn't until I was back in my bedroom with the door closed that I realized I was still holding the piece of clothing she was folding earlier. Taking a step toward the door to return it to her, my feet faltered when I saw what was in my hand.

Panties. Black. Lace. Tiny.

Fuck me.

One part of my brain told me to take them back to her like a decent human being, but it was in a fierce battle with the dirty part of my brain that lifted the scrap to my nose for a deep inhale. They were clean and smelled like laundry detergent, but the depravity of the act made my cock twitch in my pants. They may not smell like her, but they belonged to her, and that was enough to satisfy me. For now.

That same dirty portion of my brain had me placing the panties beneath my pillow, and when I undressed and climbed into bed, one of my hands slipped underneath and gripped them in my fist as I fell asleep.

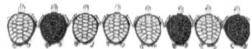

My entire face hurts.

That was the first thought I had when I opened my eyes the next afternoon in my bedroom. It was Saturday, and Jamie had done the rhinoplasty at her office a few hours ago.

Pushing my palms into the mattress, I scooted my body up and leaned against the iron headboard. That position seemed to help the intense pressure in my nasal passages a bit. I gingerly reached up and found that my nose was covered with bandages.

When a soft tap sounded on the door, I called out, "Come in," my voice sounding thick and strained. I expected it was Jamie coming to check on me, so I was surprised to see Eden walking into the room with a tray in her hands.

"Hello, patient," she said in a chirpy voice, striding across the room. "Are you hungry?"

"Actually, yes. I could eat something."

She placed the tray on my lap and grinned cheekily. "Consider yourself lucky. Jamie told me I wasn't allowed to spill hot soup in your lap."

"I'll be sure to thank her," I replied dryly, surprised when she perched on the edge of the bed beside me.

"How are you feeling?" Her voice had lost that teasing edge, sounding almost sweet.

"I feel like someone stuck a couple large sheep up my nose." I picked up the spoon and stirred the chicken noodle soup. Of course, I couldn't smell it, but it looked delicious.

"Remember, your sense of taste will be a little off for a while," Eden told me, watching as I scooped up a spoonful and placed it in my mouth. She was right. I could taste it, but the flavors were somehow muted due to not being able to smell.

"You're not wearing your contacts," I observed.

"I'm only supposed to wear them a few hours a day until I get used to them."

"They really do make a difference," I told her, taking another bite of the warm soup. "Covering your bright blue irises was a good idea."

"Did you know that the plural of irises is actually irides? Unless you're referring to the flower. Then it's I-R-I-S-E-S, but when you're talking about ocular anatomy, it's I-R-I-D-E-S."

I shook my head. "Nope, that's a new one on me."

"Most people just say irises though. The only people who say irides are pretty much eye doctors."

Chuckling, I said, "As far as I know, you're not an eye doctor, Eden."

"I know, but I'm me," she said with a shrug, as if that explained everything. Then she tapped an index finger against her temple. "I like knowing things other people don't."

"Well, keep them coming. I like hearing your random facts."

She looked pleased by that. "How did you break your nose?"

I nibbled on a cracker, hiding my wince when I swallowed. At least I thought I hid it until Eden picked up the glass of water on the tray and handed it to me. Taking a sip, I handed the glass back to her.

"My brother punched me."

Eden's neck craned forward. "The same one who told you about the helicopter?"

"Yep. One and the same."

"Why did he punch you?"

"I fucked his girlfriend."

Her eyes almost popped out of her head. "Dane!" she scolded.

"Okay, it wasn't actually his girlfriend. He liked her, but I didn't know that." My voice turned into a sneer. "My father did though. He was the one who set it up."

Eden held her hands up, palms out. "Wait, wait. Go back."

Whooshing out a sigh, I said, "My brother and I were tight, and my father didn't like it. He's a paranoid asshole who thinks everyone is out to get him, so he doesn't like people getting too close to each other. Could foster loyalty to someone other than him."

"So he set you up so your brother would be mad at you," she said.

I scooped up another bite of soup and swallowed. It was getting easier with each bite. "Luca told me it was time I became a man and said he had set me up with a girl." My shoulders lifted and fell. "I was fifteen with raging hormones, so I fucked her on the floor of our living room."

Eden's mouth gaped open like a fish out of water. "And your brother found out?"

With a scoff, I answered, emphasizing the first word. "*Coincidentally*, Fiero got home early from work that day."

"Ah, but it wasn't a coincidence, I presume."

"Correct. When we talked later, after he'd calmed down and I'd iced my nose, he told me our father had called him home for some kind of emergency. That's when we figured out he had manipulated the whole thing to get us to hate each other."

"And that's why Luca would never suspect that your brother would help you."

I nodded. "We've continued to play our parts to make him believe that for the past ten years."

"One more question." Her lips curved up into a sly grin. "Did you at least get to finish first?"

That was so unexpected from her, I snorted out a laugh, which felt like getting punched in the nose a hundred times in a row. "Owww, fuck," I grunted, my hand hovering over my face. "Don't make me laugh, dammit."

"Sorry," she said, and I could tell she was barely reining in a giggle. "But did you?"

"No, you nosy ass. I didn't. I was standing there with a bloody nose and a hard dick, which totally ruined my first sexual experience."

Eden tilted her head and cooed, "Awww, were you ever able to get it up again or was it like Pavlov's dick where you associated erections with broken noses?"

I managed to laugh through my mouth, sparing myself the pain that time. "I recovered, thank you very much." Bobbing my eyebrows up and down, I lowered my voice. "You'll be happy to know *everything* about your husband is in working order."

She sniffed. "Fake husband, so your equipment is absolutely none of my business."

"Then why were you so interested in whether or not my cock was in working order?"

Her face registered shock, cheeks flaming into the most intriguing deep-pink color. "I... uh... I don't..." She lifted her chin, finding an ounce of composure. "Just shut up, Dracula. Are you done eating?"

"All done," I told her, feeling quite smug with myself.

She stood and took the tray from me, nodding toward a sheet of paper on the oak nightstand. "Jamie said to read over those post-op directions. She went over everything before like no contact sports and stuff like that, but she wants you to read it again."

"Got it."

"Oh, and she said you're not allowed to bite the heads off any bats or other small animals for at least six weeks."

It took a monumental effort not to laugh at that. Instead, I crossed my arms over my chest and leveled her with a glare. "I'll have my secretary rearrange my bat-biting schedule."

"Excellent. And speaking of that, I came up with a last name for us," Eden said as she walked toward the door.

"This oughta be good," I muttered. "What is it?"

With a wink over her shoulder, she replied, "Osbourne."

"Owwww!" I yelled, cupping my nose after another laugh burst from me.

Swear to god, this brat was going to be the death of me.

CHAPTER 14

My bruises had faded, and I was left with only a tiny scar on my lower lip from the smack from Ethan. I was also adjusting to my new look, wearing the brown contact lenses around the house a few hours per day to get used to them. Soon I'd have to wear them full time, or at least when I was out in public.

Jamie had removed the packing from Dane's nose yesterday, and while it was still discolored and swollen, it was straight. He'd stopped slicking his hair back so it now had a slight curl to it, and his beard was coming in nicely. He no longer looked the part of a Mafia son. Now he just looked like a normal guy. A very good-looking guy, but I tried not to notice.

I was doing my best to accept this whole situation I'd gotten myself into, though I annoyed Dane every chance I got. It gave me joy and kept me from thinking too much about my family.

But today? Today I was finding it difficult to put on any semblance of appeasement.

Foregoing the contact lenses—because fuck it—I dressed in a baggy blue T-shirt and comfortable athletic shorts before leaving my bedroom. I didn't want to be alone today, but I also didn't want to see anyone. No one in this house anyway. I wanted my family.

The enticing aromas of sugar and coffee drew me to the kitchen where my feet stalled in the doorway. *What the hell is all this?* I walked on bare feet to the breakfast bar, my fingers skimming over the cool, smooth surface of the clear vase. Burying my nose in the light-purple blooms, I inhaled the unmistakable scent of lilacs.

"Do you like them?"

My watery eyes lifted to find Dane standing beside the far counter, his face apprehensive.

"I do. They're beautiful."

"Happy birthday, Evie."

I didn't correct him for using my real name because my throat was clogged with emotion, managing only a soft, "Thank you."

"I made tiramisù last night after you went to bed. It should be ready to eat now."

"For breakfast?" I asked, the surprise and delight clear in my voice.

"Hell yes. You can do whatever you want today." He took a couple steps toward me, stopping only a foot away. "Is this okay? You said your dad always got you lilacs and took you out for tiramisù on your birthday. I know it's not the same, but I was trying..." His voice trailed off.

He's trying... That struck me in the chest, and my dislike of him softened a bit. "It's great, Dane. Thank you for doing all this."

He crooked a half smile at me. "Good. Have a seat, and I'll bring your breakfast to you."

I did, and a couple minutes later, he placed a large slice of tiramisù and a glass of orange juice in front of me. "Holy crap. I'll never be able to eat all this." After one bite, I was proved wrong. The dessert was rich, creamy, and absolutely delicious, the flavors melding together perfectly against my taste buds. "Oh my god, this is freaking fantastic," I mumbled around a mouthful.

Dane looked pleased with himself as he took the seat beside me with his own slice. "Did you know that the original tiramisù recipe contained no alcohol?" I lifted my eyebrows at him. "The dessert was created in 1972 at

Le Beccherie, a restaurant in Treviso, which is a town just north of Venice, and that recipe was alcohol-free."

I was stunned. "I didn't know that. I always thought it contained Marsala wine."

He did a fist pump that made me laugh. "Finally, I know something you don't. Most modern adaptations do contain Marsala or liqueur, as some chefs believe it enriches the flavor, but the original ingredients were espresso, mascarpone cheese, egg yolks, sugar, Savoiardi biscuits, and cocoa powder. That's how I make mine."

"Well, I'm a fan. It's the best tiramisù I've ever had."

"There are also legends that say it was actually created in Treviso in the 1800s by a maitresse in," he cleared his throat and widened his eyes significantly, "a house of pleasure."

"Like a brothel?" I asked incredulously, and Dane nodded.

"They say she served it to men at the end of the evening to reinvigorate them."

I pointed my fork at him. "Okay, you win the random knowledge award for the day. That's pretty interesting."

"Want to get out of the house for a while?" he asked. "I'm feeling a little cooped up."

Brightening, I nodded. "I'd love to. Where are Jamie and Robert?"

"They went down to the house in the Keys to get it ready. It's around seven hours from here, so they're going to stay the night down there."

"They said the house is in Marathon, and I've been researching it. I think it's a wise area to hide. The city is over eight thousand in population, so big enough to easily blend in and not so small that everyone is in your business."

"Which island is Marathon on?" Dane asked, eating the last bite of his dessert.

"The city limits extend to several islands. Knight's Key, Vaca Key, Hog Key, East and West Sister's Island, Boot Key, Deer Key. A few others too, but I can't remember them all."

He began cleaning up our breakfast dishes. "Have you ever been to the Keys?"

"Just Key West. My dad took my brothers and me a few years ago. We flew into the airport and spent all our time on that island, so I've never seen the rest of them." I stood and helped him load the dishwasher.

"Your mom didn't go with you?"

I wrinkled my nose. "No, she didn't have much to do with us. It was actually nicer without her there. All she ever does is complain."

"Hmmm," he hummed, drying his hands on a dish towel.

"You never talk much about your mother or sister."

"They're both dead," he said quietly, hanging the towel with over-meticulous care on the oven handle and avoiding my gaze. "Why don't you go get ready?"

Shit. "Dane." He finally looked up at me, and I could read the sadness in his dark-brown eyes. Reaching for his wrist, I wrapped my fingers softly around it. "I'm sorry."

He nodded and attempted a smile, but it was weak. "It's okay. It was a long time ago."

Glancing down, I noticed the bandage on his arm and decided to change the subject. "Did Kevin work on your tattoos some more?"

Kevin was a friend of Robert's who was a tattoo artist. He'd been working on Dane's ink to disguise it a bit. The tribal tats were kind of nondescript, so Kevin had just added some color to them. The most notable was the longsword that took up one entire forearm.

"Yeah, take a look at this," he said, peeling the edge of the bandage up before removing it to reveal the changes. I was astounded. The sword was no longer visible at all, the previous design now covered by an intricate peacock feather.

"Wow," I breathed, drifting my fingers over the gorgeous teals, oranges, and yellows. The design was bold, the colors vivid. "It's beautiful."

"I'm happy with it. Kevin said peacock feathers are supposed to transform negative energy into positive."

"Well, we could certainly use all the positive energy we can get," I joked, and Dane laughed.

"No shit. Maybe I should cover my entire body with them."

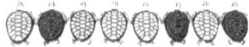

Dane kept me busy for the rest of the day. We walked along a stretch of beach, sampled foods from small shops, bought souvenirs like tourists, and stopped by a Redbox on the way home to pick up some DVDs.

Then we spent the evening on the couch and laughed our asses off at *Wedding Crashers* and *Diary of a Mad Black Woman*. We also ate more tiramisù after dinner, and it somehow tasted even better than it had that morning.

"Did you have an okay birthday?" Dane asked as we walked down the hallway toward our rooms later that night. He was carrying the bouquet of lilacs while I had a bag of T-shirts and jewelry looped around one hand.

"It was better than okay," I assured him, placing the bag on the dresser. He'd effectively distracted me from brooding. Of course I'd thought about my family a few times, especially Monty since it was his birthday too, but the mopey mood I'd woken up in this morning had been brightened considerably. Because of Dane.

"I'll just set these right here," he said, placing the flowers on my nightstand before checking to make sure my door was slightly ajar. I still didn't like being in closed spaces. I didn't have full-fledged panic attacks, but my anxiety definitely spiked if the door to my room wasn't cracked open at night.

"Dane?" He stopped on the way to the bathroom and turned. My voice sounded meeker than usual. "Can I give you a hug?"

A tiny line formed between his eyebrows but only for a second before it smoothed out and a smile snaked across his lips. "Yeah, Wildcat. You can give me a hug."

Stepping toward him, I wrapped my arms around his waist and rested my cheek against his chest. "Don't call me Wildcat."

"Don't call me Dracula," he retorted, amusement in his voice as he returned my embrace.

We'd hugged once before, that first night when I'd so desperately needed comfort from someone safe. I'd been so shaken, I hadn't even noticed the hard ripple of muscle beneath his shirt. But I was noticing now. Dammit.

"Thank you for today. Everything was perfect." Okay, maybe that was a bit of a stretch. Being with my family would have made it perfect, but under the circumstances...

"You're welcome," he murmured, kissing the top of my head, and that simple act of affection was so sweet, my heart melted a little. He released me and stepped back. "Get to bed, Eden."

When I laid my head on my pillow a few minutes later, I whispered into the darkness, "Happy birthday, Monty. I hope you had a good day."

Jamie and Robert returned the next day, and as we polished off the rest of the tiramisù, Jamie slid a wrapped white box with a hot-pink bow across the table. "Happy belated birthday, Eden."

My mouth dropped open. "You didn't have to get me anything. You've already done so much."

"It's something you need," Robert replied, fixing his eyes on mine. "Please remember what we've talked about and use it wisely." The jolly man was uncharacteristically solemn, and I wondered what the hell was in the package.

Tearing off the paper, I recognized the iPhone box immediately and smiled. "Thank you so much, and I promise I won't do anything stupid."

"Good. Dane, here's one for you too," Jamie said, passing an unwrapped box to the man beside me.

"Why doesn't mine have a fancy pink bow?" he complained, so I peeled my bow from the paper and planted it on top of Dane's head.

"There. Now you look all pretty," I teased, working my phone from the package and turning it on. "Smile!" I snapped a picture of him with a scowl on his face.

"You're so ridiculous," he grumbled, pulling the pink satin from his head.

Jamie spoke through a giggle at our antics. "Robert is going to finish up your IDs tonight. Dane, your bruising is much better today, but I'll cover it with some makeup so he can snap a photo. We also need to take some wedding pics of you two."

"W-wedding pics?" I stammered, feeling my eyes widen.

"Yes. It would look suspicious if the newlyweds didn't have any pictures of their happy day."

Happy day, my ass.

And that's how we ended up on the beach that evening with the sun setting behind us in a cacophony of supple pinks and purples. I was in a simple white dress that belonged to Jamie. It was too big, but she'd cinched it up in the back with a clip so it clung perfectly to my body. Dane was in a white button-down with tan pants.

"You just got married, for fuck's sake. Stand a little closer," Jamie instructed while Robert held a large Canon camera to his eye.

Dane snaked an arm around my shoulders and hauled me up against his huge body, and I reluctantly wrapped my arm around his back, plastering what I hoped was a happy expression onto my face.

"That's good," Robert said, snapping away. "Now look at each other."

Jamie blew out a huffed breath when I looked up at Dane. "Smile, Eden. You look like you're being forced to take a picture with your least favorite cousin."

That made us both laugh, and I could hear the whir of the camera as Robert did his thing. "Good job. Those will be cute. Now turn your bodies to face each other and gaze lovingly into each other's eyes."

Good grief!

With some fumbling, we repositioned ourselves with my hands on Dane's shoulders and his on my waist. It was awkward as hell. "You're too tall," I complained, and a second later, I let out a squeal when my feet left the ground as Dane curled his arms around my body and lifted until we were face to face.

"Better?"

Yes. No. I'm not sure.

He was awfully... firm. And I was pressed right up against *all* that firmness. His lips curved sinuously into a smile, and it softened the darkness of his eyes into molten pools of chocolate.

"Your irides look lighter out in the sun," I informed him, and he chuckled under his breath.

"Excellent! Good stuff," Robert called as we continued to stare at each other. This should have felt more awkward, just gazing at this man, but it was very... okay.

Dane leaned his forehead until it touched mine, and then he whispered. "Close your eyes, Wildcat." Like someone had physically tugged on my eyelids, they dropped without me even telling them to.

Something brushed my lips. *His lips*, I realized. *What the hell is happening right now, and why am I not pushing him away?*

My body stiffened, and when I placed my hands on his chest to do just that, he shifted, holding me up with one strong arm. Then he cupped the side of my neck, his thumb drawing a mesmerizing line over my jaw that had my stiffness ebbing away.

It wasn't an open-mouthed kiss. His lips simply moved against mine, tiny pulls that would have counted as suction if they hadn't been so tender and slow. When he finally broke away, I noticed my hands had found their way to the back of his head, my fingers tangled in the thick, dark locks that hung halfway down the nape of his neck.

How the hell did that happen?

Removing them, I scowled at Dane. "What. Was. That?"

He ran his tongue over his top lip before sucking the bottom one into his mouth. A smug grin morphed onto his face as he slowly rolled that full bottom lip out, leaving a trace of moisture there.

"A kiss." Then he fucking winked at me. "For the pictures."

Oh. Right. The pictures. I'd forgotten about that for a second.

"You can put me down now," I said curtly, feeling heat creep up the back of my neck and around to the front.

He did, but he took his damn time about it, letting me slide down his body. I ignored the ridges of his abs I felt on the way down. Didn't want to think too much about what was beneath that shirt of his. Nope. Didn't want to think about that at all. Instead, I took a large step back and turned my attention to the couple standing a few feet away.

"These look great, you guys," Jamie said, peering at the display screen on Robert's camera. "Nice touch with the kiss. Very convincing."

"What kind of wedding would it be if I didn't kiss my wife?" Dane asked, still wearing that infuriating smirk.

"*Fake* wife," I reminded him, and he had the nerve to lick his lips again. "Can we go now?" Without waiting for an answer, I stalked up the beach and toward the parking lot.

Damn you, Dane, with your soft lips and hard body. Damn you, I say.

CHAPTER 15

As we crossed onto the Seven Mile Bridge in the Florida Keys, Eden sat up straighter, her eyes roaming the dark-blue water and beyond. It really was an awe-inspiring sight.

"There's a swing span on this bridge that allows boats to go through," Eden told me. "In 1977, it got stuck open, causing a delay in traffic for more than three hours. Want to guess who was on the bridge at the time?"

"Santa Claus."

"Nooo," she lamented. "It was a musician."

"Britney Spears."

Eden shook her head. "She wasn't even alive yet in 1977. She was born in 1981."

"Ah, well. Excuse me for not knowing that. Why don't you tell me?"

She crossed her arms over her chest and grinned knowingly. "Jimmy Buffett. He apparently was on the way to Key West when the bridge mishap occurred, and he sat on the hood of his car and wrote 'Margaritaville' to pass the time."

"No freaking way," I uttered, amazed at the wealth of knowledge this woman possessed.

"Yes freaking way. And he asked Elvis Presley to record the song, but Elvis died that year."

I shook my head. "Nope, I couldn't imagine The King singing 'Margaritaville.' It just wouldn't be the same without Jimmy's iconic voice."

"Agreed," she said, turning her face to look out the side window.

We rode in comfortable silence until I pulled up in front of a one-story stucco home painted in a pretty blue color with clean, white trim. "I think this is it," I said, double checking the number on the mailbox.

"Wow. It's nice," Eden said, peering out with wide eyes. "I was picturing more of a small cottage."

We climbed out of the charcoal-gray Toyota 4Runner onto a concrete driveway. Robert had taken Guido's car to a chop shop, so it was no more. I'd purchased this one in cash yesterday at a used car lot near Jacksonville.

"Let's go inside and then I'll come out and get the bags." Leading the way across the paved walkway that cut through the perfectly manicured grass, I stepped onto the low porch, which was bordered by a white wooden rail. Two padded rocking chairs sat off to one side, looking cozy and inviting.

Using the key Robert gave me, I unlocked the door and pushed it open. Stepping inside and out of the balmy Florida weather, we were met with an instant draft of cool air. Our hosts had obviously left the air conditioning on for us.

Eden closed the door behind us and walked across the honey wood floor, drifting a hand over a plush couch upholstered in an earthy sage green. A matching love seat sat perpendicular with a glass-topped coffee table in the center of the room.

"This is pretty," Eden declared, bending to look at the base of the table. It was formed by a piece of what looked like beach driftwood, bleached from the sun. I followed her into the kitchen with my hands in the pockets of my khaki shorts, watching as she explored. "Fully stocked," she announced after pulling open the fridge.

"Of course," I said with a half-smile.

"We really owe them so much." Eden leaned back against the counter, her hands resting beside her hips.

"I already took care of them."

Her brows lifted. "Monetarily?"

I leaned against the kitchen island, facing her. "Yes. I know I should have asked you first, but—"

"You don't have to ask me," she interrupted. "I've told you that money isn't mine."

"The bank account says differently."

Eden sighed. "Okay, fine. It's both of ours while we're in this situation. The point still remains. You don't have to ask me."

"Married people should talk about big purchases," I said sagely with a smirk because I knew it would aggravate her.

She leveled me with a glare but didn't otherwise comment on that. "How did Robert get all that money deposited in a bank account without questions anyway?"

"We probably don't want to know. I'm sure he used his skills as a... what did he call it?"

"Covert computer and technology guru," she replied with a giggle.

I pointed a finger at her. "Yeah, that." Pushing away from the counter, I said, "Why don't we check out the rest of the house?"

We took the hallway off the living room, finding a full-sized bathroom, one bedroom decorated in black and white at the end of the hall, and a slightly larger bedroom with an en suite down a short hallway to the left.

"You can have this one," I told her, gazing around at the soothing purple decor.

"I can take the smaller one," she insisted.

"Nah, this one has its own bathroom so you'll have more privacy." I didn't tell her, but I also wanted to be in the room closest to the front in case someone ever found us. "And look, you have your own veranda," I said, walking over to the sliding glass door and feeling better when I saw the safety bar that kept it wedged closed. Sliding door locks were notorious for being easy to jiggle open.

Eden followed me out onto the flagstone surface when I opened the door, and her shoulders instantly relaxed, letting out a relieved sigh when she took in the view. "This is stunning." She drew out the last word, her eyes raking over the blue water beyond a pristine beach that was visible in the distance.

Her lips formed a serene smile, and my gaze dropped to her pretty mouth, remembering the feel of those lips beneath mine when I'd kissed her during our "wedding" photo shoot. It had been chaste as far as kisses went, but I hadn't been able to stop thinking about it. To stop thinking about more.

My feelings about Eden's age had... shifted. She wasn't a typical nineteen-year-old. She had more moxie in her pinky finger than most girls her age had in their entire body.

Needing to distract myself from staring at her mouth, I forced my eyes away and wandered around the wide patio. Two black, iron chairs covered with thick turquoise padding sat on either side of a matching black table.

"What's this door?" I asked, peering through the glass, but the drapes were drawn on the other side. Mentally going through the house's floor plan in my head, I wandered back inside and backtracked to my bedroom. When I opened the floor-length gray drapes, my suspicions were confirmed.

"Looks like we're sharing," I told her when I unlocked my door, slid it open, and walked out.

"Mmhmmm." Eden was sitting on one of the chairs, her feet propped up on the concrete balustrade that made up the perimeter of the area, eyes closed.

I took the opportunity to watch her. The veranda had a half roof, so her face was in the shade while the sun glistened off her bare legs and arms.

Quietly taking the chair beside her and mimicking her position, I folded my hands across my middle and relaxed into the moment, tilting my head to allow my gaze to rake over her. I fixated for a moment on the thin gold band on her left hand, which matched the thicker one I wore on my own. Jamie had taken us to a jewelry store in Jacksonville to pick them out. If we weren't going out in public, Eden always removed hers and kept it in a small dish in the bathroom. For some reason, I kept mine on all the time.

Not wanting to think about the reasoning behind that, I continued watching Eden. She had a nice tan, probably from being at the beach in Mexico for her Spring Break vacation that had ended so badly.

I didn't realize until that moment how much tension she'd been carrying, not until I saw her in a completely relaxed state. Her posture was loose, and even the curves of her face seemed softer.

"Why are you staring at me, Draco?" she asked without opening her eyes, and I chuckled.

"I was just thinking we need to get some more clothes."

She peeped one eye open and directed it at me. "Are you saying you're tired of seeing me in the same few outfits?"

Today Eden was wearing the denim shorts she seemed to favor and a red tank top. "No, but I thought we might need swimsuits since we're going to be beach bums for the foreseeable future."

Her shoulders tensed, and I wanted to kick myself for bringing up our self-imposed exile. Then she smiled that teasing smile she reserved only for me. "You definitely need some new things since you would look goofy walking around in a black suit like the dark lord of the beach."

"Hey, I can be casual," I told her, sweeping a hand down my body to encompass my khaki shorts, black T-shirt, and brown sandals. To be honest, I was pretty sure I'd never owned a pair of sandals before in my life. But I could embrace this new look. After all, Eden was handling all the changes being thrown at her like a champ.

Probably a little too well, if I really thought about it.

"You can talk to me, if you want to," I said softly.

"I am talking to you," she replied, closing her eyes again.

"I mean... about what happened. You can talk to me, Eden."

Her only reply was the pinch of her lips and a curt nod of her head. That response worried me, and I prayed she wasn't suppressing her emotions in an effort to appear unaffected.

She was one tough fucking woman, but I needed her to know she didn't have to be strong all the time. I needed her to know she could be vulnerable with me.

But first, she had to trust me, and I wasn't sure if she was fully there yet.

CHAPTER 16

WE COOKED DINNER TOGETHER that evening, and we moved around the kitchen like a team. While I cooked my mama's spaghetti and meatballs, Eden prepared the salad and heated the garlic bread.

Deciding to eat informally in the living room, we settled onto the couch. Eden brought in two glasses of red wine and handed them to me as she picked up two coasters from the holder and then laughed.

"What's so funny?" I asked, and she held them up for my inspection. One read, *I want to be sweated on* and the other, *I prefer being on bottom.* She set the latter in front of me with a sassy wink before turning the rest of them upside down.

"I say we don't look at them. We just choose a new one every day, like a fun little surprise."

"Yeah, we need more surprises in our lives right now," I deadpanned, making her bubble over with giggles. I reveled in the pure sweetness of the sound and vowed to myself to make it happen as often as possible while we were in this fucked up situation.

"I can't believe you've never seen *24.* Jack Bauer is awesome," she said, turning on the TV and DVD player.

"That's Kiefer Sutherland's character?" I asked.

She settled on the couch beside me. "Yep, and each episode is one hour in the day. Twenty-four episodes per season, hence the name."

"You're the only person I know that doesn't sound like a pretentious asshole when they say the word *hence*," I told her, picking up my plate. The aromas were perfect, a blend of tomato and Italian spices.

"Gee, thanks," Eden retorted. "Best compliment ever."

"Happy wife, happy life," I shot back.

She puffed out an exasperated sigh. "Shut up and eat, demon spawn."

Covering a smirk, I turned my attention to the television. Two hours later, I was hooked on this damn show. Eden had been correct. It was jammed full of action as the main character, Jack Bauer, worked with the Counter Terrorism Unit to track down terrorists. He was ruthless and a fucking badass.

When I was in the kitchen refilling our wine glasses, I stiffened at the ringing of the doorbell. Sprinting back into the living room, I saw Eden headed toward the front door. "No!" I hissed, grabbing her by the hand and dragging her to her bedroom. "Get in the closet and stay there."

I didn't even give her time to respond, closing the door and dashing to my room for my gun. With it pressed to my thigh and my heart beating like a racehorse's, I made my way to the front door and pressed my eye to the peephole.

An elderly couple stood on the doorstep, and my pulse calmed a tad. They looked like Santa and Mrs. Claus and appeared to be completely harmless, but I wasn't taking any chances. Leaving the chain lock engaged, I cracked the door open.

"Can I help you?" I asked pleasantly, the gun hidden behind my back.

"Hi, Osbourne family! We brought you a welcome gift," the lady sang, holding up a plate stacked high with brownies.

They know our new name. That must mean they've talked to Jamie and Robert, right? My mind quickly worked through the scenario and judged them to be nothing more than friendly neighbors. I hoped.

"Oh, hi. Just let me unlock this," I said, closing the door, stashing my gun in the cabinet beside me, and disengaging the chain.

"Oh. My. Goodness! Aren't you a handsome young man," the lady chirped, shoving the plate of goodies into my hand and pinching my cheek.

"Oh, uh, that's..." Before I could finish, I caught something in my peripheral vision. *Eden. Goddammit.* My heart rate picked up again as she strode across the floor with a hand outstretched. I told her ass to stay put while I checked out what was going on.

"Hi, I'm Eden Osbourne," she said, shaking the hands of both newcomers. "You must be the sweet neighbors Jamie told us about."

Huh. I kinda sorta vaguely remembered that, but it still didn't stop my fingers from tightening on the plate when the older woman reached for Eden. What if she was some kind of assassin in disguise? I had the overwhelming urge to tug on her gray hair to see if it was a wig.

But she simply hugged Eden before pulling back and beaming at her. "You are pretty as a picture, just like Jamie said."

The old man looked at me with a chagrined shake of his head before finally speaking. "Uh, honey bun, maybe we should introduce ourselves before you go pinching and hugging these young'uns." His voice was a deep, Southern drawl that somehow soothed my nerves.

"Oh right, sorry about that," the lady tittered. "We're your neighbors. The house to your right. I'm Helen Mims, but everyone calls me Mimsy. This is my husband, Charles."

"Everyone calls me Charles," he deadpanned, and I chuckled, shifting the plate to one hand so I could give him a firm shake.

"I'm Dane Osbourne, and this is my wife, Eden."

"We know," Mimsy said cheerfully. "We had dinner with Jamie and Robert when they were in town, and they told us you two would be honeymooning down here."

"Ooh, what is this?" Eden asked, lifting the corner of the plastic wrap covering the plate in my hand. The scent of chocolate and sugar escaped, and I was suddenly very hungry for brownies. "These smell wonderful. Thank you for thinking of us."

The woman patted her husband's chest. "Charles here is the baker in the family. He owns Sweet Heaven, which is the best damn bakery in the Keys." Pride emanated from her every word.

"Would you like to come inside and have a brownie with us?" Eden asked politely.

"Well, that would be wonderful," Mimsy chirped happily. "It's nice to have some young folks in the neighborhood. Of course, Robert and Jamie are younger than us, and then there's Charlisse and her darling little boy, Cooper, who live across the street. Other than that, just a bunch of old fuddy duddies live on this street."

I did my best to hold back a snicker as I wondered how old one had to be to earn the title of *fuddy duddy* in her eyes.

Charles settled his large frame on one end of the couch, like he'd sat there many times before, and I followed the women into the kitchen with the plate of brownies in my hand.

"Here's where they keep the K-cups," Mimsy was saying, opening a drawer. "Do you know how to operate a Keurig?"

"Yes, ma'am. I had one at home," Eden replied. While they started the coffee, I pulled down small saucers.

"You don't need one for Charles," the older woman told me. "He has diabetes, so no brownies for him."

Placing one of the small plates back in the cabinet, I asked, "How does that work with him owning a bakery?"

"He only tastes small bites to make sure his flavors are spot on, but he doesn't snack after work." Then she laughed boisterously and smacked her hip. "He also relies on me as a taste tester, which accounts for the healthy size of my rump."

After plating the brownies, which were topped with a decadent chocolate frosting, I carried three saucers to the living room and sat on the love seat. The ladies followed shortly after with the coffee.

Mimsy sat beside her husband, and Eden hesitated between the couch and the love seat, eyes darting around as if she couldn't decide where to sit. With a subtle jerk of my chin, I indicated exactly where she needed to be, and she rolled her lips inward before perching on the love seat as far away from me as possible.

Well, we can't have that, can we?

Looping an arm around her waist, I hauled her toward me until she was right up against me, the side of one small, soft breast pressed against my rib cage.

"Relax, wifey," I whispered into her ear, noticing her lips twitch before she reached for a chunk of brownie and stuffed it into my mouth. A small gasp escaped from her when I rolled my tongue briefly around the tip of her index finger, holding eye contact with her. Until a voice interrupted us.

"So, Jamie and Robert told us a little about you. I know you're twenty-two and twenty-seven," Mimsy said, nodding first at Eden and then at me. Those were the ages we'd decided on with Robert and the ones reflected on our new IDs. "But how did you meet?"

I smiled as if thinking of a fond memory and launched into our fake backstory. "Eden lived next door to my Uncle Gael. Whenever I came to visit, I always thought she was the most beautiful girl in the world." I kissed her temple, earning a swoony sigh from Mimsy.

"I thought he was a pest," Eden said flatly before looking up at me. "But he slowly grew on me. Kinda like a big, hairy mole."

A bark of laughter escaped me, and I lowered my hand to pat *my wife's* hip. "Her beauty caught my eye first, but Eden's sass is what sealed the deal." I looked down at the little vixen who was smirking up at me. "And her heart. She took care of my uncle... did his shopping, cooked for him, took him to doctor's appointments."

Our eyes were fused together, and I felt a magnetic pull between us. With a clearing of her throat, Eden broke eye contact and continued the story. "Uncle Gael always wanted us together. He fancied himself a bit of a matchmaker and was so excited when we started dating a couple years ago."

"My uncle was so enamored of Eden, he even wrote her into his will, right along with me."

Jamie had brilliantly come up with that part of the story, which explained how such a young couple had money, even though neither of us were currently employed.

Mimsy leaned forward in her seat, eyes bright. "Oh, I just love this story! Did Gael live to see you get married?"

"He did," Eden answered, her lips creasing into a sad smile. "But just barely. He passed away the next day."

"Oh dear." The older woman's hand went to her chest.

"That's why we're just now taking our honeymoon, even though we've been married for a couple months now," I added. "We've been busy wrapping up things with his estate. Jamie is an old family friend of Eden's and she offered to let us use this home for an extended vacation while we decide where we want to live."

"Jamie's a peach of a gal," Charles said, swiping a finger through the frosting on his wife's brownie when she wasn't looking and sticking it into his mouth. I met his eye and subtly indicated that he had a smudge of chocolate in his white beard. "Thanks," he mouthed, scrubbing at the spot with one hand.

"These brownies are fantastic," Eden said, changing the subject.

"That's Charles's signature dessert," Mimsy said, patting her husband's leg. "Everyone around loves them."

"I can see why," I told them, finishing off the rest of mine with my free hand. Sugar, butter, and rich chocolate melted onto my tongue. "This frosting is amazing, and the texture of the brownie is perfect."

Charles nodded. "Thank ya kindly. I do love a fudgy brownie."

Mimsy eyed her plate before darting a suspicious glare up at her husband, who managed to look as innocent as an angel.

"Do you have wedding photos?" she asked, and I silently thanked Jamie and Robert for thinking of that particular detail.

Grabbing my phone from the coffee table, I scrolled until I found the pictures and handed my phone over. "These are just the sneak peeks the photographer sent us. We'll be placing an order for prints soon."

Mimsy oohed and ahhed over all the pics, finally coming to the one of Eden and I kissing. "This! This one is simply stunning!" She stared at it for a long moment before returning my phone to me. "I can just feel the love between you two."

My eyes rested on the screen. It was a very believable photo. Eden and I looked so... *right* together. Especially with my lips on hers and her hands tangled in my hair. I couldn't deny that I felt something for my fake wife. *But love? No way. Not me.*

We chatted for another thirty minutes, learning that the Mimses were originally from Mississippi but moved to Florida about eleven years ago because, and I quote, "That's what old folks are supposed to do."

Finally, Charles stood and reached out a hand to help his wife up. "Let's hit the road, Mimsy. I'm sure Dane and Eden have better things to do than entertain us."

"Ahhh, yes," she said, tossing a wink at us. "Newlywed things."

Eden let out a tiny squeak, and her cheeks flushed. It was so fucking adorable, and I couldn't help myself. Wrapping a hand around the back of her head, I laid my lips against the tip of her nose in a gentle kiss.

"That's right, babycakes. All the newlywed things." I didn't think it was possible, but her face pinkened even more. This bold, gorgeous woman got flustered over a little sex talk, and I freaking loved it.

Then with a slight shake of her head, sassy Eden was back, swatting me on the butt and scolding, "Cool it, Romeo. We have company."

"Oh, that's all right. A healthy sex life is very important in a marriage," Mimsy intoned wisely. "We'll let you get on with it. Give us a holler if you need help finding anything in town."

"We, uh, o-okay," Eden stuttered before composing herself. "We already know where the best bakery is, but we'll let you know if we need anything else."

After a quick hug between the women, the couple left, and Eden whirled on me. "What was all that?"

"All what?" I asked innocently.

"Babycakes?" Then she lowered her voice and repeated my words back to me. "All the newlywed things."

"She started it," I tattled, pointing at the closed front door like the mature adult I was. "What was I supposed to say? *No, we're refraining from sex during our honeymoon.*"

Eden let out a long exhale. "I guess that would sound stupid."

I took a step toward her until we were only inches apart and lowered my voice. "I'm never getting married for real, but if I did, I can promise you, the honeymoon would be the opposite of abstinent. My wife wouldn't be able to walk properly for weeks when I was done getting my fill of her."

She lifted her chin, though I noticed she took a half step back to put more space between us. "Good thing we're not really married then. I like having full use of my legs."

A Grinch-like smile crept across my lips. "You'd be surprised how will-ingly a woman would give up the ability to walk if the dick was good enough."

Eden's nose crinkled, and she turned to stalk out of the living room, tossing over her shoulder, "You're a pig."

"But I'm not wrong, Wildcat," I called back. "Make sure to limp a little if you see Mimsy tomorrow. Wouldn't want her to be disappointed in my abilities." That comment earned me a middle finger from Eden, but I was pretty sure I heard her chuckle.

Just a little.

Chapter 17

THE SUN WAS JUST cresting over the horizon as I sat on the back veranda with my phone in my hand. Now that I had a cell and access to the internet, I typed *Evie Bouvier* into the search engine, and my mouth dropped open at the number of results that popped up on my screen.

Now I understood what Dane was talking about when he said my abduction was "high profile."

Tapping one from a national news site, I watched a press conference done shortly after I'd disappeared. FBI Special Agent Iris Loyola recounted what they knew, which wasn't much. *Evie Bouvier has disappeared. No, we're not ruling out the possibility of human traffickers. Yes, we are exploring all possibilities. Blah, blah, blah.*

When she was done, my older brother, Auburn, spoke passionately, his knuckles turning white as he gripped the sides of the podium, and a tear slipped down my cheek. *I love you, big bro. I'm here. I'm okay. And I miss you.*

Even after watching the press conference twice, I couldn't have told you what Agent Loyola looked like. My eyes were focused on my family lined up on one side of the stage. I could tell Auburn was trying to be the strong one, but I could read the pain in his blue eyes that all three of the Bouvier offspring had inherited from our father.

Looking at my dad almost killed me. He looked at least ten years older, his handsome face haggard, and I had only been gone for weeks. My mother looked like a million bucks in an expensive white suit. Of course, she was dressed to the nines since there were cameras present, though she did dab at her eyes with a starched handkerchief a few times. Might have been faking it. Who knew with her? She was so cold, it was hard to tell.

But Monty, oh, my sweet little brother, Monty. The absolute misery etched on his face had the tears coming fast and hard down my cheeks.

Auburn, as the oldest, was the serious one, president of everything in high school. I was the quintessential middle child, the loud one who lived to make everyone around me laugh. Monty was quieter, more sensitive. He was a football player—and a damn good one—but his passion was drawing.

The three of us were going to run our family's business as a team. Whenever I could get out of this mess I found myself in.

I clicked on another link, and my five friends appeared on-screen. They were being interviewed as a group, Juliette and Arya in the front with Madalynn, Emersyn, and Holly sitting on slightly higher stools behind them. The last picture we'd all taken together was projected on the wall behind them, and I almost didn't recognize myself standing with my friends in that lilac swimsuit. I'd grown so accustomed to my new *Eden* look in the past few weeks.

Juli was taking the lead, doing most of the talking in her sweet Texas drawl. She recounted the creepy guy who had been trying to give us drinks and wondered if he could have had something to do with my disappearance. Searching my mind, I tried to picture the man's face, but it had been too dark to see clearly. Could he have been Ethan, one of my kidnappers? The body mass was right, so... maybe?

Didn't really matter anyway since Ethan and Felipe were both dead now. Damiano's face that night, so cold when he stared down at the two dead bodies, sparked in my memory, and I shivered. I realized now I'd probably been in shock; otherwise, I definitely would have freaked the hell out.

My attention was drawn back to the screen when the interviewer said, "I'm sorry, Holly. I didn't hear what you said."

The camera zoomed in on my friend's face, and twin tears snaked down her pretty cheeks. "I said it was... it was all my fault. I-I should have gone with her to the ice machine. I should—" Her comment was cut off by a sob that shuddered her entire body, and I shook my head back and forth.

"No, Holly. It wasn't your fault," I whispered to the phone. "I was the stupid one, going outside by myself. It wasn't your fault." But she continued to cry, her plaintive wails of pain stabbing me in the heart as Emersyn wrapped a comforting arm around her.

"Fuck," I muttered, clicking out of the video, unable to watch it for even a second more. Then, like a dummy, I tapped on another one. My dad was being interviewed by the hosts of a morning show, looking somber in a black dress shirt and no tie. My heart ached to reach out and wrap him in a huge hug.

I watched my picture appear on the lower half of the screen as the hosts asked him questions about the investigation. The phone number for a tip line scrolled constantly across the bottom.

Then the male interviewer asked, "How are you and your family doing, Mr. Bouvier?"

His smile held no humor whatsoever. "Chloe is upset, of course. Auburn has been my rock. He's stronger than any twenty-three-year-old has a right to be, but it's hard for him. He adores Evie."

"And your younger son, Monty?"

My father shook his head. "Monty and Evie are so close in age, so this has been really hard on him. He's... not doing well at all with this." I gritted my teeth against the ripping ache that was building inside me. *My poor Monty.*

The female interviewer patted his hand. "What about you, sir?"

"Me?" Dad shook his head and stared down at his lap for a long moment before looking back up with damp eyes. "I'd like to say I am doing okay, but that would be a lie. Evie has been my sunshine since the day she was born, and I—"

His voice broke, and a waterfall of emotion welled up in me and escaped in the form of tears that tracked down my face. "Daddy," I whispered, bringing the phone closer to my face so I could see him better through the torrent.

"I don't know what to do without my Evie," he finished.

"I understand you're offering a million dollar reward for any information regarding your daughter?" the woman asked, her voice kind. A hiccuping gasp escaped my lips. *A million dollars?*

The camera zoomed in on my father's face, and he looked directly into the lens, speaking to the viewing audience. "Yes, I am. If anyone knows anything, please call the tip line. I'm begging you. And forget the million dollars. I will give you every last penny I have if you'll just... bring... my baby girl... home." The last words were delivered in a series of broken heaves as his face crumpled with raw pain.

That's when I shattered like I was made of glass and someone had just sucker punched me in the sternum. Doubling over at the waist, I buried my face against my knees and finally let out everything I'd been holding inside. All the worry about my family had come to a head and popped with an explosion of anguish.

I cried. Hard. So hard I was worried I'd crack a rib or two. And I kind of wished I would. Maybe then my physical pain would override the pure misery inside my heart.

Heaving breaths expanded and then deflated my lungs, over and over, until I became aware of my father's voice again. Lifting my head, I yelped when I found Dane sitting on the floor of the veranda in front of me, his gaze on the screen of my phone.

He looked up and... the fucker smiled.

"You like seeing me like this?" I snapped, rubbing harsh lines up and down my face to dry my tears. My cheeks were heated as much from embarrassment as from my crying.

"Actually, I do," the evil spawn replied, and I huffed out a sound of outrage. "But not for the reason you're thinking."

I narrowed my eyes. "Then why?"

He looked back down at the phone for a long moment before turning it off and setting it on the iron table beside me. "You're very lucky to have people who care so much about you, Eden."

My forehead crinkled when I remembered he didn't have a dad like mine. No, his father had tried to kill him. "I'm sorry your father is a piece of shit."

Dane's lips quirked up on one side. "You don't know the half of it. Luca thinks I'm dead, yet he's not even having a memorial service for his own son. Fiero said he told everyone I moved to Italy."

My fingers itched to reach out and stroke his face like I'd seen Jamie do so many times to Robert. But that seemed way too intimate, and this man was not really my husband. He was a person though, no matter how much I despised him, so I reached for his hand and squeezed.

"That's horrible, Dane. Your life should matter to him."

"Well, it doesn't," he said, holding tighter to my hand when I tried to let go. Sensing he needed the human contact in that moment, I allowed it. "And I hate seeing you cry, E. But I am happy to see you finally showing some emotion. You've had so much shit happen to you recently, and you never cry. You needed to let all that out."

He'd called me E, and I kinda liked it. "I feel like crying a lot, but I'm trying to be brave." As if summoned, a rogue tear escaped down my left cheek.

Dane's face softened and he shook his head with a wry smile. "You are brave, sweetheart. The bravest person I know." He reached up with his free hand and swiped a thumb over the wetness on my face. "You've been through a kidnapping, been told you and your family are in danger, had to change your hair and your name. Fuck, you even had to learn to put contacts in to make your eyes brown."

"That might have been the worst part," I said with a half-laugh.

His hands were still on me, one gripping my hand and the other resting against my cheek. "The point is that you shouldn't hold all that shit in, E. You need to release it from time to time. I promise I'm not judging you. I just don't want you to..."

He paused, and I found myself needing to hear what he was about to say. "You don't want me to what?"

Dane's eyes shifted away, staring over my shoulder as his gaze seemed to defocus. "My mother killed herself." His voice was barely audible.

Oh. God.

"I'm not suicidal, Dane," I assured him. His attention flashed to me, and I could see the vulnerability on his face, something I hadn't seen before from him. "I'm not. I'm just sad, and I'm angry, and I'm... frustrated as hell."

"Then show me that," he said vehemently, his voice hoarse. "I have no idea what you're thinking at any time except that you hate me. You... can you please just give me something—show me what you're feeling from time to time—so I don't constantly worry? Please?" That last word was spoken quietly, like a prayer, and I couldn't help but nod my head.

"Okay, I'll try." I watched as his shoulders sagged in relief. Then I rolled my eyes and sighed. "And I don't entirely hate you. You're kind of okay sometimes."

"Thanks, wifey." His grin was a hundred percent mischief.

"Dear god, shut up," I whined. "I take it all back. I hate you again."

The low, deep chuckle from his chest told me he enjoyed aggravating me, but then he tucked a loose strand of hair behind my ear. "Would you please not watch any more of those videos unless I'm with you?"

This man... this man was a contradiction of the highest proportion. He was gruff, a complete asshole, and a stone-cold killer. But somehow, he seemed to actually care about me.

So I replied with one bob of my head. "Will you tell me about your mom?" Dane froze, and I could feel him shutting down, could literally see the shutters closing over his brown eyes. "It's a two-way street, Dane. You can't ask me to be vulnerable and then turn into a block of ice when I ask you a personal question."

He exhaled and stood, and I thought I'd pushed him too far. "Go get dressed, and we'll take a walk on the beach."

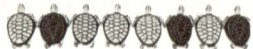

Sombrero Beach was only about a block away, and we toed off our shoes and left them beneath a tall palm tree when we reached the edge. I shuffled my feet, feeling the grit scrape the soles. I'd always loved being barefoot in the sand.

Dane reached for my hand as we took a left, and I stiffened. "Married, remember?" he said, winding his fingers between mine. It was warm and strong, and I hated that I liked it.

We walked for a couple minutes before he finally began speaking. "My sister's name was Amara. She was two years older than me. When she turned eighteen, my father arranged for her to marry a man from one of the other crime families in New York. As a kind of good will gesture."

"That's disgusting," I commented.

"I agree, but I think we're both aware that Luca's moral compass points due south, straight toward hell." He guided us a little closer to the water as we walked. "Her new husband, Desmond, was heavy into drug trafficking, and after about a year, I started noticing changes in my sister."

My lips twisted to the side. "She started taking drugs?"

"Yeah," he breathed. "Amara was very kindhearted and way too good for that asshole, but she was also gullible. Fiero and I both tried to tell our father that she didn't need to be with him, but of course, he didn't listen." Dane stopped our progress, turning to look out over the water. "Desmond started her out with pot and then eventually got her hooked on the harder stuff. She overdosed on her twentieth birthday."

Turning my head, I pressed my forehead against Dane's bicep. "I'm so sorry. You were just eighteen?"

"Yeah," came his quiet reply. "My father ordered a hit on Desmond. Didn't even fucking do it himself, like Amara's life wasn't worth the effort to him." His muscles flexed in anger. "I would have done it with a smile on my face, but he ordered one of his goons to do it instead."

"You were barely an adult yourself," I protested.

Dane scoffed out a humorless laugh. "Welcome to my world, Eden. I killed my first man when I was fifteen." My stomach rolled over in my abdomen. *Fifteen?* I felt his hand tighten on mine. "Don't get the wrong idea about me. I'm not saying I'm an angel, but it's not like I walked around whacking people every day or anything."

"So what did you do all day if you weren't a professional whacker?"

He snorted and shook his head. "I worked in one of my father's legitimate businesses. I managed a nightclub." We inched forward until the cool water lapped at our toes. "You caught me on a bad day with those two piss stains who hurt you. Before that, I hadn't gotten *shooty* for over a year."

For some reason, that made me feel marginally better. We watched as a seagull swooped down and skimmed the water before rising into the air with a silver fish in his beak. Dane's gaze followed the graceful bird until he was out of site with his prize.

With a long exhale, he spoke in a hushed tone. "My mother was devastated by what happened to my sister, and she shut down. Wouldn't leave the house, barely talked to anyone. On the six-month anniversary of Amara's death, she swallowed an entire bottle of sleeping pills."

I had no words for that. *I'm sorry* didn't even come close to being adequate, so I turned and wrapped my arms around Dane's waist, trying to give him even a little bit of comfort. He returned the embrace, his arms warm against the slight morning chill.

He lowered his cheek to the top of my head, and we stood like that for a long time before he finally said, "You're short."

I chuckled and looked up at him. "No, you're just freakishly tall." His eyes looked soft in the early light of the day, like someone had added the tiniest splash of cream to their coffee. Something fluttered deep in my gut, and I averted my gaze. "Will you tell me a good memory with your mom and sister?"

From my peripheral vision, I saw Dane turn his head toward the water.

"My best memories of my mom are from our kitchen. The house I grew up in was just a house, not a home. It was like living in the Vatican with all the artwork and elaborate decor. As kids, we weren't allowed to touch anything, but Mama reigned over the kitchen. That was the only room that held any warmth."

"If my mother didn't have to pass through the kitchen to get to the wine cellar, I'm pretty sure she wouldn't even know where to find it," I commented, and Dane made a sympathetic noise.

"One time Amara and I were helping Mama make muffins. She helped us mix up the batter and then got a phone call. She told us to spray the muffin tins with cooking spray while she went in the other room. We didn't know how much spray to use, so we looked at the recipe. It said to fill the muffin tins two-thirds full. Of course, it meant with batter, but we didn't know that."

"You didn't!" I scoffed, looking up to see Dane's face creased in amusement.

"Oh yes, we did. We sprayed a shit-ton of it into each opening. When Mama came back, we told her we ran out." He jiggled one hand, as if shaking an empty can. "She laughed so hard she had to sit down."

"That's hilarious. I hope your baking skills have improved since then."

His chin lifted. "I'm an excellent baker. Mama always said I should open my own bakery one day, but..." Dane's words trailed off as he inhaled a lungful of salty air. "Family business and all that, you know?"

I nodded my understanding. "Of course Dad wants Auburn, Monty, and I to all work for *Bouvier*, but he would never insist on it. He's always said we're welcome into the family business, but he also wants us to be happy."

"Family happiness is not a priority for my father," he said wryly. "Do you think all three of you will work for *Bouvier*?"

"For sure. Auburn is slated to take over as CEO when our father retires, and Monty plans to go to college and then become a designer for the *Bouvier* brand. Since I'm a people person, I'm going into marketing and advertising."

"Does it bother you that you weren't considered for CEO?" Dane asked.

"Nah, not a bit," I told him with complete honesty. "Neither Monty nor I have any desire to run the entire company. That's all in Auburn's wheelhouse, and we're happy to let him have it. He's kind of a bossy butt."

I stopped and squatted, inspecting a scrape in the sand just beyond the edge of the surf.

"What is it?" Dane asked.

"I was looking for turtle tracks. Loggerheads start nesting on the Florida beaches in April, which isn't too far off. That's not one though."

"You like turtles?"

"They're my favorite animal," I admitted. "I know they're not very exciting because they're slow, but that's what I like about them. They take their time. Turtles have this hard outer shell, but they're softer on the inside."

Kind of like you, I almost said but stopped myself.

"Guess I never thought of it like that."

"Loggerheads don't reach sexual maturity until about age thirty-five." I told him as we continued walking. "They spend the majority of their time in the water, but females lay their eggs on land. Their nests contain an average of one hundred eggs."

An Asian woman in a lime-green tank top and black running shorts was bent over stretching but stood when we walked by. "Are you talking about loggerheads?"

I turned to face her. "Um, yes."

She swiped a wrist over her sweaty forehead. "You're very knowledge-able."

Dane released my hand and looped an arm around my shoulders, tucking me protectively against his side. "Can we help you with something?" he asked, and I could hear the wary tone in his voice.

Apparently, the woman could too because she held up both hands, palms out. "Sorry. I didn't mean to eavesdrop, but I couldn't help but overhear. I have turtle radar."

She wiggled her fingers beside one ear, and I laughed, holding out a hand for a shake. "Nice to meet a fellow Testudines enthusiast. I'm Eden."

"Dane," he said, also shaking the woman's hand.

"I'm Anna Hsiao. I work for the Florida Department of Environmental Protection. Are you two surveyors?"

My brow creased. "I don't know what that is."

"As you probably know," she said with a wink, "loggerheads nest primarily at night. Our surveyors walk the beaches early in the morning, looking for nesting sites. If they find one, they notify us."

"Then what happens?" Dane asked.

"Then we're able to limit activity in that particular area. Pesky humans can disturb nesting sites, so the F.D.E.P. does our best to protect them." Anna rolled her eyes like she wasn't also a human. At least not a pesky one.

"That's really awesome," I said, loving that there was someone out there who cared about those beautiful animals and their eggs. My voice turned wistful. "That would be a dream, getting to help the turtles."

"Wellllll..." Anna drew out, lifting one dark eyebrow. "We actually have a training class tomorrow. It's the last one of the season."

Dane's hand tightened around my shoulder, and he shocked the shit out of me with his next words. "How do my wife and I sign up?"

CHAPTER 18

FOR A WEEK AFTER taking the surveyor course, Dane and I walked the stretch of beach we were assigned every morning at dawn. We didn't see a single turtle until...

"That was so exciting," I squealed, skipping in front of Dane and turning to walk backward. "I can't believe we actually saw the mama turtle covering her nest and heading back to the sea. They're usually gone way before dawn."

"I know," Dane said, bemusement quirking his lips up. Of course he knew. He'd attended the class too, which still flabbergasted me. "I think it's crazy that the females lay their clutch, head off to the water, and never see their hatchlings."

"Reminds me of my mother," I quipped.

"Would you turn around before you—Dammit!" Dane lunged forward and caught me beneath my armpits when I stumbled over a rock in the path. "Shit, are you okay?"

I rested my hands on his chest to balance myself and laughed. I was a little giddy from seeing our first turtle of the mating season. My hands slid down his abs before removing themselves from his body, and I didn't miss the hardness beneath his pale-yellow V-neck T-shirt. My laughter faded away as I realized I was fondling him.

"Sorry. I'm fine," I mumbled, swiveling around to face the direction of our house again.

"My wife can cop a feel any time," he assured me, taking my hand securely in his as we walked.

"Shut up, Dillweed." There was no heat behind the words. Though I'd never admit it to him, I was beginning to rather like the way my fake husband flirted with me. And the constant hand-holding. I really liked that. Sure, he was only playing a role, but it still gave me a sense of security.

Which officially made me an insane person. Dane Osbourne was still Damiano Cappitani, and Damiano was a very dangerous man. But, I reminded myself, he had saved me from a horrific situation, and then he literally saved my life.

I looked up at his profile. His crooked nose was perfectly straight now, slim at the top and flaring at the nostrils. His already olive skin had deepened to a darker tone after only a week in the Keys, and his black hair now reached his collar.

The kicker was that damn beard, thick and dark, which covered the lower half of his face. I'd never been attracted to a man with full facial hair before, but *dayum*! Even I had to admit my pretend husband was a hottie.

When he'd kissed me that day while Robert took photos of us, the slight scratch of his beard and mustache against my face had caused tingles in some very inconvenient places. It disturbed me because I was not supposed to be attracted to this man.

Women have been attracted to bad boys for centuries, Eden. Just look at Giacomo Casanova and Black Bart, both unrepentant rakes who were notorious with the ladies.

While true, that had never been me. I liked clean-cut, nice guys who majored in business and whose biggest crime was driving their sports cars too fast. *And look how well that worked out for you with Marty.*

Flicking away all those thoughts, I asked, "Once all this is resolved, like, if your father is out of the picture, will you go back to your previous... occupation?"

Dane glanced down with a sardonic lift of his eyebrow. "You mean go back to work for the family? No."

"Why?"

He chewed on his bottom lip for a long beat. "I guess I haven't had options before, and now I do. Working for the Mafia isn't great for one's health," he said, bitterness surrounding his pronouncement. "I never realized how taxing it was to be constantly looking over your shoulder."

"Isn't that what we're doing now? Looking over our shoulders?"

Dane tilted his head from side to side a couple times. "Yes, but it's different from being surrounded by criminals all day, every day. Almost everyone I worked with at the nightclub was connected somehow. Down here, I feel like that life is a million miles away. Like I can breathe easy. I like it."

"I would think the life of a lowly sea turtle wrangler would be boring as hell for you."

He burst into laughter. "Trust me, that's about as much excitement as I want." His big hand squeezed mine and he smiled down at me. "And it was exciting this morning. That mama turtle looked way bigger in real life than I was expecting. What do you think she weighed?"

"Probably close to three hundred pounds," I surmised.

As we approached our backyard, a red and yellow Nerf football rolled across the grass, stopping at our feet. Dane bent to pick it up as a tiny boy came barreling toward us, his harried mother trying to keep up.

"Footbawwwwwl!" he shrieked, holding his hands up for the ball.

"There you go, buddy," Dane said, handing it over.

"So sorry about that," the woman said, finally catching up. "You must be Eden and Dane. Mimsy said you two were staying in the Smith house for a while."

"That's us, and it's no problem," I said, giving the woman a smile. She had blonde hair scraped into a haphazard ponytail and a pretty, round face. "Are you Charlisse?"

"What's left of her," she joked.

I squatted to the kid—who I remembered was named Cooper—and poked his belly. "And you must be... don't tell me. Let me guess." Tapping my chin with my index finger, I hummed. "Hmmm, you look like your name would be Booper."

"Nooo," he giggled.

"I feel like I'm on the right track though. Is it Pooper?"

He fell onto the grass, holding his belly as he laughed. "I'm dying of funny-ness."

We all laughed right along with him. The kid was freaking adorable with chubby cheeks, blue eyes that matched his mother's, and sandy-brown hair.

"Okay," I conceded. "I get one more guess. I'm going to say Cooper."

His mouth popped into a little O as his eyes turned into saucers. "That's right. I is Cooper."

"Well, it's nice to meet you, Cooper," I told him, helping him to his feet. "I'm Eden, and this is Dane."

His gaze traveled up and up. "You're really tall, and you have dirt on your shirt."

"Cooper!" his mother hiss-scolded him before turning her pleading eyes on Dane. "I am sooo sorry."

"Nah, that's alright. I do have dirt on my shirt because I've been down at the beach," Dane said easily.

"That's where we're going," the little boy said. "We're going to play footbawwwl."

"Yes, we're going now." Charlisse rolled her eyes and muttered, "Before my kid says anything else to embarrass me."

Dane chuckled. "It was nice to meet you."

"You as well," she said, swiping some grass from her son's hair as they walked toward Sombrero Beach.

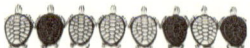

Pinching my tongue between my teeth, I piped pink icing onto one of the cupcakes Dane had made that afternoon. "This sucks," I griped, watching as the lopsided form took shape.

Dane inspected it and wisely set it down without a word, but he was obviously unimpressed. In the time it took me to make one ugly cupcake, he'd already finished a half dozen. And they looked freaking spectacular.

"Why do yours look so good?" I grumped, setting down my piping bag. "Yours look like Michael Jackson cupcakes, and I'm over here making Tito."

Dane cackled and cast my catastrophic attempt one more glance. "You just need practice."

I leaned forward with my chin in my hand. "Or I could just watch the master do his thing."

"That works too," he said, picking up a sheet of wax paper with tiny purple bits of frosting on it. *When the hell did he make those?* I watched with fascination as he peeled off each purple bit and placed them on top of one of the cupcakes with tweezers until they formed...

"Is that a lilac?" I breathed as he adjusted one of the frosting petals until it was exactly where he wanted it.

"Mmhmmm," he hummed absently, holding it up and scrutinizing it like he was a jeweler who had just acquired the Hope Diamond. "I think the petals dried a little dark and with too much blue. I'll lighten it and add a little pink next time."

I lifted skeptical eyebrows at his self-criticism. "Looks perfect to me. "

Giving a one-shoulder shrug, he placed the masterpiece in front of me with a shy smile on his face. "See how it tastes."

"This is for me?" I couldn't disguise the utter delight in my voice. "It's too pretty to eat."

"Don't be ridiculous. I made it for you to eat. We'll take some to Charles and Mimsy too when we return the brownie plate."

"Are there enough for Charlisse and Cooper too?"

Dane gave me a flat look and gestured toward the two dozen cupcakes on the counter. "I think we could manage to spare a few." Then his brow furrowed and he turned to the leftover white frosting before separating it, adding food color gel, and stirring it in. Four minutes later, he had created a perfect three-dimensional replica of Cooper's red and yellow Nerf football on the top of one.

"How the hell do you do that?" I asked incredulously. This man's big hands were super talented in the delicate art of decorating.

"It's easy once you get the hang of it," he said, leaning both forearms on the other side of the breakfast bar, facing me. I valiantly refrained from looking at the combination of pretty ink, masculine hair, and thick veins. *Mostly refrained.* He nodded toward my still untouched cupcake. "You gonna eat that or stare at it all day?"

"I thought I'd stare at it," I shot back smartly. Dane reached for my treat, and I smacked his hand. "Bah! Hands off. I'll eat it." I picked it up, pulled back the foil-paper cup, and took a large bite. The frosting was piled so high, my nose ended up in the sugary dollop.

"Well?" Dane asked anxiously.

"Ohmygurd," I mumbled around the mouthful of pure heaven. "Give me a minute; my tongue is having an orgasm." The frosting was rich and sweet, the cake moist, buttery, and cloud-like.

His voice was low and deep as his brown eyes dropped to my mouth. "I like seeing you enjoy my flavors." The words sounded distinctly dirty, and I lifted my free hand to swipe at my nose. Dane stopped me with a hand wrapped around my wrist before stretching across the countertop and sucking the frosting from my nose.

He sucked it. From. My. Nose. With his mouth. Sweet Jesus.

"Dane," I said in my best scolding voice, which wasn't very effective, to be honest. I sounded like a breathless damsel.

"It's my job to keep my wife clean," he replied with his smug-ass lips... which he was now licking. *Why does everything he says sound like an innuendo?* Then, like he'd done that night Charles and Mimsy were over, he kissed the tip of my nose.

Touching the spot with the tips of my fingers, I asked, "Are you obsessed with my nose or something?"

"It's a really cute nose," he replied, as if that explained it. "It should be cherished."

"Gee, I'm honored," I said, going in for another bite, which was as delectable as the first. "Seriously, this is the best cupcake I've ever had. It might be my new favorite dessert."

Looking scandalized, he whispered, "Don't worry. I won't tell the tiramisù you're cheating on it." He was only inches from my face, and his words brushed against my lips on a sweet breeze of sugar and vanilla. "May I?"

I thought he was asking permission to kiss me, and I nodded dumbly—*whyyy did I do that?*—but he simply bent his head and took a bite of the cupcake I was still holding. A wave of something akin to disappointment washed over me, but I ignored it.

"Mmm," he hummed speculatively, and that soft noise was distinctly sexual. Or maybe I was just delusional and needy. "Might add a drop more vanilla to the batter next time."

Clearing my throat, as if that would clear the wayward thoughts from my mind, I said, "Definitely. I could only eat seven of these in one sitting without that extra drop of vanilla." Then I pretended to shudder in revulsion, earning me a laugh from Dane.

"You're a smartass, little Wildcat." He didn't look mad about it though. The grin on his lips told me he appreciated my cheekiness. Which was fortunate because I grew up with two brothers. Smartass was a required mode for survival.

"Well, you have frosting in your beard," I retorted.

"Where?" he asked, making no move to wipe it away.

"Right there." I pointed, my finger less than an inch away from the pink blob.

"Get it for me." It was a command rather than a request, and my obedient finger swiped it away. Before I could register a coherent thought about what I was doing, I stuck my finger in my mouth and sucked.

Dane's eyes hooded and dropped to my lips, following the glide of my wet finger from my mouth with intense interest.

"Thank you, wife," he said softly. "Wouldn't want your husband to be all dirty, would you?"

Yes!

Jiminy Christmas, Evie. Eden. Whatever the hell my name is now. I was obviously not in my right mind.

Bolstering my spine, I pushed my stool back and stood. "Nope. Definitely can't have that." I began placing the pink cupcakes on Charles and Mimsy's platter. "Why don't you finish decorating while I plate these?"

And stare at your large, rough fingers squeezing that piping bag like...

Gaaah! Stop it right now, woman!

Studiously avoiding the sight of Dane decorating adorable pink cupcakes, I busied myself with cleaning up the kitchen.

I was seriously attracted to him and doing my best not to admit that I was a full-fledged fake-husband slut.

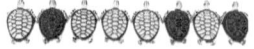

The next eight weeks passed slowly and in a blur at the same time. While June seemed to have arrived before I knew it, the pace of island life was easy and laid back. My restlessness over when I'd see my family again relaxed as I settled into my current reality. I would be with them as soon as Leo Cappitani decided to finally do something about Luca.

And by *do something*, I meant whacking... sleeping with the fishes... fitting him with a pair of concrete shoes and taking him for a swim in the Atlantic. This was a new phenomenon for me because I'd never wished another human dead. Sure, maybe I'd hoped my mother would come down with an embarrassing skin rash all over her face when she was being particularly nasty, but death? Nope. Never.

But I could honestly say that I wouldn't shed a tear if Luca Cappitani ended up six feet under. And not just because he'd tried to buy me from a human trafficking ring. No, the way he treated Dane was the final nail in the proverbial coffin. The asshole had absolutely no redeeming qualities that I could tell.

Dane and I had fallen into a bit of a routine since arriving here. Every morning we walked the beach on turtle duty, and then we'd spend the rest of the day at the beach or exploring the town.

On Friday afternoons, we baked. Well, he baked and I watched in a very supportive way. And with every single batch, he made a special dessert just for me... one with a lilac on top. He played around with different flavors and fillings, but the one constant was that lilac made of frosting. And with each nibble of sugary flower, I hated Dane a little less. In fact, I wasn't sure I'd ever hated him all that much. I hated my situation, and he was the nearest target.

Sometimes we had dinner with the Mimses, and I met up with Charlisse for coffee a few times while her little boy drove toy trucks up and down our arms. I adored all of them and hoped we could stay in touch once I returned to New York. I didn't like lying to them, but I was sure they'd understand once the truth came out about why I had to be deceptive.

One Friday evening, we were sitting on Charles and Mimsy's back porch, munching on the almond vanilla cupcakes Dane made earlier. "Damn, son!" Charles boomed, taking a big bite. "What's this filling? Blackberry?"

"It's a combination of blackberry and raspberry," he replied. "I haven't tried that before."

"Well, it's fantastic. You should come work at my bakery. These would fly out of the case like they had wings."

"Charles!" his wife scolded. "Dane is on his honeymoon. All he wants to do is spend time with his blushing bride." She waggled suggestive eyebrows at me, and my cheeks did indeed pinken at the implication.

"I'll write down the recipe for you," Dane replied. "You're welcome to use it at the bakery."

"Mighty nice of you," Charles said, reaching for the other half of his cupcake before his wife whisked it away.

"Your blood sugar," she warned, and the man gave a disgruntled sniff but didn't otherwise protest. She fanned her face with a cardstock fan on a stick she'd gotten at the local bookstore. It featured a bare-chested man who was apparently the cover model for a romance book.

Dane's hand went to his hip pocket, and I instantly recognized the unique ringtone of his burner phone. "Excuse me. I need to grab this," he said, rising and heading inside the house. Fiero only called about every ten days, and each time he did, I waited for him to tell us that Luca was out of the picture and it was safe for me to go home.

I nodded along while Mimsy chattered, trying not to look as distracted as I felt. *Is this the phone call we've been waiting for?*

"Have you read this one?" the woman asked, waving the fan at me. "It's a Mafia romance. The mouth on this man will twist your knickers."

Great, a Mafia romance. Exactly what I need, the sarcastic portion of my brain censured.

"No, I haven't read it, but I did enjoy that cowboy romance you gave me last week."

Mimsy closed her eyes and resumed fanning her face against the muggy Florida heat. "My Charles used to be a cowboy, you know. He was raised on a ranch. He asked me out twice, and I said no both times. Then I saw him riding across the pasture on his horse, and wooo-weee!"

"I had a much better figure back then," Charles said, giving his belly a self-deprecating pat.

I listened as the two of them reminisced about the beginning of their relationship, and I fell in love with their story. Charles and Mimsy were the cutest couple I'd ever encountered, and I found myself wishing my dad had a relationship like theirs. He deserved someone warm and outgoing, and I wondered, not for the first time, why he and my mother were even still married. They slept in separate rooms, and they never went out together, other than the occasional gala or other event.

When Dane returned to the porch, I knew immediately that something was not right. His lips were pinched into a tight line, and his eyes skittered around before finally landing on mine.

Covering my mouth with one hand, I feigned a yawn. "This has been so nice, but I think I'm ready to call it a night."

"Of course," Mimsy crooned. "You sweethearts need time for yourselves. Thank you for hanging out with the old folks tonight."

"It was our pleasure," Dane said, his lips turning up slightly. "We'll have you two over for dinner next week."

After a round of goodbyes, he took my hand and led me across the backyard to the house where we were staying. "What's going on?" I asked, but he shook his head.

"Inside." He unlocked the back door and led me inside and to the couch. "Sit."

All these one-word commands annoyed me, but I did as he said, watching him pace back and forth on the other side of the coffee table. Spearing both hands in his hair, he tugged before stopping his feet and dropping his hands to his sides.

"Leo is dead."

Well, that wasn't what I expected him to say. "He... how?"

"It was an apparent heart attack."

"Apparent?" Dane's eyes met mine with a heavy and significant stare. "You think your father had something to do with it?"

A gust of air rushed from his mouth, making his lips purse. "Fuck, I don't know. Fiero said Luca and Leo had a meeting two days ago, and then Leo's maid found him dead in his bed yesterday morning. The timing may be coincidental, but I wouldn't put it past my father to have... facilitated his death."

"Shit, what does that mean?"

"It means Luca is now the head of the family. He's the new Don."

My heart dropped to the floor, even as my stomach tried to rise up into my throat. "And what does that mean for us?" I asked in a voice so faint it was practically inaudible. Because I already knew.

Dane walked toward me, slowly, as if approaching a wounded animal, which was exactly how I felt. He kneeled in front of me, his own words spoken as softly as mine. "It means we can't go back, Eden. My father is now one of the most powerful men in New York City, and there's no one who can stop him."

"I don't care," I said, shaking my head from side to side. "I don't care. I want to go home."

"Are you willing to take the risk? To you and your family?" His eyes snagged mine and held, like an embedded fishhook. "Because if you are, I will send you back to New York."

I didn't even get to experience a second of elation before the images Robert had planted in my brain began to bloom. I squeezed my eyes shut to block them out, but that didn't help because they were ingrained there, seared into my soul.

Bile rose in my throat as, one by one, my family's smiling faces flashed in my mind but those pretty pictures were wiped away by the gruesome and brutal visions of their deaths. Dad. Mother. Auburn. Monty. Blood and unstaring eyes.

No!

"Damn you for making me choose," I whispered as the tears began to fall. "Why can't you just... just... force me to stay here?"

Dane's next words were delivered quietly but with so much underlying force, they almost knocked me backward. "Because. I. Am. Not. My. Fucking. Father." His tone was fierce and vehement, but his eyes held the slightest scrap of vulnerability, like maybe he needed reassurance that he wasn't evil to his core.

How can I want to scratch his eyes out and give him a hug at the same time? I opted for neither option and merely said, "I know you're not, Dane."

He grunted his appreciation and rolled his lips inward until the pink was no longer visible before averting his eyes toward my knees. "I'm sorry I can't take you to your family, E." His watery gaze slowly rose to mine. "I know this sucks, and I can't promise to fix your pain, but what I can promise is that you won't have to go through it by yourself."

Fuck.

That was really... kind. And entirely heartfelt based on the sincerity shining from his eyes. My hand lifted of its own free will and rested on the side of Dane's face, the soft beard comforting against my palm.

"Thank you for saying that."

He leaned into my touch and closed his eyes. "Do you want me to go to New York and... handle things?"

"Handle what—" My voice faltered when I caught his meaning. He was offering to kill his own father. A crack formed at the bottom of my heart and worked its way to the top as I shook my head. "No. Don't. I don't want you to kill anyone else for me."

His eyelids lifted, and his stare was so intense I found it impossible to look away. "Are you sure? Because I will."

I felt like my body was being ripped in half, dividing me into two equal parts, each of them fighting for what they wanted. The side of decency won by a slight margin.

"I'm sure."

Dane tilted his head slightly, and he kissed my palm before pushing up from his knees. "There's something else," he said as he sat beside me on the couch.

"More good news?" I asked with more than a little bitterness.

"Afraid so," he said, and I could hear the weariness in his tone. Resting his elbows on his knees, he stared at the floor before swiveling his head a little so I could see his face. "You remember when we borrowed Jamie's sedan and went for an evening drive?"

My head bobbed up and down. "Yes. We wanted to get out of the house for a little bit."

"And I wanted to gas the car up before we took it back, so we stopped at that little convenience store."

"And?" I prompted.

"And the clerk in there might have recognized you."

My hand went to my throat as the revelation dropped like a bombshell. "No."

"You weren't wearing your contacts because we didn't think we'd be getting out of the car..."

"But I had to pee," I finished, remembering that I'd gone inside to use the restroom.

"Yes. The lady thought you looked familiar but she didn't realize who you looked like until the next day when she saw your picture on TV. She wasn't certain though, just told the local police that you looked similar to the woman on the news. They called the Feds who came down to investigate. My father has people on the inside at the FBI, and this information finally made its way to him on Monday."

"But if he knows I didn't blow up in the helicopter, he'll know you didn't either," I said, my voice rising in panic. "And then he'll come looking for us."

Dane patted my hand and then left his on top of mine. "Don't freak out. He doesn't know anything for sure."

"So… what does this mean? What do we do now?" I asked, a sense of self-preservation kicking in.

"Robert is going to do some research and see what he can find out. I called him as soon as I got off the phone with Fiero."

"Do you think we have to leave here?" The thought of that overwhelmed me with sadness. The town of Marathon wasn't my home, but it was the closest thing I had over the past couple months.

"I don't think so. You were spotted over seven hours away from here, so I'm sure they'll be focused in the Jacksonville area."

Dane removed his hand from mine and clasped it with his free one, dropping his head and averting his gaze to the floor. He was silent, knuckles turning white and then pink as he clenched and unclenched them. Something was definitely bothering him… something he wasn't telling me.

An idea struck me like a bolt of lightning, searing my nerve endings. "That store is only a couple miles from Jamie and Robert's house. Are they—"

"They're fine. My father knows nothing about Jamie," Dane broke in, "and Robert looks way different than he did eight years ago. He's going to lay low for a bit, just to be safe, though I don't think Luca would recognize him even if he met him face to face."

I breathed out a long sigh. "That makes me feel a little better. I would never forgive myself if something happened to them because of me. They've been so good to us." I stared at the side of Dane's face. He still wouldn't meet my eye. "What are you hiding from me?"

Small lines formed at the corner of his eye as he scowled at the floor between his feet. "I don't want you to overreact, Eden." He paused for a long moment, and my chest tightened, waiting for his next words. "First of all, your family is fine."

"Why wouldn't they be fine?" I asked, trying to control the shaking of my hands.

Dane huffed out a long exhale before flopping back onto the couch. "There was a small fire at your parents' house. They. Are. Fine," he reiterated, finally looking at me with trepidation.

"A fire?" My voice seemed to be reaching dog-whistle levels.

"A *small* fire." His lips thinned. "The day after Luca heard from his contact at the FBI."

"Oh my fucking god. He's going after my family?"

He swiveled sideways on the couch, facing me full on and grasping both my hands. "Eden, if he was going after them, it would already be too late." My throat clogged with a painful lump. "Fiero seems to think it was a message... or a trap... for us."

"I don't understand," I wailed, my chin trembling.

"My brother is relaying what information he can to me, but he doesn't know everything. He's simply speculating about the cause of the fire. Because of the coincidental timing."

"I need to call my dad," I said in a rush, reaching into my pocket for my phone. "I need to know he and my mother are okay."

Before I could touch the screen, the phone was snatched from my hand. "No, Eden." He wedged the device beneath his leg, and my fingers itched to push him over and grab it. "I know what you're thinking, and don't even try it," Dane warned.

"Give. Me. My. Phone," I bit out.

"No," he snapped. "This is what I meant when I said it could be a trap. If Luca did have one of his men set that fire, it means he has your family under surveillance to make sure you're not in contact with them. He probably even tapped their phones, and as soon as you call, he'll know for sure."

My eyes widened in horror. "He's diabolical."

"I'm aware," Dane said dryly, slowly removing my phone from beneath his thigh. "I found a short clip from one of the New York news stations about the fire. Would you like to see?"

My answer came immediately. "Yes."

His thumbs flew over the keys, and then he tapped the play icon on a video before handing me the phone.

A female newscaster with her blonde hair pulled back into a low ponytail spoke into the camera. "Firefighters were called to the home of fashion icon Paul Bouvier in the early hours of Wednesday morning. Greg, what did you find out?"

The view switched to a man—presumably Greg—in front of my old house. A squeak escaped from my lips, but I quickly suppressed it as the reporter spoke. "Thank you, Linda. The fire began at about one in the morning. Mr. Bouvier was reportedly in the home alone and smelled smoke. Firefighters responded within minutes, and the flames were extinguished quickly. I spoke with one fireman, and he told me it appeared to be an electrical fire."

The camera angle changed, showing smoke coming out of an upstairs room, and I paused the video when I recognized my dad off to one side, speaking to a female firefighter. He was wearing plaid pajama pants and a gray long-sleeved T-shirt.

"Dad," I whispered, ghosting my finger over his image on the screen. That's when I noticed where the smoke was coming from. "Oh my god."

"What?" Dane asked, leaning closer to peer at the screen.

My eyes were wider than a full moon. "Th-that's my bedroom."

The grim set of Dane's mouth told me he had the same question as me. *Was my bedroom targeted specifically?*

He wrapped an arm around my shoulders. "I'm going to hire some people to keep an eye on your family."

"Y-you are?" I stuttered.

He lifted my chin with two fingers and kissed the tip of my nose, letting his lips linger there for a second. "Of course, baby. Just promise me you won't do anything stupid. If I wasn't sure before, the fact that it's your room where the fire was sealed the deal. I'm almost positive this is a test."

Everything inside me yearned to call my dad. My bones ached with it, but I was so afraid Dane was right about this. His father scared the shit out of me.

"Do you think he'll do anything to my brothers?" I asked, nestling my face into his neck and inhaling his musky cologne.

"Luca is a complete prick, but he's not stupid. Two attacks on the same family would definitely draw attention, and that's the last thing he wants. He's just testing us to see if he will get a response. If there's not one, he'll assume we're really dead and move on to other things."

I nodded as he stroked the back of my neck and down my spine. "Okay, I won't call them." Lifting my head, I looked intently into his eyes and forced my voice into something stern. "I want to know *everything* you find out from the people watching my family."

"I promise," he said, not looking away. "Why don't you get to bed, and I'll make some phone calls? Get all that set up."

"Okay," I said again, rising on shaky legs.

As soon as my head hit the pillow, I allowed my tears to fall, soaking the soft fabric beneath my cheek until I fell asleep.

And that's the night my nightmares began.

CHAPTER 19

I HAD DEVELOPED QUITE the bedroom routine over the past few weeks. *Number one, check to make sure Eden is asleep. Number two, grab a towel from the bathroom before heading into my room. Number three, fuck the hell out of my hand while I think about my wife.*

I was currently standing beside my bed, working on task number three, my fist wrapped around my length as I imagined Eden on her knees in front of me. She wasn't wearing her contacts, so her naturally blue eyes stared up at me, tears leaking from the corners because I was fucking gagging her.

"That's it, baby girl. Choke on me."

A squelching noise came from her throat when I breached that tight channel, and I groaned, pure pleasure coursing through every cell in my body.

"That smart mouth of yours ain't so sassy with a cock stuffed in it, is it, little Wildcat?" Her pretty lips shifted around my dick, the corners curving up into a distorted smile. Even when I was balls deep in her mouth, she was still a damn smartass, and I loved it.

"Does it turn you on to have your face fucked, Eden?" She nodded earnestly at my dirty words, and I pulled out, bending to kiss her fuck-swollen lips. "You want to touch your cunt, don't you?" I whispered against her mouth.

"Yes, Sir," she moaned, and I had to tighten my fingers around the crown of my cock to keep from blowing my load too soon. I loved these little fantasies of mine and wanted them to last for as long as possible. They always seemed to be over way too soon though. My imagination was simply too vivid when I thought of Eden.

Reaching for one of her hands, I brought it to my mouth, sucking the first two fingers until they were dripping with my saliva. "I'll allow you to come because you're going to be a good girl and swallow every drop of me. Now get those fingers between your legs."

A second later, I was back inside the heat of her mouth, gripping her dark hair as I listened to the sounds of Eden getting herself off. She made the prettiest noises, sweet and drawn out, while I shoved my cock deep.

I couldn't see what she was doing to herself from this angle, so I watched the rise and fall of her shoulder as she worked herself over.

"I'm close," I warned her. "Don't make me come yet, baby. I want it to last."

But of course she didn't listen, bobbing her head quickly up and down my length and allowing her tongue to wrap around the head on each upstroke. Her name was an oath on my lips as a familiar feeling of elation sizzled along my nerve endings.

"Eden, fuck. I need you to come. Now," I demanded, and she did, her body trembling beautifully and the vibration of her moans traveling up my cock. My god, it felt so goddamn good.

Gritting my teeth, I held on until she was done, and then, with a voice hoarse with need, I said, "Give me your fingers, baby. I have to taste your pussy while I come."

Dutifully, she pulled her hand from between her legs, raised it, and allowed me to suck her juices clean. Though I was fantasizing, I could taste her as clearly as if I had my head buried between her legs. She tasted like she always smelled... like sweet honey, rich and raw.

My hand groped blindly for the towel I'd left on the bed, already shuddering out my release by the time I found it and covered my dick. "Shit! Fuck, that's so good," I groaned. My knees almost collapsed, and I planted one fist on the mattress to hold myself up.

It took a long while before I was able to slow my breathing and make my way to the bathroom in the hall to clean up. As soon as I was done, I returned to my bedroom, slid on a pair of black boxer briefs, and fell onto the bed like an uprooted tree.

Of course, I'd masturbated hundreds of times before, but never—not once—had my self-induced orgasms been like this. My Eden fantasies exhausted me like I'd been fucking for hours.

Mmm, yes. I'd give my right nut to fuck my wife into the mattress all night long.

That filthy thought was interrupted by a scream that tore through the house and pierced my heart.

"Eden!" I yelled, my legs finding life as I leaped from the bed. Snatching open my bedside drawer, I yanked out my gun and scrambled down the short hallway. I shoved the door open and entered the room, gun first, my eyes searching for the threat. My fingers flipped up the light switch, bathing the room in light.

Eden was thrashing on the bed, but no one was in the room with her. My mind played catch-up, though I wasn't sure my heart rate would ever return to a normal level. She was having a nightmare, her whimpers punctuated by the occasional scream of pure terror.

"Baby," I breathed, rushing to her and setting the gun down on her nightstand.

My hands untangled the covers from around her kicking legs as pleas scratched up her throat. "No, please don't. Pleeeeease!" A million cracks formed in my chest at the sound of her abject fear.

"Eden, wake up, baby. It's just a nightmare." I gripped her shoulders, and that was apparently the wrong thing to do because she went feral, bending both knees to her chest and then kicking out, hitting me squarely in the gut. I covered my curse as I stumbled backward a few steps and held my hands up in front of me, a gesture of surrender.

Eden scrambled back against the headboard, her eyes wide open and round now. "Don't touch me! Don't!"

"Okay, not touching. I promise," I assured her through ragged breaths. "It's me, Eden. It's Dane."

"Dane?" She sounded confused and whipped her head back and forth, searching the room for anyone else.

"Yes, it's Dane. No one else is here. You're in our house in the Keys, and you're safe." Jesus, I wanted nothing more than to run to her and gather her slight body in my arms, but I remained rooted to the floor and kept my voice soft. "You're safe, sweetheart."

Eden pulled a pillow against her belly and shrunk into a ball, her gaze still wary as she searched the room once more. "I'm safe," she repeated, sounding amazed at the thought. Then she looked down at her hands and feet. "The chains are gone."

Chains? What the actual fuck? "All gone," I promised her, my heart in a million pieces.

Her eyes lost a bit of focus as she stared across the room. "It was so dark. I couldn't see anything." I knew in my gut she wasn't talking about the lighting in this room but about something that happened to her when she was taken.

With achingly slow steps, I walked toward the bed and picked up her phone, switching on the flashlight app. I wasn't even sure what the hell I was doing since the overhead lights were already on, but I handed it to her. "It's not dark anymore."

Eden clutched the lit phone to the pillow she was still clasping against her torso, and her breathing eased, but her gaze remained fixed on a spot on the wall. "There wasn't enough air in there."

Every inch of my body felt an unrelenting rage at the assholes who had done this to her... who had turned this vibrant, beautiful woman into a terrified shell. I wished I had magical powers so I could bring them back to life and kill them again, much more slowly this time. Piece by tiny fucking piece.

Keeping my eyes on Eden, I walked backward, removing the security bar from the sliding door and pulling it open.

"There's lots of air out here. Do you want to sit on the veranda?" I was way out of my depth here, but this seemed like the right thing to do. Maybe.

The tension in her shoulders relaxed a little as she focused on the open door behind me. The sounds of waves crashed from the ocean, and salty night air filled the room. "Yes please."

"Do you need help?"

Her messy dark head shook from side to side. "No, I can walk." Eden set the pillow aside but held onto the phone as she placed her feet on the floor and paused to get her bearings. Then she walked toward me on unsteady legs, and I stepped aside to let her exit first.

She gripped the back of one patio chair and closed her eyes, and I watched as her chest filled and then emptied a dozen times.

"Better?" I asked. "I can turn the porch lights on."

"Much better." Eden's eyes turned up toward the round, glowing moon. "I don't need more light. This is okay." Turning off the flashlight app, she set her phone on the small table.

"Sit down, Eden. You need to rest."

Her eyes flitted to mine and then back down to the tan stone floor. "Would it be okay if I sat... in your lap?"

Emotions of all kinds slammed into my chest, but the most prominent one was elation. I wanted so badly to do something to help her, and she was actually trusting me enough to ask for this.

"Of course." I sank into the chair on the left.

Eden swallowed. "Can you please not..." she made a circle in front of her with her arms, miming a hug. "I don't want... I can't..." Her breathing picked up again, and I shook my head.

"I won't hold you," I assured her, understanding what she was trying so hard to say. She didn't want to feel trapped. With a grateful half-smile, she lowered her butt to my thighs and draped her legs over one arm of the chair so she was sitting sideways on my lap.

Sitting as still as I could—and valiantly managing to keep my hands off her—I allowed Eden to use me as her own personal piece of furniture. When her soft body relaxed into mine and she rested her head against my shoulder, I sighed with a kind of peacefulness I hadn't felt in a long time.

Then I almost jolted with the realization that it mattered to me that Eden was comfortable with me. I'd never given a damn what any woman thought about me besides my mother and sister. Did I despise the way my father treated women? Fuck yes, I did. And while I was never concerned with women besides the pleasure they could offer me in bed, I wasn't cruel to them like Luca. We had a mutual good time, and that was that.

But Eden? I was starting to actually care about her as a person. Her feelings were becoming my own. When she hurt, I hurt. I wanted to take away her pain, to absorb it into my bones until she didn't feel it anymore.

It was a completely unfamiliar feeling but one that wasn't unpleasant at all. And maybe, if I was being honest with myself, it had been happening for a while. I'd gotten her flowers for her birthday, for fuck's sake. I'd never bought a woman flowers before.

My mind flashed back to that day in March when she'd stomped into the kitchen like a woman on a mission to be miserable. But the lilacs had made her smile, and that made my heart stretch like it had been dormant for a long time and was finally waking up.

With a slow hand, I tentatively stroked my fingers through the hair over her right ear. "Is this okay? If I touch you like this?"

I felt her nod against the side of my neck. "Yes. That feels good."

My fingers continued to roam through Eden's soft locks, massaging miniature circles against her scalp. For a long while, the only sounds were the crashing waves and the occasional tree frog or cricket chirping in the distance.

Then she burrowed a little closer and pierced my soul with her words.

CHAPTER 20

EDEN'S VOICE WAS SOFT but clear. "There was a false wall in the cargo area of a big truck. It slid forward to form a kind of narrow hallway along one side." Twin gusts of air feathered across my skin as she exhaled through her nose. "There were five of us. Cara. Nesha. Two girls named Jennifer. And me. They made us get in there and chained us to the wall by our arms and legs. And around our necks."

She paused for a long moment, and when she spoke again, her voice sounded strangled. "When they closed the false wall, it was only a couple inches from my face. It was so fucking dark."

Jesus. "Is that what your nightmare was about?"

"Yes." The word trembled against her lips, turning the single syllable into three, and I lowered my lips to the top of her head.

Eden pressed one palm against my chest, directly over my heart, while we sat in silence for a time. Without even thinking about it, I began rocking from side to side, and her body moved with mine in a slow, steady rhythm.

I had so many questions but forced myself to remain quiet, to let her go at her own pace. When she spoke again, the tips of her fingers curled against my chest.

"We couldn't even sleep to pass the time," she said in a trembling voice. "Every time I'd start to doze off, my head would droop forward and the chain around my neck choked me and woke me up."

Motherfucker. I wanted to wrap her up and hold her tight, but that wasn't what she needed; it was what I needed. How the hell was she even functioning? What she'd been through was goddamn horrifying, and it wouldn't have improved much if I had handed her over to Luca like I was supposed to.

"How long were you in there?" I asked.

"Hours. I think we were still in Mexico when we left."

"And they drove you to New Orleans? Jesus, E. That has to be a ten or eleven hour trip, minimum." I was trying to control the timbre of my voice, but my rage was about to crest and pour over me like an erupting volcano.

"I felt the truck stop a few times, but they never let us out to use the bathroom or anything. It was way over a hundred degrees back there, and one of the Jennifers kept puking, so you can imagine how it smelled." Her fingers tightened on my bare chest, the nails cutting little half-moons into my flesh.

Now I understood why she liked the windows down in the car and why she needed to have her door slightly ajar. I buried my nose in her hair, smelling her fruity shampoo mixed with the scents of her honey shower gel and a slight whiff of nightmare sweat.

When I felt her tears drip down my chest, I was simultaneously pained and relieved. Pained because she was hurting but relieved that she was letting her emotions out instead of bottling them up. This shit couldn't be healthy to keep inside.

"I-I finally couldn't hold it a-anymore," she said, stuttering and hiccuping her way through the sentence. "I had to pee so bad."

Motherfucking hell. I could read between the lines as to what came next. "It's okay, baby. Everyone has to pee. It's just biology, and you did what you had to do."

"I felt s-so dirty. And humiliated," she sobbed, her fingernails cutting deeper into my skin.

"That's why you take several showers a day," I stated before I could think better of it, and she nodded. "Would you like to take a shower now? Would that make you feel better?"

She'd barely croaked out a yes before I was standing, cradling her gently in my arms, and striding inside and straight to her bathroom. There was a free-standing shower along one wall, and I set her on her feet beside it before kissing the tip of her nose. I'd given up trying to figure out why I always felt the need to do that.

Taking a much-needed step back, I slid open the shower door and turned on the water to warm. "Get undressed," I instructed, holding my hand beneath the spray and adjusting the temperature until it was just right.

"You're... staying in here?" she asked.

I walked to the side wall of the shower and pressed my back against it, consciously looking away from her. "I'll be right here in case you need me." She didn't say anything, so I added, "I've been meaning to count the gulls on this seascape."

My lips curved up when I heard a little laugh escape her, and then they turned down when the sound of rustling clothes reached my ears.

Naked Eden, naked Eden, naked Eden, chanted through my brain before I knocked the words away with a chant that was more appropriate. *Hurt Eden, vulnerable Eden, scared Eden.*

That did the trick, and as I heard her click the shower door shut, my eyes flicked across the framed painting on the wall across from me. I recognized the burnt orange lighthouse that sat on a reef off Vaca Key, the iron pilings skeletal against the sunset behind it. Or maybe it was a sunrise; I wasn't sure. But the yellow orb was barely kissing the water, turning it into a blanket of muted colors.

I began counting the seagulls. *One. Two. Three.* I'd barely gotten to eight when I heard a thunk and then a soft, "Ow!" My hesitation lasted only two beats before I muttered, "Fuck it," and swung my body around to sling open the glass door. "E, are you okay?"

Her eyes widened when I stepped into the shower, still wearing my black boxer briefs, and one of her arms crossed over her chest. "I-I dropped this on my foot." She held up a small yellow bottle of face wash. "I was trying to get the lid off, and the bottle slipped."

My heart rate lowered to something approaching normal. "Sorry, you scared the hell out of me. Is your foot okay?" *Don't look down. Do. Not. Look. Down.*

She nodded, her blue eyes locked on mine, which assisted in my efforts to not let my gaze drop. "It's fine, but do you think you could—" Eden held out the bottle toward me. Taking it from her, I grasped it in one hand and used the other to twist off the lid. "Showoff," she muttered, giving me a teasing half-smile.

As if she was metal and I was a magnet, I took a step closer to her and pulled the door closed behind me, cocooning us in the steamy enclosure. "May I?" I asked, squirting a dollop of the amber gel onto my fingers.

Her voice was quiet but clear, floating softly between us. "Yes."

Something roared inside me, like a lion proclaiming his dominion over the animal kingdom. Maybe it made me a prick, but I loved that she needed me, trusted me, even with something as simple as taking care of her in this small way.

My eyes searched her bare face. The bruises had long since healed, but when she was fragile like this, I could practically see them again. Or the ghost of them. Like a phantom reminder of what she'd endured, and it somehow made her even more fucking beautiful.

Reaching for her face with both hands, I massaged the cleanser in tiny circles over her skin, methodically, slowly, starting with her forehead, being cautious near the cute nose piercing, and working my way down to her neck.

With the soft, content smile on her face, I was finding it easier not to look down. I focused instead on the blue tinge of her closed eyelids, tracing each tiny vein with my eyes.

Once I'd lathered her entire face and neck, I carefully rinsed away the suds and reached a hand to the back of her neck, gently tilting her head back to wet her hair.

While I worked the fruity shampoo through her strands, Eden drifted her fingers over the marks she'd left on my chest, a frown wrinkling her brow. "Did I do that?"

"Now you know why I call you Wildcat."

She leaned forward, pressing a series of kisses across the area, and I had to remind myself to breathe. "I'm sorry," she whispered, tilting her head up until I got lost in her beautiful face.

"It doesn't hurt," I assured her, though perhaps I should have lied and told her the pain was unbearable. Then maybe she would have kissed my chest some more.

Dude, you're such a fucking prick.

After finishing Eden's hair with conditioner, I handed her the bottle of body wash. "I think I'll let you take over the, um, the rest."

I'd never thought of myself as a saint by any stretch of the imagination, but not looking down at my beautiful wife's bare body probably qualified me to at least make it through the first round of the application process.

"What are you smiling about?" she asked suspiciously.

I chuckled and stared at a spot high on the shower wall where the caulk was peeling away. "I was just thinking *Saint Dane* has a pretty nice ring to it."

She giggled when she got my drift, and I wished I could bottle that sound and carry it around with me so I could take it out and listen to it when I was feeling the darkness. As I stepped out onto the bathmat, the scent of honey and vanilla filled the air, and I was glad I'd gotten out before she started rubbing down her body. I was obsessed with the smell of her body wash.

After drying off, I retreated to my bedroom, stripped off my wet underwear, and donned a pair of lightweight black sleep pants. When I returned to Eden's room, I heard the hairdryer running and decided to change her sheets, which were damp with her sweat.

She walked out just as I was tucking the top sheet in at the bottom of her bed. Her feet stalled, and she dipped her chin, looking at me from beneath her lashes. "Thank you, Dane. For... everything."

I pulled back the covers and nodded for her to slide in. "Hop in and try to get some sleep."

"I need to shut this," she said, heading toward the glass door leading to the veranda, but I stopped her with a hand on her elbow.

"Leave it. You'll sleep better with it open."

Her eyebrows inched together. "But you said I need to keep it locked with the security bar every night."

"Not if I'm in here," I informed her, pulling the white wicker chair from the corner and placing it beside the bed. "I promise you'll be safe." I gestured once again for her to get in bed as I turned on the lamp on her nightstand.

She finally did, but now her eyebrows were cinched so tightly together they resembled a unibrow. "But you need to sleep."

"I'll take a nap tomorrow."

"So you're just going to watch me sleep?"

"Yep, just like Dracula would do," I told her wryly, turning off the overhead light.

Settling my butt onto the purple cushion of the wicker chair, I watched as Eden turned onto her side facing me and snuggled down into her pillow, an amused smile playing over her lips.

"Night, Dracula."

I chuckled. "Goodnight, Wildcat."

When she closed her eyes and stretched one hand out toward me, I took it.

And didn't let go until morning.

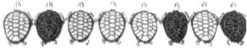

A woman wearing a red vest approached me as I wandered into the plumbing section of the hardware store. "Can I help you find anything, sir?"

"Yes, I need some caulk," I told her, and I was sure I'd never tried so hard to enunciate the L-sound.

"Of course. Right this way." After I found what I needed, she asked, "Anything else?"

"Where's your lighting section?"

Forty minutes later, I exited the store into the Florida sunshine with several heavy bags. I hadn't gotten any sleep last night after Eden's nightmare, and I was looking forward to getting home and crashing for a few hours.

After putting the bags in the SUV, my gaze snagged on a neon sign in a storefront beside the hardware store. Forgetting about my lack of sleep, I walked across the parking lot toward it, stopping beside the plate glass window and staring inside for several moments.

Mind made up, I smiled to myself, opened the door, and walked inside.

CHAPTER 21

"WHAT'S THE MOST ROMANTIC thing Dane has ever done for you?" Charlisse asked, resting her chin in her hand and staring at me with stars in her eyes.

"Oh. Um. Wow, I'm not sure," I hedged.

She gave me puppy dog eyes. "Pleeeease, Eden. I need to live vicariously through you. God knows I haven't seen any amorous action since before Cooper was born." Her eyebrows bobbed up and down. "I bet Dane is super romantic. I can tell by the way he looks at you."

The way he what? Sure, he's affectionate in front of other people, but that's just for show, right? Then something popped into my head, and I bit my bottom lip as my thumb toyed with my wedding ring. I wasn't able to explain why, but I'd stopped taking it off at night.

"He knows I like lilacs, so when he bakes every week, he makes me a special cupcake, or whatever dessert he's making, with a frosting lilac on top."

Charlisse swooned back against her chair and dramatically covered her forehead with her wrist. "Gawd, that's so flipping sweet! Seriously, the little things are what matter most, not the big, grand gestures. It shows that his love for you is ongoing."

I tried my best not to react with a startled look at the L-word. Pushing the corners of my mouth upward, I attempted to look like a lovestruck fool. After all, Dane and I were newlyweds. Well, *pretend* newlyweds.

She got up and refilled our tea. "And I think he'll be a great dad. He was so patient with Cooper that night the baby turtles hatched."

A few weeks ago, Dane and I had been walking on the beach when we saw movement in one of the nests we'd previously marked. I'd immediately called Charlisse, and she'd gotten her son out of bed and brought him to the beach in his Hulk pajamas. Dane had held the boy's hand and explained how the babies were making their way to the water to find their mom.

"He is a good guy," I said as images of last night in the shower flitted through my brain like a slideshow.

The way his fingers cleaned my face so softly. The way his hands took their time washing and rinsing my hair. The way he didn't look down even once.

Why the hell hadn't I felt intimidated by that big man towering over me in the confines of the shower? Why had I, instead, felt a wave of comfort and contentment wash over me as soon as he stepped into the space, as warm as the water coursing down my back? The answer was immediate. *Because he took care of you, Eden. Made you feel safe.*

A genuine smile melted across my lips and loosened my jaw. Charlisse must have noticed because she squealed, "Oh my god, you're thinking about sexy times, aren't you?" Her voice lowered conspiratorially. "I bet Dane is amazing in bed. That deep voice and those bedroom eyes. Whew! You're a lucky girl, Eden."

He did have a very deep voice, but bedroom eyes? I pictured them in my head. Heavy lids, brown irides that seemed to darken when he touched my face... *How would they look if he was on top of me?*

With a giggle that I hoped didn't sound as hysterical as it felt, I busied myself by dabbing at my lips with a paper napkin. "Girl," I said, waving the napkin at her, "I can't even tell you how good Dane is in bed."

And that was the god's honest truth because I had no idea. But now my curiosity was piqued. Dane's flirt game was top-level. Would that translate to some dirty talk between the sheets?

My thighs clenched together, and I quickly turned the subject back around to Charlisse. "So, it's been a while for you?"

Her nose crinkled. "Yeah, not many guys our age want to date a woman with a toddler. I'm thinking of getting myself a sugar daddy." We both burst into laughter, and then she shook her head. "Who am I kidding? I always seem to pick guys who have no ambition outside of what new video game their mommy is going to buy for them next."

I shrugged. "No one can change your choices except for you. Just make a conscious effort to choose differently."

"You're right," she sighed, taking a sip of her iced tea. "Maybe I'll try dating again when Coop is a little older. I'm too freaking tired now."

Both our heads swiveled toward the front of her house when we heard a knock at the door. "That's probably Dane," I said, standing and placing my cup and our plates in the dishwasher. "Thanks for letting me hang with you while he was running his errands." *Which he was rather vague about.*

"Hey, I'm happy to have an adult to converse with about something other than *footbawwwl,*" she said with a laugh as we headed to the front door.

Dane was indeed on the other side, and his concerned eyes met mine as I stood just behind Charlisse. "Hey, babe. How are you feeling?"

My friend's head swiveled in my direction. "Are you sick?"

"No," I laughed. "I promise I wouldn't come over if I were. I just... didn't sleep well last night. That's all." Looking back at my fake husband, I gave him a small smile. "I'm feeling good."

Because you sat with me while I slept. Because you held my hand until I woke up this morning. Because you kept the patio door open all night so I could breathe.

Dane held out a bright-yellow bag to Charlisse. "Got this for the kid. He seems to like football, and the lady at the bookstore said this was a good one."

She pulled out a large book with cartoon football players on the cover. It was one of those pop-up books and was completely adorable.

"Dane! You didn't have to do that. Cooper is napping right now, but I'll give it to him when he wakes up. He will love this." She flipped through a few of the pages, a huge smile on her face.

My pretend-husband's cheeks pinkened. "My mom used to read to me when I was a kid. Every night before bed." My heart ached a little for him, knowing what I knew about his mother.

Charlisse gave him a quick hug. "I do the same with Coop. Thank you for this. Really, it was so thoughtful."

Dane reached for my hand, his eyes holding mine as he kissed my knuckles. "You ready to go, E?" Seriously, every inch of my body was melting at once, like a mass-swooning at the cellular level.

"I'm ready," I said way too breathlessly, and Charlisse nudged me with her elbow, a smug smile on her lips. I gave her a warm hug and allowed Dane to hold my hand as we crossed the street. "What errands did you have? You've been gone for hours."

"I went to the hardware store and a couple other places in that shopping center," he said, unlocking and opening the door. "Then I came back here to take care of something. Come on and I'll show you." He led me to my bedroom, his lips rolled inward between his teeth.

"Why are you acting weird?"

Dane's eyes flickered to me, just a fleeting glance before he opened my door. "I did a quick home improvement project." He pointed at what used to be a light switch that had been replaced with a dimmer switch. "I talked to Robert and Jamie to make sure it was okay," he assured me.

I punched the button and then twisted it back and forth, watching as the overhead light brightened and then dimmed. "You did this?" I asked incredulously, and he shrugged with nonchalance.

"It wasn't hard. The lady at the hardware store told me how to do it."

A lady? Was he with her the past few hours? Is that why he's acting so sketchy? For some reason, that bothered me, the thought of him being with someone else. I mean, our marriage wasn't real, but he could blow our cover if he was out there whoring around. *On that subject, what is he doing about his... needs?*

"Did you sleep with her?" That fell out of my mouth like the cringiest word waterfall ever. *Dammit to hell, Eden. What the fuck?*

"Who?" His brow was creased so deeply, I wasn't sure he'd ever get rid of the wrinkles.

I picked at the fringe on the bottom hem of my shorts. "The, um, the hardware store lady."

"Agnes?" he asked with a chuckle. "No, I'm not into cougars."

"What are you into?" *Shut. Up. Stop talking now!*

He linked his index finger with mine and pulled me across the room. "I'm into wildcats," he said flatly, not looking at me. "I got you a few other lighting options as well." His free hand gestured at the area around my bed, and I had to force myself not to laugh.

And what was that about wildcats?

"A few?"

Dane pushed out a sigh and stroked his beard, surveying everything he'd bought. "Maybe I went overboard. I just wanted you to have choices close at hand in case you have another nightmare."

Two of those push-button lights had been stuck on either side of the white padded headboard. But that was only the beginning of Dane's illumination shopping spree. My finger touched the pretty silver lamp on the nightstand, and it lit up. I tapped it twice more, and it got brighter and then turned off. Then I picked up each flashlight—there were six of them, by the way—and flicked them on and back off.

He lifted the heavy-duty Maglite and gave me a chagrined smile. "I guess this one could be used as a weapon if needed." Setting it down, he gestured to the plugs dotting the walls around the room. "I got some nightlights too."

There were three of them, and they were all shaped like turtles. My heart squeezed almost to the point of pain in my chest.

"Thank you," I eked out, and Dane gave me a self-deprecating smile.

"Hope I didn't overstep. I just... you scared me last night, Eden, and I think maybe you need to talk to someone."

"I talked to you."

His lips pressed together, and he shook his head. "I mean a professional. Like a counselor or psychiatrist or something."

My eyebrows inched together. "It was only one nightmare, Dane."

But that turned out to not be altogether accurate. Over the next week, I had four more horrible dreams, those featuring the lifeless bodies of my family.

And every night, Dane was by my side, holding my hand, taking me outside, letting me cry until my eyeballs ached. In the light of day the mornings after, he always begged me to talk to someone.

But my answer never changed. No.

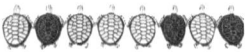

"Good morning. How was your shower?" Dane asked from beside the stove where he was scrambling eggs. Shirtless.

"It was good."

He plated the eggs and pulled a pan of bacon from the oven before dividing the slices between two square white plates. "They had some nice fruits at the market," he said, carrying our food to the breakfast bar and setting them down. "The pineapple is really sweet."

Orange and pineapple slices had been arranged around plump purple grapes on a blue-and-white floral platter, and I loaded my plate with fruit. "Thank you for breakfast. I would have cooked."

"You always overcook the eggs," he muttered, sitting on the stool beside me. He wasn't wrong.

After we finished eating and were cleaning the kitchen, my eyes dropped to the white bandage he'd been wearing on his chest the past few days. The top edge was peeling up.

"I'm sorry about that," I said, nodding at where he'd covered my fingernail marks on his skin the day after my first nightmare. I hadn't thought they were bad enough to require a bandage, but maybe... "Are you keeping it clean? You probably need to change this bandage."

I reached for it, and he took a step back, smoothing the tape back down. "It's fine."

My eyes narrowed, and I matched his backward step with a forward one of my own. "Don't be a baby. Let me look."

Dane's eyes rolled, and he dropped his hand. "Fine. You're going to see it at some point anyway."

Giving him a curious look, I swiftly peeled the bandage off his chest to reveal—*What the hell is that?*

The fingernail marks were practically invisible, just tiny, pale crescents now. But above each one were marks in the same precise shape, only these were inked.

"Are those tattoos?" He didn't speak, merely nodded, his eyes wary. "Why did you get tattoos of my fingernails?"

"They're... tattoos of your pain and your fear." His brown eyes were solemn when he looked down at me. "I can't take those things away from you, but I can carry a part of them with me."

Tears pooled on my bottom eyelids and then broke free, making a downward trek over my cheeks. The tats, the long nights beside my bed, the grim set of his mouth... all of that told me he was determined to help in any way he could, but my stubborn ass wasn't allowing him to.

I kissed his new ink, each of the five replicas of my own fingernails, before wrapping my arms around his bare torso and hugging him.

My words were spoken softly, but I knew he heard them because I felt the tension practically flow from his body.

"I'll talk to someone."

CHAPTER 22

SIX MONTHS IN HIDING

"Good session today, Eden. You're doing really well."

I smiled into the phone, feeling better than I had since my abduction in March, six months ago. I hadn't even realized everything I was carrying inside until I started these phone sessions with my psychiatrist. She was a pro at drawing the repressed feelings out of me and giving me the tools to deal with each one.

"Thank you, Lilibet. It's been weeks since I had a nightmare," I bragged.

"That makes me so happy. I'll talk to you again next week, okay?"

"Sounds good."

"And remember—"

"Do whatever it takes to feel safe," I parroted. That was how she ended every session with me.

Her laugh sounded like tinkling bells, and I wasn't sure how I could like someone so much even though I'd never actually met her. "You're learning, dear," Lilibet sang before we said our goodbyes and hung up.

Jamie had recommended Dr. Lilibet Lynch after Dane called her and told her about my nightmares. The two had gone to med school together, and Jamie often called on the woman when one of their "clients" needed help.

Dane turned off the circular saw he was using to cut plywood when I walked into the back yard. He was wearing a heather-gray Henley that stretched over the bulk of his shoulders and jeans that fit in all the right places. Despite the cooler September weather, sweat dampened his forehead. Swiping the wetness away on his shoulder, he flashed me a smile.

Dammit, why is a sweaty man working with power tools so dang hot? And to top it all off, he had a ball cap on backward.

"How did it go?"

"Good. Lilibet is pleased with my progress."

"She should be," he said, pulling off his work gloves and stowing them in his back pocket before tilting his head back to look up at the sky. "They're saying the hurricane should make landfall late tonight."

I looked down at the two stacks of plywood cut into squares lying on the lawn. "I don't think we have this many windows," I remarked.

"I cut extra. Thought I'd go board up Charlisse and Cooper's windows too. I called Charles, and he said they already have plywood cut from the last hurricane a few years ago, but I'll drop by and hang them for him."

"I'll help," I offered, and he lifted a skeptical eyebrow at me. "I can hand you the screws or something."

"M'kay," he said, walking to the stack and picking up the tape measure before stretching it across the piece of wood he'd been working on. He bobbed his head, apparently satisfied, and added it to one of the stacks. "These are for Charlisse's house."

Dane bent, giving me a spectacular view of his ass in those jeans, and picked up a huge stack in both arms. I rushed over and tried to grab the remainder, but the damn things were heavy, and I was only able to carry one.

"Come on, Hercules," he teased.

Two hours later, we had all the windows covered on our house and the two neighbors' homes, and we had a big plate of Charles's brownies on our kitchen counter.

"The man's a national treasure," I commented, sliding one off and taking a big bite. "This frosting should be in the Smithsonian."

"I'm going to fill up the gas cans for the generator," Dane said, reaching for his keys.

"I'll get some blankets and pillows ready. Your closet or mine?" I asked, giving him an eyebrow wiggle.

He laughed. "Yours is bigger."

"That's what she said," I shot back, earning me an eye roll from Dane.

"Go take a shower, Wildcat. It's going to be a long night."

It was indeed a long night. I did surprisingly well, despite being closed up in a closet for hours during the worst of it. Dane and I ate brownies and played Uno with music from his phone in the background to distract from the storm raging outside the house.

Lilibet was big into music therapy, and she'd told me to experiment with different styles to see what calmed me the most. Turned out it was rock ballads from the eighties, and I listened to a playlist of Foreigner, Journey, Heart, and lots of others while I went to sleep each night.

The final notes of "Every Rose Has Its Thorn" faded away as the wind finally subsided, and Dane pushed to his feet. "Sounds like the worst of it has finally passed. I'm going to check the house and then fire up the generator." The electricity had gone out about halfway through the storm, but, of course, we had lots of flashlights in our little hideaway.

Once we got outside, we found that our house had weathered the storm well, but Charlisse hadn't been quite so lucky. A large water oak tree had fallen through the roof of her bedroom and blocked the door to her closet, trapping her and Cooper inside. Thankfully, they were physically unharmed.

As the rescuers worked to free them, I looked up at Dane in the moonlight that was finally peeking through the clouds. "Do you think we should—"

"Offer to let them stay with us for a bit?" he filled in, and I nodded, grateful that he seemed to read my mind. "For sure, but we'll have to move my stuff into your room. It wouldn't look right if newlyweds had separate bedrooms. Are you okay with that?" His brown eyes darted back and forth between my own.

Was I? I guessed it would be okay. After all, he was a constant presence in my room when I had a nightmare. But he'd always sat *beside* my bed, not slept *in* it.

Reading my thoughts once again, he said, "I can sleep in the chair or on the floor."

Hearing him say that out loud left a bitter taste in my mouth, and I shook my head. He'd worked his ass off helping neighbors all day, and he deserved a soft place to sleep.

"No, it's fine. The bed is big enough for both of us."

"All right. Let's go move my stuff."

Several neighbors were gathered in Charlisse's front yard watching the rescue efforts, including Charles and Mimsy. The latter was dressed in sneakers and a red floral muumuu, handing out paper cups of coffee to neighbors and first responders. We stopped to inform her that we were going inside to get a room ready for Charlisse and Cooper, and she wrapped us both in a hug, bursting into tears for about the fiftieth time that night.

When we finally extricated ourselves, we went in and transferred Dane's clothing and personal items to my suite. It looked strange to see men's clothing hanging on one side of my closet, but I didn't mind. My friend and her precious little boy needed a safe place to stay, and that was all that mattered.

We'd just gone back outside when we saw Mimsy escorting an exhausted Charlisse across the street. Dane jogged out and took a sleeping Cooper from her arms while I curled my arms around her and squeezed her.

"I'm so happy you're safe. How is Cooper?"

A small smile broke through her tears. "The little stinker slept through the whole thing, including a tree falling through the damn house and all the banging and chainsaws." Her bottom lip trembled. "I was so scared, Eden. That tree came within a couple feet of landing right on us."

I swiped at the tears on my face as I led her inside. "But it didn't. You're both fine and safe. That's all that's important."

She cast one last glance at her house across the street, and I thought the poor woman was going to collapse, but she straightened her shoulders with resolve.

"You're right. A house is just a house, and my baby is okay." Her hand gripped my upper arm as I closed the door. "Thank you both so much for letting us stay here."

"As long as you need," I assured her, guiding her to the bedroom where Dane was laying Cooper on the bed. "Let me grab you some pajamas."

It was three in the morning by the time we were ready for bed. Dane showered first, and when I came out from the bathroom, I noticed he'd set the overhead light on the dimmest setting.

"We can turn that off if you can't sleep with it on," I told him.

"Nah, I could sleep with the light of a thousand suns on me right now."

I could see the fatigue etched onto the planes of his face, and I suddenly felt bone tired as well. It had been a long-ass day. Feeling the awkwardness like a dense fog between us, I climbed onto my side of the bed and faced the veranda door, away from Dane, before tapping the touch lamp to turn it off.

The mattress sank with his weight, and from the sound of his breathing, I could tell he was facing me. He was so big, I could feel the heat of his body against my back—even though we weren't touching—and my breathing picked up.

"What's wrong?" he said into the darkness.

"Nothing," I lied.

A second later, I heard the soft click of one of the push lights and twisted my head to see Dane resting on one elbow, the blue haze of the light forming a halo behind his head. He was so close, and one of my hands fisted in the sheet as I attempted to control my heart rate.

"Remember what Dr. Lynch said. I won't know the things that trigger you unless you tell me."

He was right. Exhaling through my mouth, I turned until I was on my back, looking up at Dane. "When I was taken, Ethan grabbed me from behind. I guess it just makes me... nervous."

Dane nodded like he understood. Like I wasn't acting crazy, even though sometimes I felt like it. He never made me feel like that, instead validating my feelings at every turn.

"M'kay," he murmured. "I can take the floor. No biggie."

"No," I said sharply. "It's my issue. I can sleep on the floor."

His lips crooked up on one side. "Yeah, that's not going to happen, babe." He slowly reached for my left hand and tugged, rotating until we were both resting on our right sides, me behind him instead of the other way around. Then he placed my hand on his hip. "That better?"

I breathed out a long breath I hadn't realized I was holding in my lungs, the air gusting against his broad back. This was better. I didn't feel confined like this.

"It's... good. Thank you."

Dane reached up and turned off the small light before burrowing down into his pillow. "You're in control, Eden. Never forget that."

And as I closed my eyes and drifted into the first comfortable waves of sleep, I felt like it.

CHAPTER 23

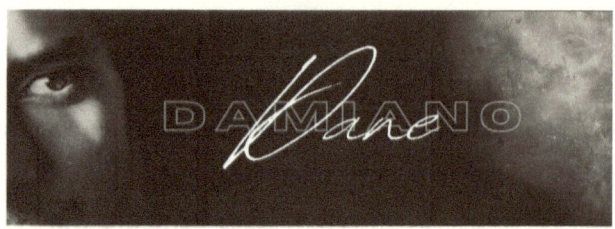

I AWOKE WITH A small, warm body plastered to my back. With my eyes still closed, I smiled, loving the feel of Eden's warmth and her arm wrapped around my waist. Tightly. Some time during the early morning hours, she'd closed the gap between us and cuddled against me, turning me into "the little spoon."

A quiet noise escaped her, a tiny "hmmm" of contentment that mirrored my own. It had been a long time since I'd slept in a bed with a woman.

Eden's hand rested against my abs, and I reached down to stroke my fingers over it, taking the opportunity to appreciate the softness, like expensive silk beneath my touch. When her hand absently moved up and down the ridges of my abdomen, I linked my fingers between hers to stop her before she could accidentally go lower and find the morning wood tenting the front of my briefs.

Not that I didn't have daily fantasies about various parts of Eden wrapped around my cock. Her hand. Her pussy. And let's not forget about that goddamn smart mouth. So sweet, so luscious, and as ripe as a wild cherry. I suppressed a groan as I thought about filling her mouth while I called her my wife.

Why do I like saying that so much?

Sure, at first it was because it annoyed her, and annoying Eden was one of my favorite things to do. It made her eyes sparkle with indignation and her pretty lips purse.

And now we're back to the mouth fantasies. Super. My cock swelled, seeking some real action after experiencing nothing except my hand for six fucking months.

I'd never wanted to get married. My mother and father's union had been arranged by their parents because they were *a good match*. Which was utter bullshit. My mother had been the kindest, gentlest person on the planet, and Luca was... decidedly not.

Over the years, he'd mentioned finding appropriate matches for Fiero and me, but his pushiness had ebbed a bit after the disastrous results of Amara's marriage. Fiero would probably end up marrying some Mafia princess to satisfy the old man. As the oldest, there was more pressure on him than me. I'd planned to resist as long as possible, never having any desire whatsoever to get involved in some farce of a marriage.

Ironically, that's exactly the situation I found myself in now. Only, the *farce* was seeming less farcical and more... *real* every day.

My wife—*see how pretty that sounds?*—nuzzled against my back with her nose and then kissed my spine, mumbling something in her sleep. My ears perked up. Swear to god, if she said some man's name, I'd have to rethink my whole *not going to kill people anymore* promise. I would hunt down the person behind any name she uttered while in this bed, and I would fucking end him.

Wow. Possessive much? Damn straight I was possessive when it came to Eden, which was a foreign concept for me. I was the *pump and dump* kind of guy, not the jealous, covetous type.

But the woman sleeping behind me was different. Perhaps it was just protectiveness because she was vulnerable, but I was pretty sure it was more than that. I'd been attracted to her from day one. To her bravery and sass, which I witnessed long before she'd softened and opened up to me about her nightmares.

I absolutely hated when she had those dreams, when she woke up afraid and crying, but a certain part of me—the part that made me a complete prick—liked that she turned to me. That she curled onto my lap on the veranda in the dark of night and trusted me with her secrets.

Her trust swung open some previously unknown door inside me and let loose the primal urge to shield her from any harm, including the demons inside her.

Unbeknownst to Eden, I had called Dr. Lynch after their first session. The woman then proceeded to scold me until I'd assured her I wasn't looking for any of Eden's private information or thoughts. I only wanted to make sure I was doing everything I could on my end. Now I occasionally checked in with the psychiatrist, though there hadn't been much to discuss recently since Eden was doing so well.

We'd had to share some specifics with the doctor so she could better understand what her patient was going through, but we'd been vague on a lot of the information. She knew Eden had been taken by human traffickers and that we were now in hiding because not everyone involved had been caught, though she had no idea of the Mafia connection or our true identities.

Behind me, Eden let out a sigh, her warm breath gusting over my spine and raising a patch of goosebumps on my skin. My cock made his needs known—the persistent bastard—and I shifted a little, releasing Eden's hand so I could make a necessary readjustment.

I knew the instant she woke up and realized that she'd turned me into her own personal body pillow because her breathing stalled for a second before quickening. So I decided a little teasing was in order.

"I don't remember filling out the application to be your teddy bear, but I happily accept the position," I said without turning over.

Her giggle had a direct line to my chest, causing a rapid staccato beat to form there. "Hush, Dark Lord," she said, swatting my shoulder before backing away from me. I missed the feel of her warm body immediately. "Sorry, I didn't mean to get all up on you like that."

I rolled over, giving her my finest smirk. "Do you hear me complaining, Wildcat?"

Her eyes drifted down my bare torso, and I subtly pulled the sheet up around my waist since things were so... *active* down below this morning. I imagined they would be for however long I'd be sleeping in Eden's bed.

She was lying on her side, one hand tucked beneath her pillow and the other toying with the round neckline of her sleep shirt. "I must have gotten chilly during the night. I won't make a habit of it."

"Again, were you under the impression I'd lodged a formal complaint with the HR department?"

Her eyes rolled in a circuitous route inside their sockets. "It's too early to be dealing with your nonsense," she snarked, though I saw the corners of her mouth twitch. She liked our banter as much as I did.

"I need to go outside and add some gas to the generator. It's going to be hot today, so we don't want to go without air conditioning."

"And I need to put my contacts in. I guess I'll have to wear them around the house while Charlisse and Cooper are here."

I planted my elbow on the mattress and rested the side of my face in my palm. "I'm sorry about that. Hopefully the contractors can get their house done pretty quickly." My smile turned mischievous. "I know you like to go bare when we're alone."

Her pretty lips pursed and her eyes narrowed. "You're awfully cheeky this morning."

"I live to entertain you, Mrs. Osbourne."

She snorted. "You live to aggravate me."

My hair, which was now about chin length, fell over one eye, and Eden lifted her hand and tucked the errant strand behind my ear. Then she scowled, as if she hadn't meant to do that.

"Thanks, wife," I told her before kissing the tip of her nose. "Why don't you shower first?" *Because I have a giant boner that needs to go down before I can get out of this bed.*

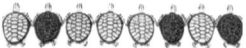

Thirty minutes later, I was across the street at Charlisse's house while the ladies made breakfast. In the light of day, the sight was chilling. The tree had fallen directly on her bed. If she and Cooper hadn't been in the closet...

"Hey, you need protective gear if you're gonna be in here," a man with a clipboard said, rapping his knuckles against his hardhat for emphasis. "We can talk outside."

I led the way to the front porch where we stood in the shade. "I'm Dane. My wife and I live across the street."

"George Baron," he said, shaking my hand before removing his hat. "Are you related to the home's resident? Miss..." He consulted his clipboard. "Miss Michaels?"

"She's a friend and neighbor. She and her son are staying with us until their house is done. I'm assuming you're the contractor?"

"Yep." He ran a hand over his jaw, which was covered with salt-and-pepper stubble. "Her insurance company contacted us. Fourth house this morning, and I've got five more to get to today."

"How long will it take before this house is livable again?" I gave two sharp knocks against the doorframe.

"The work here should take about a month once we get started on it, but like I said, I have several houses in front of hers."

"I understand that," I said, lowering my voice and putting on my metaphorical businessman hat. "But how much will it cost me to get Miss Michaels's house moved to the front of the line?"

He shrugged. "It's only fair that I go in the order I assessed them."

I stuck my hands in the pockets of my cargo shorts and rocked back onto my heels as my eyes locked onto his. "Look, George. My wife and I are newlyweds, and while I like Charlisse and her son, I would appreciate them getting back to their own home as soon as possible. Do you get my meaning?"

A sly grin took over his face. "Totally understandable, Dane. But like I said..."

"You seem like a smart businessman, so I have a business proposition for you." His forehead furrowed, but I didn't let that deter me. "If you get this house done in three weeks, you'll receive a little... bonus for your efforts."

He lifted an intrigued—and very bushy—eyebrow. "A bonus?"

"How does ten thousand sound?"

"D-dollars?" he stuttered.

My head tilted to the side. "I'm very motivated, George. Three weeks. Ten grand." My gaze turned into a cold glare that had frozen many a man in place, and I watched George's throat work in a hard swallow. *Could he read me? Did he know what I really was on the inside? Is he afraid of me?* "And I do expect your best work. I'll have an independent contractor check everything over to make sure it's done to my satisfaction."

"I..." His beady brown eyes darted around the yard, and his voice dropped to a whisper. "I'm a legitimate business owner, Dane."

"As am I, George. Nothing shady going on here." Okay, maybe that was stretching it a teeny bit, but what-the-fuck-ever. Eden needed to be comfortable in her own home, and I was going to make it happen. "This is simply a bonus for a job well done. Quickly."

He sighed and rubbed his hand over his jaw once again. "Three weeks?"

"Not a second more."

He propped his clipboard on his ample belly and scrawled something there before looking back up at me. "You got yourself a deal."

George was true to his word, and on a mid-October evening, exactly twenty days later, Charlisse and her son moved back into their home. It actually belonged to her parents and they had great insurance, so she only had to pay a deductible. The work was impeccable, and I transferred the money to a very happy George.

Charlisse and Cooper had been excellent houseguests. The kid had energy out the wazoo, that was for damn sure, but his mom insisted on helping out around the house, cooking dinner several nights a week.

Once I'd helped them carry the last of their personal belongings back to their house, I felt a hint of bittersweet energy course through me. Though I was glad things would return to normal, it also meant I no longer had an excuse to sleep in Eden's bed.

A devilish voice inside my brain whispered, *You don't need an excuse. She's your wife, remember?*

I let that thought settle in, gelling into an ill-formed plan as Eden and I ate dinner and watched a movie. Then we got ready for bed.

When she came out of the shower, dressed in a purple T-shirt and tiny sleep shorts that always made my eyes bulge, I was lying on her bed with the covers pulled up around my waist. Just like I had been for the past few weeks, as if nothing had changed.

Her mouth dropped into a tiny O, an indentation forming between her eyebrows as she processed what she was seeing. She tucked a piece of hair behind her ear, and I waited for her to tell me to go to my own room.

But she didn't.

Instead, she straightened her shoulders, adjusted the low lighting in the room, and finally climbed in behind me without a word. When her hand slipped beneath the covers and rested on my waist, I imagined this must be what it would feel like to win the Super Bowl.

A victorious smile crossed my lips as I reached for her hand and tugged until her body was snuggled right up against my back. "We both know this is how we're going to end up anyway," I said into the dim gray of the room.

She sniffed in indignation, curling her legs until they molded to the backs of mine. "It's not very nice to point that out."

"Yeah, well you should be aware by now that I'm not a very nice guy."

"Hmm," she hummed against my back, and I felt the peaks of her nipples harden against my back.

Perhaps I hadn't thought this plan all the way through. Every fucking night for the past few weeks, I'd lain with this woman against me, and it had been the sweetest torture imaginable. I loved her warm softness, but it wasn't mine to touch.

Though I wished like hell it was.

CHAPTER 24

NINE MONTHS IN HIDING

"Merry Christmas Eve! Are you—" I halted in the doorway of the living room when I saw the blotchiness on Eden's face. Walking slowly toward her, I crouched beside the couch. "What's wrong?"

"Just... you know... missing my family. I'm okay though." She swiped at a few stray tears and pushed a brave smile across her lips.

I glanced down at the phone in her lap and saw that she was watching one of the videos of Auburn and her dad. At my request, the guys I'd hired to keep an eye on her family occasionally sent clips of the Bouviers, and true to my word, I sent them on to Eden. She usually enjoyed watching them, but I knew the holidays would be hard for her.

"We don't have to go tonight," I told her.

Eden shook her head. "No, it'll be fun. And a nice distraction."

I nodded and reached for her hand to pull her to her feet. "We can leave any time you want. Just give me a signal."

"Like press the Dark Mark on my forearm?" she asked with faux sweetness, referring to Voldemort's mark on the Death Eaters from the Harry Potter novels.

I gave her a light push between her shoulder blades. "Go get ready, smartass. I got you something special to wear. It's on the bed." *Our bed. Because once I'd staked my claim there in September, I hadn't left.*

Using my old room to dress, I put on the black suit I'd bought, along with a starched white button-down and no tie before going back to the living room to wait.

Thirty minutes later, my jaw fell to the damn floor. Eden walked into the room with more confidence than any nineteen-year-old had any right to have. I guessed that stemmed from her upbringing in the Bouvier family. Though her father had kept his kids mostly out of the public eye, Eden had told me that they had been taken to the occasional gala or fundraising event once they were teens and they were expected to attend parties at the Bouvier estate from a young age.

"Thank you for the jumpsuit. I can't believe you got me a *Bouvier*."

"I wanted you to feel…" I shrugged, unable to find the exact words, but she nodded in understanding.

The outfit was a pretty crimson, fitted through the bodice and flaring at the calves, with just enough sparkles to make it perfect for a holiday party. The peep toe heels I'd ordered for her matched the jumpsuit, and each had a tiny silver bow adorning the top.

She'd used more eye makeup than usual, the eyeliner forming perfect wings over mile-long lashes. Her lips were the deepest red, somewhere between black and cherry, and they looked absolutely delicious. Her hair was different too. Instead of the messy, edgy look she usually rocked, tonight it was smooth and controlled, molded into a dark cap that was sexy as fuck.

"Eden, you look…" I brushed a hand over my chest as I walked slowly toward her, letting my eyes eat her up. "You look like I might have to go back on my promise not to kill any more people."

She giggled. "Please try and control yourself. It will mostly be older folks there."

"Yeah, hopefully they'll all have cataracts and won't be able to see how beautiful my wife looks."

Tilting her chin down a notch, she looked up at me with her big, brown eyes. "My husband looks pretty wonderful too."

My fucking heart almost fell out of my chest and at her feet. *My husband.* That was the first time she'd used those words in private.

"I wasn't sure what to do with my hair," I said, and she tilted her head, regarding me as she drifted her fingers through the strands over one ear.

"Will you let me fix it?"

Fuck yes.

"You're not going to put one of those glittery things in it, are you?" I asked, indicating the red-and-silver rhinestone clip that was holding her hair away from her perfect face on one side.

"Of course not," she scoffed, taking my hand and leading me to our bathroom. "I have a perfectly respectable velvet bow. Or maybe I'll do space buns. That would be cute."

"Space what?" I almost shrieked, a moment of panic coursing through my chest. Maybe this wasn't such a good idea. Unless... "You're fucking with me, aren't you?"

Eden pulled the chair from beneath the knee space and pushed me down onto it. She was slightly taller than me when I was seated, and she blinked guileless brown eyes down at me.

"Would I do that?" Her voice was a teasing coo, and I didn't bother answering because *of course she would.*

Motherfucking hell, I wanted to kiss that smug smile off her pretty little mouth. Smear that dark lipstick all over my own lips and then leave a trail of it down her body as I went on a treasure hunt for the promised land.

And now I've got a boner situation. Great.

Shifting slightly to accommodate my growing length, I watched as Eden rummaged through the top drawer and pulled out a pink hairbrush. Her hairbrush. There was something so intimate about her using her own brush on my hair, and I closed my eyes and relaxed into the moment, letting her do whatever the hell she wanted to me.

After draping a towel around my shoulders, she worked some kind of product through my hair with nimble fingers. It smelled fresh and cool, citrus and maybe mint? Eden hummed a Christmas tune while she smoothed and brushed, and my neck was pliant, allowing her to turn my head as she wished.

Peeking one eye open, I watched her as she worked, her tongue working back and forth over the small scar that bisected her bottom lip. Finally, she stepped back, tilting her head from one side to the other while she assessed her handiwork.

"Yeah," she said to herself with a pleased smile, backing away and doing a little hand flourish. "What do you think?"

I looked at myself in the mirror and remembered my sister telling me this style was called *half up-half down*. The top was pulled back and fashioned into a ponytail at the back of my head, looking more tousled than slick. The bottom half of my dark hair was left loose, and whatever product she'd added brought out the latent curls, which hung almost to my shoulders. The look was a little wild and a lot stylish, like something a long-haired celebrity might wear with his tuxedo on the red carpet.

And then I noticed something else. "Is that... a braid?" I asked with trepidation, turning my head slightly to see the tiny plait on one side. It started over my right ear and was pulled back and fastened into the black rubber band that held my ponytail.

I brought my eyes slowly to Eden's, wondering if she was messing with me, but her heated gaze told me she wasn't. With her teeth sunk into her bottom lip, she nodded.

"I think it looks hot," she breathed, and any doubts I had about wearing a freaking braid vanished in a puff of desire.

"Then I love it," I said, standing and dropping a kiss on her nose. "You've elevated me from about a three to at least a solid five, so thank you for that."

Eden snorted out a laugh. "You're way more than a five, Dane."

Would it be douchey to ask for an actual rating from her? Yeah, definitely a douchebag move.

She pulled the towel from my shoulders, and her gaze snagged on my suit. Trailing her fingers down to the signature buttons on my black jacket, she rubbed a circle on one with her thumb.

"You're wearing a *Bouvier* suit," she murmured.

"You know, just supporting your family's business," I replied, and when Eden lifted her face, her eyes were soft and suspiciously damp.

"That just shot you to a big, fat nine, buddy." Then she looked up at my hair again, and her tongue darted out to wet her lips. "But the braid makes you a ten."

Note to self: find a YouTube tutorial on how to braid hair.

I've never particularly enjoyed holiday parties, but the one at Charles and Mimsy's house on Christmas Eve was actually fun. The food was stellar, the drinks were flowing, and the company was nice. Well, except for *Chad*.

I tried not to glare at Mrs. Walker from down the street simply because she'd invited her fucking great-nephew, *Chad*, to come along to the soirée. He was in town, ostensibly to visit with his widowed aunt, but I knew his real game. The asshole was in town to prey on the unsuspecting women of Marathon, namely, my wife. *Mine.*

The problem was that he reminded me of... me. Well, the me of a year ago. Fake smile. Wearing a suit that was a little too slick. Flirty touches. I sighed internally when I found the tall blond in the small crowd. *Like he's doing right now.*

Strolling over to one of the food tables, I stepped in between Eden and *Chad*, slipping my arm around my wife. "Hi, baby," I said, turning my back on the sleezeball and kissing Eden softly on the lips. Not on the nose this time because I was staking a claim here. That required me to level up.

She looked startled for a moment, and then a knowing smirk curled the corners of her mouth. "Hi. What's up?" But she knew what was up.

"I wanted a piece of cheese," I explained, picking up a cube of gouda and popping it into my mouth. From the periphery of my vision, I noticed Chad cross the living room to bother someone else. *Good fucking riddance.*

"You know, I expected it to be warmer," Eden mused, stroking a hand down the red fabric over her hip.

My brow furrowed. "The cheese?"

Her grin grew even wider. "No, where you just peed on me."

"Jesus, Eden," I chuckled with a chagrined shake of my head. "Was I that obvious?"

"Yes," she said, patting me on the chest, "but you can make up for it by going with me to get another drink." Her hand looped around my elbow as I guided us through the minglers to reach the bar set up in the corner.

Two guys in their early twenties greeted Eden by name, and my brows lowered. *I thought this was supposed to be a block party. Who are all these young fuckers?*

"Eden! You back for another Santa's Sunrise?" the red-haired one chirped.

"Yes, please. Do you want one, Dane?" She turned her brown eyes up to me.

"Sure," I clipped out.

The other bartender, this one with dark-brown hair and a gap between his front teeth, stuck out his hand, and I shook it. "You must be Dane. I'm Kevin, and this is Barry." He jerked his chin toward his friend who was filling two festive glasses with orange juice. "I call him Straw-Barry. You know, because of his hair."

"And I call him asshole. You know, because of his personality," Barry retorted dryly, making me laugh.

Eden bumped me with her hip. "I was telling them about your tiramisù. Kevin and Barry work at Charles's bakery."

"She said it's divine," Barry said as he added tequila and then topped it with grenadine. "If you accidentally make two pans next time, we'd be happy to take the spare off your hands."

"I'll see what I can do," I told them, relaxing a little because I wasn't getting that *flirting with my wife* vibe from these two.

I stayed close to Eden for the rest of the night, and as the crowd thinned, we made our way over to Mimsy and Charles to say our goodbyes. Once I'd helped Eden into her jacket and we were outside, Eden stumbled a little, a giggle escaping from her lips as I steadied her with an arm around her waist.

"Oopsie!"

"Is Mrs. Osbourne drunk?" I asked, amused.

"Tipsy," she corrected, tucking herself beneath my arm. I liked her like this, loose with her affection.

"You know you're not even legal to drink," I said, a playful taunt in my tone.

"My license says I'm twenty-two," she argued, her feet pausing as her eyes went to the two-story home on the other side of the Mimses. Like they always did. It was the palest of yellows but looked white in the blue haze of the moon. Eden called it "the butter house" because she said it was the color of whipped butter.

I let her look her fill until she shivered. It was in the sixties, which was typical for winter evenings in the Florida Keys, but we'd both grown accustomed to the more temperate climate over the past nine months.

Eden was giggly as we got ready for bed, and I wished for the millionth time that we were husband and wife in every way. I'd love to have a wild, playful romp between the sheets with her. But instead, we ended up in our normal position, me on my side and her curled up against my back.

"What were you laughing about in the bathroom?" I asked.

I felt her chuckle against my back. "I was thinking of how you acted when Brad was flirting with me."

It took me a second. "I thought his name was Chad."

I felt the vibration of her hum on my spine. "Hmmm, maybe. I thought it was Brad."

There were no words to describe how happy it made me that she didn't even remember that dickwad's name. It was definitely Chad. The name was imprinted in my mind.

"Fucker is lucky I left my gun at home," I muttered.

She giggled again and moved her hand up to my chest, fingers toying with the hair between my pecs. "I'm proud of you for not being shooty."

A smile quirked my lips. "Go to sleep, Eden."

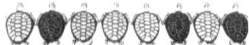

The sun was barely peeking through a gap in the curtains when I woke up with a hand moving over my body. A small hand. *Eden.* She was touching me, and I tried to keep my breathing even so she didn't know I was awake.

Fleeting touches over my shoulder turned into curious squeezes of my biceps before trailing down and tracing the veins of my forearm. It was a slow, inquisitive exploration that I had no intention of stopping.

Inching her fingers down my ribs, Eden looped her arm around me and slid her palm up and down my torso a few times before rolling one of my nipples between her thumb and middle finger. *Jesus fucking hell.* She made a quiet sound from the back of her throat when her hips pressed forward against my ass, and I had to suppress a moan of my own. *Is she turned on?* I sure as fuck was, my cock throbbing against the confines of my underwear.

Then her hand moved lower, to my abdomen, her index finger bumping slowly over each ab muscle on one side and then the other, as if she were counting them. Then she was touching my happy trail, and she was so fucking close to where I longed for her to be. When she crept her hand a little lower, I finally spoke.

"Sweetheart, if you lower your hand another inch, you're going to find out exactly how much I like being in bed with you."

She stilled her hand, pausing for a long moment, and I wondered if maybe she had been touching me in her sleep. But then she took that last inch, moving her fingers over the tip of my erection that was peeking out the top of my boxer briefs.

A hiss seeped out from between my teeth before I groaned her name. "Eden."

"Do you want me to stop?" she asked, her words as tentative as her hand.

"Absolutely not," I answered before she'd even stopped talking.

The scrape of teeth on my shoulder blade came at the same time Eden's thumb swirled around the head of my cock, drawing out a thick bead of sticky fluid. She smeared it around the tip three times before lowering her hand another couple inches to cup my shaft over my underwear.

"Fuck," my voice trembled as she took my measure, giving me a squeeze that made my balls clench.

"You're thick," she whispered, her warm breath gusting against my back.

That proclamation brought images to the forefront of my mind... dirty, sweaty images of two bodies moving in the dim light of morning. Thoughts of stretching her with that thickness, making her pussy accommodate me, induced another gush of pre-cum to ease out and pool on my stomach.

Eden's fingers skittered up and down my cloth-covered dick, from my balls all the way back to my crown, before sliding her fingertips into the waistband of my briefs.

"Is this okay or am I overstepping?" she asked.

Rolling onto my back, I looked over at her, noting the way she pulled her bottom lip between her teeth. *Does she actually think I would say no to her? To this?* I cupped the back of her head, sinking my fingers into the mess of her hair.

"Eden, I think of you while I'm jerking off in the shower every single morning. So this..." I gripped her wrist and pushed her hand farther into my underwear until her palm was resting against the length of me, earning me a gasp from her. "Having you touch me is a fucking dream come true. And anything you could do to me wouldn't even come close to the filth I think of while I'm stroking my cock to thoughts of you. So, to answer your question, no, you're not overstepping."

Her eyes were wide with shock, but the blue pools darkened slightly at my words even as the prettiest pink shade ascended her neck and coated her cheeks. Then she smiled... sweet and a little bit shy, which made my cock twitch against her hand. My bold girl had a bashful side, and it turned me the fuck on.

With my free hand, I worked my briefs down my thighs and kicked them off beneath the covers. Then I peeled back the sheet to expose myself with Eden's hand pressed against me. I studied her as she looked down, as her tongue slipped out to wet her lips. That tiny peek of pink and the slickness it left there was about the sexiest thing I'd ever seen.

Drawing my gaze down, I watched as she wrapped her fingers around my shaft and gave me a small, testing stroke. Her hand didn't quite reach all the way around my girth, which only made me harder. *Because yeah, I'm a guy.*

"Feels good, baby girl," I encouraged on a shaky breath.

On my admission, her next movement was less tentative, a long stroke from my base to my tip. Eden sat up, curling her legs beneath her, eyes rapt on what she was doing. Her movements were unhurried, as if she were learning my cock with every touch.

Up and down, up and down. The tiny twists of her wrist. I was mesmerized by all of it. Her free hand drifted up my abdomen, almost absently, fingers tenderly caressing the hard planes of my body.

"You're beautiful," she murmured.

Tugging on her hair until she looked up at me, I rasped, "Not nearly as beautiful as you, sweetheart. You make it hard for me to breathe." I pulled her toward me, needing to taste her mouth, but after giving me only a soft peck, she pulled back, turning her attention back to what her hand was doing between my legs.

Not that I was complaining about a hand job, for fuck's sake, but I wanted a kiss. Maybe she was self-conscious about morning breath.

Eden gripped me a little tighter and continued pleasuring me with long, slow strokes, her eyes occasionally flashing to me, watching for my reaction.

"That feels so fucking good, sweetheart," I assured her.

I'd always thought I was the master of my own body, that I knew how to masturbate and bring myself pleasure better than anyone. After all, it was *my* cock. But I was sorely mistaken. My rough, quick strokes were nothing compared to Eden's hand wrapping around my dick, gliding with aching slowness. There was something so sensual, so intimate, about watching her fuck me with her small, soft grip.

As her left hand continued its up and down motion, she covered the end of my erection with her right hand, swirling her palm around to smooth the drops of my desire over the crown before sliding it down to double-fist me. The dual sensations had my eyes rolling back in my head.

"You're close," she murmured, gaze glued to her hands on my cock. When she reached down to cup my balls, the fingers of my free hand fisted in the sheet, curling so tightly my knuckles ached. I didn't want this to end, but she was right. I was about to fucking blow.

My dick swelled in her grasp, blood pulsing hard and fast along my length. Eden never sped up, keeping her unhurried pace as my juices lubricated the slide of her hand.

"Fuck, baby," I growled, my voice a plaintive rasp in my throat. "Coming. For you." Pressing my head back into the pillow, I gritted my teeth and closed my eyes.

My brain went numb, unable to think of anything but the pure pleasure as a full-body orgasm convulsed through me. "Eden," I cried, lifting my hips as spurt after spurt landed on my chest and stomach.

"God, that's so hot," I heard her say, gliding her fingers through the puddle on my abdomen and glossing my stomach with my own desire. I peeled my eyes open to watch her, my mouth watering to taste her. And that was the plan... as soon as I caught my breath.

But right then, I was completely spent, my muscles as loose as a taut rubber band that's been suddenly snapped in half. And I'd never been happier.

CHAPTER 25

WELL. THAT WAS ABOUT the hottest thing I'd ever seen.

"Best Christmas morning ever," Dane croaked, making me grin. He pulled me down until I was stretched out against his side, my head on his broad shoulder.

"Glad you enjoyed it." I continued running my fingers through the mess he'd made on his stomach. *Because I made him come.* I'd never drawn such satisfaction from pleasuring a man before. But I'd also never been involved with a man like Dane. So strong. So masculine. So infinitely sexual. And I had undone him.

"Give me a second to re-inflate my lungs, and I'll take care of you," he promised, his hand wrapping around my back and resting on my hip.

The tightness forming between my legs intensified at the thought. I wanted him to. I wanted to feel that beard against my pussy as he put his wicked tongue to good use.

"No, it's okay," I told him, my vagina protesting my refusal with a clench around nothingness.

He angled his head down, a frown marring his perfect face. "I want to, baby girl. It's all I can think about some days."

Baby girl. I hated to admit how much I liked that. His eyes searched mine, seeking my approval, but I shook my head.

"I don't want to."

Laying a soft kiss on my nose, he nestled my head against his neck, which was slightly damp with sweat. "I understand if you're not ready."

A little voice deep inside me—a very horny voice—yelled that we *were* ready, but I closed my eyes against the almost overwhelming need to lie back and let him take care of me. I wasn't sure why I was refusing since I very clearly wanted him. Craved him with every fiber of my being.

"I'll get you a towel," I said, pushing up and climbing off the bed, doing my best to ignore the confusion on his face. Hell, I was as confused as he was.

Too intimate. The words flashed through my mind, and I almost laughed. A minute ago, I'd had the man's dick in my hand and then ran my fingers through his release, coating my hand with the musk of him.

Once in the bathroom, I lifted my sticky hand to my nose and inhaled. The scent of a man had never turned me on before. I'd actually never paid much attention to it, but the smell of Dane on my fingers made me want to return to the bedroom and tell him I'd changed my mind.

How had I gone from exploring his body while he was asleep to giving him a hand job? What the hell had come over me?

Sweetheart, if you lower your hand another inch, you're going to find out exactly how much I like being in bed with you.

Oh yeah. That was it. Dane's words—almost like a challenge—had me reaching for his cock in the next moment. Of course I'd noticed his bulge before, but actually holding that big, thick rod in my hand was on another level. I could still feel the smooth, hot skin that covered the hardness beneath, could hear his grunts and moans of encouragement, could smell—

Dammit to hell, why am I still sniffing my hand? Get your shit together, Eden.

Giving my head a firm shake, I washed my hands before grabbing a towel and walking it back into the bedroom. "I'm going to take a shower," I told him, tossing him the towel and heading back to the safety of the bathroom. Seeing him sprawled out on the bed, completely naked, was too tempting.

No, Eden. Remember who he is. What he is.

Sure, he was Dane Osbourne and not Damiano Cappitani now, but that was simply the name he was using. It didn't change who he was on the inside, right?

I should have feared him, hated him but... I didn't. And that scared the shit out of me. Because beneath that icy exterior, there was a warmth he reserved only for me, and I was finding myself enthralled by it.

"Eden?" My feet stalled at Dane's voice.

I faced the open bathroom door, not turning around. "Yeah?"

"You okay?"

Plastering a smile on my face, I looked over my shoulder. *Big mistake.* Dane was lying there, legs spread apart and towel covering his private parts. He looked like a large, lethal cat, one that could take me down with a single bite. My core clenched at the thought.

You're such a perv, Eden.

"I'm fine."

His gaze held mine for a long moment before he nodded. "Okay. Go shower, and I'll put the cinnamon buns in the oven. Then we can open presents." Something lit in his brown eyes, something almost childlike. Excitement, maybe?

We'd talked about family Christmas traditions last week, and Dane had admitted that he and his family hadn't really celebrated in any significant way since his mother died. His father transferred a thousand dollars into his and Fiero's accounts, and that was that.

With some gentle prodding, he told me his mother used to let each kid open one present on Christmas Eve, and then they ate cinnamon buns by the tree the next morning while opening the rest of their gifts. My heart hurt for him, so I suggested we follow that tradition for our first Christmas together.

He'd given me the dress and shoes last night, and I'd given him a fancy new stand mixer, one I saw him eyeing last time we went to the kitchen store he liked to frequent.

"Sounds good," I said, going into the bathroom and closing the door behind me. Turning on the shower, I undressed and stepped beneath the steamy spray. After washing and conditioning my hair, I soaped up the washcloth and began cleaning my body. When I moved the rag between my legs, I gasped at the aching sensation I found there.

Shit. Jacking him off had turned me on as much as it had him, but while he'd found his release, I was still sexually frustrated. Maybe I should have taken him up on his offer. Lord knew I wanted to.

With a wet plop, I dropped the cloth on the floor of the shower and ran my soap-slick fingers over my sex, finding my clit with ease. It was swollen and hot, ready to be touched. *Fuck it. I need some relief.*

"God," I moaned quietly when my middle finger circled around the needy bud. This wasn't going to take long; I was already halfway there just from feeling Dane's slick, engorged cock in my hands. I'd never seen one that big. Not in real life anyway. What would that feel like inside me? It was much larger than my pink vibrator, which I'd started hiding in a shoe box in my closet now that Dane and I shared a bedroom.

I slid my middle finger inside my sex, the slender hole hungrily sucking my entire digit in. "God, Dane. Fuck me," I whispered, pressing my cheek against the damp red tiles. But one finger wasn't enough to simulate what that big dick would feel like inside me, so I added two more.

Wincing at the uncomfortable tightness, I pursed my lips and panted in and out as I took my time, my body slowly acclimating to the fullness. The hint of pain began to morph into pleasure, a raw, greedy thing that took over my body as I added some thumb action to my clit.

My mind pictured Dane behind me, thrusting hard and deep, soft grunts of bliss emanating from his full lips as he fucked me. I imagined those eight-pack abs of his—yes, I counted them—tensing with each roll of his hips. His hand gripped my chin and turned my head so his mouth could take mine in a searing kiss, our tongues tangling with carnal thrashes.

I came with a soft cry less than a minute later and had to brace a palm on the wall to keep from collapsing with relief.

I tried to brush away the guilt for wanting the things I wanted. I was supposed to hate Dane. After all, it was his father's fault I wouldn't be spending this Christmas with my family, that my entire life had changed for god knows how long. I hung my head, letting the hot water course over my neck and down my back as a voice inside my head reminded me that he wasn't his father. That Dane had never treated me badly, only with kindness.

And, despite my constant snarkiness with him, I was beginning to actually like him. A lot.

Damn, I'm in so much trouble.

Dane was like a kid on... well, on Christmas morning, as we sat on the floor in front of our Christmas tree and opened gifts. He stared in awe at the bottle of rare bourbon in his hand, the tiny blue lights on the tree casting an azure glow against the side of his face.

"Pappy Van Winkle? Eden, where the hell did you find this?"

I shrugged nonchalantly, though I couldn't help the pride that swelled inside me from his reaction. "With a little help from our computer whiz friend."

He laughed. "I should have known Robert would have something to do with this." Cradling the bottle with both hands, he read the label again, shaking his head back and forth. "I can't believe you got this for me. My grandpa on my mother's side had a bottle of this that he only broke out on special occasions."

"Like your eighteenth birthday," I said, remembering him telling me that story a couple months ago.

Dane was still staring at the bottle, lost in his memories. "Yeah, he called me to his office and poured us both two fingers of whiskey. It felt so... important that he was sharing his prized bottle with me." His lips twisted into a crooked smile. "I wasn't even old enough to drink, so that made me feel even more like a big shot."

"You'd never drank before that?" I asked, and he released a loud guffaw.

"Fuck yes, I had. Fiero used to buy me liquor because he was older. He told me it would put hair on my balls."

"How charming," I said flatly. "So, I'm assuming your brother doesn't believe in manscaping?"

"I don't know," Dane replied in an equally dry tone. "I don't enjoy staring at other men's dicks. Unlike someone I know." That last pointed comment was accompanied by an impish grin and a wiggle of his dark eyebrows.

"Dane," I gasped, feeling heat rush to my cheeks, though somehow his blatant teasing made what we did in bed earlier seem a little less awkward. He wasn't being weird about it, instead acting like his normal, teasing self.

"What?" he asked with a casual shrug. "Ain't no shame in loving my penis. It's probably my best feature."

I snorted loudly. "You are so ridiculous," I told him, reaching for the final present wrapped in purple.

We'd followed one of my family's traditions when it came to wrapping paper. When we were growing up, Auburn, Monty, and I each had a designated color for our Christmas morning gifts. Dane and I had done the same, going to the store and picking out paper for each other. His was a masculine red and green plaid, and mine was purple with silver ornaments in a scatter-print.

Ripping off the paper from the small box, I gasped when I pulled off the lid. "Dane," I breathed, one of my hands going to my throat.

"Do you... like it?"

"It's gorgeous." The paper-thin platinum chain was delicate, the tiny facets of each link reflecting the light. But what held my attention was the charm. About the size of a nickel, the turtle's curved back was encrusted with green gems.

Dane scooted around to sit beside me, resting one hand on the floor behind my butt while using the pinky of the other to point at various jewels as he spoke.

"While these are all emeralds, you can see they have different hues and vibrancies. The green ones are classic emeralds. The ones with yellowish and bluish tints have iron and chromium in different amounts. And these..." he pointed out two that had a red undertone. "These have more vanadium and iron. They're called pigeon's blood emeralds and are pretty rare."

I looked up, catching his brown eyes with my blue ones. "How do you know all that? Are you secretly a gemologist?"

He scraped his teeth across his bottom lip. "I know how you like knowledge, so I had the jeweler print out all the properties of the emeralds I chose. The card is at the bottom of the box."

"Wait." I shook my head. "You had this custom made for me?" My heart pitter-patted in my chest.

He looked mildly embarrassed. "Yeah. Technically, the ones that aren't the bright green color are considered impure, so they're not perfect." A tear slipped down my face, and Dane's expression turned into one of panic. "I'll get him to change them all to just regular emeralds. It's not a big—"

I stopped the rest of his sentence.

With my lips.

On his lips.

CHAPTER 26

As soon as our mouths touched, I was hauled onto Dane's lap, my knees on either side of his hips. His hands went to the nape of my neck, and a second later, I felt a gentle weight against my chest and realized he'd fastened the turtle necklace onto me.

"Thank you." When I murmured against his mouth, he took the opportunity to breach my lips with his hot tongue. *And dear god!*

Dane tasted of cinnamon and sweet icing as he took control of the kiss, his tongue making a thorough exploration of my mouth before twisting around mine. He lifted my arms to encircle his neck before banding one of his around my waist to hold me tight against his hard body. His other hand cupped the back of my head, tilting it slightly so he could deepen the kiss.

A groan escaped from me, and he answered it with one of his own as he continued to taste me with long, aggressive twirls of his tongue. My hips made an experimental rock over Dane's lap, feeling the hardness growing in his sweatpants.

Well hello there, swift recovery time. I'd just made him come about an hour ago, and the man already had a burgeoning erection.

"Fuck, do you know how long I've waited for this?" Dane growled, going back in to nibble on my bottom lip before soothing it with the tip of his tongue. "Do you have any idea how many times I had to hold myself back from kissing you, Eden?"

"I've thought about it too," I admitted as he kissed down my chin and over my neck, finding a fleshy spot on the right side that had my sex seeking out his rigid cock again. Wetness flooded my panties as I grinded down onto him.

"Please tell me you've changed your mind, that you'll let me feast on your sweet pussy. Right now." His tongue swirled mesmerizing little circles up the side of my neck, and I canted my head to give him better access.

"Yes," I panted, clutching his long, soft hair between my fingers.

Way to go, Eden. You held out for an entire hour. Way to be strong. I couldn't help but smile at that snarky voice inside my head. Dane made it almost impossible to resist him, from the way he literally ate at my mouth to the way his dirty words dripped like honey from his perfect lips.

He wasted no time in stripping my sweatshirt off, his hands gripping my rib cage as his eyes scored my body with their heat. "My god, Eden. I've never seen anyone more beautiful."

I imagined what he saw when he looked at me... specifically my tiny boobs. Surely he'd been with more voluptuous women.

"I'm just... me," I said lamely as his hands moved up and down my sides.

Dane's lips quirked up on one side. "I know. That's my favorite thing about you." Then his hands went to my breasts, thumbs strumming over my nipples and drawing them into hard points. When he leaned forward to nuzzle one tip with his nose, he made a soft sound in the back of his throat. "You always smell like honey."

"It's my body wash," I managed to say because *fuck*, his mouth was *right there*. My voice transformed into a tease. "Or maybe because I'm so sweet."

His eyes lifted to mine, all mirth gone from his expression. "I have no fucking doubt you are, Wildcat."

Sweet baby Jesus. If those words and the darkening of his irides wasn't a sign that he wanted me, I wasn't sure what was. Well, perhaps the extremely hard dick I was currently sitting on was another obvious indication.

When his lips closed around one of my nipples, my head fell back on a moan. "So good," I called to the ceiling as he sucked, adding a scrape of teeth to the mix. My hips circled, dragging my clit across his rigid length with each rotation, and my spine tingled.

"Your tits are perfectly bite-sized, baby girl," he mumbled around me.

"Is that code for small?" I mean, my boobs weren't mosquito bites, but they were by no means large.

Dane released me with a pop, a naughty smile playing across his lips. "Haven't you ever heard that the best things come in small packages? Like chocolate chips. They're not big, but they make the most delicious cookies."

I giggled and roped my fingers into his hair, guiding his mouth to my other breast. "Shut up and suck."

He did as directed, taking my other nipple between his lips and giving it the same attention as the other. I felt him fumbling around behind me, but I was too distracted by all the sucking and hip grinding to care what he was doing. But I figured it out a minute later when he held my back with both hands and laid me on the floor. Dane had folded my sweatshirt to form a makeshift pillow for my head. The gesture was so sweet it made my heart swell.

He continued working over my breasts, low groans rumbling from his throat and vibrating through my sensitive flesh.

"Your nipples are so goddamn hard against my tongue, baby girl. I could eat them all day." He lifted an eyebrow. "If I didn't already have another meal in mind."

Holy flipping hell!

"You just had breakfast," I said cheekily and then let out a little yelp when his teeth scraped along a spot on my rib cage that skated the line between tickling and overwhelming pleasure.

He looked up at me and chuckled. "I'm a glutton for your pussy, baby. I'm going to coat my fucking face with your orgasm." His grin was impossibly wicked. "I've heard a woman's cum is an excellent beard conditioner."

My entire body trembled at the filth coming out of this man. "You have a dirty mouth, Mr. Osbourne."

"My mouth has many talents, Mrs. Osbourne. Dirty talking is only one of them." Then he kissed his way down my body—sucking, nipping, licking—until he reached my stomach. He pressed a line of kisses above the waistband of my red lounge pants, his facial hair lightly scratching over the taut flesh before his eyes found mine. "Are you sure this is what you want?"

"I think I might murder you if you don't."

"Jesus, so fucking violent," he complained, though I caught the amused irony in his tone. Hooking his fingers into the top of my pants, he dragged them down my legs, leaving me in only a pair of black microfiber bikini panties. "Damn, you're sexy," he said softly, kissing his way up the inside of one thigh.

Dane angled his head an inch until his nose was right in my crotch, moving up and down my slit. "So wet for me, aren't you, baby?" He gave me a long lap of his tongue over my underwear, and my hips lifted off the floor, seeking what my body needed. "So goddamn greedy for my mouth on your cunt."

"Please," I whimpered, desperation making me beg.

"Such an impatient little wildcat," he murmured, kissing down my other thigh and licking his way back up. Then he slid the tip of his tongue along the seam where my panties met my leg. "Fuck, I can't wait another second to taste you."

Thank god!

As soon as he tugged my panties down, the cool air hit my pussy but did nothing to extinguish the fire between my legs. Only one thing could do that. And I finally got it.

Spreading me with his thumbs, Dane took a long, slow lick up the center of me, and I cried out in relief. "Oh shit, that feels good!"

His smiling lips peeked through the dark beard when he lifted his head. "Just wait, Wildcat." He flicked my clit with a pointed tongue. "I'm about to do things to you that will make you see Jesus and call me your god."

I tried to retort something smart, but my throat was clogged with lust. Dane pressed soft kisses all over my pussy. "Or you can just call me your husband."

He really liked saying that.

"If *my husband* doesn't put that tongue to good use, I'll take care of it my damn self," I warned, earning me a soft laugh from the man who was trying to torture me to death.

"I'll always take care of *my wife*," he proclaimed a second before he buried his face in my pussy. Like, *buried* it there, as if he were trying to crawl inside me, face-first. His tongue was a wicked machine, working overtime as he licked through me, over and over before teasing my entrance.

"Don't stop," I rasped, watching his dark head move between my thighs. It was such an erotic sight, and his soft beard added the perfect amount of scratchiness against my tender flesh.

"Baby girl," he managed to mumble while still licking me, "I could tongue-fuck this sweetness all day long. Feel what you do to me." He straddled my lower leg, allowing me to feel his massive erection.

My fingers found his hair, sinking into the long, silky strands as he rolled his tongue into a circular tube and pressed it into me. Then he unfurled it and began fucking me with it... fast, relentless darts of that firm muscle, feeling like he was touching every inch of my inner walls.

"Yesss," I hissed, clutching his hair and lifting my hips from the floor. I was already primed and ready to come after all the pussy grinding and nipple play. All it would take was...

Dane pressed his thumb against my clit, rubbing with firm circles, and I exploded. Still piercing me with his tongue, he growled into me, the sound like a feral animal feasting on its kill.

I closed my eyes and imagined what he would look like on top of me, inside me, and the thought brought on another wave of pleasure. My fingers tightened in his hair, and I fucked his face like I owned the damn thing.

"Ohmygod, ohmygod, ohmygod," I babbled, losing myself in the devastating sensations racking my body. Dane lapped at my sex as I floated back down out of the stratosphere of bliss.

He hummed, sounding content and satisfied, though I knew he wasn't because his erection still laid hot and heavy against my leg. As my climax wound down, my clit became hypersensitive, and I closed my legs around his head because the man wasn't showing any signs of stopping.

With his hands on my inner thighs, he pulled them open again, pinning them to the floor. "Not done with you yet, baby. Are you sensitive?"

Well, this obviously wasn't his first rodeo. He seemed to have an intimate knowledge of how the female anatomy reacted to an orgasm.

"Yes," I said, opening my eyes and realizing my head was almost beneath the Christmas tree. With a huge smile on my face, I stared up at the blue lights and white and silver ornaments, the decorations a dizzying backdrop to the kaleidoscope that was my vision.

Dane avoided my clit but didn't remove his mouth from between my legs, instead biting and licking the outer lips of my pussy.

"That was fucking hot. You're going to come on my face again," he announced.

I looked down at him and lifted an eyebrow. "Oh, am I?"

He lifted his head and fixed me with a challenging glare. "Yeah. You are." His lips glistened with my arousal and seeing that caused the tiniest of throbs to begin deep inside me.

"Well, if you insist," I said, my chest still heaving. "Can I catch my breath first?"

His laugh was low and taunting. "Oh, I don't think so. I'm too hungry."

Then he lowered his head, diving back in. Dane took his time this time, eating me slowly, edging me, using his fingers and his mouth until I was begging him for my release. Which he kindly provided with two fingers inside me and his lips wrapped around my clit.

"Holy shit, you're good at that," I panted, smoothing his mussed hair with my fingers.

Dane crawled up my body and kissed me deeply, smearing my wetness all over my lower face before pulling back with a slight frown. "Does it bother you with me on top of you? Make you feel trapped or anything?"

Though he was a hulking presence over me, it surprisingly didn't affect me. Not in any negative way. "No, I'm all good." I reached down to cup his cock through his pants, and it jerked in my palm. "Though it feels like you're not."

"I'm about to fucking come in my pants," he admitted with a wry grin. "The taste of you has me ready to blow."

"Do you want me to... touch you again?"

He glanced down between us where one of his hands was cupping my breast. "Would you let me fuck these sweet titties?"

I blushed to the roots of my hair. "You and your filthy mouth," I said with a mock glare. "I've never done that before, but I'm open to trying new things."

Five seconds later, he was totally naked and straddling my body, his big hand fisting that gorgeous cock with long, hard strokes. Releasing himself, he held out his hand beneath my chin. "Spit," he ordered. My eyes widened, but I did as he asked. His voice was a soft croon. "Good girl." I could have come again just from the visual of him and his words of praise.

Coating his dick with my saliva, he groaned as I ran my hands over his abs and chest, loving the soft sprinkling of dark hair beneath my fingertips.

"This isn't going to take long," Dane said with a barely restrained voice. "Hold your tits together for me."

He laid his erection between my boobs, and I pressed them together around him. "Feel good?" I asked, and he nodded.

"So fucking good." He tilted his head back as he began to move his hips, sliding his wet cock between the mounds. "Eden, baby," he moaned in a gravelly voice.

He looked like a beast hovering over me with his long hair, dark beard, and enormous body. Every muscle was taut and on full display beneath his tanned skin.

Then he fell forward with one palm on the floor above my head, his other hand softly caressing my cheek. His hips picked up speed, riding me roughly as he grunted out nonsensical syllables.

Dane's cock was hard and long, the head of it almost reaching my chin with every forward thrust. It looked so damn swollen and hot, and I dipped my chin down and stuck out my tongue, letting his tip press against it every time he pushed forward.

"Goddamn it. That's so fucking sexy, Wildcat," he barked, picking up his pace.

Ten strokes—and licks—later, Dane's mouth dropped open, and he roared out his release, along with a string of curse words that would make a sailor blush. Spurts of his seed hit my neck, chest, and mouth as he slowed down, his dark gaze fixed on mine. I ran my tongue over my lips, tasting him for the first time. Salty and surprisingly appealing.

"That was amazing." He leaned down and kissed me, not recoiling in the slightest at the taste of himself on my lips. "I think I'm completely addicted to you, wife." He flopped onto his back and, with little effort, rolled me on top of him.

"Dane! I've got... stuff all over me."

With his hand cradling the back of my head, he pulled me down for a kiss that made me want to do very naughty things to him. Well, *more* naughty things.

"I don't give a damn," he said once we broke apart, a satisfied grin on his handsome face. "If you haven't noticed, Wildcat, I like things as dirty as possible."

I laughed and leaned my forehead against his. "I think I do too."

CHAPTER 27

DANE HELD MY HAND while we took a Christmas afternoon stroll around the neighborhood, and for the first time, I was a hundred percent okay with it. This wasn't for show or because newlyweds should hold hands a lot. No, this was real couple stuff.

And that made my stomach grind with guilt. I wasn't supposed to like this guy. I wasn't supposed to get flutters in my belly when he looked at me.

Not to mention the flutters I'd now be getting in other places, thanks to our little escapade beside the Christmas tree. I couldn't stop thinking about his very talented tongue and all the things he'd done to me with it.

"Around seventy percent of the population can roll their tongues," I blurted out and then mentally kicked myself in the ass. *Well, that wasn't obvious.*

"Wildcat," Dane drew out, shaking his head in mock consternation. "I wonder why in the world that thought popped into your pretty little head."

"Shut it," I mumbled, avoiding his smirking face as we rounded the block back onto our street. As always, my gaze went immediately to the big yellow house that sat two doors down from ours. I wasn't sure what it was about that place that intrigued me. It was larger than the one we lived in but somehow cozier with its Victorian style, wide porches, and white trim.

The Corrigans, a middle-aged couple, had moved out three months ago because they were relocating to Oregon to take care of Mrs. Corrigan's elderly mother. It made me sad to see the grand place abandoned.

Instead of walking by, Dane lightly tugged my hand and led me up the walk.

"What are you doing?"

"Checking out this house."

"We're trespassing," I hissed, attempting—and failing—to drag him back to the main sidewalk.

He ignored me, ascending the three steps onto the covered porch and cupping one hand to peer into one of the paned-glass windows. "Huh. I can't see much. Let's go inside."

"Dane! Have you lost your mind? What are you going to do, break in?"

The corners of his lips lifted when he produced a key from the pocket of his gray sweatpants. If I hadn't been so shocked, I probably would have checked him out in those pants. For about the twentieth time since he'd put them on earlier.

Looking quite pleased with himself, Dane inserted the key into the front door lock, tossing me a look of fake surprise when it opened. "Would you look at that?"

He made a sweeping gesture, indicating for me to enter, and I did, dumbfounded into silence. The house was nothing short of grand on the inside with high ceilings and honey-colored hardwood floors. We stood in a wide foyer with a short wooden bench just beside the door. Ahead was the living room, and the open floor plan allowed a view into a gorgeous kitchen with a marble island as the centerpiece.

I finally found my voice. "What are we doing in here?"

"I got the key from the realtor and thought you might like to take a look around. You're always staring at it."

"Well, it's really pretty, but... Wait, did you say realtor?" I backtracked, peering out the window into the front yard, where I saw no hint of a *For Sale* sign.

"Yeah, a guy named Clint who I overheard talking about it at the bakery." Dane had been working at Sweet Heaven a couple days a week so Charles could travel to Miami to see a wound care specialist. The older man had stepped on a nail during the hurricane cleanup, and it hadn't healed well.

"So, it's for sale?"

"It's going on the market next week." He lifted an eyebrow at me. "Making sure to always have the realtor's favorite cookies on hand can get a person some very interesting inside information."

"Ooh, sugar-fueled shadiness. I like it." I looked around at the beautiful home, noticing the floating staircase leading up to the second floor. This place was as amazing on the inside as it was from the street. "But that doesn't explain why we're in here."

"I thought since our situation has changed from short-term to indefinite, we might want to get our own place. I'm sure Robert and Jamie would like to have their vacation home back."

I could literally feel my eyes light up with excitement. "Seriously? You mean we could buy this place?"

Dane stuffed his hands into his pockets, biting his bottom lip. "If you want to. They've priced it to sell, and we have plenty of money from... you know."

From the money his father was going to use to buy me... which we then stole from him.

My shoulders hunched up around my ears. "Let's look around."

Fifteen minutes later, I was officially in love with this house. It was modern and spacious, but it also had an undeniable charm that spoke to me. And the master bathroom? I freaking adored it. The floor in there was white tile with tiny black accents, and the countertop and shower were covered by candy-apple-red tiles with black grout. The black dual sinks were a stunning contrast to the red, and intricate tin panel tiles made up the ceiling. It was a fun and undeniably sexy room.

"It would probably be best if we financed it. Handing over that amount of cash would look suspicious," Dane mused as we descended the stairs. I wanted to squeal like a little kid at this staircase. Every step lit up from below each time you stepped on it. It was cool as hell. Once we reached the first floor, Dane gripped my hips and pulled me toward him. "What do you think?"

"I really like it."

He studied my face. "Then why are your eyebrows pinching together?"

"It just seems so..."

"Permanent?" he filled in, and I nodded.

"Yes."

"Houses can be sold, especially ones near the beach in Florida. We can probably sell it quickly when our situation is resolved." He looked out the windows overlooking the backyard. "Or maybe I'll just buy you out and stay here when you go back to New York."

The thought of that brought on a rush of mixed emotions I couldn't quite understand. Elation. Hope. And a little bit of sadness.

Smiling tentatively, I said, "Then I say we go for it."

Dane lifted me by the backs of my thighs, and I wrapped my legs around his waist. Holding me up with one hand, he turned his ball cap around backward and kissed the hell out of me. I melted into him like a snow cone in the Sahara.

He pulled back and laid a sweet peck on my nose. "I know this isn't perfect, Eden. I know you want to be with your family, but I'll do my best to make you as happy as possible while you're stuck with me."

Tears filled my eyes, and I could only nod.

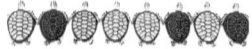

"Robert and Jamie said to tell you hi," Dane said, walking in from the hallway once we were back home and tossing his iPhone onto the coffee table. He still had his hat on backward, which had the effect of making my nipples perk up. Not to mention the way his sweatpants hung off his hips.

"Are they having fun in Park City?"

Dane chuckled. "Yes, but Robert said his knees hurt after skiing the past three days. They're going to spend some time in the hot tub tonight."

"Any new Evie sightings?" The FBI had finally ruled the actual sighting of me months ago in Jacksonville as unreliable. There were no video cameras, and the woman at the convenience store had been near the end of a double shift and was tired. According to Fiero's spying, that information had trickled down to Luca, which was a relief.

"Oh, yes," he said, plopping down beside me. "A woman named Thorunn called the Feds and swore she saw you in an ice cave in Iceland."

"Wow, I'm really living my best life. I was just spotted hanging out near the Great Pyramid of Giza last week."

The Evie sightings had become a bit of a running joke for us. Robert used his skills to regularly tap into the FBI database and delighted in calling us every couple weeks to let me know where I'd been "spotted." The FBI call center received at least a dozen each day, and most were dismissed as dead ends. Luckily, there hadn't been any more Florida sightings.

"You're quite the world traveler," he said, picking up the mug of hot chocolate I'd prepared and looking at the coaster. It read, *I enjoy being used.* He snickered and looked at mine, his eyebrows lifting when he read the words. *Make me wet.* "Never thought coasters could make me horny," he muttered, adjusting himself in his pants. "What are we watching?"

Using the remote, I clicked on the television. "*The Santa Clause*. I love Tim Allen in that movie."

"Agreed. Just don't make me watch fucking *Elf* again," he grumbled.

"That's next," I replied breezily, knowing he despised Will Ferrell in that film.

"Jesus," he groaned, tipping his head back against the couch. "Why the hell do I put up with you?"

"Because I give good hand jobs," I retorted.

Dane ran his tongue over his top teeth and eyed me before wrapping an arm around my shoulders and pulling me into his side. "Can't argue with that."

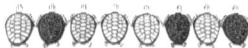

My first Christmas Day without my family was better than I could have expected. I missed the hell out of them, but Dane had made it... nice. The thoughtful gifts. The sexy stuff. The prospects of us buying the butter house.

And then the stomach virus hit. We'd just finished *Elf* when my stomach rolled over on itself. I pursed my lips and breathed in and out, trying to tamp down the nausea. It didn't work.

Clamping a hand over my mouth, I muttered, "Shit," and sprinted to the bathroom. It wasn't pretty, and through the heaves, I managed to groan, "Get. Out," when Dane trailed behind me and held a cool washcloth to the back of my neck. He didn't listen.

In fact, for the next three days, he didn't leave my side except to bring me Sprite, broth, and crackers, despite my warnings that he could get sick too.

By New Year's Eve, I was feeling better and eating everything in the house. "Stop smirking at me," I said around a mouthful of Pringles. "I'm hungry."

"Could you eat some spaghetti?"

"And meatballs?" I asked hopefully, looking up at him from my lounging position on the couch. I batted my eyelashes for added effect.

"If milady wishes." He reached down and gripped my wrist, staring down at where his fingers met. "You've lost so much weight. I need to fatten you up a bit."

Scrunching up my face, I shook my head. "Never say 'fat' to a woman. Not in any context."

"I didn't say you were fat. I said—" I glared at him until he redirected and drifted a single finger over my cheek. "Your color is better. Am I allowed to say that?" he asked dryly.

"Depends. Are you making garlic bread too?"

"Who do you think you're dealing with? An amateur?" he scoffed, pinching my chin. "Do you think you'll feel up to going out to dinner tomorrow night since it's our anniversary?"

My eyes widened. "Our... what?"

He actually blushed. "The date on our marriage license is New Year's Day. I know it's fake, but... I'd like to take you out."

I chewed on my bottom lip, attempting to hide how happy that made me. "Okay, that will be nice. I can wear that blue dress you got me for Christmas." In addition to the turtle necklace, Dane had spoiled me with tons of new clothes.

Something swelled up inside of me and it was becoming almost impossible to deny. Affection for this hardened man who showed me a softer side.

Affection and maybe something... more?

Dane led me inside the house after our "anniversary" date. The seafood had been wonderful, and then he'd taken me to a little jazz club with cool music and dim lighting. The effect was incredibly sexy, especially when he'd held me close on the dance floor and pressed his cheek against mine.

Cheek to cheek dancing... Why was that so damned romantic? His masculine scent had surrounded me as snugly as his arms, and his warm breath against my ear had a constant supply of tingles running up and down my spine. And lower.

We'd stayed on the floor, swaying to the sultry music until my stilettos threatened to rub all the skin off my big toes, and then he'd brought me home. When we crawled into bed, I wanted him to roll over on top of me. I wanted him to push inside me and stay there all night long.

But no. I needed to keep some kind of distance between us. That *thing* on Christmas morning was an anomaly. Just a momentary lapse of judgment. And it wasn't going to happen again.

Though it had been the most erotic moment of my life.

You hate him, my brain reminded me, but the rest of my body felt the lie. Especially the part beneath my panties.

With my cheek pressed against Dane's back, I inhaled a mixture of his body wash and the hint of leather from the jacket I'd bought him for Christmas. He'd looked smoking hot in it tonight, the soft black leather hugging his tall, muscular frame just right.

Dane's breathing slowed and evened as every blood cell in my body seemed to congregate in my clit. I needed some relief. Sliding my arm from his waist, I cupped my sex, allowing my fingers to press against my most sensitive spot. Wanting friction, I rocked my hips and groaned quietly at the relief that was on the horizon.

The big man beside me stirred, and I held my breath for a few long seconds. When he didn't wake up, I carefully rolled onto my back and stared at the ceiling, the need still pulsing in my core.

Fuck it. Without shaking the bed I slid off the mattress and crept into my closet, rummaging around until I found the box that held the vibrator I'd ordered from Amazon.

"Hello, old friend," I whispered to it, pressing the button to turn it on and see how loud it would be if I used it in the bathroom. Nothing. No vibrating. No buzzing. Dead.

I cursed under my breath, a quick inspection telling me the charger wasn't in the box. *Where the hell is it?* I checked the charging hole on my toy. It was one of those round ones, similar to a laptop charger. I suddenly remembered a drawer full of various cables in the kitchen. Maybe Jamie and Robert had something that would fit it.

Tiptoeing into the bedroom, I made sure Dane was still asleep and quietly made my way to the kitchen. I slid open the drawer and began pulling out cables and scrutinizing their ends.

No. No. Not even close. Ah, this one has potential. Fitting the plug end into the hole, I smiled. *Bingo.* So excited about my find, I didn't even hear him enter the kitchen until he spoke.

"E, what are you doing?"

"Gaaaaah!" I shouted, whirling around and shoving the toy behind my back, my eyes like giant globes bulging from their sockets. "Dane, you scared the hell out of me." I put on the fakest smile I'd ever attempted, probably looking like a creepy ventriloquist dummy.

"Sorry, I woke up and was afraid you were sick again." He took a step toward me. He was only wearing his boxer briefs, the olive skin over his cut chest and abs almost incandescent in the glow of the small light over the sink.

"Nope, not sick. Not me. I'm grrrreat!" Jesus, I sounded like Tony the Tiger from those Frosted Flakes commercials.

His eyes dropped down my body. "What do you have behind your back?"

"Nothing." I said that way too quickly, and Dane's dark eyebrows lifted.

"Can I see your hands?"

"My hands? Sure you can see my hands." I showed him one and then the other, switching the vibrator from one to the other behind my back. *The old switcheroo. Genius.*

He drummed his fingers on his bottom lip, and I was pretty sure I saw a muscle tic beside his mouth. "Can I see both of them at the same time?"

"Ha. You're being weird," I deflected while stuffing the vibrator into the waistband of my pink satin sleep shorts at my back and then waggling both hands at him. *Take that, buddy.*

There was only one problem. I'd lost a few pounds, and the waistband of my pants no longer fit me snugly, so the toy slipped down past my butt, out the right leg hole of my shorts and directly onto the floor between my feet.

Plunk.

We both looked down, and there it was... my vibrator in all its purple, rabbit-eared glory.

"Huh. I have no idea how that got there," I mused.

Mortification heated my entire face. I usually considered myself a fairly sharp-witted person, so I had no idea why I was babbling out that nonsense. Dane and I both knew exactly where it had come from.

Risking a glance at his face, I noticed another little twitch of his lips before he bent to pick it up. The asshole was amused by this whole situation.

He held it up and turned it over in his hands, giving it a very thorough inspection. The damn cord was still dangling from it. Dane took it between his fingers and swirled it in a circle.

"I saw this hanging down and thought you were either charging something, or you'd grown a tail."

"You're hilarious," I said without a trace of humor. I'd thought the vibrator was huge when I bought it, but it looked small in his hand, especially compared to his own... toy.

Dane took a step toward me, getting into my space. My butt was backed up against the countertop, and he widened his stance, placing his feet on either side of mine.

"Are you feeling..." his eyes raked me up and down, scoring my body like hot coals before finishing with, "*needy*, Eden?"

The way he growled that sent a flood to my pussy. Clenching my thighs together, I lifted my chin. "What if I am?"

"Why didn't you ask me?"

"I-I didn't want to wake you up."

His bulge throbbed against my belly as he leaned forward, his nose almost touching mine. "If my wife has needs, I will take care of them. Any time. Any place."

Jesus, Mary, and Joseph. His tone oozed complete filth, and I felt the need to do the sign of the cross. *You're not even Catholic, Eden,* the voice in my head reminded me.

"I guess you're one of those men who thinks women shouldn't have... devices," I said defiantly, trying to control the hitch in my breathing.

The villainous curve of his lips was slow and deliberate as he dragged the vibrator up the inside of one of my thighs.

"Oh no, sweetheart. Don't think for a second that I'm intimidated by sex toys. I consider them my teammates, not my enemies." Dane leaned forward until his lips were pressed against my ear, dropping his voice to almost a whisper. "They can add endless hours of fun to playtime."

He punctuated that naughty little bomb by tapping the bulbous head of the toy against my sex. I swallowed hard. Did he say *hours?*

"It was dead, so I was looking for a charger," I admitted. "The little ears don't flicker without power." I gestured toward the clit-tickling rabbit ears at the base of the toy with one circle of my fingers.

He rubbed the vibrator back and forth between my legs, and my breaths seemed to get lost somewhere between my lungs and my mouth.

"There are... other things that flicker," he informed me coolly, dragging his tongue along my bottom lip to emphasize exactly *what* kind of flickering he was talking about. "If that's something you're interested in."

"I d-don't... know," I stuttered out.

His grin widened. "Oh, I think you do know. Should I put the Christmas tree back up to remind you?"

Visions of me sprawled on the floor with Dane's head between my legs flickered through my muddy brain, and I groaned. "Dane..."

His mouth closed over mine at the same time he increased the pressure of the vibrator against my core. His tongue gave me a very convincing demonstration of his skill, and then he moaned into my mouth, "Say yes, Eden."

I breathed, "Yes," into his, and a minute later, my shorts and underwear were puddled on the floor, I was sitting on the counter, and a huge hulk of a man was kneeling between my thighs. He even took time to wash the toy since it had fallen on the floor.

Dane's eyes looked almost metallic when they met mine in the dim light, and he spat on the head of the vibrator. *Whyyyy? Why is that so hot?*

"Put your heels on the counter," he demanded, and my feet asked no questions before doing exactly as asked. Lifting the toy, he slid the wet head of it through my slit, bumping against my clit with every pass. Then he pressed it forward until the crown was inside me. "I believe I promised you some flickering."

With that, his mouth went to work, that marvelous tongue of his battering my clit as he began fucking me slowly with the vibrator. Tilting the device slightly, he found a spot that had my knees snapping shut around his ears. He glared up at me.

"Keep your fucking legs open, or I'll stop."

Dear. God. No one had ever been bossy with me like that, and I fucking liked it. Widening my legs, I thumped my head back against the cabinet as he resumed his previous activities. The slow fuck. The quick tongue. It all promised an impending orgasm that I was sure would blow the top of my head off.

When Dane pressed the cock deep and gave a swirl of his wrist, the pressure of his tongue on my little button intensified. "Oh shit, I'm close," I panted as he sped up the thrusts inside me. "I'm... I'm..."

No more words were forthcoming as my body exploded like a supernova fracturing in the depths of space. All sounds were muffled except for his grunts and slurps as he pulled the vibrator out and replaced it with his tongue.

Dane lapped up everything I was giving him, and it was a lot. My climax seemed to go on forever as his mouth coaxed and tasted. "Fuck, you have the sweetest little pussy, Wildcat," he mumbled into me, and I felt another gush of wetness escape me.

He grinned up at me. I wasn't sure how he managed to smile and eat me out at the same time, but he was talented like that. As I began to come down, a dull pain pulsed through my fingers, and I realized I'd been clenching the counter until the edge was almost cutting into my flesh.

Loosening my grip, I took several deep breaths and asked, "What are you smiling about?"

He rose, his face covered with my arousal, and held my jaw in one hand. "I just realized my wife has a praise kink."

"No I don't," I protested, and he chuckled.

"Oh, I think you do, Eden. Why don't I see for myself." He slipped one long finger inside me and leaned close. I could smell myself on his breath when he purred, "You are so fucking beautiful when you come on my face, baby girl. And you taste like my own personal nectar."

Goddammit. He was right. I liked the hell out of that, and my pussy did too, clamping down around his invading finger.

But he wasn't done with his little test. He curled his finger forward, stroking my G-spot. Then he added another finger, the fit snug as he fucked and rubbed me from the inside, his intense gaze burning into my own. When he picked up the pace and added his thumb to my throbbing clit, I could feel another climax coming on, heat radiating outward from my core.

"Come again for me, Eden. Like a good fucking girl."

Yeah, that did it. My second orgasm shuddered through me, not as intense as the first one, but it was still so satisfying. "Damn you, you smug ass," I whimpered, my head lolling back as my body went limp.

Then Dane surprised the crap out of me by lifting the vibrator and running his tongue up and down the velvety purple surface. His brown eyes held mine as he licked around the head. "I don't want to waste a drop of you," he explained before opening his mouth and taking the fake dick inside. With closed eyes, he moaned around it.

Dear god.

"Have you done that before?" I asked, my eyes locked on his full lips around the girth of the toy. It was strangely arousing.

After an incredibly deep suck that I was surprised didn't gag him, he pulled it out with a pop. "A real dick or a vibrator?"

"Either?"

"No to both," he answered. "Guys aren't my thing, and I've never had the urge to suck a fake cock either. But then again, I've never come across a vibrator that's been inside my wife either."

Someone just stop the world and let me off. Seriously, the things that came out of this man were next level.

"Thank you for... all that," I said awkwardly. Was that weird? Thanking him for making me orgasm?

"All in a day's work," he said cheekily. "Feel better?"

I nodded, dragging my hands down his body until I reached the very prominent erection that was barely contained in his briefs. "But I don't think you do. Want me to help with this?"

"Yes," he hissed, almost before I'd finished asking.

"What do you want?"

Dane cupped my face and pressed his lips hard against mine. "I want you, Wildcat. On your knees."

CHAPTER 28

EDEN SLIPPED OFF THE counter, her blue eyes sparkling, but before she could sink to her knees, I gently held her chin and gave her a long, languid kiss.

"You're not going to be able to talk for a while because I'm going to be stuffing your pretty mouth full of cock," I informed her. "If I'm being too rough or you need me to stop, tap my leg. Understood?"

Her bemused blue eyes sparkled with mirth. Or maybe that was an aftereffect of the two orgasms I'd just given her.

"Did you get a master's degree in dirty talking?"

"A doctorate," I corrected dryly.

She winged one eyebrow up at me as she lowered her knees to the floor. "Well, keep on, Dr. Dirty Talk. I like it."

In the next instant, I wasn't able to speak at all, dirty or otherwise, because Eden had my underwear around my ankles and her tongue on my balls. A groan liberated itself from my chest as she gripped my shaft and gave me a long tug.

"Fuuuuh," I garbled out, grabbing the breakfast bar behind me with both hands since all the ligaments in my knees forgot how to do their job.

The goddess on her knees ran her tiny pink tongue around my balls before taking each into her mouth, all while still jacking me off with her right hand and pinching one of my nipples with her left. She was like a damn multitasking porn star.

Then she looked up at me, wetting her lips with that magical tongue. "Spread your legs for me like a good boy."

God. Damn.

A large glob of pre-ejaculate leaked from my tip, and Eden eyed it hungrily as I stepped out of my briefs and widened my stance. Holding my cock firmly, she licked me up and down like my dick was a melting ice cream cone and she was trying to lap up every messy drip. Then she took the head into her mouth and sucked on it—just the tip—and I resisted the urge to cram my entire length into her mouth in one go.

Popping it out and leaving a thick coating of saliva, she looked up at me. "Do you want it fast or deep?" Eyeballing my swollen dick speculatively, she said, "I don't think I can do both with this thing."

"D-de—" I cleared my throat, willing the word to come. "Deep. Please."

Then she fucking swallowed me. All of me, and I cried out at the sensation of being in her mouth, root to tip. "Fucking hell, Eden. Where is your gag reflex?"

Other than a soft hum, she didn't answer, and I honestly didn't want her to because she pulled back, dragging her lips up my cock before plunging forward once again, burying her nose in my neatly trimmed pubic hair.

Peeling the fingers of one hand from the counter, I stroked them through the top of her messy hair. It was thick but soft, and I moved my hand to the back of her head. She hadn't had a nightmare in seven weeks, and I didn't want to trigger any of her issues by being too rough or demanding, so I was tentative, almost tender, when I urged her an inch deeper.

"That's it, Wildcat," I said softly. "You take my cock like a good girl, don't you? So deep and wet."

She made a noise in the back of her throat, which had a vibrating effect against the tip of my cock. I tugged lightly on her hair, reluctantly pulling her mouth off me.

"What?" she asked, looking up at me with vulnerable blue eyes. "You don't like it?"

I huffed out a laugh at the ridiculousness of that question. "I love being in your mouth, baby. It's my favorite fucking thing. I just want you to take your top off so I can see those pretty tits while you suck me off." I dragged my bottom lip through my teeth. "So I can fantasize about devouring them. Or fucking them again."

Eden pulled her sleep shirt off and then made a show of cupping both breasts and pinching her nipples into the most beautiful rosy peaks. Her slight smile was catlike, and my erection jerked in front of her face, drawing her attention back to him. He was a bit of an attention whore, especially with a gorgeous woman on her knees with her mouth *right there.*

"Get back on my dick, Eden," I growled, desperation seeping into the syllables. Since my first blow job when I was a teenager, I'd been a fan, but I'd never once felt like I might cry if a girl didn't give me head. This woman though... she had a way of making me crave her with every ounce of my being.

As requested, Eden surrounded me with her mouth, earning a low groan from me as she deep throated me again. My eyes closed until I realized I hated not seeing her, so I popped them back open, my gaze shifting between the wrap of her lips, the hollows of her cheeks, and the peek of tits I got while she slid her mouth up and down my length.

Eden had the bare remnants of a tan remaining on her body where her swimsuit didn't cover, and her breasts were a milky, porcelain white, the dark pink nipples a riveting contrast. She was stunning.

"Fuck, baby, I love watching my cock disappear into that pretty mouth." Remembering her praise kink, I added. "You are so fucking sexy. Hottest thing I've ever seen."

Her head moved faster, sucking me up and down as I watched. Leaning back, I let the countertop take the majority of my weight and plunged both hands into her hair, guiding her head in long strokes. "That's it, Wildcat. Give me some teeth."

The edges of her top teeth scraped along my dick, and I groaned, "Fuck's sake, that feels so good. Please tell me you swallow."

"Mmhmm," she managed to mumble around me, and I felt the telltale rush of adrenaline that coursed through my body. It built and built, and I snapped my hips forward, fucking her face as sweat beads popped out on my forehead.

My eyes were glued on where I was shoving into her, mesmerized by the dribble of saliva that leaked from one corner. She was letting me abuse her mouth, turning her lips red with the rough friction.

"Good girl, baby. Keep your eyes on me while I come down your throat."

Watery blue eyes lifted to mine, and my jaw dropped, a feral bellow ripping up from my chest as the orgasm crashed over me like an avalanche. "Fuuuuck. Fuck yes."

My vision doubled until I saw two of my little wildcats on their knees before me, two cocks jerking into two sexy mouths. She was greedy for my release, sucking on me with thirsty little sounds as I spilled into her mouth.

When the final twitch was done, she slowly pulled back and released my cock with one last kiss on the tip. There was something so sweet about that after the way she'd just defiled my dick, and I pulled her off the ground and directly into my embrace.

Despite my arms having the consistency of a couple overcooked noodles, I cupped her ass and lifted until her legs curled around my waist. Our cores met, and if I wasn't so completely spent, I think I would have popped another erection at the feel of her wet pussy on my dick.

"That was perfect, Eden. *You're* perfect." Her face flushed, and I chuckled, kissing each rosy cheek. "Don't get all blushy on me now that I know you're a little freak."

"Just trying to keep up," she retorted in true Eden fashion.

Finding the use of my legs, I carried her to our bedroom and placed her gently on the bed. After a quick cleanup in the bathroom, I brought a warm cloth to the bed and kneeled between her legs.

"Dane, what are you—"

"Shhh, let me clean you up." I peppered her belly with soft kisses while I moved the cloth over her sex, feeling the overwhelming need to take care of her, make her feel special. Because she was.

After tossing the cloth aside, I reached into her nightstand drawer and pulled out her cherry lip balm, smoothing it over her abused lips before replacing it. Her eyes watched me, not saying a word. Then I stretched out beside her, facing her, and pressed my lips softly to hers.

When my tongue sought entrance, she pulled back. "I just..." She lifted her eyebrows at me. "You're in my mouth," she explained.

"You think that bothers me?" I asked, cupping the back of her head and bringing her mouth back to mine. The truth of it though? I'd never kissed a woman after blowing in her mouth. I'd always avoided it. Hell, by this point, I was usually slapping them on the ass and telling them to get dressed so I could call them a ride. Done. Finished.

But with her, it was different. My senses were immersed in the combination of my saltiness and the taste of cherry lips, the scent of honey on her skin, her soft noises as we kissed. And just...

Eden.

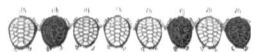

As dawn crested, I stared down at the woman on the bed, my body lingering in the doorway. She was still completely nude, though covered by the cushy comforter and wrinkled sheet.

All I wanted to do was crawl back into the bed, into her warmth, but I had to go to work. Charles had an appointment at the wound care center today, and I was the person who ran the bakery while he was gone.

It was early January, and turtle mating season didn't begin till April, so Eden could sleep in. Striding back to the bed, I sat on the edge and kissed the side of her head.

"Hmm?" she hummed.

"Sorry, go back to sleep," I said, quietly, stroking the wildness of her hair until she settled. Then I went to Sweet Heaven, ready to tackle cupcakes, cookies, and cakes. And the employees. Namely Kevin and Barry, the two guys I'd first met at Charles and Mimsy's Christmas Eve party.

Those two were full of shit but in the best of ways. I'd learned they were roommates, had both grown up in Marathon, and had been best friends since kindergarten. Barry lost his parents in a plane crash when he was a teen, so Kevin's family had taken him in for their senior year of high school.

I entered through the back door of the bakery to the sound of bickering. I swear, those two were like an old married couple. They weren't together romantically, though Barry was gay.

"I'm telling you, you need to dump him," Kevin was saying. "He's a fucking douchebag."

"You know I'm drawn to the bad boys," Barry argued.

"You're drawn to idiots," his friend shot back before issuing a warning. "I'm not eating ice cream with you when he breaks your heart. I gained six pounds in a week with your last breakup. What was his name? Calvin?"

"Carmine," the red head corrected with a sigh. "I miss him."

"He literally blew half the island while—"

"Morning, guys," I interrupted, pulling a white apron from the hook and tying the strings behind my back.

"Morning, boss," they chorused before resuming their conversation but a bit quieter now.

"Happy New Year, Mr. Osbourne," Maria said, walking into the kitchen from the front. She was a college student who worked the register on her days off from school.

"Same to you, Maria," I said with a nod. She was a sweetheart, quiet and efficient, and she refused to call me anything other than Mr. Osbourne.

"There were thirteen calls on the answering machine asking if we'd be having those praline stuffed cookies today." She giggled. "I think everyone in Marathon knows that you're on the schedule on Tuesdays."

"I'll start making them now," I told her.

"Cool, I'll return the phone calls. And..." She dipped her head shyly as her shoulders rose.

"What is it, Maria?"

"It's just that, um, it's my mom's birthday, and she really loves those cookies..." She lifted her eyes in a shy plea.

"Would a dozen be okay?"

Relief lowered her shrugging shoulders. "That would be awesome. Thank you. I'll pay for them, of course."

"Consider them a gift for your mom," I told her, turning to Kevin and tossing him the handheld nutcracker. "Start shelling those pecans." I nodded toward the two huge red bags on the pristine metal worktop.

"Bosssss," he groaned, "you know you can buy already shelled pecans, right?"

"And you know anything that's not fresh isn't acceptable in my kitchen, right?" I leveled a glare at him.

Kevin hauled one of the bags toward him with a grumble. "I know, but my hand will be virtually unusable. Last time I had to jack off with my left hand for a week."

"Fuck's sake. Keep that information to yourself. And go wash your hands."

"I just washed them, boss."

"Wash them again," I barked, striding over to the ingredient bins to get started. It was going to be a busy day, which was good. I needed something to keep my mind off where I wanted to be this chilly morning. At home, in bed with my wife.

The realtor, Clint, showed up about noon while I was helping Maria stock the glass bakery case with muffins and cookies. As soon as I saw him, I pulled out the pan with the syrup-topped almond cookies—his favorites—and lifted an eyebrow in question.

"A dozen of those, black coffee, and a couple minutes of your time," he answered.

Donning a fresh plastic glove, I asked Maria to pour the coffee while I boxed Clint's cookie order. When it was all ready, I grabbed my own cup, a pink mug with fluffy clouds and the *Sweet Heaven* logo on one side, loaded everything on a tray, and headed to his table.

"Clint," I greeted, placing a saucer with two warmed cookies in front of him. The rest were in the pink box, ready for him to take home. After unloading the tray, I took it back to Maria and returned to sit in the white iron chair across from the realtor. "What's up?"

He already had half a cookie in his mouth and dabbed at his lips with a paper napkin before swallowing. "Dane, good to see you. I wanted to talk to you about the property."

My nerves rose and prickled my skin. Eden loved that house, and I hoped he had good news for me. "Yeah?" I asked warily.

"The Corrigans have accepted your offer. They're ready to sell as soon as possible, so—"

"Eden and I will go to the bank tomorrow. We want it."

Clint grinned. "That's great news." He nodded his head, covered with a thick mat of gray hair. "I'll let them know and get started on the paperwork on my end."

"When can we take possession? There are a few things we'd like to change before we move in."

"About a month," he assured me, taking a sip of his coffee. "It's a beautiful house. I hope you and Mrs. Osbourne will fill it with children one day." He must have noticed my startled look because he quickly backtracked. "I mean, if you want kids. Some people don't, and that's fine."

"We're... still newlyweds," I managed to say, suddenly thinking of little ones in the big backyard of the butter house. A boy and a girl with Eden's blue eyes and my dark hair.

Forcing a smile as Clint picked up his box and told me he'd be in touch, I couldn't get that image out of my mind.

Does she even want kids? Better yet, would she want kids with me? A family was something I'd only thought of in some abstract, way-in-the-future possibility. It wasn't anything I sat around dreaming about, only something that would inevitably be forced on me by my father.

But now my life was my own. Luca Cappitani no longer controlled me. Well, I guessed technically he did. Otherwise, I wouldn't have had to change my name, disguise my appearance, and go into exile with the woman he'd tried to buy.

My stomach turned at the thought, as it always did when I thought of my father having Evie Bouvier as his plaything. But the feeling was even worse now that I knew her, now that I was falling for her.

I stared down at my now cold coffee and let that revelation sink in.

I'm falling for her. My wildcat. My Eden.

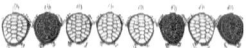

Eden was excited about the house, and we celebrated with pizza, wine, and a delectable sixty-nine in the bedroom. But by the time we moved into the home in mid-February six weeks later, we hadn't progressed past oral and foreplay.

I was certainly ready, but she... wasn't.

Two nights after we moved in, we had just christened the couch, and Eden was lying sated and smiling with me kneeling between her knees. I kissed up her stomach and neck until I was hovering over her. She'd sucked me off, but I was already hard again after going down on her, and I pressed my erection against her belly.

"I want to be inside you, baby," I told her quietly, nuzzling my nose against the peachy softness of her cheek. She inhaled quickly and let the air out slowly, and I wedged myself onto the couch until we were facing each other. "Talk to me, Eden. Is there a reason you don't want me?"

"I do want you,'" she replied, squishing her eyes shut like it hurt her to admit it.

I swiped a sweaty strand of hair away from her forehead. "I don't want to pressure you. I'm just trying to understand."

She finally lifted her lids, and I read the conflict in her blue eyes. "I don't understand it myself. I want you but..." Her lips rolled in between her teeth. "I've only had sex with two guys."

Giving her a gentle smile, I felt myself relax a bit. "I don't care if you're inexperienced, Eden. I promise we can go slow."

Two little lines appeared between her eyebrows. "It's not the physical that's holding me back. It may sound stupid or naive to you, but I have to have an emotional connection. I only have sex with someone when it really means something."

Ouch.

"And I don't mean anything to you," I said tightly, doing my best not to grit my teeth. An ache formed somewhere deep inside me because, for the first time in my life, I had a woman I thought I could actually fall in love with. And she didn't feel the same.

Eden looked surprised and lifted a hand to my beard, letting her fingers stroke through it. "No, it's because you *do* mean something to me." Her bottom lip trembled. "Even though I tried not to let that happen."

That ache disappeared in a flash, replaced with another swell of relief. "Because you want to hate me," I filled in.

She nodded, her eyes skittering to the tattoos of her fingernails on my chest. "I feel guilty. I feel like... like I need to be punished for caring for you." Leaning forward, she kissed the ink before slowly lifting her baby blues to my face. "Would you punish me, Dane?"

CHAPTER 29

WOULD YOU PUNISH ME, Dane?

My tongue turned into a blob of gelatin at those words, and it was a long moment before I could speak. "You want me to... punish you? Like a spanking?"

She lowered her chin. "You don't have to."

With two fingers, I lifted her chin right the fuck back up. "You look me in the eyes, Eden. Never be ashamed to ask your husband for any goddamn thing you need because I'll give it to you." I kissed her on the nose. "Do you need a spanking to feel better about wanting me?"

Her lips barely quirked up at the corners, and I could feel the tension leave her body. "Yes, I want you to spank me and then fuck me."

Seriously, I almost came like a thirteen-year-old with a bottle of lotion and a nudie mag. I somehow managed to hold onto my control and pulled Eden tightly against me, tucking her head beneath my chin.

"Good girl, baby," I murmured, burying my face in her hair. "Tonight, okay?"

"Okay," she agreed, though my dick thought the delay was wholly unnecessary.

We both had a glass of white wine with our pasta dinner. An anticipatory tension congealed in my gut, and Eden's fidgeting fingers told me she felt it too. I had hoped the wine would relax us both.

"We don't have to do this," I assured her, reaching out and tucking the lilac strand of hair behind one of her ears.

She looked surprised, her eyes widening. "You don't want to?"

"Eden," I said sternly, "I'm struggling not to pop a boner every time I think about painting your gorgeous little ass red. Of course I want to. I've been sitting here trying to picture the most unsexy thing I could think of to control things down south."

Amused, she propped an elbow on the table and rested her chin in her palm. "And what did you come up with?"

"Will Ferrell in his *Elf* costume," I replied flatly, earning me a laugh. Her posture relaxed, and she stopped fidgeting with the napkin on her lap.

"I want to. I read that spanking can relieve negative emotions, stress, and responsibility. I think I need to release whatever is holding me back from being normal."

I quirked an eyebrow, my voice stern when I asked, "What is it Lilibet says about being normal?" Eden still talked to the psychiatrist once a week.

She sighed. "That normalcy is a spectrum, not a pinpoint."

"Exactly. You've been through different shit than others, so your normal will look different from theirs."

"The Dark Lord is always so wise," she teased.

I rose and kissed the top of her head. "And don't you forget it. I'll do the dishes. You go take a shower. Wear the white lace panties and nothing else."

Then I picked up our plates and left her sitting at the ash-gray wooden dining table.

After taking a quick shower in one of the other bathrooms, I walked into our bedroom with a white towel around my waist, my eyes roving over the bed to find that Eden wasn't there yet. I smiled, hearing her moving around in the bathroom. She always took longer than me, mostly because I washed and got the fuck out while she pampered her skin with lotions and potions.

Not that I was complaining. Her skin was always like silk, and she smelled like a snack. I'd gotten her some honey-vanilla lotion from the same company that made her body wash, and I secretly used it on my face and beard so her scent was with me while I was at work.

My hand brushed over the white padded headboard, my fingers falling into the dimples made by the tiny white buttons that pressed in and formed a pretty pillowy surface. It was almost exactly the same as the one in Jamie and Robert's house. I'd talked to Lilibet about the move, and when she suggested that it might be a good idea for Eden to have a familiar bed, I ordered it immediately.

My wife wanted new covers though, and when she'd chosen a dark-teal duvet and cream sheets, I agreed. The color palette was soothing, with small lilac accents around the room... a lamp... a glass vase... a couple abstract pictures we'd found at a local gallery.

Walking around the large space, I flicked on each of the turtle nightlights and turned the overhead light down low just in time for Eden to emerge from the bathroom. She was goddamn stunning in her simple white lace panties and nothing else. Steam from her shower spilled out from behind her, making her look like the most alluring angel ever created.

Crossing her arms over her bare breasts, she stopped in her tracks and blushed. I strode slowly to her, gently pulling her arms away before sliding my hands down her arms and gripping her hands.

"Don't cover yourself in front of me," I ordered, softening the command with my lips on hers. Her fingers twisted between mine, and she opened for me, accepting my tongue into her mouth. Releasing one of her hands, I swept my fingers around her side and up and down her spine.

Goosebumps peppered her dewy skin at my touch, and she whimpered into my mouth. "Dane."

"I'm here, baby," I assured her, pressing my palm into the small of her back, needing that soft, beautiful body snug against mine. The hardening of her nipples inspired some hardening of my anatomy as well, just a bit lower. "Are you sure this is what you want?" I asked against her lips.

Eden pulled back and tilted her face up to mine. "Yes." It was a simple, brief reply, but it was filled with determination, delivered with her gaze confidently meeting mine.

I trailed my hand up her back and cradled the side of her neck. "We're going to use the traffic light system. If you're okay, your color is green. If I need to slow down, yellow, and if you need me to stop, say red. Do you understand?"

"I understand," she replied, her tone resolute.

Taking her hand, I led her across the wood plank floor and sat on the edge of the bed with her standing between my spread thighs. I took a moment to worship her, take in her scent, taste her skin. My mouth roamed over her abdomen, kissing her stomach and nibbling lightly at her breasts while my hands traced each supple curve.

"You're so warm. So sweet," I murmured, circling her belly button with my tongue before placing a kiss on that adorable divot. "I want you to bend over my lap, one hand on the floor and one on my leg for support."

She did, her right hand clutching my calf while her other one rested palm down on the floor. Beginning at the top of her spine, I dragged a single finger down it, counting each bump until I reached the top of her white panties. The lace had an iridescent sheen and practically glowed like my own personal beacon in the dim light of our bedroom.

Hooking my fingers in the waistband, I worked them down over her hips until they rested around her thighs. I could have taken them all the way off, but there was something so motherfucking sexy about seeing her with those sweet panties halfway down, the globes of her ass round and exposed for my hand.

"Beautiful," I whispered, stroking a palm over each one. She wiggled, and I placed my forearm protectively over her mid-back. "I'm not doing this to hold you down, just to keep you from sliding off. I'll move it immediately if you need me to."

"Okay," she breathed, and I could sense her anticipation was as thick as mine, like an autumn fog that coated everything in its path.

Holding my breath, I spanked her right butt cheek, not hard enough to hurt, and she gasped. "Color?" I asked, soothing the area with my palm.

Eden replied without pause. "Green."

Nodding to myself, I delivered a matching spank to the left side and watched the softest of pinks appear on her skin. It was so pretty, but I wanted to turn it a few shades darker.

"I'm going to tell you what to say, and you say it," I commanded. "Understood?"

"Yes," she breathed.

Drawing back my hand, I spanked her right side again—a little harder this time—and watched the outline of my handprint bloom. My dick ached at the sight. "It's okay to want to fuck my husband."

I could hear the smile in her voice when she said, "It's okay to want to fuck my husband."

Jesus, my cock almost spontaneously combusted at those words. I delivered a matching blow to her other cheek. "I can trust my husband," I said, my voice gritty. She repeated my words as I rubbed the redness on her pretty ass before slapping her right side again, this time a little harder. "I'm a good girl."

My eyes were laser focused on her exposed pussy, and I almost groaned when her desire dripped from her. She was as turned on as I was. "I'm a good girl," she said on a shaky breath.

"Last one," I informed her. My hand came down on her left cheek, leaving my mark on her. "I'm perfect."

She didn't repeat the words, instead gripping my leg even tighter. "No one is perfect, Dane."

Leaning down to kiss the middle of her spine, I reworded. "Okay, let's try this. I'm perfect for my husband."

Her voice was so quiet, I almost didn't hear it. "I'm perfect for my husband." The last word cracked on a sob, and I flipped her over, cradling her in my arms and holding her against my chest. I rocked her for a long time as she cried, wetting my chest with her tears.

Finally, I asked, "Are you okay?"

She nodded, nuzzling her face into my neck. "I feel better." Her butt was between my legs, and the grind of her hips shifted my towel until it loosened. With her pussy warm against my inner thigh I felt the spread of her wetness on my flesh. When she lifted her head, I swiped the tears away from her face with tender strokes.

"What do you need now?"

"You," she replied, and I wasted no time, immediately shifting until my back was against the padded headboard, completely shedding my towel until I was naked. The panties were still down around her thighs, impeding her from spreading her legs, so I ripped them off and tossed them on the floor. She gasped but her eyes met mine with a fierce blue blaze.

"Then take me, wife. I'm all yours."

Eden rose on her knees and straddled me, taking my length in her hand and using the tip of me against her clit. "Goddddd," she moaned, tilting her head back as she worked me against her hot button. "I could come just like this."

I clutched the hair at her nape and pulled her head forward until we were nose to nose. "No, you come with your cunt wrapped around my cock or not at all," I growled, lifting my hips in invitation.

She gasped, eyes widening for a split second before they hooded with desire. Then she notched herself on the head of my erection and rotated her hips in tiny circles, coating me with her slickness. On a sigh, she slid down my dick a couple inches, and her pretty lips parted.

I was fucking hooked even though I was barely inside her. My eyes fell to her mouth and watched her tongue toying with that tiny scar on her bottom lip. With a mind of its own, my ass lifted off the mattress and took her fully, pulling a grated sound from the back of my throat.

"Goddamn, you're tight."

The most beautiful flush of pink rushed up Eden's chest and neck until her cheeks were rosy. "Penis," she breathed as she stretched around me. "So. Much. Penis."

Chuckling, I lapped at her lips with my tongue. "You can take me, Wildcat." Then I breached her mouth, taking it in a long, hot kiss where our tongues tangled around each other. My wife's hands trailed over my shoulders and into my shoulder-length hair, twisting around the strands until she had a firm grip.

Then, with our mouths sealed together, she began to ride me. Our sounds melded together, both of us lost in the pleasure of raw, carnal fucking as Eden set a seductive rhythm. I gripped her with both hands, my thumbs resting on the front of her hips.

When she pulled her lips from mine, her eyes were glazed in arousal. "Yes, Dane. I like when you touch me right there."

Our lips were separated by only an inch, and we shared each other's air as our bodies moved together in an age old cadence of lust and need, each of us giving and taking.

I angled my head, kissing her bottom lip before sucking that little scar into my mouth for a second. "Fuck me like you hate me, Wildcat." Making my way across her cheek, I bit her earlobe and whispered, "But I think we both know you don't."

Her hips jerked, and her fingers tightened in my hair to the point of pain, but I reveled in it because she began moving with a furious pace, taking my length like she was made for me. She whimpered and panted as I feasted on the side of her neck, my teeth sinking into the soft flesh and leaving my mark over and over. All the while, my thumbs stroked the tender spots on the front of her hips because she said she liked it. And if my wife liked something, I was goddamn well going to give it to her.

She was so wet, her juices dripping down my balls, and I felt her tightening around me. I knew she was about to explode even before she cried, "I'm... coming."

"Yessss," I hissed, fucking up into her without an ounce of finesse, but Eden was taking every thick inch of me without complaint. We were nothing more than animals as we both neared our climaxes, needy beasts who were sating their most primal desires. "Squeeze my cock in that tiny pussy of yours, baby girl. Give me everything you got."

Eden threw her head back, arching until her perfect tits were right in my face. I took full advantage, wrapping my lips around one nipple and sucking in hard, quick pulls. Her body shuddered into an orgasm that threatened to break my dick in two.

While my mouth moved to her other breast, I kept my eyes cast upward, watching her, and I swear on everything holy, I've never seen a more breathtaking sight than Eden in the throes of her release.

Skin flushed and slightly mottled. Full lips parted. Eyes closed. Neck taut and bearing bruises from my mouth. She looked wild and free and goddamn gorgeous.

I was fucking barely hanging onto my own control, my body trembling with the effort to wait until she was done. When her trembling subsided, she tilted her head down and met my eyes with soft blue ones. Her pussy was still fluttering around my length when she gave me a deep grind.

"Your turn," she announced, swirling those sexy hips again, letting me feel every tight inch of her.

My gaze flicked down to the small implant in her upper arm, the one she'd gotten a month ago to help with her periods. "Can I come inside you?"

The lines of her face were soft and content, and she kissed the corner of my mouth. "Yes. I trust my husband."

That statement undid me, and I lost my shit, holding her hips with bruising force as I pistoned up into her. My voice held every ounce of strain my body was feeling.

"Fuck, Eden. You have the most perfect pussy. Made for me." On a groan, I spilled into her, bare inside a woman for the first time ever. Nothing had ever felt more right.

After a few minutes of cuddling, I carried her into the bathroom so she could take a post-coital pee while I cleaned up and picked up a small bottle. Back in our bedroom, I turned her onto her stomach and smoothed lotion all over her backside.

She smelled so fucking good, like sex and honey, and I ran my nose all over her ass before spreading her cheeks and slipping my face between her legs. She gasped when I flicked my tongue over her back entrance.

"What are you doing, Dane?"

"Cleaning my wife." I lowered my focus. "One more," I begged, softly licking her clit.

This orgasm took a little longer, but I was patient, reveling in the taste of our combined releases and the rocking of her body against my mouth as she relaxed and sought more.

I devoured every drop of her before leaving wet kisses up her spine. Eden collapsed into a lump of sexy sweetness on the mattress, and I stretched out beside her, rubbing her back as she laid her cheek on the sheet so I could see her satiated smile.

"Will you hold me?" she asked.

My hand swept her sweat-damp hair from her forehead. "Of course."

Then, to my surprise, she turned her back to me and pulled my arm around her waist. One of my hands went automatically to her breast as she did a cute backward butt-snuggle against my groin, settling her small, warm body against my big one.

And for the first time, my wife was the little spoon. All night long.

With no nightmares.

CHAPTER 30

THIRTEEN MONTHS IN HIDING

"Hey, bro," I said when my brother's face popped up on my laptop screen.

He chuckled. "Hey, man. I don't think I'll ever get used to seeing you with long hair and a beard."

I stroked a hand along my jaw. "You don't think my mountain man look is sexy?"

Fiero's lips curved wryly. "I can barely contain myself. How are things going there?"

"All good. April is turtle mating season, so Eden's busy and happy."

Fiero took a sip of an amber liquid from his highball glass. "How is she doing with everything?"

I sighed and scooted the computer over a little on the kitchen counter so I could work. "She had a couple nightmares last month, but before that it had been months."

My brother tilted his head to the side in thought. "I guess that makes sense since March was the year anniversary since she got taken."

"That's what her psychiatrist said. Overall, she's doing well, but there will be certain things that trigger her."

Fiero's nose wrinkled. "Never put much stock into shrinks, but it sounds like it's been beneficial to Eden. How's married life treating you?" His smirk irritated me.

"It's fine, and wipe that smartass grin off your face."

He guffawed. "I just think it's funny that the guy who said he never wanted to get married is now living in wedded bliss."

My eyes rolled to the top of my head as I pulled the lilac petals from the wax paper with tweezers. The color was perfect. "Did you want to have this meeting for any particular reason? Or just to bust my balls?"

"I have a reason. The ball busting is just a perk." He drained his glass and disappeared from the screen while he kept talking. "Wanted to let you know Luca is looking for Guido."

I paused my decorating and stared at the screen until Fiero returned with a refilled glass of liquor. "Well, he's not going to find him." *Because I splattered his brain against the wall of an airplane hangar.* "Do I need to be worried?"

"He did some checking and noticed one of Guido's cars was missing. You know anything about a Ford Explorer?"

A relieved breath pushed from my lungs. "We... borrowed that, but Robert took it to a chop shop," I told him. "There shouldn't be a trace of it. Why's Luca just now noticing?"

My brother waved a dismissive hand. "You know he doesn't deal with the guys in New Orleans too often. Only when he needs something. He had a shipment he needed picked up at the port in New Orleans, so he called everyone's favorite douchebag."

I chuckled as I arranged the petals on the cupcake. "Eden called him Flava Flav."

Fiero barked out a laugh. "Fucking classic. Luca's not too worried about Guido's disappearance since he was a low-level associate. He reckons he took the money he earned from placing the bomb in the helicopter and hightailed it to Vegas. Just thought I'd check in with you and make sure there was no trace of him to be found."

"There's not," I assured him.

Glancing over, I noticed he was leaning toward his screen, peering at what I was doing. "What the fuck is that?"

"A lilac," I told him, holding the cupcake up so he could see.

"You bringing work home from the bakery now?"

"Nah, this is for Eden. She likes lilacs."

My brother gawked at me. "She likes lilacs, so you made her a cupcake with a frosted lilac on top?"

"Yes," I said defensively. "I make desserts every Friday, and I always decorate something for her."

He leaned back in his chair and threw his head back in laughter. "You are so pussy whipped."

"Fuck off," I grumbled, ready to end this chat.

"Are you even getting laid, or are you two still just pretending to be married?"

Placing the cupcake on a platter with the others, I leaned my butt against the counter and crossed my arms over my chest. "I've had more sex in the past two months than I'd normally have in a year," I told him, taking my own opportunity to be smug. "How about you?"

"I had a threesome with these twins last night. Blondes with big tits." He held his hands in front of him in an estimation of their extreme bustiness. "Colleen and Carissa. Or was it Calista?" My prick of a brother stared at the ceiling as he tried to remember. "Hmmm, whatever. They're still upstairs, so I'll ask them when I go back up."

"Congratulations," I said dryly. "Sounds very meaningful."

Fiero leaned forward with both arms on his large mahogany desk, his brown eyes slightly darker than mine when he peered at me on his screen. "That's the whole point though, right? Quick and easy lays without any meaning? That's always been our credo."

"It has," I said, leaving out the *but* I wanted to tack onto the end, but my brother beat me to it.

"But?" he asked, and he was really getting on my damn nerves.

"I'm trying to make this work. Eden got thrown into this through no fault of her own, so I'm doing my best to make it easier on her. To be a good husband."

My brother's lips pursed and he nodded. "That's admirable. So you're being discreet with your side pieces?"

I wanted to punch the damn screen with his face on it, but I balled my hands into fists at my sides. "No side pieces," I informed him through gritted teeth.

"No... side... chicks? At all?" he drawled slowly, as if he were attempting to understand each word individually.

"None." That's all he needed to know.

He appeared genuinely perplexed. After all, our father always had women on the side. The only good thing I could say about Luca was that he had kept that shit on the down low and hadn't flaunted it in front of Mama. It wasn't until after she'd died that he'd started bringing women to his home.

"But..." Fiero shook his head. "I was under the impression you and Eden had separate rooms for the first few months. I remember you making comments about *my room* or *Eden's room*. You weren't fucking anyone else during that time?"

"No, Fiero," I sighed and then had to fight a grin as an idea popped into my head. "Well, except for Rosie."

"I knew it," he crowed, shifting in his leather chair and leaning closer to his laptop. "What does this Rosie look like?"

I held my hand in front of my face and pretended to talk to my palm. "Rosie, would you like to meet cousin Fiero?" I turned it around to face the screen and waved. "Fiero, this is Rosie Palms."

His eyes rolled back so far I was afraid he'd dislodge them. "Jesus, you're fucking stupid." Then a wicked grin crossed his lips. "Wait, if Rosie is my cousin, then she's yours too. So every time you jack off, you're fucking your cousin. That's sick, dude."

I couldn't help but bark out a laugh. "Shut the hell up and tell me what's going on with Luca."

Fiero groaned and ran a hand over the top of his dark head. "Not much. The motherfucker keeps everything compartmentalized. There's not one single person who knows everything he does because he's so paranoid."

"Which, I hate to admit, is smart. That way no one can take him down from the inside."

My brother nodded. "Exactly. The one who probably knows the most is Manny."

"Makes sense since Manny is his consigliere. And he's completely loyal to Luca?"

"A million percent. Our father could tell Manny to shoot off his own dick, and the fool would ask if he wanted him to aim for the balls too."

"You paint a lovely mental picture," I said with a grimace. "So what you're saying is that you don't have enough tangible evidence to bring our father down?"

"Not yet," Fiero said, with a sad shake of his head. "I do my best to eavesdrop as much as possible, and I've started asking to sit in on meetings under the guise of *wanting to learn more about the family business.*" He sneered that last part. "And there's no way to plant a listening device. The old fucker has all his offices and cars swept three times a day for bugs."

"Paranoid asshole," I muttered, feeling my mood sink. I didn't know why I always got my hopes up every time I called or had online meetings with my brother, but I did. "Thanks for trying though."

"No prob. I want you back here as much as you want to come back."

"Fiero," I warned, pulling my Florida Marlins ball cap off and readjusting it on my head, "you know I'll never be able to come back to New York.

Even if Luca eventually goes to jail for good and we determine it's safe for Eden to return, my betrayal will never be forgiven. You don't just fucking leave the family."

Our thoughts were that if Luca got a life sentence, he would have no reason to go after the Bouviers, even if Eden pointed the finger at him. A life sentence was a life sentence, and he wouldn't fuck with a powerful family unless it was to save his own skin.

That was probably wishful thinking though. Who the hell knew what that crazy bastard would do? The ideal situation would be for one of his enemies in the joint to shank him to death in the shower. That was the only way we could be sure Eden and her family would be safe. And I wasn't above paying someone to make that happen.

Fiero drained the rest of his glass and slammed it down onto the leather blotter on his desk. "Shit, I know. On a better note though, I haven't heard Luca talk about the Bouviers in a long time. I think he considers that issue closed."

"Because he's convinced she died with me in the helicopter explosion," I added, and he bobbed his head up and down.

"Yeah, that was way too close for comfort. If I hadn't overheard his conversation..." Fiero trailed off, a shiver shaking his shoulders.

"You saved our lives," I said quietly. "I'll never be able to thank you enough."

"Fuhgeddaboudit. Don't go gushing all over me. You'll make me blush," he teased before changing the subject. "How's the new house?"

"Excellent. Lots of amenities. We have a small sauna next to the workout room, and there's a hot tub on the lanai out back."

"Such a fancy pants with your lanai. What is that anyway?"

I laughed and spoke a bit louder as I went to the fridge to pour myself a glass of iced tea. Eden and I had both started drinking a lot of the sweetened drink in the past few months.

"It's like a cross between a patio and a sunroom. It's got a concrete floor and is on the back of the house like a patio, but it has windows like a sunroom, though ours are just screens and not glass. It leads out to the pool."

"Why do you need a pool when you live right near the ocean?"

"Well for one, sometimes conditions aren't good for swimming in the ocean, and for another, we have a tall privacy fence so we can skinny dip without getting arrested."

Fiero laughed. "Ahhh, that's the important thing."

My ears perked up when I heard Eden's footsteps on the lanai, and I quickly turned my cap around backward. She loved when I wore it like that.

I kept my gaze on the door even as I spoke to my brother. "Damn straight. We still have a gorgeous ocean view from the upstairs balcony since it's above the fence line. It's pretty much a dream house." My heart sped up when I saw my pretty wife enter through the kitchen door dressed in tiny denim shorts that made me a bit slack-jawed and a lightweight green sweater that hung off one shoulder. And the turtle necklace. She wore that every day.

Eden's eyes roved up and down my body, from my bare feet, gray sweatpants, white tee, and backward ball cap—what she teasingly called my man-slut outfit. She gave me a look that almost incinerated those very clothes from my body.

"I need to come visit this dream home," my brother mused, and I swung my head back around. Hell, I'd almost forgotten he was there. When I opened my mouth to protest what he'd just said, Fiero beat me to it, holding both hands up, palms out. "I know, I know. Too risky. I'd never want to inadvertently lead someone to your front door."

Eden stepped up beside me and waved at the screen. "Hi, Fiero."

A grin widened across his mouth. "Hey! How's my favorite sister-in-law?"

She laughed. "Your only sister-in-law is doing good. I was at my friend Charlisse's house."

"I told you I'd come walk you home," I told her, glancing at the receding light through the window over the sink.

"Her house is across the street," she said, giving me that *you're ridiculous* look she reserved just for me. "It's not even dark yet."

I glared at her but she merely lifted her eyebrows and then pinched me on the ass. "Ow, wench."

Fiero's chuckle came through the speaker. "What did you do, Eden? Slap his dick?"

She giggled. "No, just a butt pinch."

"Try slapping him right in the junk pouch next time. That'll really piss him off."

Eden tilted her head to one side, like she was seriously considering it, as I grumbled, "Don't give her any ideas, asshat."

"I think I'm going to go for a swim," Eden announced before twiddling her fingers at the computer. "Bye, Fiero."

"Later, Eden."

She gave me a light tap on my crotch, not enough to hurt, but enough to get my attention. Then she winked at me and headed back toward the door leading outside. *Not* upstairs to change into a swimsuit. *Fuck. Yes.*

The shirt came off first and dropped to the floor near the refrigerator. Then the shorts and shoes as she walked out the back door.

"Bro, what are you looking at?" a voice said from what seemed like very far away.

When her black satin panties hit the window in front of me, I didn't say a word, just shut the lid on the computer. He'd figure out that the meeting was over. My grin was so big it made my cheek muscles hurt as I stripped off my shirt on the way across the kitchen at a full run.

The backward hat and gray sweats... they do it every time.

CHAPTER 31

SIXTEEN MONTHS IN HIDING

"You made this?" Dane asked, looking with suspicion at the cake with its silky smooth white frosting and multicolored sprinkles.

"I made the frosting and the cake layers—which were only slightly crooked, I might add—and then took them to Barry. He worked his magic on it." I made a grand gesture over the pretty confection. "And voilà! A perfect masterpiece for my husband's birthday."

Dane's smile was huge. "No one has made me a birthday cake since..." A hint of sadness dimmed the curve of his lips.

"Since your mom?"

He looked over at me and nodded. "Yeah."

"I'm sorry," I fretted. "I didn't mean to upset you."

His arms wound around my waist and pulled me hard against him as he silenced me with a toe-curling kiss. Pulling back an inch, he pecked the tip of my nose. "Don't apologize. I love it. Thank you, baby. And for the record, I wouldn't have minded if it had been crooked with lumpy frosting."

I couldn't help my giggle. "I can bake, but my decorating skills are abysmal."

"Is this where I'm supposed to lie and say you're an excellent decorator?" he asked, and I smacked his chest.

"Yes! You're supposed to tell me my cupcakes are pretty."

His large hands slid down to cup my bottom and give me a squeeze. "This cake is really pretty. I'm a huge fan."

"You're a huge perv," I corrected, pushing away and pulling the pan of lasagna from the oven. "Let me just pop the garlic bread in, and then we'll be good to go."

Over our dinner of salad, lasagna, and bread, we talked about his day at the bakery. As we cut into the cake, I shifted the conversation.

"I met a lady named Maz today. She's one of the veterinarians at the Turtle Hospital. I called them because I found a male loggerhead in distress this morning on the beach."

"That's that big green building up on the highway?"

"That's the one. They do rehab on injured or sick sea turtles and then release them back into the wild. They also do a lot of research and collaborate with universities."

"That's cool," he said, taking a bite of cake and closing his eyes as he savored it. "This is really good, Eden. The flavor is amazing."

"Thank you," I replied before veering back to the turtle topic. "There's an outreach program where workers visit local schools to teach kids about conservation and about the animals." I poked at my cake. "Maz asked if I might be interested in helping out with that."

I watched him for a reaction, my shoulders sagging with relief when he smiled. "That would be awesome, babe." He picked up my hand and kissed the back of it. "You'd be really good at that because it's something you're passionate about. You can talk turtles in your sleep."

That made me laugh. "So you think I should do it?"

"If you want. I thought you were going back to school though."

"This job is only part-time. I can do both. Plus, my degree will be in marketing, and this could be considered a type of marketing. Like I'm selling turtle conservation."

Dane tilted his head to the side in thought. "That's true. I think you should go for it. They'd be lucky to have you." He reached out and stroked the back of my hand, gently asking, "Is the turtle okay?"

Warmth spread through my veins at his praise and his concern. It wasn't that I needed his permission to take the job—because fuck that shit—but it felt damn good to have his acceptance.

I turned my hand over and linked my fingers with his. "They took him back to the hospital. He's going to be fine in a couple months."

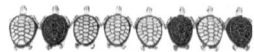

As I used a ladle to pour scented water over the hot coals, Dane leaned his head back against the top bench of the sauna and closed his eyes. He was seated on the bottom bench, his body on glorious display with only a white towel wrapped around his waist. *What was it about a man in a white towel that was so freaking yummy?*

"That one smells good. What is it?" he asked when I sat beside him with my towel draped around my torso. We'd been testing out different drops you could add to sauna water to infuse the space with various scents.

"Chamomile and lavender," I replied. "It's supposed to be good for relaxation."

"Mmm, it's working," he said dreamily, reaching for my hand.

We relaxed for a few minutes, both of us with our eyes closed. It had taken a while for me to be comfortable in the confines of the sauna. I still didn't go in alone, only with Dane. That helped a lot.

When I opened my eyes and crooked my head to look at him, I found the first droplets of sweat dotting his body. He had a little bit of dark hair—not too much—on his chest, and it tapered down across his abs and straight into that damn towel.

"What?" he asked, peeking one eye open and seeing my heated gaze. One side of his lips crooked up in understanding. "Oh. You hungry, baby?"

My attention dropped lower, finding a tent beginning to form beneath his towel. I tugged the knot at his waist and pulled back the edges, watching as his cock continued to grow against his belly.

"I'm very hungry. You should feed me," I purred.

His brown irides flamed hotter than the sauna as he urged me to my knees on the floor between his thighs. "Wait," he said, reaching for a clean towel and wedging it beneath my knees. Then he spread his legs and leaned back like a god waiting to be worshipped.

And I did. Starting at the root, I traced the thickest vein with the tip of my tongue, inhaling the scent of chamomile, lavender, and aroused male. It was a heady combination.

When I reached his crown, I made my way back down, finding the trail of another beautiful vein that required my attention. Then I flattened my tongue and licked a wet stripe all the way up the underside of his impressive length.

"Happy birthday," I told him before taking his head into my mouth and sucking. Hard.

"Dear god," he cried, his hands immediately sinking into my hair. "You have the best fucking mouth, Wildcat. So damn hot and wet. Touch me, please."

He pulled my head down until my nose pressed against his groin, and I worked my throat around his tip with gulping pulses. With one hand, I cupped his tight, swollen balls, rolling them in my palm as my other hand stroked up his abdomen and over his chest. I'd learned what he liked during the past few months, and he loved the touch of my hands while he was in my mouth.

"Goddamn, Eden."

Pulling off him, I looked up into his hooded eyes. "I like the way you say my name."

Then I went back to work as he chanted my name like a filthy prayer. "Eden, Eden. Yes, Eden. So fucking good. I have the dirtiest little wife. "

I increased my pace, bobbing my head up and down faster and faster with every tug of his hands in my hair. As soon as I felt him pulsing against my tongue, I readied myself for the inevitable spurts of his release, but he pulled me away from my task.

His chest rose and fell with his heaving breaths. "I'm coming in that sweet cunt of yours, but first, I'm feeling a little hungry myself."

"I just fed you cake," I teased as he bent down and lifted me by the waist.

"Stop being a smartass and sit up here." With little effort, Dane had me seated on the top bench while he kneeled on the lower one.

He growled before pulling off my towel and burying his face between my breasts. With long, slow licks, he dragged his tongue up and down my torso.

"Dane, stop it. I'm all sweaty," I protested, trying to push him away, but he refused to relent.

"I know," he murmured, continuing to lap at my feverish skin before finally diving in between my legs. My husband was always ferocious when he went down on me, using his tongue, lips, and teeth to maximum effect. He fucking loved it as much as I did.

"That feels amazing," I breathed, pressing my palms against the wooden seat as Dane yanked my legs further apart. I looked down and watched him devouring me, perspiration dripping down my face and naked body. One of his hands slid up to squeeze my breast as his other one wrapped around his turgid cock.

"Nothing tastes better than you," he groaned, licking through me before lapping at my clit with long, slow strokes. "I come so hard when I have your taste on my tongue while I fuck you."

He continued using his mouth to bring me higher and higher, his dark head tilting from side to side as he ate every single inch of me. I reached down to grasp the back of his head, grinding myself against his face until I screamed out my orgasm to the cedar roof.

Dane's grin was wrought of satisfaction when he lifted his wet face to look up at me. My own smile crept across my lips as he took one last lick, coating his tongue with... me.

Then he surprised me when he stood, walking to the pan in the corner and spitting onto the hot coals. The sizzle filled the air as he turned to me and said, "Fuck chamomile and lavender. I want this place to smell like my wife's pussy."

Well.

Dr. Dirty Talk has entered the chat.

A second later, he had me pushed to my back on the bench and was stretching his long body over mine, his cock pulsing at my entrance. With his burning gaze locked on mine, he pushed into me in one sharp thrust, causing both of us to groan.

The wood was warm against my back, but it had nothing on the heat radiating from Dane's body as he began to move inside of me. His hair was pulled back at the nape of his neck, and I reached up to pull the elastic out, allowing it to form a curtain around us. There was something so intimate about that, and my heart squeezed in my chest.

I love you.

The thought slammed into me like a runaway freight train, and I spoke before I could stop myself. "Dane, do you love me?"

He immediately stopped moving, his brown eyes widening in shock and... something else.

Shit. Shit, shit, shit.

Before I could even attempt to think of a way to brush off my hastily asked question, Dane pulled my legs around his waist and began thrusting into me again.

"Baby girl, every single molecule of air in my lungs belongs to you. Every drop of blood in my veins is yours. When my heart beats, it's your name it calls."

He fucked me with a vigor I had never experienced before, his body sliding up and down mine, lubricated by our combined sweat. The sounds of flesh on flesh met my ears, and I cupped his beautiful face, completely mesmerized as he continued talking in a low rasp.

"You are my everything, Eden. My morning, noon, and night. I would conquer the world for you... drain the seas and burn down the forests if it meant you would be mine."

Oh. My. God. That was the best declaration I'd ever heard, and I tangled my hands in his hair and yanked his mouth to mine. We shared a groan as the head of his cock found a spot deep inside me and hit it with every hard thrust. When he circled his hips, my knees slid up his ribcage, giving him a new angle, and I dug my heels into his firm ass, urging him on.

Dane set a relentless pace with his hips, though his tongue remained unhurried in my mouth, tasting me with gentle, passionate lashes. An orgasm tingled along my nerve endings, and my butt lifted and fell in a perfect counter-rhythm to his body. We were both drenched in sweat, and he slid one hand down my slick body to cup my ass and tilt my pelvis up another inch.

"You're perfect for me," he murmured against my lips. "Your pussy forms around me until it's in the shape of my cock. We were made for each other."

And that pushed me over the edge, the wildfire of my climax eating me up as Dane rode me through it. I was sobbing when he lifted his head to look at me, and panic flashed across his gorgeous face.

"I'm sorry, Eden. Did I hurt you?" he asked, stilling inside me and brushing my soaked hair from my forehead. "I'm so sorry. I got carried away."

"You didn't," I promised him. "It was just intense but so perfect."

He breathed out his relief, kissing away my tears before resting his forehead against mine. "Thank god. I was so worried I went too far. I never want to—"

"You don't have to treat me like a china doll," I broke in, feeling two lines form between my eyebrows. "You can be rough with me, Dane. You can even... fuck me from behind." I could hear the glimmer of hope in my voice with those last words. He hardly ever took me like that, and when he did, I could tell he was holding back.

His erection—still hard as stone since he hadn't come yet—jerked inside me. *He wants it as much as I do.* "I want to, but I always worry it will trigger you since... you know..."

"Don't treat me like I'm damaged," I told him, my voice sharp. At his startled look, I softened my tone and cradled his cheeks in my hands. "I'm tired of being a kidnap victim. I just want to be a woman. I want my husband to hold my hips and drive into me from behind without worrying that I'll have a panic attack. I'm not afraid of you, Dane."

He studied my face for a long moment, a muscle twitching in his jaw, and then he pressed a kiss on my forehead, my nose, my mouth, before pulling slowly out of me. "Turn over, Eden. Get on your knees and drop to your elbows."

I almost broke my damn neck turning over and assuming the position. Dane growled, a feral sound that reinvigorated the throb between my legs.

"You have no idea how goddamn sexy you look, baby girl," he said, gripping my hips with both hands as he notched the head of his cock against my pussy. Then he took me with a brutal thrust that almost knocked me over. Bracing myself on my forearms, I accepted the onslaught of his ferocious fucking. He was definitely not holding back now.

His big cock tunneled into me over and over, and he slid one hand up my spine and gripped the back of my hair. "Yes!" I cried out, pushing back against him as he rode my ass with loud slaps of his hips against my bottom.

"Mine," he grunted. "All fucking mine." Dane was a beast, primal and wild, and my mouth dropped open, trying to deal with all of him. He'd never been this deep inside me, this rough and uninhibited.

"That feels so good," I moaned. The scent of hard sex mixed with sweat in the humid air, and my fingernails clawed against the wood beneath me.

"You're so beautiful and strong, Wildcat. You may have cracks, but you're not broken." He leaned over my back, sinking his teeth into my shoulder and sucking hard enough to mark me. "I want to break you, though. I want to tie you to the bed and break you into a million pieces."

His lips moved up the side of my neck until his voice was right in my ear as he continued to fuck me like an animal. "And then I want to glue you back together with my kisses, Eden. I'll be your maker, and you'll belong only to me."

Dear god. This man...

"I'm already yours," I panted, tilting my face for a kiss. His tongue dominated mine, and I felt his dick swell inside me, the telltale sign that he was about to come.

"Eden, I'm right on the edge. Can't hold back anymore." Reaching between my legs, he massaged my clit with two fingers, applying the perfect amount of pressure.

And he took me over the edge with him.

CHAPTER 32

NINETEEN MONTHS IN HIDING

Well, I fucked that up.

It had been three months since that night Eden asked if I loved her, and I still cringed when I remembered that I hadn't said the words she needed to hear. All the other things I told her had flowed from my lips like a waterfall, and I'd meant every syllable, but the L-word had eluded me.

I knew I loved Eden with every fiber of my being, so why the hell wasn't I able to say the words? Maybe because I had never said them to a woman before, other than my mother, and that had been years ago. Had I ever even said it to my sister? Not that I could recall.

I love you.

It was a simple enough statement... only three words, eight letters. But they held so much meaning. *Man the fuck up, Osbourne. Tell your wife how you really feel.*

That was the plan. I was going to tell her tonight. Come hell or high water, those eight letters were going to come out of my mouth, into her ears, and hopefully, straight to her heart.

It was October, and turtle mating season was over, though Eden spent a few days a week at the Turtle Hospital on top of the eighteen-hour class load she was taking. In honor of the end of the season, I'd told her I was taking her on a little weekend getaway to Miami.

After an excellent dinner of Cuban food, we found ourselves in a steamy nightclub with bodies all around us on the wood dance floor. Despite all the other people, I only had eyes for my wife. She was so fucking beautiful in a sparkly pink dress and silver heels that gave her a good five inches of height. The rhinestone nose ring in her right nostril matched the dress.

She was brilliant and vibrant, standing out like a beacon in the crowd—at least in my eyes—as she threw her hands over her head and shimmied her body to the pulsing beat. I, of course, was doing the *dude dance*, which consisted of minimal arm movements and only a slight sway of my hips as my feet moved side to side. I wasn't a big fan of dancing, but I was a huge fan of watching my wife dance, so here we were.

I was half-chubbing in my pants from watching her. The circle skirt flowed around her thighs when she spun in a circle, showing off the thin criss-crosses across her otherwise bare back.

I love you. The thought played like a broken record in my head, repeating itself every single time I looked at her. I was a fucking goner for her.

Another song came on, this one slower, and Eden's eyes lit up. "I looooove OneRepublic," she managed to coo and yell at the same time, tossing her arms around my neck. She was a little tipsy, definitely not sloppy drunk, just enough to enjoy herself.

The sweet lyrics of "Stop and Stare" came on, and I roped my arms around Eden's waist, moving my hips a little more now that she was plastered to my body. My half-chub hardened to a steel pipe against her swaying body, and her brown eyes flashed with pure wickedness when she noticed.

"Can we go back to the hotel after this song?" she asked, her lips a hairsbreadth from mine.

"That would probably be best unless you want to get fucked on this dance floor."

Eden sank her teeth into her bottom lip and lifted one leg, hooking it over my hip and anchoring her ankle against my butt. "Is this how you'd fuck me in front of all these people?" Her voice was a purr, her soft lips moving against mine as she spoke.

Taking her mouth, I bent my knees to cradle my cock against her sex, holding her ass with both hands. And then we dry-fucked right on the dance floor with bodies all around us. I barely noticed them. I was lost in Eden, the stroke of her tongue synchronized with the raunchy rhythm of our grinding hips. I'd never been more turned on in my life.

Our bodies were sticky with sweat, my white dress shirt clinging like Saran Wrap to my chest and stomach as I mimicked what I was planning to do to her when we got to our room. A good, hard fuck. Damp bodies writhing together in the most carnal of dances.

Bending my head, I took one of her nipples into my mouth, sucking hard as she cried out, her hands tangling in my hair. It was loose around my shoulders, other than a tiny braid Eden had fashioned and tucked behind my ear. My dick throbbed in my pants, attempting to break free when her nipple hardened into a bullet against my tongue through the thin fabric of her dress. She obviously was not wearing a bra.

I thought about picking her up and carrying her to the restroom to take her there, but I didn't want to fuck my wife against the wall of a dirty bathroom. Not when we had a perfectly good hotel room that was less than ten minutes away.

Thankfully, the song came to an end, and I unwound Eden's leg from my waist before straightening the circle skirt of her dress. Her eyes held the same heavy heat as mine.

"Let's go," I told her gruffly, taking her hand and leading her to the corner booth we'd shared. I'd been wearing a suit jacket and tie for dinner but had shucked both before she'd dragged me onto the dance floor at this club. Picking them up, I wrapped the tie around her neck and slung the jacket over one of my shoulders.

We'd only made it halfway to the front door when Eden stumbled, grabbing hold of my arm. "Shit!" she said when I turned to see what was wrong. "My heel broke." I looked down to see the heel of her left shoe hanging at an odd angle.

"I gotcha," I told her, scooping her up like a bride and striding the rest of the way to the door. She giggled against my neck, and it was the best fucking sound I'd ever heard.

Once outside, I set her gingerly on her feet. "I'll go get the car. You stay right here by the door." Most of the street was dark, but the sidewalk in front of the nightclub was lit by a single overhead light and bright neon signs in the windows.

Her eyes glistened in the dim October night, and she pinched my ass. "Hurry up, husband."

Motherfucker, that's hot.

Giving her a quick, hard kiss on the lips, I took off at a jog to reach the parking garage two blocks away. The evening air against my wet shirt did little to cool the flames inching across every inch of my body. Despite my inability to say those three little words to my wife, our passion hadn't suffered a bit over the past few months. We were constantly wild for each other.

I started the vehicle, exited the garage and looped around the block, pulling up on the street in front of the club, my eyes immediately finding the sparkle of her pink dress. But she wasn't alone.

I'd heard people say their vision went red when they were angry, but my sight was clouded only by darkness. Like the pits of hell, so deep that there were no more flames, only the blackest of ash.

Slamming the vehicle into park, I reached for something in my console before leaping out of the car and sprinting to the sidewalk where a big, hairy motherfucker was talking to Eden.

"Yeah, baby. I'm gonna get all up in those little panties of yours. What color are they? Bet they're red, aren't they? Like whore panties." Neither of them noticed my approach. This hairy asshole would never survive in the wild because he obviously didn't sense the presence of a true predator right behind him.

Eden took a limping step backward, her broken heel scraping across the concrete. "No. Back off, asshole. My husband will be here in about twenty seconds." *More like two seconds, baby.*

The man's filthy mouth continued spewing slurred words at her as he laughed and took another step toward her. "Fuck your husband. I'm going to be the one in your panties tonight, sweet thang. You ain't ever—"

He was unable to finish whatever bullshit he was about to say because as soon as his grubby hand grasped her shoulder, my arm was around his thick throat, the tip of my knife pressed into the flabby flesh beneath his chin. I had several inches of height on him, but he probably outweighed me by twenty or so pounds. Nevertheless, I had the element of surprise—as well as an all-consuming rage—on my side, and within seconds, I had dragged the startled prick deep into the brick-lined alley where only a sliver of light reached us.

"What the fuck?" he said on a strangled breath.

I pressed the knife upward until I felt the flesh give way. Just a bit. I wasn't ready to kill him quite yet. The scent of fear rolled off his skin and filled the alleyway. I'd almost forgotten that smell, the way anxiety changed the chemistry of a person's sweat into something mustier. It was probably not discernible to most people, but to a man like me... Yeah, I reveled in that shit.

"Who the fuck do you think you are to speak to my wife like that? To fucking *touch her*?" I hissed into his ear.

"I'm... I'm... Jeb," he replied like I had actually been asking his fucking name.

"Good to know. I like to know the names of the people I kill," I say coldly, drawing a whimper from his lips. *Not such a big man now, are you?*

"I'm sorry. I didn't know."

In a flash, I had him swung around to face me, the blade of my knife now flat against his fleshy neck. "*You didn't know?*" I bit out, my voice suffused with rage like an overfilled balloon. "When she told you to back off, you didn't fucking *know?*"

"I was just having... a little fun."

"Fun." Every muscle in my jaw was tensed so tightly I was surprised they didn't snap. "It's fun to rape a woman? Is that what you're telling me?"

"I-I was... I thought she wanted it."

My hand trembled with the need to gut him from stem to sternum. "She. Said. No." Each word snapped like the deadly strike of a cobra. "No is a complete sentence."

In a weak attempt, Jeb shoved both hands against my chest, but I didn't budge an inch, my anger rooting my feet to the sticky concrete.

"Look, man. It was a... misunderstanding. I'll just let you go on your way," he cajoled.

I lifted one eyebrow. He'll *let me?*

"How about this instead?" I mused, finding my control because that was scarier to a pussy like this than if I'd gone off in a frenzy. The anticipation heightened the sense of fear exponentially, so I kept my tone conversational as I trailed my knife down his dirty tank top. "How about I cut your measly little dick off, use it to clean out your ears, and then stuff it down your throat until you choke to death on it?"

The smell of urine stung my nose, and I knew he'd pissed himself. I watched as a tiny trickle of blood inched down his throat from my earlier prick beneath his chin. That only fueled my bloodlust. Until...

"Don't." But it wasn't the asshole's voice. No, this one came from behind me, soft and sweet, accompanied by a gentle hand on my back. *My Eden.* "Please don't."

My skin rippled at her touch, and her plea hit me directly in the chest. Eden was the angel to my devil, and I gave a curt nod but kept my eyes on her attacker. I'd honor her request and wouldn't kill him, but there was no way I was letting the asshole get off scot-free.

"Baby," I said quietly, tilting my head but still staring down at the piece of shit in front of me. "Take off your panties."

I could hear the shock in her high voice. "What?"

"Take them off and give them to me. Now." I didn't yell, but my voice was no less commanding, and after a moment's pause, I heard the rustling of clothing behind me.

With a few precise slashes of my knife, I had Jeb's clothes in shreds, and I yanked at his tank top and shorts until the pieces fell to the filthy ground, leaving him naked except for his briefs. He began sobbing but I ignored his tears as I stuck one hand behind me. I felt the soft lace of Eden's panties in my palm a moment later. *Good girl.*

"Now you take off your underwear," I directed the man, and his face crumpled like a baby's.

"Please, mister. No," he squeaked, sounding like a pathetic little mouse as he raised two hands in surrender.

"I'm not touching your piss stain with my hands, so either you take them off, or I will cut them from your body. And to be honest with you, Jeb, my hand is not feeling too steady right now. I might accidentally cut something vital." I held the knife up and faked a hand tremor.

His eyes were as wide as saucers, and I was pretty sure he hadn't blinked a single time since I'd dragged him into this alley. Keeping his gaze on me, he bent and pulled his yellow-stained white briefs down, letting them pool at his feet before standing again. The smell of fear rolling off him was overpowering now, and his face was streaked with tears.

I glanced down and noticed his dick was shriveled up to the approximate size of a peanut. Or maybe that's how it always looked.

"Put them on," I ordered him, shoving Eden's little lace thong into his chest.

I thought it was impossible for his eyes to get any bigger, but they did. "Y-you mean..."

"You said you wanted to get into my wife's panties, so here's your chance."

He clutched the scrap of lace to his chest and shook his head. "I said I was sorry. Please don't make me—"

In an instant, my knife was back at his throat. "Do it. Now."

He swallowed hard and then flinched when the sharp edge of the knife scraped against his Adam's apple. "Okay," he relented, and I backed off enough to allow him to bend and step into the panties.

"Pull them up," I ordered, and he did, his chest heaving with terror and humiliation. He had to work to get the panties over his flabby thighs, the material stretching grotesquely as he finally hitched them up.

The garment was lace on the front, a soft pink color with tiny white bows at the hips. Jeb looked utterly ridiculous.

I tilted my head to the side and regarded him. "What do you think, Jeb? Is it all you hoped it would be?"

His lips pinched together, and I could tell he wanted to yell and curse at me, but he held his tongue, so I prodded. "Do you have something to say to my wife?"

His watery blue eyes darted from me to Eden. "I'm sorry, ma'am."

I gave him a slow nod. "Such good manners, Jeb. I think you've learned a valuable lesson here tonight. From now on, if a woman tells you no, you back the fuck off. Because next time, you might run into someone who's not as sweet as me."

With that, I bent to pick up the remnants of his shirt and pants, leaving the soiled underwear where they sat because *fuck no*. After tossing the shredded clothing into the dumpster against the wall, I fixed my glare on him and said, "You're going to count to one hundred. You will not move until you're done. Understood?"

He nodded as I folded and pocketed my knife before scooping Eden into my arms and backing out of the dark alleyway. Once we were back on the sidewalk, I hurriedly placed her in the passenger seat and brushed a strand of damp hair from her forehead.

"Are you okay?"

She nodded but didn't say a word.

I'd left the vehicle halfway in the street, and other drivers were honking as they maneuvered around my SUV. I tossed up a middle finger as I entered the car and then put it in drive. Pulling into traffic, I gripped the steering wheel so tightly my knuckles ached.

I'd completely lost my temper back there. I would have killed that motherfucker without a second thought if Eden hadn't reined me in. Her rules floated back to me from that day at Jamie and Robert's house.

I'm not living with some Mafia thug.

That means no whacking anyone.

When I pulled up to a red light, I risked a glance at Eden. She was staring straight ahead, her head tilted over against the window.

Before I could think better of it, I blurted, "I didn't kill him."

She didn't move, didn't meet my eye. She only murmured, "I know," and fixed her gaze on the passing buildings.

As I drove, I stayed silent, lost in my own thoughts. The one at the forefront of my mind, the one that made my heart pound so hard, I probably needed to find a hospital with an excellent cardiac wing was...

Is she going to leave me?

CHAPTER 33

Dane was quiet on the drive back to the hotel. It was only ten minutes, but it seemed like hours as the silence pressed down on us like a thousand-pound weight.

I slid my hands beneath my thighs so he wouldn't see the tremble there. Tilting my head against the cool window, I kicked off my shoes and attempted to sort through my feelings. That asshole's fetid breath and the feel of his hand on my shoulder had incited a panic that I hadn't felt in a long time. After being kidnapped once, the thought of someone taking me or hurting me again only added to the overwhelming pressure.

But Dane had been there. He'd saved me. Again. Despite his promise to not kill anyone, he'd been willing to do that to protect me.

I mean, I'm glad I stopped him from committing homicide. We certainly didn't need police involvement in our lives, them poking around and possibly finding out we were living with false identities. But Dane was going to push aside his newfound moral compass and do whatever it took for me to feel safe.

And I'd never loved him more.

I just didn't know how he was feeling about it. He was obviously not doing well because he'd hardly spoken. What if he decided I was too much damn trouble?

Once we reached the hotel, I padded through the lobby on bare feet, and as we rode up the hotel elevator in even more oppressive silence, the fingers of my right hand twisted my wedding band around and around my ring finger. I wished he'd at least touch me.

The walk down the corridor of the eighth floor felt like marching to the death chamber. The muted lighting from the brushed metal wall fixtures lit our way, but I might as well have been walking in darkness.

Dane unlocked the door to our room and led us inside, and just as I opened my mouth to ask him to please talk to me, he surprised me by pushing my back against the door. His brown eyes were darker than I'd ever seen them, almost coal black as he caged me in with his arms and stared at me for an uncomfortably long time.

Then he dropped to his knees on the entryway floor and leaned his head against my stomach, his hands sliding down to hold my waist with a ferocious grip.

"Eden. Please, baby, don't leave me." His words sounded like they had been pried from his chest with a rusty crowbar, the tone both harsh and pleading. *Leave him? What the hell is he talking about?* Before I could voice that question, he raised his head, and I was shocked to see tears swimming above the rims of his eyelids. "I love you, Eden. I love you so much. Please forgive me."

Those words and the rawness of his pain buckled my legs until I was kneeling in front of him, my hands going immediately to his face. His fingers clutched onto them like a drowning man would grab a life preserver.

"Dane, what are you talking about? Why would I leave you?"

His chest rose and fell in rapid huffs. "I promised you I wouldn't kill anyone." He gritted his teeth so hard I could hear the scraping grind before he whispered, "And I almost did tonight. I wanted to hurt him so fucking bad for touching you. For scaring you."

Oh. My. God.

The tips of my fingers dug into his cheeks, and I pulled his face closer until our noses were a mere inch apart. "To protect me. You were protecting me, Dane. You didn't do anything wrong."

Wrinkles formed across his forehead, and his eyebrows pinched together. "But... but you said you didn't want to be with a Mafia thug, and that's what I acted like tonight. I turned back into Damiano." A single tear slipped over his bottom lid and trekked down onto my hand. "He's still inside me."

"Oh, baby," I said softly, kissing the tip of his nose like he always did to me. "Of course he is, and that's not a bad thing."

Dane made a scoffing noise in the back of his throat. "I hate him."

"I don't," I said simply, and his eyebrows lifted in shock. "Damiano saved me first."

"Eden," he started, and I could hear the argument in his tone.

"I love you too," I told him before he could finish. "I love both sides of you—Damiano and Dane—because both of you have saved me in so many ways."

My breath whooshed out of my lungs when Dane grabbed me and crushed me against his chest. With our height difference, my knees no longer reached the ground, so I lifted my legs and curled them around his waist.

"I should have told you. I should have said I loved you that night in the sauna. I'm so sorry, baby."

"Shhh," I soothed, resting my cheek on his shoulder as he buried his face in my neck. "I already knew. What you said to me that night was so much more than three little words. My god, Dane. You have no idea how much you touched my soul with what you said. You bared yourself to me."

"I meant all of it," he wept, dampening my flesh with his tears as my own dripped onto his shirt.

"You don't have to tell me for me to know that. You told me with every night you held me on the veranda... every cupcake... every nose kiss."

When he pulled back to look at me, there was the slightest hint of a smile on his face. Then he tapped my nose with his lips. "You deserve to hear the words anyway. I love you, Eden."

"I love you too, Dane."

And then our mouths crashed together in a mind-bending fusion of desperation and adoration. We were in a frenzy of tongues and lips, teeth, and hearts. Dane held the back of my head and tilted it a little to go deeper, and I felt his kiss all the way to my toes.

Our heartbeats pounded a staccato rhythm against each other's chests as we slowed into a more sensual slide of mouth over mouth. I loved this man with every cell in my body.

"What?" I asked when I felt him smiling against my lips.

"I love you," he said again, a soft laugh breaking through. "I've been so scared to say it, but now it seems so easy. I love you, Eden Osbourne, my wife."

Dear god, help me. My heart...

I pulled back a little and smoothed his hair away from his beautiful face. "I love you, husband." His grin widened at that. "I'm sorry for how I acted early on. I was scared, and didn't know what to do with all my feelings. You were the closest target, but I want you to know I was never afraid of you."

A shadow crossed his face. "I killed four people, Eden."

My fingers twisted in his long hair. "For me. You did that for me, even before you knew me."

"I think I started falling for you the first time I saw you. In that video with your middle fingers held up." Then his fingers drifted over my cheek like he could still see the bruises left in the aftermath of my defiance. "I have zero remorse, Eden. I'm not good enough for you."

"Don't start that shit. You're not getting rid of me that easily," I teased before turning serious again and telling him my truth. "I'm glad Ethan and Felipe are dead. I didn't really know the guard or Guido, but they would have caused us harm, so I'm not sad they're dead either. That means, if you're a bad person, so am I."

Dane pushed to his feet with me still wrapped around him like a koala. "You, my sweet, are not a bad person. You are the best, kindest person I've ever met."

"Even when I call you Dillweed or Dark Lord?"

He arched one eyebrow. "I rather like when you call me Dark Lord. In fact, you can call me that in bed." Easing me to my feet, he said, "Stay right here for a second."

I watched his back as he walked across the room and rummaged in the pocket of his small suitcase. Then I watched his front with equal attention when he returned. He was a gorgeous specimen of man, coming or going.

"What's in your hand?" I asked, focusing on the fist Dane held against his thigh as he approached me.

"So impatient," he scolded playfully, though I could read the wariness in his expression as he took a long pause before speaking again. "Eden, I know you didn't ask for any of this. Neither of us did. We didn't have much choice but to be a married couple."

I felt my eyebrows furrow together. "So, what are you saying?"

"I'm saying..." He swallowed hard and then wet his lips with the tip of his tongue. "I'm trying to say that I know we were put together by circumstances, but I want you to know that I like being married to you."

My eyebrows returned to their normal position, and I tried not to look too giddy. Dane had told me before that he'd never wanted marriage, so this felt like a big freaking deal.

And then he opened his hand.

My eyes almost bulged out of their sockets when I saw the perfect, cushion-cut diamond ring in his palm. "Dane, that is... beautiful."

"I thought you'd like it," he said, lifting it between his thumb and forefinger and handing it to me. "Read the inscription."

I took the ring and turned it until I could read the words on the inside of the platinum band.

In the light and in the darkness... I choose you.

My hand went to my throat, and I attempted to control my breathing. Those were the most beautiful words I'd ever read. "Dane..." I whispered, unable to say much else.

We had a tiny tug of war when he tried to take the ring from me, but I finally relented. He smirked as he dropped to one knee, and I had to lean back against the door for support.

"I know we're already married, but I wanted you to have this ring so you'd know every single day that *I choose you*." Tears streamed down my face as my beautiful man stared up at me with earnest eyes. "Eden Osbourne, will you please choose me too?"

I nodded vigorously as I swallowed the lump in my throat and finally found the ability to form actual words. "I choose you, Dane Osbourne."

In two seconds flat, he had nestled the ring onto my finger beside my wedding band, and he was lifting me once again. His mouth closed over mine with a gentle suction before he breached my parted lips with his tongue. Our kiss was gentle and loving, and I felt like I'd just gotten engaged to the man of my dreams. Except I was already married to him. Kind of illegally, but whatever.

Dane carried me into the bathroom and set me on the pecan-colored countertop. Then he wet a washcloth, and with his tender touch, cleaned my face. It seemed somehow even more intimate than when he cleaned between my legs after sex. When he was done, I took the cloth from him, rinsed it, and proceeded to wipe down his cheeks with the same care.

"Let's go to bed," I told him, laying a soft kiss on his lips. "Give me a minute, and I'll be in there."

After he left, I removed my brown contact lenses and then pulled the terry cloth sash from the white robe on the back of the door, wrapping it a few times around my wrists. When I got into our bedroom, my heart swelled when I saw my turtle nightlights scattered around the room, giving off a soft greenish-yellow glow. I didn't know he'd packed them.

Dane was looking out the tall window at the city, and he turned when he heard me enter the room. His shirt was unbuttoned all the way, giving me a tempting view of his toned chest and abs.

"You know how you said you wanted to tie me to the bed and break me?" I asked, and his brow furrowed as he nodded. I pulled a hefty supply of air into my lungs and lifted my bound wrists to show him. "Then break me."

CHAPTER 34

DANE STARED INTO MY eyes for so long, I wasn't sure he'd heard me, and then his gaze dipped to my hands. The hitching of his breath was the only indication he was affected.

I stood like a statue as he unbuttoned the cuffs of his white shirt, his brown eyes locked onto mine. Then he slowly shrugged it off one shoulder and then the other, revealing his thick arms before removing it and folding it with all the precision of a high-end men's store clerk. The muscles of his arms and torso bunched, even with the simple act of carefully placing the folded shirt on the top of the black lacquered dresser.

My teeth sank into my bottom lip when Dane's hands dropped to his belt and unbuckled it. With aching slowness, he pulled it from the loops, rolled it around one fist, and prowled toward me like a man on the hunt.

He dominated the room with each measured stride, each ripple of muscle, each dark look. Though he radiated danger, I wasn't afraid of him.

"Eden." My name was a vow on his perfect, full lips. He lifted the back of his leather-wrapped fist and rubbed it against my face. It felt cool against my cheek, or maybe that was due to the fever of my skin. His voice was low and gritty when he asked, "Who is in control tonight?"

"You," I said instantly, and Dane shook his head and gave me a disappointed smile.

"Try again."

"By process of elimination, I'll say me."

I could tell he was fighting a smile. "Correct. I may tell you what to do, but you're ultimately the boss. You're in control, okay?"

"Okay," I agreed, moving my face against the leather. He knew how much that word—*control*—meant to me. Once it had been taken from you, you treasured it that much more when someone gave it back.

"Good girl," he said, making my nipples tighten, and like he had some kind of nipple radar, his gaze dropped immediately to my chest.

"Take off your dress for me," he ordered as he unwound the robe tie from my wrists. Taking a page from his seduction notebook, I reached for the hem and lifted it slowly, inching the pink dress upward, revealing my bare body to my husband. His voice went hoarse as I dropped the garment to the floor. "Fuck, you make my heart full, baby girl."

He reached down to my butt and picked me up, and I wrapped my legs around him as his mouth descended on mine. In one hand he held the soft tie from the robe, but he had the leather belt wrapped around his other hand. The dichotomy of those two dueling sensations against my ass cheeks made me wet, and he groaned when my wetness leaked onto his stomach.

"Always so wet for me, Wildcat," he murmured, urging me up and down so my pussy was rubbing against the rough hair on his lower stomach. "You're dripping onto the waistband of my pants. What will the dry cleaner think when I drop off my messy pants with him?"

I kissed my way to his ear and whispered, "Maybe he'll think you're very good at turning your wife on." Biting his lobe, I added, "Or that you're like a teenage boy who came in his pants."

He chuckled and walked me over to the bed, laying me down gently and arranging me on my back with my head on the pillow before straddling my waist. Unwrapping the leather belt from his hand, he laid it beside me before drifting the cushy robe tie down my chest and circling the end of it over my breasts. Goosebumps and extremely hard nipples ensued, which made him smile.

"If it's too much for you, do you remember what to say?" he asked.

"Red for stop. Yellow to slow down."

He gripped the sash and slid it through his fist. "You won't need yellow tonight, Eden, just red or green. There won't be any in between. You're either going to love this or you're not, and I trust you to stop me the minute you feel uncomfortable."

"I will," I promised.

"Good. Now hold your wrists together for me." I did, and he wrapped the plush tie around and around my wrists until they were completely bound together before tying a knot and leaving two long ends. "We still on green?" he asked, nudging a finger between the tie and my wrists to check the tightness.

"Green as grass."

A smile flickered over his lips, and he kissed my knuckles before stretching my arms over my head and tying the ends of the robe sash to the wood slats of the headboard. When he picked up the leather belt, my body tensed.

"Relax, Eden. I'm not going to hurt you."

"Evie," I corrected, and his mouth dropped open. "Just for tonight. Please."

He leaned down and nuzzled my nose with his. "Are you sure... Evie?"

I nodded. "Yes... Damiano."

His hot breath gusted across my face on his groan. "Say it again."

"Damiano," I whispered. "I love both sides of you."

"Mmm, I love both sides of you as well," he said, kissing his way down my neck. "The outside and the inside. And I plan to be on the inside of you very soon. But first..."

He sat up, still straddling me, and folded the belt into a loop, dragging it up and down my chest. Then, without warning, he popped it against my left breast. It wasn't hard enough to hurt, but it did make my nipple rise to rapt attention. Damiano's nostrils flared with desire as he did the same to my right breast, with the same effect.

"Your pretty tits are so responsive. I'd love to put some nipple clamps on you some time." He pulled his attention from my breasts and gave me a hopeful, questioning look.

"We can try that. Can I put some on you too?"

Damiano laughed and scooted back, parting my thighs and rearranging himself to kneel between them. "If that's what butters your bread, Evie, I'm game."

There was a certain thrill to hearing *Evie* from his mouth after avoiding it for so long, like we were doing something clandestine by using each other's real names.

With unhurried precision, my husband dragged the belt down my abdomen until it was between my legs. Then he smacked it against my pussy with a light slap, and my hips jerked off the bed. It felt better than I would have expected.

"Color?" he asked, his voice strained.

"Green," I panted. "Very, very green."

"You want more, Wildcat? You like having your naughty little pussy spanked?"

I spread my legs further apart. "Yes, please."

He glared down at me and growled. "Say my name, and I'll give it to you."

I was fully aware that Damiano Cappitani was in the motherfucking house, and I was entering without a single reservation.

"Damiano, please spank my bad little pussy."

"Fuck," he bit out, giving my sex three more spanks with the belt. Each stung more than the last, but I'd also never been more aroused in my life. My clit felt like it was about to burst like a balloon. "Your cunt is so swollen and red, Evie. And you're soaked. You like this don't you?"

I could feel my arousal dripping down the crack of my ass, and I nodded. "Yes, I need to come," I warned, writhing against the bedcovers.

Damiano unlooped the belt and slid one end beneath me, holding it against my lower back with his hand while pulling the other end through my legs. With the smooth leather against my sex and him holding both ends, he ordered, "Ride it."

My hips lifted and began to move back and forth while Damiano held the belt taut, and it only took seconds until I was coming so hard I did one of those silent scream things. Mouth open. No sound coming out. Then the belt was gone, replaced with his hot mouth closed around me, sucking my pussy as the orgasm went on and on.

"Damiano. Damiano. Damiano," I chanted, finally finding my voice as my hips churned against his face. Euphoria filled me, tingling along every nerve ending until I collapsed back to the mattress.

My husband lifted his dripping face, eyes darker than I'd ever seen them as he rose and straddled me. I watched with rapt attention as he undid his pants and took his heavy cock in his big hand. I couldn't look away from his rough, quick strokes, the purple head swelling before he released all over my bare stomach.

"Evie. Goddamn, I love coming with your taste on my tongue." Damiano's head was thrown back, eyes closed and my juices dripping from his beard and landing on my stomach to mix with his own release.

When he opened his eyes and locked them on me again, I could see the feral love shining in the chocolate-brown depths. Then, with the tip of his index finger, he dabbed one of the spurts of his cum on my chest and drew a heart with it. He did it again with three on my stomach.

"How can you be so sweet and completely debaucherous at the same time?" I asked.

"You ain't seen nothing yet, baby girl."

And for the next hour he used his mouth and hands on my body. Wicked, depraved, and ravenous, he worked me over until I couldn't even count the number of orgasms I had. My back ached from arching off the bed, my hips hurt from being stretched so wide, and my skin prickled from the beard burn that covered literally every inch of my body. As he'd wished, he'd completely broken down all my walls until I was nothing but a pile of mush on wrinkled white sheets.

Finally, unable to take anymore, I called, "Red. Please stop, Damiano."

Immediately, he lifted his head from the mark he was leaving on the side of my breast and released my hands from the binding. Stretching out beside me, he cuddled me close and kissed the tip of my nose.

"Are you okay, Evie?"

I wrapped my arms around his shoulders and rolled to my back, pulling him on top of me. "I'm good. I just needed my arms released." My legs wound around his waist, notching my pussy against his thick erection.

"Can I make love to you?"

Despite all the pleasure he'd delivered, I wanted nothing more than to have him inside me, to be bound to him in the most intimate way. In fact, I craved that connection.

"Yes." My voice was pure gravel from calling his name so many times.

Cradling his hips in between my legs, he pushed into me slowly and stilled, resting his forehead against mine. "You feel so perfect around me. So warm and tight."

With full-body contact, he began to move in and out of me in unrushed thrusts as his hair formed a dark veil around us. "Who do I have now? Dane or Damiano?"

He kissed me softly. "Both."

Smiling against his lips, I said, "Taking two men at once? Damn, I'm a slut."

Damiano chuckled and stroked his thumbs along my cheekbones. "Don't call my wife a slut. She's my good girl."

God, I loved when he called me that.

With a roll of his hips, he went deeper, but still didn't increase his pace. His eyes held mine, and he continued caressing my face with gentle fingers. "I've never felt more connected to anyone in my life," I admitted on a whisper.

"Me neither," he replied before lowering his mouth to mine and piecing together all of my broken pieces with his kisses. Just like he'd promised.

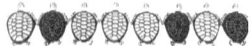

After our sweet lovemaking, my husband carried me to the bathroom—because my legs were not cooperating—and set me beside the toilet. "Take care of your business, and then we'll take a shower."

"I don't want to shower tonight," I said, and his dark eyebrows shot up to his hairline because he knew how obsessive I was about my showers. "I want to sleep with you all over me."

He was unable to fight his smile as he bent to kiss my nose. "Be right back."

I had just finished and stood when Dane returned to the bathroom with his phone pressed to his ear. He was gloriously naked, and I ogled every hard inch of his tall frame as he spoke into the phone.

"Yes, tomorrow. A full-body massage... My wife's name is Eden Osbourne... Yes, that will be fine." A scowl formed on his face, and he answered sharply. "No, a female provider... Okay then... She'll be there after lunch."

"You booked me a massage?" I asked when he hung up, trying not to laugh at his request for a female massage therapist.

"You'll be sore tomorrow," he explained, scooping me up like a bride. "I would do it myself, but we both know where it will lead if I get my hands on your body, and I wanted you to have a little pampering."

"You're too good to me," I sighed, leaning my head against his shoulder as he carried me to the bed.

"I know, but you'll just have to live with it."

"Gladly," I said when he tucked me into bed and crawled in beside me. "Forever."

CHAPTER 35

FOUR YEARS IN HIDING

"No," I said forcefully.

"Yes," Eden replied with just as much fervor.

I walked over to where she was sitting on our couch with her phone in her hand and glared down at her. "You are not getting one of those facepage things."

"It's called Facebook, and yes I am." She stood and propped her hands on her hips. "You can't tell me what to do."

"I can turn you over my fucking knee until you listen to me," I shot back.

"Don't threaten me with a good time, Osbourne," she said, poking me in the chest with her finger, and I fought the need to laugh. God, even when she was being infuriating, she was adorable. "I had a Facebook profile before."

"That has nothing to do with our situation now. What if someone recognizes you?" I demanded, managing to keep my face stoic.

"They won't because I'm not going to post any pictures of myself. I just want to be able to see my family."

"I can put the surveillance team back on them and get videos of them for you," I countered. We'd stopped having her family watched last year since Luca seemed to have lost his concern with the Bouviers.

"That's dumb. This is totally free, and I can follow them on there. I've already talked to Robert about it."

That got my attention. Robert, as our own personal computer guru, was well-versed in the social media craze. "And he said it was okay?" I asked, feeling myself softening to the idea.

"He did. He suggested that I not follow their personal accounts. I can follow the Bouvier business account though because I would just be one of millions.. Monty doesn't seem to have a Facebook page, but Auburn does, and it's not set to private, so I can see what he posts, even if I don't send him a friend request."

That all sounded like Greek to me, but I sighed and flopped onto the couch. "Show me."

"Wow, your brother really gets around," I said, watching as Eden flipped through picture after picture of Auburn and a never-ending line of beautiful women.

She giggled. "The ladies love Auburn. He's quiet and a little broody, so they all think they can change him."

"Looks like he's working for your family's company now since he graduated with his master's degree," I said when she flipped to a picture of Auburn sitting in an office with the city of New York as a backdrop. He was wearing a finely cut suit, and the Bouvier logo was visible on a side wall.

"And Monty's not," Eden replied sadly. "I can't believe he's decided to go into law enforcement. I'm sure it has something to do with my disappearance."

I put my arm around her and pulled her close. Those fucking traffickers had altered so many lives, and I was struck with an idea.

"Would you like to find a nice charity to donate to? One that supports victims of human trafficking?"

She looked up at me with moony eyes and nodded. "I would. Thank you."

I gave her a soft kiss and then watched as she looked up her college friends on the Facebook thing. Arya was in medical school in California, Holly was working on her master's in criminal justice, the Papadopoulos twins were traveling in Europe after graduating, and Juliette McNamara...

"Oh my god, look!" Eden shrieked. "Juli is publishing her book!" She shoved the phone so close to my face, I saw double.

"Okay," I laughed, pushing the device back about a foot. "Looks like a romance book."

"It is," Eden said, a smile taking up her entire face. "She let me read some of it the night before I was taken. She's so talented."

I squinted at the screen. "What's an ARC reader?"

"That's someone who receives an advanced copy of the book to help promote it before and during the release."

"Do you have to meet face-to-face with the author or anything?"

Eden shook her head. "No, you either get a digital copy or a hard copy mailed to you. Then you read it and review it."

I thought through it for a minute before saying, "You should do that. Join her ARC team."

Her eyes shone with tears. "You think that would be okay? I'd love to help promote her, even if she doesn't know it's me."

The idea seemed to bring her so much joy, how could I deny her? "As long as you don't have to meet her in person, I think it would be fine. If she's going to mail you a book, there are mailbox services we could use. To the outside world, your address would be a mailbox in... I don't know... Kansas or something, and then they forward it to you. That might be overkill since she won't know it's you, but I'd rather be safe than sorry. Can we check with Robert on the ARC thing just to make sure before you do it?"

"Of course. That's probably a good idea."

"We'll talk to him tonight. Now you need to go get ready or you're going to be late for your big day."

I was pretty sure my heart was about to burst right out of my chest as I watched my wife walk across the stage and receive her college degree. My throat was clogged with emotion so I couldn't even yell, but it was okay. There was a whole slew of people who'd come to watch her graduate, and they were loud as fuck.

Charlisse and Mimsy were the most vocal, and they both held up hand-made signs when Eden's name was called as Charles and Cooper clapped. Maz, the veterinarian from the Turtle Hospital, was also seated with us, as were about a dozen other people who also worked there with Eden. Robert and Jamie had even made the trip down from Jacksonville.

"It's a good day, boss," Kevin said from behind me where he was sitting beside Barry and Maria from the bakery. He patted my shoulder. "I know you're proud of her."

Eden had worked her ass off and graduated early with honors. Proud didn't even begin to cover it.

"I am," I said, waving at Eden when she looked up at our section and held her arms up in victory. Our crew cheered even louder, and the announcer had to pause for our noise to die down before he could call the next name.

My wife was fucking radiant, and everyone who knew her loved her.

But none more than me.

CHAPTER 36

A MONTH AFTER SIGNING up for the ARC team, I received a package from "Juli Mack," Juliette's pen name. I'd done the whole *rerouting through an out-of-state mailbox* thing, just for safety's sake. It was almost impossible anyone would know it was me, but Robert said being extra cautious was best since the FBI kept tabs on anyone who had been close to me, including my friends. So an extra degree of separation from where I actually lived wouldn't be a bad idea.

I skipped into the house and waved the red and black bubble mailer in the air. "It's here!" I announced to Dane, who was sitting on the couch. My voice was brimming with excitement. Flopping down beside him, I tore open the package and held my best friend's paperback book in my hand for the first time.

"Slow and Low?" Dane asked, peering at the title of the book.

"Yes, the main dude in this book is a pitmaster who owns his own barbecue restaurant. Slow and low refers to the proper way to cook brisket. Slow and on low temperature so it's nice and tender." I ran my fingertips over the smoky cover, knowing my friend had also touched it, and I loved the connection this book gave us.

Dane kissed my temple. "I'll get started on dinner so you can start reading. Potato soup okay?"

"Sounds good," I said, opening the book and almost tearing up at Juli's loopy signature. Then I gasped when I saw my name on the dedication page.

"What?" Dane asked, crowding close as we both read. I could practically hear Juliette's sweet drawl in every word.

To my real life Evie. You believed in me when I didn't even believe in myself. I stopped writing for a while after you disappeared, but then I kept hearing you nag me, and I knew you'd be pissed if I didn't finish.

So, here we are. I did it. And you're not here with me. I miss you more than you could ever know, Evie, and wherever you are, I hope you're safe. I love you, bestie from the nestie.

A fat tear plopped onto the page, and I swiftly swiped it away with the heel of my hand. Dane wrapped a long arm around me and pulled my face into his neck.

"I'm sorry, Eden. You miss her don't you?" I nodded, and he kissed the top of my head. "You want to tell me about her?"

I nuzzled into his warm skin and smiled at the memories flooding my heart. "I met Juliette McNamara when I was seven. We both went to a summer camp near Hot Springs, Arkansas, and were assigned as room-mates. As soon as I walked into the little cabin, I was surrounded by long arms, a flurry of blonde hair, and the smell of citrus." Resting my hand on Dane's hard chest, I said, "I remember thinking she was so pretty and smelled so good."

Dane's hand rode gently up and down my back. "What's the bestie from the nestie thing?"

A giggle escaped my lips. "Everyone at the camp had to name their cabins, and Juli and I decided to call ours The Nest. There was a big robin's nest on our windowsill, so that's how we came up with it. By the time dinner rolled around the first night, she informed me that we would be best friends forever, and so we should be *besties from the nestie.*"

My husband chuckled. "That's both sweet and incredibly weird."

"That's Juliette. She and I became pen pals—like honest to goodness letters, not emails or texts. We wrote to each other every week and promised to see each other the next summer. My mom wanted to send me to some fancy schmancy camp the next year, but I pitched a hissy fit until my dad said I could go back to the Arkansas camp again."

"And you went every year after that?" I nodded, cuddling closer to them.

"Until we turned sixteen, and then we were both counselors. At some point, we decided to try and go to the same college. Juli's dad couldn't afford out-of-state tuition, so I applied to the same Texas colleges she did. Luckily, she got a full ride to SMU, and I was accepted too, so that's where we went." I looked up at Dane, my lips tipping into a smile. "She's the best friend I've ever had. I had lots of friends in high school, but they were more... superficial, I guess. Juli is like my friend soulmate. She and I can talk about anything."

"I'm sorry you don't get to see her, but I'm glad you can communicate with her, even though she doesn't realize it's you." He kissed the tip of my nose. "I'll get started on the soup while you read."

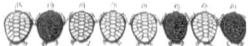

I knew from reading Juli's first fifteen chapters four years ago that she was a gifted writer and that this book was going to be great, but *dayum*. She'd totally upped her game, and I literally couldn't put it down.

"Soup okay?" Dane asked as I flipped to the next page.

"Uh-huh. Good," I murmured, my eyes eating up every word. I spooned some soup into my mouth—at least, I tried to, missing my lips and dribbling it down my chin. "Shit." I swiped at the mess with my napkin but still couldn't peel my eyes from what was happening on the page. This story was compelling as hell, and I couldn't wait to see what was next for Colton and Book Evie.

I was vaguely aware of my soup bowl being removed, and I was unsure how I ended up in bed with one of Dane's T-shirts on. "Here's a book light," he said, and I could hear the amusement in his voice when he clipped it on.

"Thanks, babe," I replied, absently patting his hip when he rolled over and turned off the lamp. With my back against the headboard, I propped the book on my stomach and continued reading. Things were starting to heat up on the page, and I let out a little gasp when Colton rolled on top of Book Evie. *Okay, wow.*

"What?" Dane asked, shifting to his back.

I spared him a glance and lifted an eyebrow. "Things are starting to get *really good.*"

"Somebody getting whacked?" he joked.

"Nope, somebody's about to get licked."

That got his attention, and he scooted closer, resting his cheek on my shoulder so he could read along with me. I heard his breathing hitch as his eyes moved over the spicy scene, and then he slid one big hand down my body and directly into my panties like he owned my pussy. The wetness he found there was evident in his low groan.

"Hmm, this book is turning you on, isn't it?"

"Maybe," I demurred teasingly.

"I thought that was my job. Should I be jealous of this..." He focused on the page and sneered, "Colton?"

"Definitely. He's got a very talented tongue."

My husband growled at my smirking face before jerking the covers back and hooking his fingers onto the sides of my panties and working them down my legs.

"Dane!" I exclaimed. "What are you—"

Shoving my legs apart, he fitted his broad shoulders between my legs and demanded, "Read it to me."

"Oh, I don't think so," I said with a nervous giggle, pushing playfully at him with my foot.

He grabbed my leg and kissed my ankle before settling my foot on his shoulder and then doing the same with the other one. Reaching up and tapping the top of the book, he said, "Read it to me, and I'll do whatever it says on that page." He gave me a challenging look, and I bit my bottom lip, shoring up my nerves.

"Okay, fine."

Dane narrowed his eyes. "But don't fucking say *his* name."

I rolled my eyes. "Oh my god. Are you jealous of a fictional character?"

"Nope. I'm grateful he started the job of turning my wife on. And now I'm going to finish it."

Jeez, how could I say no to that? Knowing my face was all kinds of red, I cleared my throat and began reading, exchanging Colton's name for my husband's. "*Dane kissed down my body, his tongue delighting my skin with every swipe.*"

Dane followed along, his mouth moving down my abdomen before grinning up at me. "Is your skin properly delighted?" he asked.

I giggled. "It is."

"Then please go on," he replied, dropping a kiss on my mound.

I turned back to the book and began reading. "*When he reached the apex of my thighs, he pressed them down with his hands, holding me firmly to the mattress. His tongue swept through my sex. Once. Twice. Th-th—*" I broke off as Dane followed through on everything I was saying.

"Keep reading, Wildcat," he directed, dark eyes locked onto mine.

"*Three times,*" I continued, my gaze flitting between him and the book. "*Then he speared me with his tongue. His aroused hum let me know he was enjoying this as much as I was, and his hands slipped beneath my ass to hold me to his mouth.*"

Dane's eyes closed, and he moaned into me as his hands lifted my lower body, just like the words on the page. Shifting the book to one hand, I reached down and stroked his jet-black hair, smoothing the thick, soft strands against the skin of my thighs.

"He tongue-fucked me with leisurely strokes, the sensation like warm velvet inside me." My breaths were coming out in harsh pants, and my vision began to blur a little around the edges, but I blinked a few times to bring the text back into focus. *"Dane knew my body better than anyone—my moans, the tightening of my inner walls—and when I was right on the edge, he began lapping at my clit with the flat of his tongue."*

I closed my eyes and dropped the book onto the bed, both of my hands in his hair now, rubbing the silk of it against my thighs. Why the hell was that so erotic? Dane's magical tongue worked over my clit as my orgasm began in my core.

"What next, baby?" he murmured, and I cried out the next words from the book, the ones I'd memorized before abandoning it.

"I came, and he bruised my ass with his brutal grip as he devoured my climax like it was his last meal. God, Dane!"

With my head pressed back into the pillow and my spine curved up to the ceiling, I unleashed myself, grinding wantonly against his hot mouth. The feral noises he made between my legs only drove me higher, made me come harder.

As my spasms subsided, Dane's tongue slowed and finally stopped. "I think I like this book," he admitted, pressing soft kisses up and down my sex. "What happens next?"

My body floated back to the mattress, and I dipped my chin to look at him. "That was... the end of the... chapter," I said through heaving breaths.

He crawled up my body and gave me a long kiss, sharing my taste with me, before reaching over to turn the page. "Hmm, this next chapter is from the male point of view." He flipped another few pages to read ahead a bit, and his eyebrows shot upward. "Yeah, I really like this chapter."

"What's it about?" I asked, still trying to control the racing beat of my heart.

"You let me worry about that," he ordered with a smirk before flipping me over onto my stomach like I weighed nothing.

"Do you have to treat me like a pancake?" I complained, and he chuckled and swatted my ass.

"Hush. You're giving me syrup fantasies." Leaning over, he opened the drawer beside the bed and pulled out a bottle of lube, a silicone dildo, and something called a lube launcher, which does exactly what you're probably thinking.

"Ohhh, it's *that* kind of chapter," I said, looking over my shoulder at my hot-as-hell husband. The tent in the front of his black briefs was obvious. Dane had introduced me to anal sex a couple years ago, and to my surprise, I loved it as much as he did.

"It is," he replied, and I could hear the excitement in his voice. "On your hands and knees. You know the drill, Wildcat." Because of Dane's size, I still needed to be properly prepped before we could engage in that particular act. Thankfully, I was married to the most patient man on earth, and over the next twenty minutes, he lubed and stretched me until I was ready for action. The entire time, he kissed up and down my back and massaged my shoulders with his free hand.

Leaning over my back and turning my head to the side, Dane dipped his tongue into my mouth, softly at first, and then with more passion. I could feel the hard length of him throbbing against my ass.

"I love you," he said, looking deeply into my eyes. "You're the most important thing in my life, Evie."

"I love you too," I returned, my heart swelling for this man. Even when he was being dirty as hell, he never let me forget my worth.

"Tell me if I need to stop," he instructed while dragging the book to the side of my body and finding the page he wanted. Then he began to read. "*Evie's ass was round, firm, and absolutely perfect. I'd been obsessed with her pretty backside from the very first moment I saw her in my restaurant in her tight-fitting jeans. I stroked my hands over her cheeks, pretty as a ripe peach and ready to take my cock."*

"God, that's hot," I groaned, loving the feel of his rough hands on me.

"My cock fucking ached with the need to be inside her. I'd had her sweet pussy, but taking her ass would be the final step in making her mine. And make no doubt about it, Evie was mine. 'Spread your legs,' I ordered, and she willingly complied like the good fucking girl she was."

I parted my knees until my hips were stretched as far as they could go.

Dane's deep voice scratched up his throat, evidence of his desire. *"I stroked my hand up and down my length a couple times before bringing the head to her back entrance. I already knew she was going to be tight as fuck. I'd felt that from fingering her ass earlier. Though my body was thrumming to take her fast and hard, I eased in gently, reveling in her soft whimpers as I breached her tiny hole. 'Goddamn, baby. You feel so good.' I worked my way in slowly, reaching around and rubbing her clit with the perfect amount of pressure to make her back arch up like a cat."*

"God that feels so good," I moaned, my fingers clawing at the wrinkled sheet as Dane continued to read.

"Evie's tightness gripped me, pulling me in as I took her deeper before easing out and back in a few times. The sight of my cock disappearing inside her, stretching her, almost made me come immediately, and I had to bite down on the inside of my cheek to keep myself under control. 'You are perfect, baby,' I told her, dipping my middle finger into her cunt before using the wetness on her sensitive clit again."

I lowered my chest to the bed, opening myself up to him even more as he began to move faster. The sensation of being stretched to my limit while his fingers danced over my clit had my toes curling. "More," I begged, rocking my hips with Dane's.

His voice was becoming ragged as the headboard knocked against the wall with forceful thumps. *"I couldn't pull my eyes away from the sight of her ass cheeks vibrating each time my hips slapped against her. 'Good girl,*

Evie. You're such a good fucking girl, taking my cock up your pretty ass.' Her hair was a mess, and I couldn't help but bury my hand in the back of it, holding her down as my thrusts became harsher, more relentless. I was barely hanging onto my control, but Evie didn't seem to mind. She was moaning my name and tightening around me like a vise."

"Dane, I'm close," I rasped as his hand followed the path of his words, gripping the back of my hair as he rode me hard and fast.

Then I was pretty sure he abandoned the book reading because he slumped over my back, rutting into me like an animal. "Fuck. So good, Evie. Love you so much." His mouth moved up and down my neck, sucking and biting as our pace turned frantic.

I unclenched one of my hands from the sheet and reached up and back to tangle in his long hair. "Love you... too," I managed to say as his fingers moved faster between my legs while his other arm banded around my waist and held my body to his. "I'm coming."

"Yes. Fuck. Come for me, Wildcat. I'm going to fucking fill this ass up with my cum."

Burying my face in the mattress, I screamed, the orgasm one of the most intense I'd ever had. Dane bucked against my back, his own roar of pleasure mingling with mine as we found our highs together.

For a long while, we laid like that, his big body covering my small one as we sucked in lungfuls of air. His kisses against my neck turned tender and sweet as he pulled slowly out of me.

"You okay?" he asked, rolling me over and holding himself up on his forearms. Dane's face was red and sweaty, and his hair was a complete mess, but he'd never looked sexier to me.

"I'm so good," I told him, smoothing down a large chunk of his hair on the left side. "Never better."

After a hot bath, Dane and I were back in our bed, facing each other with our limbs tangled together.

"So, you liked the book?" I asked.

He kissed the tip of my nose. "I never knew reading could be that fun. I'm going to get a library card tomorrow."

I giggled and snuggled into his embrace. Though I still missed my family and friends every day, I felt safe and loved in Dane's arms, and I was content... body, mind, and soul.

CHAPTER 37

SIX YEARS IN HIDING

"Smells good, babe," I said, walking up behind Eden and kissing her neck. She no longer flinched when someone approached her from behind, and it had been years since her last nightmare. She was so damn strong, and I loved her more every day.

"Thanks," she replied, leaning her body weight slightly back against me as she removed chicken breasts from the baking pan. "It's a pistachio and parmesan crusted chicken. It will be healthier for Charles without flour or breadcrumbs."

"And what's this?" I asked, stepping to the side to stir some kind of green sauce she had in a bowl.

"Avocado and lime sauce that I'm going to drizzle over the meat when we get there."

"Sounds good." I glanced at the digital clock on the oven. "We should probably get going. Can I help with anything?"

"Just put a lid on that sauce," she directed, wrapping foil over the platter with the chicken. "I'll get the roasted cauliflower out of the oven."

"What do you think they want to talk to us about?"

"Guess we'll see when we get there."

"This is delicious, Eden," Mimsy praised, taking another bite of the juicy chicken. "It was nice of you to cook after working all day. How are things at the Turtle Hospital?"

Eden beamed. "Really good. I'm so happy they took me on full-time after graduation. We had a group of junior high students on a field trip today. They got to watch a rehabilitated turtle get released back into the ocean."

"Y'all do such good work down there," Charles said, forking up a bite of cauliflower. He glanced over at his wife, who gave him an encouraging nod. Turning his head to Eden and me across the table, he started, "Mimsy and I wanted to talk to you two about something."

His eyes found mine, and I set down my fork, my stomach bubbling with nerves. Hopefully, he wasn't firing me from Sweet Heaven. I loved being at the bakery. It was my happy place... when I wasn't with my wife.

"Okay, Charles. What is it?" I asked, hearing the strain in my voice.

"You know I've had to slow down at the bakery since the doc cut off two of my toes." I nodded, a pit forming in my stomach as he continued. "Well, we were thinking it might be time for me to retire."

"You're closing?" Eden asked, putting voice to my fear.

The older couple looked at each other and shared a smile. "Not exactly," Charles replied. "We were hoping you'd want to take over, Dane. You're already there and managing things practically every day."

The bubbling in my belly eased, and I felt my shoulders relax. "Of course," I said, bobbing my head up and down. "Whatever you need."

"Also, I want to sign over ownership of the business to you," he said, and I almost slid right out of my chair and onto the floor.

"But... it's yours. You've worked for years to build it up."

"I'm aware, but I'm old as hell, and to be honest, I'm tired. It's time for the new generation to take over." As I sat in stunned silence, he reached behind him and pulled a manila envelope from a drawer before sliding it across the table. "I had my lawyer draw up some papers. As long as Mimsy and I are alive, you'll pay us a salary, based on profits. Then when we pass on, it's all yours, free and clear. You and Eden will be the owners."

I was stunned into silence, my mouth agape as Eden placed a comforting hand on my thigh beneath the table. "What about your children?" she asked, and Charles scoffed.

"Psshh, they want nothing to do with it. They only come to visit us every couple of years, and neither of them want to move down here to run a bakery. They have their own lives."

"Joseph and Jennifer would sell it, and then god knows who would own it or what they would do with it," Mimsy said with a shake of her gray head. "They could tear it down and turn the property into a condo or something."

Eden's hand squeezed my leg, encouraging me to speak up as my eyes flicked to the envelope on the table and back to the couple across from us. "Wow. I'm not sure what to say."

"You both have been so good to us," Mimsy said kindly. "Dane, you've kept the business running and growing while Charles has been dealing with his diabetes issues the past few years. And sweet Eden cooks dinner for us at least three times a week. You have no idea how much that means to us."

"It's no problem," my wife said, a sappy look on her pretty face. "It's hard to cook for just two people, so we always have plenty."

"Oh, stop blowing smoke up my tailpipe," Charles said, waving a large hand at her. "We all know you've been cooking up diabetic friendly dinners because of me. Mimsy and I feel like you're our adopted children with the way you take care of us, and we adore you both."

"The feeling is mutual," I replied, my voice swollen with emotion. "This place wouldn't have been home if we hadn't met you two."

Mimsy's grin broadened over her lined face. "And to think, you two came down here for your honeymoon six years ago and never left."

"We love it here," I said, meeting Eden's eyes and giving her a soft smile, which she returned. We stared at each other for a long moment before Charles started talking again.

"No pressure at all, but we wanted to at least offer you the chance. Otherwise, we'll just shut down. Kevin and Barry are good workers, but they're just that. Workers. Neither has the gift for management like you do, Dane."

"That's really nice of you," I said, pulling the envelope toward me and resting my palm on top. "I'll take a look at this. Is it okay if I take a few days to mull it over?"

The old man nodded approvingly. "I'd expect nothing less. You've got a good head for business, son."

That last word hit me directly in the chest. *Son.* I wished like hell he'd been the kind of father I'd grown up with.

But at least I had him now.

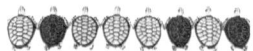

SIX MONTHS LATER

My heart ached as I wrapped my arm around my wife in front of the double grave site. She sobbed against my chest while I did my best to rein in my own sorrow.

"I can't believe they're both gone," she sniffed, taking the linen handkerchief I offered her to dab at her face.

"At least they went together," I said. "I couldn't imagine either of them without the other." Though the comfort of that was minimal, it did help a bit.

Charlisse approached in a black dress, holding Cooper's hand. He was ten now and was dressed in a solemn little charcoal-gray suit with a navy tie. The women hugged, and I squatted down to the boy whose chin was trembling with his mighty effort to hold back his tears.

"Hey, bud. You look sharp today. How you holding up?"

"I miss them," he said in a shaky voice, and dammit, it broke me in two. "But I'm trying to be brave for Mom. Like a man." To my surprise, a tear that I'd been fighting against for five days finally escaped down my cheek, and Cooper reached up to swipe it away with his little finger. His voice was semi-incredulous. "You're crying, Dane."

"There's no rule that says a man can't cry," I told him and watched as his face crumpled. I pulled him against my chest and closed my eyes as his body shook. Fuck, this was so hard. Charles and Mimsy were the best people I'd ever met. "It's okay, buddy. Just let it out."

"Why did they have to be in a car wreck?" he asked in a trembling voice against my shoulder.

I wanted to tell him it was because some fuckwit was drunk at nine in the morning and had plowed into their car while they were going out for breakfast. Instead, I said, "I don't know, Cooper, but I'll miss them too."

"Mimsy was so fun, and Papa Charles always took me to the store and bought me my own can of Pringles." I smiled at the innocence of this sweet child. "I don't see my real grandparents a lot, but I think Mimsy and Papa were like my grandparents."

Casting a glance at Eden and Charlisse, who were fussing over the many flower arrangements, I pulled back and wiped Cooper's tears away before holding him by the shoulders. "I know how you feel. I didn't have a very good father growing up, so Charles was like my dad."

I was unsure why I was opening up to a ten-year-old, but my proclamation felt like the thing to say just then.

"I don't have a dad, so that's why I have to be the man of the house," he informed me, lifting his chin stoically.

"And you're a damn fine one," I told him, "but it's okay to have feelings. I do, and I'm a lot older than you. You're really lucky to have a great mom who loves you more than anything."

An adoring smile crossed his small face when he looked over at his mother. "She's the best, but sometimes..." The kid faltered, and he looked down at his black shoes, the shine of them dulled by a fine dusting of dirt.

"But what, Coop?"

His big blue eyes found my brown ones, and I could see the worry in his expression. "I don't have anyone to talk to about, you know..." He dropped his voice to a whisper. "About *man stuff*."

"Ahh, I gotcha," I said, nodding in understanding. "Well, your mom knows a lot, but if you ever feel like you need to talk to someone else about *man stuff*, you can talk to me."

A smile brightened his adorable face. "That would be awesome, Dane." Lowering his voice to a conspiratorial level, he leaned into my space. "When do you think I'll get hair on my chest?"

I couldn't help my chuckle. "Probably in a few years, buddy. Give it time."

The women returned, and I stood, straightening my suit jacket. "Everything okay?" Charlisse asked, running a hand over her son's neatly combed hair.

"Yup," he replied. "Me and Dane were just talking about man stuff. Like chest hair."

His mom smiled around her bemusement. "Oh. Well, okay. You ready to get out of that suit, Coop?"

The boy's body sagged in apparent relief. "Yes, it's hot out here." It was September, but the Florida sun bore down with a heavy, humid heat.

I looped an arm around Eden as Charlisse took her son's hand. "We'll go home to get changed and then meet you at Charles and Mimsy's house. The other neighborhood folks were headed over to get lunch started." Then her mouth turned down in disapproval, lowering her voice, even though we were the only ones left at the cemetery. "I can't believe their kids showed up for the funeral and then left directly after."

Eden let out a tiny snort. "Yeah, they gave Dane their phone numbers and told him to call when he'd gotten the house and its contents sold. Then they skedaddled like they had more important things to do."

I'd been named executor of the Mimses' wills, and other than a provision about the bakery and a few small bequeathments for some of the neighbors, they'd left everything to their children. But the kids hadn't seemed keen on clearing out the house and going through their parents' things.

"It was pretty shitty," I said before wincing. "Sorry, Cooper."

The kid smiled up at me. "That's okay. My mom says that sometimes when she's doing laundry."

That brought a moment of levity to the moment, and we all smiled as Charlisse lightly chastised, "Way to call me out, son." She lifted an eyebrow in our direction. "Let me tell ya, stain removal for a ten-year-old boy is enough to make a nun cuss."

After they departed, I pulled Eden against my chest and looked at the two mounds of dirt over her shoulder. We'd only known them for six years, but the vibrant couple had become so important in our lives.

Another wave of emotion hit me, and I rubbed my hands up and down my wife's back. She was dressed in a flowy black dress and suede booties, and, as always, her fresh honey scent soothed something inside me.

"Dane?" she questioned, lifting her tear-soaked face to mine. "Promise me we'll die like that. Together. Like Mimsy and Charles."

My heart seemed to deflate and then swell like a balloon in the span of a few seconds, and I kissed the tip of her nose. "There's no other option, sweetheart. I could never live a day without you."

CHAPTER 38

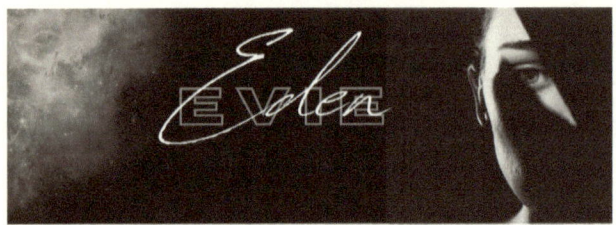

EIGHT YEARS IN HIDING

"Hey, there are my favorite lovebirds," Fiero said as soon as his face popped up on the FaceTime call. I was sitting on Dane's lap with his arm wrapped around my waist.

"What's going on, Fi?" my husband asked. We'd both been anxious since he'd texted earlier and said we needed to talk. It had to be important if he was interrupting our trip.

"First of all, how is Treviso? I haven't been to Italy in years."

"Completely magical," I sighed, tilting my head to rest against Dane's. "I've gained approximately forty pounds in the past three days."

"She's crushing my legs, bro," my smartass husband said, giving my thigh an affectionate pat to assure me he was kidding.

He'd brought me to Treviso, the home of tiramisù, because the dessert had a special meaning to us. Dane had made it for me for breakfast on my first birthday away from my family, and when I thought back, that was probably the first pivotal moment that led me from hatred to love of this man. He'd done his best to make the difficult day not so crappy for me.

"Glad you two are having fun," Fiero said, picking up a glass and taking a long sip of the amber liquid inside, which surprised me. With the time difference, I knew it had to be around nine in the morning there. Then he ran a hand back and forth over the top of his head before sliding it down his face. He had the same eyes and dark hair as my husband, but that's where the similarity ended. Besides the obvious lack of facial hair, his facial features were sharper.

"What's wrong?" Dane asked, and I could feel the tension in his body.

"Luca was arrested last night."

Boom. It was like a bomb had exploded inside my chest and filled me with tiny shrapnel of hope. "For what?" I asked quickly.

"Murder."

Those two syllables had my eyes widening, but before I could say anything else, Dane jumped in. "What happened?"

"There was an altercation in an alley in midtown two nights ago. Luca shot a guy who was some kind of mid-level arms dealer. There was apparently a witness who came forward and identified him as the shooter."

Every vein in my body thrummed with excitement. "So he's in jail?"

Fiero snorted and took another drink. "He *was*, but he made bail and is on his way home as we speak."

"Who's the witness?" Dane inquired, tightening his hold around my waist.

"No clue, but the prosecutor will have to divulge that if they go to trial..." He let the words hang in the air, and Dane immediately picked up what he was putting down.

"And then Luca will know and can get to them." His voice sounded resigned, and I sagged back against him, remembering Robert and Dane's stories about how Luca Cappitani dealt with witnesses against him. Fear. Intimidation. Threats. More death.

Fiero nodded. "Maybe it will be different this time. He's never been brought up on murder charges before. It's usually weapons or racketeering or something."

"You weren't involved, right?" Dane asked his brother, concern lacing his voice.

A lascivious smile took over his face. "No, I was at the club that evening, and then I spent the rest of the night in the company of a very lovely lady."

I smiled, only rolling my eyes slightly. "Anyone special?"

"Oh, she was special all right. She had a tongue piercing, and the things she could do—"

"That's enough," Dane broke in. "My wife doesn't need to hear about your exploits."

"Yeah, we have enough of our own exploits to deal with," I retorted, making my husband choke and my brother-in-law roar with laughter.

The latter shook his finger at the screen. "You've met your match with this one, bro."

"No lie. She gives me shit all the time," Dane said, dropping a kiss on my shoulder. "So you think the charges will stick?"

Fiero shrugged. "Who the fuck knows? It depends on if the idiots in charge can manage to keep the witness alive. I'm sure Luca's lawyers will postpone the trial as long as possible. Could be years."

Dane rubbed a comforting hand up and down my side. "Thanks for letting us know, Fi. Anything else?"

He waved his hand. "Nah, you two go do... whatever it is married people do."

A wicked grin spread over my lips, and I waggled my eyebrows at my brother-in-law. "Oh, you'd be surprised at—"

The rest of my teasing statement was muffled when Dane covered my mouth with his palm and chuckled. "That's not for my brother's ears, Wildcat," he informed me before saying, "Later, Fi. Keep us updated when you can."

With the press of his finger, he disconnected the call and pulled me closer. I swiveled until I was straddling him on the cushy taupe couch in our hotel room. But his normally direct gaze lingered somewhere around my chin.

"What's wrong? This is good news, isn't it? We might be able to go home if Luca goes to jail."

His brown eyes finally met mine, and I read the conflict there. "You'll be able to go back, E, but I'm not sure about me." My heart sank at his words. "When you reappear, Luca will suspect I'm alive too. I'm sure there will be media coverage out the ass, and even with how different I look now, he'll know it's me when photographers inevitably take photos of us. Even from inside prison walls, he'll still wield his power."

"And he'll come after you," I stated, and Dane nodded.

"Neither of us will be safe if I'm with you."

I leaned forward and rested my forehead to his. "Let's not think about that right now. Like Fiero said, it will probably be a while before this goes to trial, so we have time to formulate a plan. I won't go back without you."

I was shocked at how easily that last sentence fell from my lips. All I'd wanted for the past eight years was to get back to my family, but now... Now I knew I couldn't live without the man who wrapped his arms around my waist and jerked me close until my chest was flush with his.

"I want you to be with your family, Eden. I want that so much for you."

Cupping his face with my hands, I pressed a soft kiss to his pillowy lips. "You are part of my family now. You're my husband." Our eyes held, and I let him read the truth of every word before kissing him again. "Now let's go enjoy this beautiful city together."

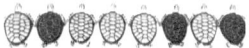

April in Treviso was beautiful, the weather a comfortable sixty-seven degrees. I was dressed in a sky-blue maxi dress and a downy white cardigan since some of the more historical tourist spots required "modest attire" for women. Dane was in jeans and a long-sleeved black T-shirt that was just tight enough to hint at the muscular physique beneath.

We'd hit a couple museums yesterday, but today, our trek was aimless and unscripted. We ate gelato and walked along the cobblestone streets, admiring the beautiful frescoes and architecture.

A few hours into our wandering, a few droplets of rain dotted the stone beneath our feet and tapped our heads and shoulders.

"Guess we should get back to the hotel," Dane said, stopping to look up at the graying sky.

"A little rain never hurt anyone," I said, lifting my chin to allow a few splatters to splash onto my face.

"Tell that to flood victims," he smarted, and I giggled.

"It's only a sprinkle, and besides, I like the rain. It's cleansing, like a renewal of your soul. In fact, to some, rain is considered good luck."

Dane laughed and twirled me in a circle beneath his arm before tugging me close. He looked so much younger than his thirty-three years when he just let go and had fun. I had just turned twenty-seven the month before, though since Robert had fudged our ages eight years ago, our IDs and paperwork listed Dane as thirty-five and me as thirty. My husband liked to joke that those were our ages in "Dane and Eden years," similar to the concept of "dog years."

"I'm sure you have examples in that brilliant mind of yours," he said, his tone a lilting inquisition.

"Mmm, I'm sure I do."

He brushed his lips across mine and swiped a damp strand of hair from my forehead. "Enlighten me, Wildcat."

I was a bit love-drunk from the way he was holding me, touching me, looking at me like I was his world, but my brain managed to remember something I'd heard once.

"Let's see… in Hindu culture, they believe marriage is like a knot, so rain on your wedding day is supposed to make the marriage stronger because a wet knot is harder to untie."

The smile faded from Dane's face, replaced by a narrowing of his eyebrows. "I should have given you a real wedding."

"What?" I laughed. "No. Totally not necessary."

But he was fixated on something behind me, and a second later, he grabbed my hand and took off at a jog—pulling me behind him—toward a large white building with Corinthian columns. The church of Sant 'Agnese.

"Dane, what are we doing?" I hissed as we trotted up the short stairs.

"Getting married," he said, wiping his feet against the concrete, and I followed suit. Then he pushed open the large, brown wooden doors, and we entered the old church. The air instantly changed, the sweet smell of incense melding with a peace that relaxed the senses.

To my surprise, Dane dipped his fingertips in the holy water font and crossed himself before pulling me forward into the nave. The church was stunning in shades of white with dark wood pews and huge arches near the ceiling, which was so tall, I had to crane my neck to see the top. My gaze roamed slowly, taking in the beautiful side altars and landing on a majestic painting in an intricate stucco frame above the altar.

"Wow," I breathed.

"Indeed." Dane kissed the top of my head and said, "Wait here for a minute," before he headed up the center aisle. When he got to the front, he turned to face me and nodded.

Okaaay, I guess we were getting married. As soon as I started walking up the aisle, he held up his phone, and I heard "Here Comes the Bride" from his speakers. I felt a little silly and reckless, walking in off the street and traipsing down the aisle of an ancient church to marry the man who I already called my husband. But I loved the spontaneity of the moment, so I went with it.

Dane's grin was wide and boyish, and I found myself striding more quickly, not staying in time with the slow tune at all. When I reached him, he took both of my hands, and we stared at each other with goofy grins until the music ended.

"Benvenuto," a scratchy voice said, and we both startled slightly as we turned our heads to find a very old priest standing in front of the altar, only a couple feet away. We'd apparently been so lost in each other, we hadn't heard his approach. He had deep wrinkles on either side of his mouth that indicated he smiled a lot, and two furrows between his brows told me he probably scrunched them together while in prayer.

I dipped my head respectfully toward the man, allowing Dane to do the talking since his Italian was way better than mine.

"Ciao, padre." He said a few more things I didn't catch, but I assumed he was telling the priest we were already married because he held up our hands so he could see our rings.

"Ah, continua," the old man said before handing Dane a pristine white rose with a trimmed stem and giving him a wink. My husband took the flower and tucked it behind my ear.

"He wants us to continue." He smiled nervously and said, "Maybe I didn't think this all the way through. I would have prepared something brilliant and romantic to say."

I laughed and rubbed my thumb over his wedding band. "I'll go first. I'm pretty good at talking, though I'm not making any promises that it will blow your drawers off."

"You do have the gift of gab, Wildcat."

He wasn't lying. "Okay, here goes." I swallowed hard and began. "We didn't have the typical beginning to a romance. There was no meet-cute where we bumped into each other in a coffee shop and I spilled my coffee on your suit just before you had an important business meeting."

Dane chuckled. "Accurate."

"I thought you were my poison, but it turns out... you're my perfect antidote. You healed me, Dane. Every single day, you made me better. Every single day, you were there. You never let me feel alone, and I'm so happy and proud to be your wife. I love you, Dane Osbourne." I lifted his left hand and kissed his wedding ring before saying the words he had inscribed on the inside of mine. "In the light and in the darkness... I choose you."

"Wow, babe," he said, his eyes shiny with emotion. "Not sure how to follow that. I'm going to sound like a bumbling idiot."

A giggle escaped me, and I lowered my voice to a whisper. "Newsflash: I'll love you anyway."

His shoulders straightened, and he closed the rest of the distance between us, resting his hands on my waist. "I think I started falling for you the first time I saw you. It was a video that turned my stomach, but then I saw two blue eyes, a stubborn, pretty little mouth, and two middle fingers. You had me then, Eden. You captured my heart, and I don't ever want it back."

His voice clogged a little and I rested my hands on his chest, my right one directly over his heart. It was beating a rapid tempo beneath my palm. "Good, because it's mine now, and you're not getting it back."

"You are my everything, Eden Osbourne, and I love all your sides. Soft and strong. Sweet and sassy. I never knew how lonely my life was until I found your love. You fill me up, and I will always choose you." Then, like I had done to him, he took my hand and lifted it to kiss my ring before repeating the inscription in perfect Italian. "Nella luce e nell'oscurità, scelgo te."

We stared at each other for a long while, a single tear escaping down my cheek as its mirror twin slid down Dane's. Then another hand closed over ours, and we both swiveled our heads to look into the sweet face of the priest.

"Il matrimonio è un'alleanza. Invoco su di voi le benedizioni di Dio. Puoi baciare la tua sposa," he intoned, his voice quiet but strong.

My Italian may have been a little rusty, but I recognized that last part. He'd told Dane to kiss his bride. And he did. With a sweep of his arm beneath my lower back, my husband dipped me low and kissed me with a passion that was probably a bit scandalous, given the setting.

His other hand cradled the back of my head, making me feel safe and loved, even though I was bent backward almost in half. Our tongues tangled, and I wove my hands into his slightly damp hair until he finally pulled back with a soft peck and lifted me upright.

I wasn't sure how long we'd been kissing, but there was no sign of the priest. Before I could think too much on it, my husband scooped me into his arms—bridal style, of course—and ran up the aisle. We were both laughing like maniacs, even when we made it outside the beautiful church to find that the evening sky had opened up and was dumping its contents all over Treviso.

"Put me down, and let's run together in the rain," I ordered, and Dane dropped me to my feet, grasping my hand in his. It felt warm compared to the coolness of the rain, and we ran back to the hotel, laughing like little kids on an adventure. When we reached the columned portico at the front, we shook the wetness from our hair as the uniformed doorman looked on with an indulgent smile.

"Buona sera, Signore e Signora Osbourne," he said, handing us two plush white towels from a rack beside the gold and glass double doors. *Talk about service...*

We returned his greeting and graciously accepted the cloths before doing our best to pat off the worst of the soaking we'd endured. "Come on, Wildcat," Dane said, tossing our towels in the wicker hamper provided outside the entrance. "Let's go consummate our marriage."

"You realize we've slept together many times, right? Or have you forgotten?" I teased quietly as our feet squished over the fine Carrara marble floor.

We entered the lift and the elevator operator pressed the button for our floor without us having to tell him. Dane's breath was warm against my chilled skin when he bent to whisper, "I remember every second I've ever been inside your perfect pussy, wife. The feel of you wrapped around me will be the last thought in my head before I die, but I want to give you the wedding night you deserve." His words only induced more chills, and it had nothing to do with the cool air hitting my damp skin.

My teeth were chattering by the time we entered our hotel room, and Dane pulled me directly into the small bathroom and turned on the shower to heat up. Then he undressed us both and slid the rose from my hair, setting it carefully on the marble countertop before taking out my contact lenses.

The bathroom was large, sumptuous even, but the navy-and-white tiled shower was tiny, barely big enough for one person. "That's an awfully small space," I mused, and Dane flashed a lascivious smile.

"I'm aware. We'll just have to stand really close to each other."

I stepped backward into the stall, pulling my man along with me until my back hit the wall. "I think I can make that sacrifice." With our bodies plastered together, we turned in slow circles, letting the water hit us from all sides and warm us. Dane hummed the wedding march, and I smiled against his bare chest. "Thank you for today. For everything but especially the wedding."

He buried his nose in the top of my hair. "One day, I'll give you a real one, Wildcat. With flowers and a dress and your family there." His voice turned softer, more vulnerable. "If you think they'll accept me."

Lifting my head, I looked up at him. "Of course they will."

He snorted out a sound of derision. "I'm not exactly sure I'm the kind of man they had planned for you."

I directed my best scowl at him. "Don't talk about my husband that way. I chose him, remember?" That made him smile, and he lifted me until my legs curled around his waist.

"I love you, Mrs. Osbourne."

He was already hard, and I rocked my hips, sliding my pussy up and down his strong length. "I love you, Mr. Osbourne."

Dane stopped our circling dance and pressed my back against one of the walls of the shower, the tiles quickly warming beneath my flesh. His cock was on fire though, and the head of it swelled as I found it with my clit, getting me wet and slick against him.

"Fuck your wife, Dane," I demanded, and he groaned shifting his hips until we were lined up for the perfect entrance. Then he pushed upward, filling me slowly as I stretched to accommodate his size. "This is my favorite part, when you're working your way inside me. Okay, maybe second favorite because I really like the orgasm part."

He chuckled. "Ah, yes. The grand finale is always stellar." Then all reasonable conversation was forgotten as Dane switched to the dirty-mouthed man I adored. "My favorite part is when your pussy tightens up and tries to resist me until she recognizes her master. Then she accepts me so fucking beautifully like the good little cunt she is."

He began to move, fucking up into me with measured thrusts that drew his name from the back of my throat as his mouth dropped to the side of my neck.

"Dane, yes!" As always, he located my G-spot like he was born to do it, and the thick ridge around the crown of his cock rode against it. "Right there. Don't stop or I'll divorce you."

My husband chuckled before biting the tender spot where my shoulder met my neck, no doubt marking me as his. "Is that so? Even when I can do this?" He rolled his hips, touching spots I was convinced no other man could find, and his ass cheeks clenched beneath my heels. I loved the way Dane fucked with his whole body, but that ass... Good god! He had the perfect man butt, firm, hard, and completely biteable.

With a deep grind, he abraded my clit with his pubic bone, and my head fell back against the tiles. Through hooded eyes, I watched as Dane ramped up his efforts, and a feral glint sparkled in his brown eyes. "Hands above your head, Wildcat," he demanded, and I clasped my fingers together and lifted them.

Holding beneath my ass with one hand, Dane grasped my wrists and pinned them to the shower wall as the rhythm of our joining quickened. His hot mouth closed around one of my nipples, and I was totally at his mercy, lost in the pleasure only he could deliver.

"I'm close," I panted, and he switched to the other breast, adding a scrape of teeth to his repertoire. The warm water sluiced over our writhing bodies, and the fever in my core rose until…

"Fuck, I feel it, baby girl. I feel you coming. Give it to me."

My hips churned in tandem with his, and I definitely gave it to him, every bit of myself. I'm pretty sure my soul left my body when I came so hard it could have been measured on the Richter scale.

Dane only went harder, taking me higher as the sounds of wet flesh slapping together blended with the pattering water and the grunts of raw sex. And then with one… two… three more thrusts, he stilled, spilling himself deep inside me.

I blinked sleepily, my body completely used and loose, and watched my husband's gorgeous face, contorted in the agony of pure rapture. He released my hands slamming his palm against the tiles beside my head as he pulsed inside me, his lips parted and panting against my breast.

He was absolutely the most beautiful specimen of man I'd ever seen in my life. His lean, hard muscles finally started to relax and lose their tension as his back heaved with harsh breaths.

Lifting his head, he flashed a crooked smile that gave me all the flutters and said, "Give me about a month to recover, and we'll do that again."

Of course it didn't take nearly that long. After we dressed and had dinner in our room, Dane was ready for round two, but this time was in our spacious bed beneath the crisp, sky-blue sheets. I was on top, my body flush with his as we made slow, sensual love together.

After we were done and my husband was snoozing lightly beside me, I crawled from the bed and retrieved the white rose he'd placed in my hair earlier. Finding the small stack of books I'd brought, I opened one of them and put the flower in the back before closing it and stacking the other books on top to press it into a keepsake.

I knew it was only an impromptu "ceremony," but that made it even more special to me because Dane was not exactly known as the king of spontaneity. I wanted to remember it. Forever.

CHAPTER 39

ELEVEN YEARS IN HIDING

"Got us some popcorn," I said, sitting beside Eden on our soft leather couch. My wife, always one for deeper descriptions, said it was the color of cocoa after the marshmallows had melted. Yeah. I called it brown.

Her eyes flicked to the television mounted on the opposite wall and then back to me. "I think this prosecutor is really sharp, don't you?"

I could tell by her tone she needed my reassurance. "Her opening statement was excellent yesterday. She did a good job of laying out the case." The case being the murder of Martin Love by my father, Luca Cappitani. "The jurors seemed to like her."

Twisting the lids from two bottles of Dr Pepper, I handed one to Eden as the much-publicized trial resumed on the screen. Popcorn and soda may not be the most nutritious breakfast in the world, but I was fully in the *fuck it* zone this morning.

Our attention was glued to the TV while New York prosecutor Leana Wallace went through the forensic evidence with one of the witnesses. Leana was dark-skinned with a pin-straight black bob that hit just at her chin. Her dark-teal suit was perfectly cut, and she exuded confidence and professionalism with every question.

When she was done, one of Luca's attorneys, Tony Russo, cross-examined the witness, making sure to drive home the point that there was no ballistic evidence tying the three bullets found in the victim's head to Luca Cappitani.

"No shit. He disposed of the gun," I mumbled, stuffing a handful of popcorn into my mouth. "It's at the bottom of a very deep body of water."

Beside me, Eden nodded as she nibbled on a single kernel of popcorn. "The key is the eyewitness," she said, more to herself than me.

The next person called to the stand was the medical examiner, and that took up the rest of the morning before the judge called for a lunch break and announced that the trial would resume in the afternoon.

"Going good so far," I soothed, wrapping an arm around my wife and kissing her temple. "Are you hungry?"

"No," she told me a second before her stomach contradicted her with a long growl. "Okay, maybe I should try to eat a little something."

"Go sit on the lanai. We can eat out there." Though Eden no longer had nightmares, being outdoors still seemed to calm her. I was fully aware of why she was nervous. Our entire future depended on the outcome of this trial.

She nodded and rubbed the turtle charm on her necklace between her thumb and forefinger, an almost absent gesture she did when she was deep in thought. "Okay, sounds good."

Once I'd whipped up a couple warm ham and cheese sandwiches, I grabbed a big bag of Lay's potato chips and brought everything out to the lanai where Eden was scrolling through her phone. She already seemed more relaxed in the May sunshine.

"The first thing I'm going to do when I get back to New York is have a chat with my oldest brother about the company he keeps. Look at this." She turned her phone around so I could see the Facebook picture of Auburn and a platinum blonde with huge breasts. "Her name is Magdalena. What does he see in her?"

"Big knockers," I muttered around a mouthful of sandwich. If the narrowing of my wife's eyes was any indication, that was the wrong thing to say, so I quickly backtracked. "I mean, not that I'm into all that. Don't want to sprain a hand."

She giggled and nudged my knee beneath the table. "I see your point. She is pretty, but she's looking at him like he's her own personal bank account."

Avoiding looking at the picture again—because I valued my testicles—I said, "Probably won't go anywhere. Auburn's too smart to marry some floozy. He's bound to get a lot more attention now that your dad is retired and Auburn is the CEO at *Bouvier.*"

"Yeah," Eden said, and I was happy to see that she was distracted enough to begin eating. "Monty finally got a Facebook, but it's set on private so I can't see any of his stuff. Auburn did post this picture recently though." She turned the phone around again so I could see her younger brother in a police uniform. We'd learned years ago that Monty was an officer in a small town near Miami. I knew it was hard on my wife to realize her brother was so close and yet she couldn't see him.

"All three of you look so much alike, especially with your hair dyed dark like that. Of course, you're much more gorgeous," I told her, leaning over to kiss her temple.

A pretty rosy color bloomed on her cheeks, and I loved that I could still make my wife blush after over a decade. Then she turned her attention back to the phone, staring longingly at her brother.

"Do you think he'll move back to New York once I return?"

Fuck, she made my heart ache with her hopefulness. I only hoped it wasn't misplaced. It would be up to the prosecutor and ultimately, the jury.

"I hope so, baby." I reached for a chip, crunching the salty snack before peering at the time on my own phone. "Ten more minutes till the trial resumes."

Eden stood and gathered our plates and the bag of chips. "I'm going inside. I have to use the restroom before it gets started."

"Meet you in there," I said. Once she was gone, I stared at the crystal-blue water of our pool and prayed to the trial gods to do their thing.

The suspense in the courtroom was palpable, even through the TV screen, as the prosecution's main witness took the stand. Nita Malone was short with a full figure and strawberry-blonde hair. Through the questioning, we learned she was a twenty-four-year-old single mom and worked as a waitress at a restaurant adjacent to the alley where the murder had taken place.

Once all the preliminary questions were done, Leana Wallace stood behind a podium and smiled at her witness. "Nita, can you lead me through the events of the night in question, please?"

The young woman shifted in her seat and nodded, her hand fluttering up to fiddle with the long braid hanging over one shoulder. Eden inched closer to me, and I reached for her hand. I needed the comfort as much as she did. This was a pivotal moment in our future.

"I was, um, taking out the trash after the restaurant closed," Nita started. "I went out the back door to the alley, and that's when I heard voices."

She paused, her eyes darting around the room, and Leana gave her an encouraging nod. "Could you see who was talking?"

Nita pulled her gaze back to the prosecutor. "They were yelling, actually. I was scared." She wrapped two fingers around her braid. "There was a car parked in the alley. It was dark colored, but that's all I could tell."

"How many people did you see?" Leana asked gently.

"There was one man in the car... in the driver's seat, but it was dark, so I couldn't make him out. Just, like, his silhouette, you know?" She rolled her lips inward, obviously nervous. "I saw two other men standing outside of the car, and one of them had a gun. I didn't want them to see me, so I hid behind the dumpster."

Leana did her best to keep her voice measured, though it was obvious we were getting to the meat of the trial. "Could you see the two men well?"

Nita nodded before apparently remembering she was supposed to answer orally. "Yes. They were standing in the beams of the headlights. The one not holding the gun was Martin Love." Her smile was tremulous as she shrugged. "I mean, I didn't know his name then, of course. I learned it later. He was medium height, not tall but not as short as me either. Mostly I noticed his mustache. It was really bushy."

A titter went up around the courtroom. The victim had indeed sported a very impressive mustache.

"And the other man?" Leana prompted. The witness's eyes moved to her right and seemed to be frozen there. "Nita, what did the man with the gun look like?"

Nita's eyes popped back to the prosecutor and then dropped to the floor, as if she were praying. Then her attention flicked to the right again before she inhaled a long breath. "The other man was very tall and very thin. Blond and pale, almost like one of those, um, albinos."

Eden and I both gasped as murmurs went up around the courtroom. Nita's description was the exact opposite of Luca Cappitani, who was olive-skinned and portly with black hair. The judge banged his gavel twice and ordered everyone to be quiet.

Leana Wallace was standing with her mouth agape, but she quickly recovered, stepping around to the front of the podium to put her a little closer to the woman on the stand. She straightened her suit jacket and drew her eyebrows together, eyes focused like lasers on the witness.

"Okay, Nita. Maybe you're confused about which night we're talking about. It was April eighth, three years ago. Do you remember that night?"

"Yes."

"I'd like you to tell me what the man in the alley—*the one holding the gun*—looked like."

Nita's green eyes were as round full moons, and my heart sank, knowing what she was going to say next. "He was skinny and tall and pale," she repeated. "I, um, that's what he looked like... the man who shot Martin."

A muscle twitched in Leana's jaw as her case fell down around her head. "Nita, that's not the description you gave to me before. You said the man who shot Martin Love had dark hair and was fat. Those were your exact words." Her tone was sharp and accusatory. "You specifically identified Luca Cappitani. Why are you changing your story all of a sudden?"

The defense attorney objected, and the judge sustained it, but I could barely hear the words because my attention turned to my wife, who was looking up at me, horror filling her blue eyes.

"Dane, what just happened?"

"Luca fucking happened." I pulled her onto my lap and wrapped my arms around her. "The fucker got to the witness. Probably threatened her kid or something."

The voices from the television raised in volume, and it grated on my nerves, so I hit the mute button on the remote, drenching our living room in silence. Eden curled against me, and I smoothed her hair away from her face, surveying her dry eyes.

"Are you okay?"

Eden contemplated that for a moment before speaking. "I don't know. I think I knew deep down something would go wrong." She scrunched her eyes shut and huffed out a gust of air. "I'm pissed that witness straight up lied, but I guess that would make me a hypocrite."

I rubbed her shoulder. "What do you mean, baby?"

She pointed a finger at the silent screen. "Nita lied because she was scared. And isn't that the same fucking thing I've been doing for eleven years? I've changed my hair and my name. I wear colored contacts every damn day. Hell, I'm pretending to be married." Her voice rose. "And why? Because I was scared your father was going to hurt my family."

Your father. While it was technically true, she never referred to him like that.

Her words were sharp as a jellyfish sting, and I dropped my head, shame coursing through me. "I'm sorry," I breathed, and her arms instantly circled my neck.

"Shit. No, I'm sorry. I shouldn't have said it like that." Eden nuzzled her face into my neck. "I would never have found my soulmate if things hadn't worked out like they did."

I inhaled the fruitiness of her shampoo and the honey scent of her skin as we held each other. "I hate being associated with him."

Her hand stroked softly through my hair. "I know. I'm sorry I said that." She pulled back and pressed her lips softly to mine. "I love you, Dane, and I wouldn't give up a second of what we have together."

"I love you too, Eden."

"You still choose me even when I get bitchy?"

"Always. In the light and in the darkness. I guess today is an example of the latter." I kissed the tip of her nose. "And you weren't bitchy. You were just upset and disappointed."

Her lips pressed together, and I saw the slight trembling of her chin. "Maybe they can talk to the witness and..." The words trailed off because we both knew that was unlikely. "I think I want to take Juliette's newest book and sit on the beach for a while. I need some literary escape."

"Do you want me to come with you? I can be quiet so you can read."

She dragged her knuckles down my cheek. "Would it be okay if I go by myself?"

No, I want to cling to you like white on rice. Instead of voicing that, I smiled. "Of course. Take your phone with you and call if you need me. I can be there in a couple minutes."

Eden stood and picked up her phone and the paperback from the coffee table before bending to press a kiss to my lips. "Thank you for loving me, Mr. Osbourne."

"It's my greatest honor, Mrs. Osbourne," I returned, standing and following her into the kitchen. I watched through the glass door as she snagged a beach blanket from a shelf on the lanai and headed toward the back gate. I gave her five minutes before following her to the beach.

My eyes found her immediately from my hiding place behind a small building. She was facing away from me, on her stomach, feet kicked up behind her. A vibration in my pocket notified me of an incoming text message, and I pulled it out to check the screen.

> **Eden: Stop lurking, Dracula. It's creepy AF.**

I couldn't help but laugh as I tapped out a quick message.

> **Dane: Sorry, I was worried about you.**

> **Eden: I'm fine. Go check on the bakery or something. Love you.**

I looked up from my phone to see my wife's head turned in my direction. She blew me a kiss, and I returned the gesture before reluctantly turning to head home. We'd both taken some vacation time from work to watch the trial, though no one besides us knew the reason. I guessed it wouldn't hurt to go check on my bakery.

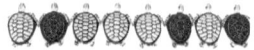

Entering the back door, I was hit in the nostrils with the scents of sugar and chocolate. Barry looked up from the cake he was meticulously decorating.

"Hey, boss. Thought you were off this week."

"I am. Just wanted to make sure everything is going okay."

"All good back here, but I heard Maria yelling into the phone a few minutes ago."

"I'll check on her," I assured him as he got back to work on the cake.

On my way to the front, I waved to a couple of the other employees we'd hired in the past few years as business had grown. Kevin, Barry's best friend, no longer worked at Sweet Heaven. He'd gotten married two years ago and moved to Key West with his bride, though they stopped in for a visit every time they were headed to the mainland.

Maria, the sweet, quiet young student that used to work the register, had grown into one hell of a manager. I'd taken a chance on her, and it had paid off big time.

"Hey, Maria," I said, poking my head in her small office to find her pulling her purse strap over her shoulder.

"Dane, hey. Sorry I've got to run. TJ didn't show up to do deliveries today. Again."

"That's the third time this month. Want me to talk to him?"

She shook her head, making her ponytail swing. "Nope. I already fired his ass. I called three people who've turned in job applications recently, and they're coming in for interviews this week so I can get him replaced. But now I have to get those cookies to the animal shelter in twenty minutes."

"Whoa, slow down. I can take the delivery."

"Oh thank god," she said, tossing her purse down and not even bothering to argue. "I put Becca on the register, but she's still learning the nuances of the POS system. Miguel is up there too, and he can help her, but he stays busy this time of day with barista duties."

"Yep, people need their afternoon caffeine fix." We'd put in a fancy coffee bar around four years ago. It had brought in a younger crowd, and profits had risen thirty percent since then. "Let's get the cookies loaded."

As we began stacking boxes into the back of my new Ford Explorer, Maria said, "Your neighbor kid is doing a good job. Too bad he's not old enough to drive, or I'd put him on deliveries."

"Cooper's a good kid," I said. "Hard to believe he's a teenager now." I'd hired him a few months ago to bus tables, and he worked his ass off. He was saving money to buy a car.

"I think that's it, Dane. Now scoot," Maria ordered, giving me a light shove between the shoulders. She'd come a long damn way from the shy girl who nervously called me Mr. Osbourne every time she saw me.

I arrived at the Furry Love animal shelter with five minutes to spare and was met at the front door by the director, Mrs. Starrett. "Mr. Osbourne, so nice to see you."

"You, as well," I said, opening the back of my vehicle and extracting the dolly. She peered into one of the clear-topped boxes and clapped her hands beneath her chin.

"Oh, these are just perfect! Look at all the pretty colors!"

Barry and I had decorated fifteen dozen paw print cookies in a rainbow of colors over the weekend, and I had to admit, they were eye-catching. And fucking delicious.

I wheeled the boxes into the facility, and Mrs. Starrett directed me to an area where two long tables were set up along the wall. "So you're having a drive to get more pets adopted?" I asked, helping her place the individually wrapped cookies on pretty platters.

"Yep. We always need people coming in to adopt our furry little friends, so we decided to bribe them with cookies. Thank you for the gracious discount, by the way."

"No problem at all. Happy to help." I held up a box with an X marked on the side. "We tried something new and thought we'd see if you wanted to try them out. These are homemade dog biscuits. I did research on them, and they're made from all natural ingredients and are safe for big dogs and puppies."

Her eyes lit up, and she opened the box, pulling out a few of the small bone-shaped treats. "Oooh, let's do some market research, shall we? Follow me."

I trailed her into an area where puppies frolicked in a low-fenced enclosure. Three of them bounded over when she stepped over the barrier and squatted down. "Here you go, babies," she cooed. "Mr. Osbourne brought you a little treaty-treat."

Two of the pups grabbed their snacks in their mouths and scampered off, but the third, a small blond dog, rolled onto his back and held the bone between his front paws. Mrs. Starrett and I both laughed when he took a tentative nibble and literally sighed.

"I guess he's a fan," I said, stepping over the low fence and squatting to give the pup a belly rub. He snarfed down the rest of his cookie before rolling over and running laps around me. "You sure are cute, little buddy."

He gave me an agreeable yip and then leaped into my arms. I chuckled, holding his warm, furry body to my chest.

"It looks like you've made a friend, Mr. Osbourne," the director said, her gaze shrewd. "Do you have a backyard?"

Ten minutes later, my gullible ass was walking to the front of the facility with a puppy in my arms. Eden would adore him, and I wanted nothing more than to bring a little joy to my wife. As we were passing through the clear-fronted enclosures holding the cats, my new pet let out a whimper.

"What's wrong, little dude? Are you scared of cats?"

I walked closer to where his brown gaze was directed, and he held out a paw that seemed too big for his body and pressed it against the plexiglass. The little black-and-white kitten inside rose up on her back legs and laid her front paws in the same spot. Then the pup licked the glass, and the kitten did the same.

"Awww, it would be a shame to separate them," Mrs. Starrett said.

"You are an evil, manipulative woman," I said, feigning exasperation but not really feeling it.

"That's what my husband says. Shall we take them to the play area to see if they get along?"

After another thirty minutes, I opened the passenger side of the SUV and loaded the pet carrier holding the puppy and kitten, who were curled up together on a pink blanket. Both of them were fast asleep.

"Here are your supplies," Mrs. Starrett said, handing over a large bag with the shelter's logo imprinted on it. "There's enough food for each of them for two days."

"I'm getting out of here before you can foist a hamster or some other damn critter on me," I complained, climbing in behind the wheel.

"Pleasure doing business with you, Mr. Osbourne," she said sweetly, but I was pretty sure she was doing some kind of evil witch laugh on the inside.

CHAPTER 40

I TUCKED THE BOOK beneath my arm and trudged through the sand. Juli's latest romance novel was phenomenal, though her original—the one where Evie was the main character—would always be my favorite.

The butter house came into view, and I sighed. I needed to apologize to Dane again. I'd pulled "the father card," and that wasn't right of me. I'd been frustrated and allowed the words to come out before I could think better of it.

Sure, he'd been rough around the edges when we first met, but he'd turned his entire life around. Now he was a legit businessman and a damn fine husband. He'd done it all for me and deserved better than my barbed words.

Setting down my stuff on the lanai table, I opened the back door, fully prepared to ask forgiveness. *Perhaps on my knees,* I thought wickedly a second before I heard Dane's voice.

"Don't you dare pee on the rug."

"Uh, I wasn't planning on it. I know you like to get kinky, but damn," I replied, walking into the living room and surveying the scene with widened eyes.

Brightly colored toys littered the room, and there was something that looked suspiciously like a paper napkin shredded into a million pieces beside the coffee table. My husband sat on his butt with his legs splayed while a small, light-brown puppy tugged at one of his socks. To top it all off, an even smaller kitten rested on top of his head, hissing to the room at large. Dane's hair was a flyaway mess, and I could read the desperation in his brown eyes when he spotted me.

"Help. I've been duped."

I burst into laughter just as the pup finally worked off one of my husband's socks and pranced around the room with it in his mouth, the pride evident on his cute little face.

"You've been what?"

"Duped," Dane said. "Swindled. Scammed. Played for a fool." He pointed an accusing finger at the puppy. "That one started it with his waggly tail and puppy dog eyes. Acting all sweet and shit."

"Oh," I said, watching said tail swing like a banner flag above the dog's furry body.

"And then there was Catzilla here," he growled, pulling the kitten from his head and staring at it before cradling it against his body. "Ohhh, this one was all *meow, meow, take me home* with her teeny little paws on the window."

His words were snippy, but the way he was holding the baby cat and stroking its sweet head... *Seriously, is there anything hotter than a man with a gentle hand for a fur baby? Yeah, I didn't think so.*

"So you're telling me you got swindled by these two little cuties?" I asked, picking up the pup and looking down into his precious face.

Dane snorted. "They had help in the form of that demon woman, Mrs. Starrett."

I cracked up laughing again at his description of the sweet old lady. "Mrs. Starrett is an absolute doll. She was one of the first people to hire me for a freelance logo design," I said, noticing the bag bearing the shelter's design sitting on the floor. My heart throbbed with love for my husband, and my voice rasped low. "You rescued these little ones?"

"Yeah," Dane admitted. "I wanted to cheer you up. I went to deliver some cookies, and then..." He waved a hand around the room. "Then *this* happened. They. Are. Terrorists."

Setting the puppy down, I crawled to my husband and took the kitten from him, also putting her on the floor. The two promptly began wrestling in a ball of fluff, fighting over Dane's white sock.

I crawled onto his lap, straddling his hips before kissing the ever-loving hell out of him. He looked a little dazed when I pulled back.

"Um, so I bring two feral beasts home and get rewarded like that? Because I'm sure I could find a rabid raccoon or something for your next gift."

"I love them, and I love you," I told him. "I'm sorry for how I acted earlier."

He tucked my hair behind my ear and smiled. "Don't apologize, Wildcat. You know I don't like it when you hide your feelings with me."

I glanced over at the playful animals. "What are their names?"

"They don't have names yet. They were new additions to the shelter, but they've had all their shots and everything. The cat is a girl, and the pup is a boy."

"Hmmm," I said, tilting my head to the side and inspecting them. The dog had won the battle for the sock, and the little cat was now creeping around, sniffing every corner of the room with her curious nose. "Let's think about it. We'll have to come up with something that fits them."

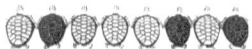

Three days later, we were no closer to coming up with names for our new family members.

"Dillweed and Draco?" Dane asked as I pulled a pan of lasagna from the oven.

I shook my head, knowing he was teasing. He adored those two little rascals as much as I did. "Stop trying to give them your nicknames. Where are they now?"

"In their room. I don't even know why we bought them their own beds because they always cuddle up in the same one." We'd designated one of the empty downstairs bedrooms for the animals.

"Let's take a swim while the lasagna rests," I said, taking his hand and leading him outside.

When we came back in thirty minutes later, we stared at the scene in disbelief. "How the hell did he get up there?" Dane breathed, nodding to the puppy on the countertop. The little toot had destroyed the lasagna, and the blond fur of his face was stained red. The kitten was snooping around below him, snapping bites of meat and noodles from the air as his partner in crime dropped them.

"No clue," I said, grabbing my phone to take a quick video of the carnage before plucking the pup from the counter. "Why are you so bad?" He answered with a lick to my face.

"I'll order a pizza," Dane sighed. "It should be here by the time we get this mess cleaned up."

The kitten was a much more precise eater than the puppy, so while I wiped her face with a wet cloth, Dane bathed the naughty little dog in the bathtub.

As I watched him, something was right on the tip of my tongue, but I couldn't quite...

"I've got it," I announced suddenly. "Who is known for eating lasagna?"

Dane pulled the puppy from the tub and wrapped him in a towel. "Um, everyone with taste?"

"Noooo," I chastised. "Garfield! From the cartoon." I rubbed the little dog's wet head. "We'll call him Garfield."

"But he's a dog."

"I know. It's ironic, so that makes it cute."

He nodded. "I like it. Should we come up with a dog name for the cat to keep with the theme?"

I peered down at the black-and-white kitten in my arms. "Yeah, I think so."

Dane kissed the cat's nose. "How about Snoopy since she's always snooping around like a little nosy butt?"

"I love it!" I squealed as the doorbell rang.

"That's the pizza. I'll get it," my husband said, handing the towel-wrapped puppy to me.

Turning to the mirror, I looked at myself and our fur babies, so happy we finally had names for them.

"Welcome to the family, Garfield and Snoopy."

CHAPTER 41

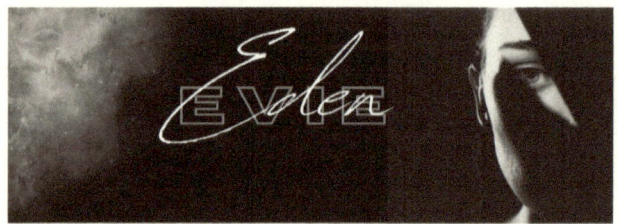

FOURTEEN YEARS IN HIDING

"Garfield, would you please stop licking Charlisse?" I groaned, and the big, goofy dog tilted his head at me in apparent confusion. "Oh, don't give me that look, mister. You know exactly what I'm saying."

Charlisse gave him a scratch behind the ears and leaned closer. "He's not bothering me. He's a gooood boy, isn't he?" she crooned, and he licked her mouth. She wiped it with the back of her hand and gave him a mock frown. "I was sticking up for you, doofus."

Properly chastised, Garfield circled once and flopped onto the floor beneath the dining table for his usual afternoon nap. I tilted my laptop screen and showed Charlisse what I'd been working on.

"Do you like this?"

She pressed a hand over her heart and nodded. "I can't believe my baby is graduating from high school. Thank you so much for helping me with the invitations. The ones you can order through the school are so damn expensive, and this looks a million times better."

"Happy to help. His senior photos turned out so great. There's a place where you can order the invites online. All you have to do is upload this file, and they'll send you a proof within twenty-four hours." After a few keystrokes, I said. "There. I sent the file and the web address to your email."

She hugged me tightly, and I could hear the sniffle in her voice. "You are the best friend ever, Eden. Coop was so excited when I told him you and Dane are hosting a senior party for him and his friends."

"Well, we're very proud of him. I'm going to miss him when he goes to basic training." I pulled back and looked into her watery blue eyes. "How are you doing with that?"

"Oh, you know. I'm proud as hell that he's going into the Army, but of course, I worry." She waved a hand in front of her face to try and stave off the tears that seemed to come more and more often the closer we got to the date when Cooper would be leaving home.

"You've raised a wonderful son, Char. He's going to go do great things."

When she burst into tears, I did too, and we hugged it out as we cried. "He is such a good boy," Charlisse wailed, and Garfield popped his head up at the last two words, making us both laugh.

"She wasn't talking to you, silly dog," I told him, reaching down to rub one silky ear.

"Let's talk about something else," she suggested, pulling a package of tissues from her purse and handing one to me. "I saw your latest Instagram post, and it was so funny. You always come up with the most clever captions."

"I try. It helps when I have such cute subjects." As if summoned, Snoopy leaped onto my lap and boosted herself onto the keyboard of my laptop, making herself right at home. I scratched the spot she loved beneath her chin. "Hey, pretty girl. Are you posing for a picture?"

Grabbing my phone, I backed up and snapped a photo of the cat on my computer. I generally tried to use videos or pictures of both the animals for the Instagram account I'd titled *The Adventures of Garfield and Snoopy*, but occasionally, one of them would get to be in the spotlight by themselves.

"You should totally let me take some pictures of you with Snoopy and Garfield," Charlisse said. "You're never in the pics with them, and I bet your gazillion followers would love to see your pretty face."

Eek!

"No," I said with a laugh that I hoped didn't sound nervous, "the account is all about them."

My friend gave me a wan smile. "You never put pictures of yourself on Facebook either." *Double eek!* "Is there a reason? Did you have a bad breakup with an ex or something?"

I took that and ran with it. "Something like that. I'd rather not have my pictures online."

Charlisse's cheeks pinkened slightly, and she pressed her fingertips to her lips. "I'm so sorry, Eden. That was a very personal thing to ask. I was just curious."

"Hey, it's no problem," I said, patting her arm before lifting a teasing eyebrow. "Maybe I'm an international jewel thief and on the run."

That sent her into a fit of giggles. "Oh, whatever. You and Dane are, like, the most law-abiding people I've ever met."

If only you knew, Charlisse. If only you knew.

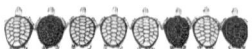

A couple months later, I was sitting at the breakfast bar checking my notifications on the Instagram account and smiled. I'd followed Monty on the platform a while ago, and he had followed me back. I always got a little thrill when he commented on one of my posts, like I was having a secret conversation with my brother.

After replying to a few comments on my latest post, I scrolled through my feed, my thumb pausing when I saw a post from the official *Bouvier Fashion* account.

"Well, well, well. Who is this?" I mumbled.

"Who is what?" Dane asked, coming up behind me and resting his chin on my shoulder.

"This woman with Auburn." I clicked on the caption and read.

CEO Auburn Bouvier attends hospital gala with the lovely Gianna Moschella. Miss Moschella is wearing a couture Bouvier gown.

"Wow. He put her in one of the couture designs? Who the heck is this woman?" I scrolled through the photos.

"What exactly does couture mean?" Dane asked. "I've heard the term, of course, but I don't know what makes something couture or not."

"They are custom-designed pieces, usually made for a celebrity. Or at least for someone very wealthy because they can cost hundreds of thousands of dollars. You wouldn't be able to purchase couture fashion at any store."

This Gianna woman was a bombshell, but that wasn't what kept drawing my eye to the photos of her and my oldest brother. It was her smile, genuine and open.

Doing a quick internet search, I found an article and read it carefully.

NYC'S AUBURN BOUVIER - ELIGIBLE BACHELOR NO MORE? Auburn Bouvier, one of New York's fashion giants, was spotted last night with a new lady on his arm. The lovely and charming Gianna Moschella accompanied Mr. Bouvier to the exclusive NYH Gala, and the two seemed quite cozy, leading every single—and some not-so-single—woman in the city to mourn the potential loss of Bouvier's "eligible" status. We don't know who Miss Moschella is, but we're keeping an eye on this one, folks.

I grinned down at my phone and thought, *I'm keeping my eye on you too, Gianna Moschella. Because I think I like you.*

I was right. By the end of the year, my formerly bachelor brother was engaged to the brunette beauty.

And I couldn't have been happier for him.

Chapter 42

SIXTEEN YEARS IN HIDING

I was in my office at the Turtle Hospital when Maz, the chief veterinarian for the facility, walked in and sat in the chair across from me. "Hey, Eden. How are the new advertisements coming along?"

Opening my desk drawer, I riffled through one of my file folders and pulled out a glossy brochure before sliding it across the desk. "This is the first mockup. What do you think?"

My teeth gnawed at my bottom lip as she inspected it, inside and out. Pulling a pen from her topknot of raven locks, she drew an arrow and slid the document back to me. "I think you should move this photo up to the top. Otherwise, it's perfect."

"Great, I'll get those sent off to the printer in the morning," I said, trying not to sound all giddy, but damn. I loved my job. I got to use my marketing degree *and* be involved with sea turtle rehab and rehabilitation. "How is Gus doing?"

Maz beamed. "He's good. We should be able to release him next month. You want to come watch?"

Though actual care of the animals wasn't in my job description, the staff always included me on release day. They knew it was one of my favorite things to watch, seeing a turtle return to its home in the sea. I always hoped they'd be able to find their families, though that was a bit of a crazy idea due to the vastness of the water. Perhaps I was projecting my own situation a wee bit.

"I would love to."

She rose to stand and walked toward the door, where she paused and turned back to me. "Oh, by the way, have you heard they caught that serial killer in south Florida?"

My heart stalled like an old car in cold weather, and I couldn't control my stammer. "Th-the one in Marytown?"

"Yep. Check it out. It's all over the news."

She was barely out the door before my fingers were clicking on my computer screen. I'd been following that story closely because Monty was the lead detective on the case.

Link, link, where's the fucking link? My hands trembled on my mouse as I clicked on the first one... and there he was. My little brother. Except he didn't look so damn little standing behind a podium and answering questions during a press conference.

"Monty," I whispered, smashing my palm over my mouth as the tears began to flow. He was in a light-blue polo with his police department's insignia on the chest, and he was fielding questions like a pro. And his voice! It was so deep.

I was so fucking proud of Monty, and tears sprang to my eyes at the way he talked about the bravery of the women who had survived what the media was dubbing "The Prince Charming Attacks." Then his eyes glazed over, staring into space for a long moment, and I couldn't help but wonder... *Is he thinking of me?*

With his next request, delivered in a hoarse voice, I was pretty sure he was. "I'd like to ask you all to please give these women, as well as their families, the privacy they need to heal. I'm aware you have a job to do, but please consider this. If it was someone you loved, how would you want them to be treated?" Then he turned and quickly exited the stage.

When that video was done, I clicked on the next one. And the next. Monty commanded every press conference, every interview, every room he was in. My baby bro was all grown up.

Auburn was too, running the Bouvier fashion empire like a boss. And he was a daddy now! He and Gianna had gotten married and adopted twins, a boy and girl. Jaxon and Jane. I was an aunt, and I hadn't even gotten to meet them.

I didn't think it was possible to be so happy and so sad at the same time. My stomach rolled over, and I reached for my coffee, but the smell of it only made nausea rise in my throat, so I put it back down and grabbed a bottle of water from the mini fridge behind my desk. The liquid was cool and soothing, and I went back to my computer feeling nostalgic for my family.

In my opinion, social media was the best thing ever invented. It gave me a way to keep up with my family from afar. My father wasn't very active on Facebook or Instagram since his retirement, so I did a Google search for Paul Bouvier. There wasn't much new stuff, only a few older articles announcing that he'd filed for divorce from my mother, and I wondered what the final straw that broke the camel's back was. My dad and Chloe hadn't been close for years. They'd had separate bedrooms for as long as I could remember.

Over the years, my family still shared info about my disappearance, and again, that warmed my heart and made it break at the same time. They still loved me. They still thought about me and missed me. And I missed the hell out of them too.

My stomach did another weird flip, and I clamped my hand over my mouth as the water I'd drunk attempted to make a reappearance. Leaping up, I dashed to the restroom down the hall, ignoring the curious stares from the other people in the office.

After I'd emptied my stomach in the toilet, I emerged from the stall to find Maz leaning against the sink with a cool, damp cloth. "You okay, Eden? Do I need to check you out?"

"You're a veterinarian," I said, my voice scratchy from vomiting.

She chuckled and felt my forehead before dabbing my face with the cloth. "Anatomy is anatomy. You don't seem to have a fever. When was your last period?"

Oh. Shit.

"Umm, I'm not sure. It's been a little spotty since I had my birth control implant removed a few months ago." Maz arched a perfectly plucked eyebrow, and I clarified. "We're not trying for a baby, but we're not exactly *not* trying either."

Dane and I had actually talked about starting a family a few times over the years, but the timing had never been quite right. At first, I'd wanted to wait until we returned home so we could share the experience with my family. Then we got the fur babies, and they certainly kept us busy. But now...

Maz nodded thoughtfully. "Go on home, just in case you are coming down with something. I don't need the entire hospital puking." Rubbing a soft circle over my upper back, she urged me toward the door. "And you might think about stopping by the pharmacy on the way home."

I did as she suggested, but rather than taking the pregnancy test, I shoved it into a bathroom drawer, behind my hair products. There was no way I was pregnant already. Though the doctor that removed the implant told me it was possible my fertility would return within weeks, he also cautioned that it didn't usually happen that quickly.

My cycles had been erratic since I'd had it removed. I would have a heavy period one month and then a bit of spotting the next. No, I definitely wasn't pregnant. My breasts didn't feel heavy, and I felt completely fine. Well, other than today's vomiting incident, but I was sure that was just an emotional response. And it was only once.

If I got sick again, I'd take the test.

CHAPTER 43

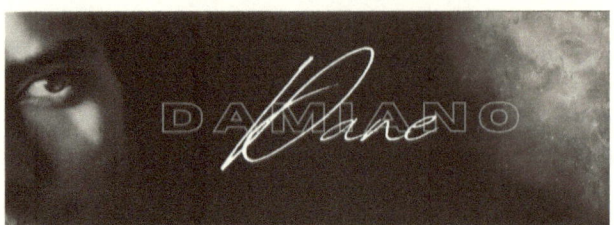

I PUT THE FINISHING touches on a wedding cake that was to be delivered this weekend and stood back to admire my handiwork.

"That's gorgeous," Barry said, walking up beside me. "Those silvery pearls are a nice touch."

"I think Andrea will be pleased."

"But will her mother?" he scoffed, and I shook my head in silent commiseration with the poor bride. She was dealing with a full-fledged mom-zilla.

"Who the hell knows? That woman is something else."

Barry checked his phone, and his ginger eyebrows shot straight up. "Whoa, they caught that serial killer."

"The one near Miami?" I asked, instantly on high alert.

"Yep." His eyes scrolled down the screen. "Wow. Dude dressed up as Prince Charming for kids' birthday parties. That was how he found his victims. Holy shit!"

"Would you mind storing the cake for me? I need to make a phone call."

"Sure thing."

Walking out the back door to the employee parking lot, I found a shady spot beneath a full oak tree and leaned against the thick trunk before dialing Eden's number. She answered right away.

"Hello?"

"Hey, babe. I was wondering if you've seen the news today."

"The serial killer thing?" she asked.

"Yeah, that."

I could hear the excitement in her voice. "I did. I got to see Monty doing some press conferences and stuff. He's kinda famous and shit now."

I laughed. "That's pretty cool." The sounds of waves crashing in the background caught my ear over the phone line, and I frowned. "Are you at work?"

She hesitated only for a second. "No, I wasn't feeling great, so Maz sent me home."

"What's wrong?" I asked, pushing away from the tree.

"Just an upset stomach. I'm fine. Sitting on the lanai with a glass of iced tea, a cute dog, and a grumpy cat."

"Did you throw up?"

"Just once, but—"

"I'm on my way. I'll stop and get some 7-Up."

"Dane," she sighed, "I'm fine. I promise."

"See you in a few minutes," I said and hung up.

When I arrived at home, my wife was indeed on the back porch with her feet up. I watched her through the window for a moment before filling a glass with ice and the clear soda. Taking it outside, I swapped it for her glass of tea and kissed the top of her head.

"How are you?"

"I told you I was fine, you sweet, ridiculous man. I think I just got emotional, you know? I haven't heard my brother's voice in sixteen years, and it was weird."

I took the seat beside her and draped my arm around the back of her chair. "I guess that makes sense. I was done anyway. I finished up a wedding cake, and all the baking is done for the day."

Eden tilted her head over against my shoulder. "Then I guess I get to spend the rest of my day with my husband."

Almost three weeks later, I was wiping down tables at Sweet Heaven at the end of the day. There was only one table of customers left, two twenty-something ladies who were sipping lattes and eating coffee-flavored cupcakes with a chocolate ganache drizzle on top, one of our most popular desserts.

"Did you hear that Bouvier woman died?" one of them said in a conspiratorial voice.

It was all I could do to keep from whipping my head around, but I continued with my task and shamelessly eavesdropped. "Who? The one married to Auburn? Because I wouldn't mind being a shoulder he could cry on."

Oh fuck. Are they talking about Gianna Bouvier?

"No," the other one giggled. "The older one. Auburn's mom."

Holy shit! I hightailed it to the kitchen and found one of the high school kids who worked after school. "Brandon, can you finish up in the dining room? I'm going to head home. Got some... family stuff."

"Sure thing, Mr. Osbourne. Hope everything's okay."

I arrived home a few seconds after Eden and pulled into the driveway beside her cute little sports car. She didn't seem to be aware that anything was amiss, if her exuberant wave was any indication.

Hopping out of the SUV, I pulled her into a hard hug, and she laughed. "What's that for?" She snuggled into my chest. "Not that I'm complaining."

"Come inside, sweetheart. We need to talk."

Twenty minutes later, I was squatting beside my wife as she threw up in the toilet. After showing her a news article about Chloe Bouvier dying in a car accident, she'd immediately taken off for the bathroom with me right on her heels.

I helped her stand and massaged her shoulders while she brushed her teeth at the silver sink. When she was done, I handed her a hand towel to wipe her mouth and met her eyes in the mirror.

"Are you okay?"

She nodded. "I think so. It was just a shock. We've never been really close." She dropped her head and leaned her palms against the countertop. "I feel bad saying this because she's dead, but I never really knew her. She was cold, you know? Like someone who just lived in our house, not like a mother at all. I was closer to our housekeeper than my own mother."

I continued massaging her shoulders when I asked my next question. "Are you pregnant?"

Eden blew out a breath and then turned to face me, her brown eyes meeting mine. "I think... maybe."

My heart turned Grinch-like, growing three sizes in the span of a couple seconds. "Really?" I was practically breathless with excitement. Just as I was about to suggest that I go get a pregnancy test, Eden reached into a drawer and pulled one out.

"I bought this when I got sick a couple weeks ago but never used it because I felt better."

I cupped her face and leaned my forehead against hers. My blood was moving entirely too fast through my veins, like the blood cells were in an all-out sprint. "Will you take it now?"

Five minutes later, we stared down at the little stick on the glossy red tiles of the counter, and our entire lives changed.

Pregnant.

Joy. Elation. Wonder. My mind was a fucking thesaurus of every happy word in existence.

As if our eyeballs were being pulled by invisible ropes, we looked at each other, and I didn't have to ask if she was as happy as I was. Her brilliant smile said it all.

"We're having a baby," she whispered.

"We're having a baby," I said in a much louder voice because *fucking hell*, I was going to be a dad! Grabbing Eden's butt, I lifted her until her legs banded around my waist. Then I spun us in circles until I was so dizzy I was at risk of tipping over.

"You're going to make me puke again," she giggled, and I leaned my back against the wall for balance and fell even more in love with the woman who was now carrying my child.

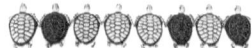

Dr. Makenna Katten smiled as she turned from her computer to face us. I'd called and insisted that the OB/GYN's office get my wife in for an appointment the very next day. I was fully prepared to pull out my old Damiano persona to get what I wanted, even if that meant busting into the office with guns blazing and demanding they check her out. Luckily, they'd had a last minute cancellation, and I was saved from reverting to my former proclivities.

"Congrats, kids. You are indeed expecting. I'd say you'll be getting a new member of the family in late October."

Eden and I shared a smile, our intertwined fingers resting on her thigh. She was freaking glowing. I knew that sounded cliché, like something everyone said, but I honestly wouldn't have been surprised if her skin glittered like the vampires in those movies.

"And everything's okay?" I asked, only pulling my eyes from my wife's when the doctor hesitated. "What? What's wrong?"

"Eden is fine, I promise. Just a bit anemic." She tilted her head back and forth a few times, her dark-brown ponytail swinging around her shoulders. "Quite a bit, if I'm being honest. That means your red blood cell count is low."

My wife sensed my rising panic and squeezed my hand. "What can we do about that?" she asked calmly.

How the hell is she calm right now when she doesn't have enough red blood cells? Because that seems like a really big fucking deal.

"You'll start on prenatal vitamins with plenty of iron, but you'll also want to include plenty of leafy greens in your diet. Asparagus, brussels sprouts, and broccoli have lots of folate, which is also vital." The doctor held up a bottle of pills and some paperwork before placing it into a white plastic bag. "There's a month's worth of vitamins and some literature for you to read. Feel free to call me if you have any questions."

She stood, and I leaped from the plastic chair I was sitting on, alarm bells ringing in my head. "Wait! I mean... what? Shouldn't she be in the hospital or something? For god's sake! She doesn't have enough blood cells." I shook my head manically. "Isn't there somewhere she could go to fix this? I'm pretty sure I read about a place in Switzerland that specializes in... blood. Or something."

I was fully aware I sounded like a lunatic, but my wife—*my freaking wife*—was not well. And the best medical advice we could get was to eat more goddamn broccoli? The woman smiled indulgently, and I narrowed my eyes at her.

"Mr. Osbourne, I can assure you, this is not an uncommon thing for pregnant women. And I give you my word, I will stay on top of this."

My mind whirled through all the things I knew about pregnancy, which admittedly, wasn't a lot. "Should she be on bed rest?"

"That's not necessary and can cause more harm than good, like blood clots. Though I would say that restricted activity would be wise since dizziness, fatigue, and weakness can be symptoms of anemia. That means no extreme sports like rollerblading or skiing. Since Eden has mostly a desk job, it's fine for her to continue working. I would like for you to avoid traveling long distances though," she said, patting Eden's knee.

"Should I get her a wheelchair or something?" I asked, and I swear to god, the woman was biting her lip to keep from laughing at me.

"Not at all, Mr. Osbourne. Walking is actually a very healthy form of exercise." Her lips crooked up at the corners. "And before you ask, normal sexual activities are also fine. In fact, I encourage it. A happy mommy is a healthy mommy."

I lowered my voice. "Define *normal* sexual activities because—"

"Dane," my wife broke in, her voice a razor-sharp warning.

"It's okay. Trust me, it's nothing I haven't heard before," Dr. Katten said with a chuckle. "Many fathers are concerned about this very thing. If you want specific things to avoid, I would say definitely no breath play. Also, many women have hemorrhoids during pregnancy, so be cautious with anal sex. Other than that, my advice is to listen to your partner. She'll be able to tell you if anything is uncomfortable."

The knots forming at the base of my skull seemed to loosen just a bit. Specifics. Yes, that's what I needed, and I appreciated her candor.

I wanted to ask more questions, but my wife dragged me from the office. Once we were in the car, I cupped her chin and gave her a soft kiss on the lips. "I'll take care of you and our baby," I told her. "I may not have had a very good paternal role model, but I can do this. I can be a good father."

I wasn't sure if I was trying to convince her or myself, but her returning smile was so sweet, so full of confidence, I felt it in my bones.

"And I didn't have a warm, loving mother in my life, but you did," Eden said. "And I had a wonderful father. So we can help each other. Fill in the blanks we each have in our own experiences. We'll be a team."

My hand slid around to the back of her head and held her still for my kiss, one filled with all the promises I intended to keep.

"A family team," I murmured against her lips before pouring all my love into another soul-bending kiss.

"I liked Dr. Katten," she told me once we were on our way home.

"Hmph. She's really young," I said, unimpressed.

"She's in her fifties. I looked up her bio before the appointment."

"Yeah, but is she really? She could be lying. Just like your paperwork says you're thirty-eight, but in actuality, you're thirty-five. Maybe she's—"

"Dane, it's fine. She's fully licensed and is known as the best OB/GYN on the Keys. Don't make a big deal of it."

I closed my mouth and nodded. I didn't want to upset my wife, but I fully planned to have Robert do a deep dive on this Makenna Katten person—if that was even her real name.

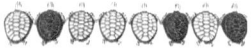

They say when it rains, it pours. And a few nights after Eden's mother passed away, I realized that was the truth.

I was roused from sleep by the ringing of my phone. A call, not a text. Glancing at my still sleeping wife in my arms, I carefully extricated myself and rolled to snag my cell from the nightstand. My brother's name flashed on the screen, along with the time, 3:04 a.m.

Answering it as I rose from the bed, I whispered, "Give me a second." Once I was downstairs and safely out of earshot, I spoke again. "What's going on? You better not be drunk dialing me."

"Luca's dead," Fiero blurted, and my heart almost fell out of my chest.

"Holy fuck. What happened?"

My brother's voice was a little breathless. "The entire organization was at a party at Luca's estate tonight. You know he hardly ever does that, has everyone under one roof, but he's been planning this for weeks."

I started preparing a pot of coffee because I had a feeling I was going to need some caffeine. "Go on."

"An anonymous person sent a tip to the police that there would be unlawful activity going on there."

My mind whirled. "And were you that anonymous person?"

There was a brief pause and then... "I was. I made an appearance and then scrammed. It was just as I suspected. Drugs, prostitutes, even underage girls partying like it was 1999."

"Holy fuck," I repeated because it pretty much summed up my feelings.

"Yeah, I've been listening on the police scanner, and I heard that everyone was arrested. Luca and two others were killed. The entire organization is going down. Well, except for me."

I felt dizzy at the thought, and I wondered if maybe I was anemic too. Pouring myself a mug of coffee, I settled on a barstool at the breakfast bar. "Are you safe? Where are you?"

"I'm on my way to Florida. I stopped to get a new phone, and I'm going to toss this one in the river. I'll text you my new number, so if you could send me Jamie and Robert's address..."

"I'm on it," I said, my chest filling with so much gratitude and love for my brother. I knew he'd done this for me. For me and Eden and our baby.

We hung up, and I rested my elbows on the bar and buried my hands in my hair. I could take her home. I could fulfill the promise I'd made to Eden all those years ago. And it would finally be safe to do so.

Then a voice popped into my head, the voice of Makenna. And yeah, I'd gotten on a first name basis with the doctor over the past few days. Robert had checked her out, and she was completely legit, thank god. She had finally given me her cell number after I'd called the office nine times in two days. Apparently, I was "disrupting the staff" with my questions. But whatever. There were detailed things I needed to know, and Makenna had very patiently answered them each time I called her.

I would like for you to avoid traveling long distances though, I remembered her saying to Eden on our initial visit, and my mood sank slightly. Though her anemia was much better due to the diligent use of vitamins and a solid diet, I still wasn't taking any chances.

I was going to take my wife home… but we'd have to wait until our baby was born.

Chapter 44

"DANE," I MOANED AS he slid into me from behind. We were lying on our sides, one of the only positions that was still achievable with my big belly. I was six weeks from my due date, and pregnancy had apparently turned me into a sex fiend. I wanted it all the damn time.

My husband cupped my round stomach, and I gripped his forearm, digging my fingernails into the flesh as he took me deep and growled, "That's it, Wildcat. You know I love it when you mark me."

His cock was thick, filling every inch of my pussy as he tunneled in and out of me with slow, languid strokes. "That feels so good. I love how hard you get for me. Or is that just your morning wood?" My tone was a tease.

He chuckled low in my ear. "Every inch of this is for my sexy-as-fuck wife." With an undulating grind of his hips, my eyes rolled back in my head. I knew I looked like a beach ball with a head, arms, and legs, but I'd never felt sexier, more alive, because Dane told me every damn day.

And it wasn't just his words. It was the way he looked at me, the way he couldn't keep his hands off me. And one of those hands was now snaking down, down, down until it reached my sex. With practiced fingers, Dane massaged my clit in little circles, just the way I liked it. The perfect amount of pressure. The perfect speed.

"Give it to me, Eden. You know what I want." I did know. My body trembled with the anticipation of what was to come, and I checked to make sure the folded towel was in place beneath me. "Come on, pretty girl. Squirt for Daddy."

Yeah. That did it. As Dane's thrusts sped up, I came hard, all over his cock and his hand. And yes, I squirted. I'd freaked out the first time it had happened one morning a couple months ago, but Dane, after cleaning me up, had called Makenna. *Because of course he had, the overprotective worrywart.* She'd assured us on speakerphone, in that calm way she had, that it was normal due to the swelling of the uterus and the surrounding blood vessels in the area.

"Mmm, that was a good one," I moaned as he fucked me through the remnants of my orgasm.

"You drenched my fucking cock, Wildcat. Do you know how fucking turned on that makes me?"

I clenched my inner muscles around his erection. "I think I'm aware by now."

"Fuuuuck, someone's been practicing their Kegels like a good girl," he panted, kissing up and down my neck with open mouth kisses. "You want more?"

"Always," I replied, knowing he'd do his best to give me another orgasm before he left for work. In fact, he always insisted on what he called *Dane's BOGO orgasms.* Buy one, get one free. He was ridiculous, the smug ass, but I was the one who reaped the benefits.

"Assume the position," he told me, sliding out and smacking me lightly on the hip.

With his help, I maneuvered myself until I was on my hands and knees with him behind me, and we faced the mirror over the dresser. Then I glanced over my shoulder, my smile coy, and said, "Fuck me, big Daddy."

"Goddamn," he breathed, sinking into my pussy with his eyes closed in ecstasy. "This little cunt of yours is perfect, Eden. You fit me just right."

He opened his eyes and met mine in the mirror. We both loved fucking doggy style, but we also loved seeing each other's pleasure etched on our faces.

"I love you," I told him, as his hands gripped my hips.

"I love you too, wife. You are beautiful like this." Then his smile turned from sweet to wicked as he began to move. "You are beautiful and so goddamn hot on your hands and knees for your husband, taking my cock up this perfect pussy."

Then we lost ourselves in each other, in the frenzied carnality of mating, our gazes locked in the glass but no less intense. My husband was stunning. Achingly breathtaking, especially when he was like this with his dark hair swinging around his shoulders with every hard thrust. Sure, he had a few gray strands starting to make an appearance in his hair and beard, but it only made him sexier.

Dane's abs clenched as he took me from behind, and the muscles beneath his tatted arms bulged like finely tuned machines. The bed rocked with the motion of our bodies, and the squeaking of the bedsprings mixed with the slaps of flesh on flesh and our rapturous moans. It was a thrilling cacophony of need and pleasure that only drove us higher.

Though I'd come like a freight train earlier, my husband wasn't satisfied until I got my BOGO orgasm. It started at the base of my neck and trickled down my spine as Dane increased his pace, a self-satisfied smirk on his perfectly full lips. He knew my body so well, and he was aware I was on the brink.

He also knew just how to get me there. Scraping his teeth hard over his bottom lip and leaving it red and swollen, he said, "Come for your husband, Evie."

The use of my real name did it, and I collapsed to my elbows as Dane draped himself over my back and rutted into me like an animal intent on the sole purpose of satiating our needs. I tilted my face for a kiss, which he delivered with love and passion, our tongues wrapping and licking as our lower bodies rocked out our orgasms.

Then Dane went all gentle on me, dragging his hands around my body to cup my pregnant belly. He guided us down until we were once again lying on our sides, his big body pressed against my back.

The only sounds were our labored breathing and beats of our hearts as the sun streamed into the room through the transom windows.

I fell back into a dreamless sleep, only waking for a second when Dane rearranged me on the bed so my head was on the pillow. A sleepy smile wove its way across my lips when he kissed my belly and whispered, "Be a good boy. Daddy will be back to check on you two later."

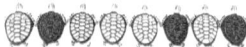

Later that afternoon, I was walking with Charlisse on the beach in the September sunshine. Dane and I had finally sat down with her and told her our story... minus the shooty parts. We both trusted her, and we would need her in the coming months.

"I talked to Cooper today," she said, pride warring with worry in her voice. "He can't tell me where he is, but he said he's doing well."

"Make sure to give him our love when you talk to him again," I said.

She grasped my hand, and we continued walking. "I will. And thank you for inviting me to go with you and Dane to New York. It's just the distraction I need."

"We're happy you're coming. We appreciate you agreeing to watch our little one while we talk to my family. I know he'll just be an infant, but I think they can sense extreme emotional distress, and I don't want him upset."

"Your family is going to be thrilled to see you again, but I'm sure it will be a shock too. It's best not to have the baby around all that. I'll just be in my hotel room, whispering to him that I'm his favorite honorary auntie while I kiss his cute little face."

My feet paused as a twinge shot down my side, and Charlisse stopped too. "What's wrong?" she asked.

"Just a little... something." A vise wrapped around my middle, and I grunted. "It's really tight. It happened a few minutes ago, but this one was a little more intense."

Charlisse's calm tone belied the worry I saw in her blue eyes. "Let's head back when you're able to walk."

I blew out a breath from my pursed lips and straightened, the weird feeling dissipating as quickly as it had come. "I'm good now."

"Uh-huh," she said, already dialing her phone one handed before putting it to her ear. "Dane, meet us at the entrance to the beach. I think she just had a contraction."

"I'm fine," I protested even as I heard yelling through the phone line.

"I know it's not time yet," she said smoothly, guiding me with a hand on my back. "That's why we need you to pick us up and take us to the hospital... Yes, call Makenna... No, you can't talk to Eden right now. You can talk to her when you get here. She's okay, but I'm trying to get her off this beach before another one hits."

"I think you're overreacting," I said, though the last word broke a little as another of those things that was absolutely *not* a contraction squeezed my belly. "He's not ripe yet."

"Babies don't wear watches," she retorted as I bent at the waist and concentrated on breathing.

Charlisse rubbed circles on my back as I whispered to my child. "Just stay in there a few more weeks, baby boy. Please."

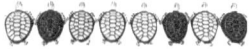

"Yep, this baby is coming today," Makenna announced, stripping off her gloves and covering me with a sheet. "You're five centimeters dilated."

Dane clutched my hand and used his free one to swipe down his face. "Could I have caused this? We had intercourse this morning."

"Dane!" I scolded, feeling my face heat.

But it didn't deter him from continuing. "And then I came home at lunch for a nooner."

Makenna snorted, and I glared. "Would you please stop talking? She does not need to hear about our sex life, Dane."

He pointed at my crotch. "She deals with that area, sweetheart, and I'm going to give her all the information about what has recently occurred in that area in case it's important."

My doctor patted Dane's shoulder as her lips twisted in amusement. "Thank you for letting me know," she said politely. "And no, you didn't cause this. Sometimes babies are just very excited to meet their parents. Especially when they have great ones like I know you two will be."

Such a diplomatic answer for someone who—I have no doubt—had been about two seconds from hearing the details of positions, pacing, and orgasm count from my husband.

"Will he be okay?" I asked.

"Your baby or your husband?" the doctor asked, and I couldn't help but giggle, even through my nerves.

"Both."

Her face turned serious. "Babies born at thirty-four weeks generally do very well. He might spend a few days in the NICU to make sure his lungs are strong enough, but I have every confidence your pediatrician will take good care of him. Dr. Bonner is very well-respected in our little medical community. My daughter is a nurse and uses him for her baby."

That made me feel a little better. Dane and I had interviewed several pediatricians before settling on Dr. Jay Bonner. He was mature with a kind face and a direct manner. And he always wore funny socks and ties to the office to put kids at ease, though we would be long gone by the time our child was old enough to notice such things.

Three hours later, the most beautiful baby to ever grace this earth was born. He had black hair like Dane and blue eyes like my natural ones. He weighed five and a half pounds, and Dr. Bonner remarked that he probably would have been at least eight pounds if he'd gone full term.

We stood in the NICU, Dane on one side of the incubator and me on the other. We both had one hand inside, and our baby was holding our fingers. He had a nice, firm grip. Our other hands were clasped together on top of the glass enclosure that was keeping our precious gift safe.

My husband and I were both crying, but they were tears of joy. He was going to be okay. His lungs were slightly underdeveloped, but he was going to be fine.

We'd named our boy after my father and Dane's maternal grandfather, one of the only good male influences in his life. My eyes dropped to the name card on the side of the incubator, and I smiled. The card listed his parents' names, all his birth stats, and his name...

Paul Augustus Osbourne.

Chapter 45

NO LONGER HIDING

I walked toward the man I hadn't seen in years, my heart hammering in my chest. My brother, Monty Bouvier.

God, he's gotten big. Which was a silly thought because he's a grown-ass man now, and the last time I saw him in person, he was only seventeen.

He stared at me with confusion on his face, and I saw the moment he recognized me. We simultaneously broke into a run, our arms entwining around each other when our bodies crashed together. He was so strong, lifting me from my feet with ease as my legs wrapped around his waist.

Tears. Nothing existed except for the tears of sorrow and regret that streamed down my face and soaked his shirt. I could feel his grief dripping down my neck.

We said nothing for the longest time, aside from murmuring each other's names, his coming out as a question each time, as if to assure himself that it was really me.

"Evie?"

"Monty."

"Evie?"

We went back and forth like that until he finally pulled his head from my neck and searched my face. His blue eyes mirrored my own, blue and extremely wet.

"It's you." His tone was awestruck and raspy as he touched my face and swiped at my tears. "It's really you." My brother's voice was so damn deep now, but there were cracks between each word that I knew matched the cracks in his heart.

Because of me.

"It's really me," I promised him.

Monty shook his head back and forth, his expression a jumble of wonder and confusion as he set me down but kept his arms around me.

"Where have you been all this time? What the hell happened to you, Evie?"

Well, here the fuck we go.

I heaved out a long breath and spit it out. "I was kidnapped."

My brother's expression transformed into one of rage, of the protective big brother, even though he was a year younger than me. "By whom?" he gritted out.

I glanced over my shoulder at the man standing nervously near a tree about twenty yards away, his face a mask of apprehension as our eyes met. He gave me a nod of encouragement, and I turned back to my brother.

"Human traffickers."

Monty's knees buckled, but he remained standing upright. "No," he whispered, his face the picture of grief.

"I'm okay, Mon. I was rescued not long after I was taken, and I am okay." I said those last three words slowly to emphasize them.

"But..." He shook his head back and forth, as if to clear it. "But where have you been? Why didn't you come home or call us or... something?"

"I went into a do-it-yourself witness protection program."

He pulled his head back, brow furrowing. "A what?"

"I'll explain it all to you, but I'd rather not do it a million times. Can I talk to the whole family at once?"

"Fuck. Yeah," he said, bobbing his head up and down. "We have to get to Dad and Auburn." His eyes turned to the right where his gorgeous, pregnant wife was being comforted by Cruz Estrada, Auburn's former driver and security guard.

I touched Monty's arm as his face took on the consistency of a marshmallow at the sight of Kassie. "I'm so happy you and Kass are back together," I told him, my throat feeling tight. They'd been apart for so long, but they'd finally found their way back to each other.

"You know about us?" Monty asked, giving me the side eye.

"I've been keeping up through social media and my friend Google."

"Right, the Instagram account," he said, shifting his gaze to the left this time. "So you're really *The Adventures of Garfield and Snoopy*?" A smile crossed his face when he spotted my fur babies.

I motioned for Dane, and he nodded, making his way toward us. "That's me." I'd sent Monty a private message from my account and told him I'd be bringing the furry duo to New York and asked if he wanted to meet up in Central Park. "Here you thought you'd be meeting the stars of the account, and you ended up with your sister."

A laugh burst from Monty as he swiped the remnants of tears from his face. Then he looped an arm around my shoulders and squeezed. "Best goddamn surprise of my life. Who's that guy? Some kind of handler or pet sitter?"

"Actually," I said, reaching for Dane's hand as he approached. "This is my husband, Dane Osbourne."

My brother's mouth dropped open so wide, I was surprised it didn't hit his loafers. "Your husband? You're married?"

"As are you," I pointed out, and he shook his head in wonder.

"I'm just... I'm still trying to get my head around the fact that you're here, but now you tell me you're married? I guess I still think of you as an almost-nineteen-year-old."

"I'll always be a year older than you, no matter how long I've been gone."

Monty gave me a light punch on the arm before turning to shake Dane's hand. "Nice to meet you. I'm Monty Bouvier."

"I know. I've kept up with you through Ed—uh, Evie."

"Wish I could say the same," my brother said wryly before turning toward the approaching footsteps.

For an extremely pregnant woman, Kassie Bouvier could trot. She barreled into me, hugging me in a wild tangle of arms and tears. "Evie! Oh my god, Evie!"

I returned her embrace. Kassie and I had been instant friends as soon as Monty introduced us as teens. I'd been heartbroken when she and Monty split up shortly before I got kidnapped.

"You look so beautiful," I told her, pulling back and patting her belly. "I'm so happy you two are back together."

Her brown eyes were wide and wet. "What happened to you, Evie?"

Monty stepped up behind her and rested his hands on her shoulders. "Evie was taken, and she's going to tell us everything once we're with Dad and Auburn. This is her husband, Dane." He still looked incredulous that I was married.

Kassie did too. "You're married?" she gasped.

I wanted to tell them I was also a mother, but I held back. We had enough to deal with first. While Kassie greeted Dane, I turned to the other man who was trying to look inconspicuous, though he wasn't succeeding. He was the same size as Monty, tall and muscular.

"So," I said, opening my arms for a hug, "I hear you're my brother."

Cruz Estrada laughed and embraced me. "Apparently so. It's really nice to meet you, sis."

"I saw the press releases a few months ago," I explained. "Welcome to the family."

"And welcome *back* to the family. I've heard so much about you from Monty and Auburn," he replied, and I liked him instantly.

"So, your mom was my nanny when I was a baby?"

"Yes, she and our dad got together while he and Chloe were separated."

"I want to hear the whole story some time," I requested.

"Absolutely. It's kind of complicated."

"I bet mine would beat yours as far as complicated goes."

"No doubt," Cruz laughed, and then his face turned serious. "Are you okay, Evie? I know we just met, but I still care about you."

Yep, I definitely liked my new brother.

Dane and I introduced Garfield and Snoopy to the group, and everyone gave them pets and scratches. Monty watched me the entire time and never got more than a foot away from me. He was probably afraid I'd disappear again.

Then he pulled Cruz aside, and they had a brief conversation before returning to our little circle. Monty pulled me into another hug and whispered, "I'm so fucking glad you're home, Evie."

"Me too," I said, tearing up again.

"Auburn's apartment is within walking distance. Cruz is going to pick up Dad, and he'll bring him to us." His lips tightened for a second before he took both my hands. "Dad had a heart attack last year."

"What?" It would have been a scream if my throat hadn't been attempting to close up. "Is he... I mean... oh my god. Dad."

"He's okay," Monty soothed. "He had surgery, and he's fine now, but we thought it would be best if Cruz broke the news to him gently to minimize the shock of seeing you. I'm guessing you heard about Chloe?" Our mother's name came with a slight curling of his lip, almost a sneer, but not quite.

"I did," I confirmed.

"Well, Dad is with Estrella now, Cruz's mom. I just thought I would give you a heads-up. And Cruz is..." He huffed out a breath.

"Our brother. I know. I saw the press releases, and I've seen pictures of Dad with Estrella. It was big news for about a week, and then the media moved on to the next thing."

Monty chuckled. "You have been keeping up."

"I was a total stalker."

His eyes searched my face one more time, like he wasn't quite sure I was real. "I'm so happy to see you, Eve-ster Egg."

"I'm happy to see you too, Montague."

He cringed. "I don't care how long you've been gone. You're still not allowed to call me by my full name."

It felt like old times, as though the years separating us had shrunk and we were back to our younger selves, teasing and laughing.

"Remember when we used to call ourselves the Wonder Twins?" I asked, and my brother laughed.

"Yeah, after we found those old comics in the attic." He rolled his lips inward and then stared over my shoulder. "When you were gone, sometimes I would think about that and wish I really was a superhero so I could find you."

"But you became a detective, so you were a hero to so many other people."

I read the regretful response in his eyes, but he didn't say it out loud. *And yet I couldn't find my own sister.* Instead, he said, "Let's go see if we can make Auburn piss himself."

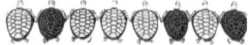

A few people recognized Snoopy and Garfield as we walked, and we had to pause for them to gush and take pictures. They really were popular.

"That's our hotel," I said, gesturing to the brick building across the street from the park. "Do you care if we leave Garfield and Snoopy with our friend upstairs?"

Monty looked surprised. "That's fine, but why did you get a hotel room? You can stay with us."

I shrugged. "I didn't know..."

He rolled his eyes. "They're welcome to come with us. Auburn and Gianna won't mind."

"No, it's almost time for Snoopy's nap. She gets grumpy if she doesn't get at least twenty hours of sleep a day."

Everyone laughed, and Dane reached to take Garfield's leash from my hand. "I'll take them. Will you be okay down here?" His eyes darted around as if looking for danger behind every lamp post.

"I'll be fine," I assured him.

We watched him enter the hotel, and Monty looped our arms together. "He seems really protective of you."

"He is," I said simply before changing the subject. "So tell me about your son. Sully, right?"

My brother's face cracked into a proud grin. "He's an awesome kid. I guess in all your snooping, you figured out he's Kassie's biological son and I adopted him?"

I nodded. "I'm so happy he has you."

"I'm the lucky one," he replied. "I'm not sure what I even did with my life before Kass came back. She and Sully and our soon-to-be daughter are my world. And now you're here too. It's like... I feel whole again."

My chest ached for him. He'd been through so much by the time he turned eighteen. Losing their baby. Kassie disappearing. And then me.

Before I could reply, Dane exited the hotel and jogged up to me, tugging me into his chest and burying his face in my neck like he'd been in Siberia for twenty years instead of in the hotel for five minutes. "You okay?" he murmured, and I nodded. His face smelled faintly of baby lotion, and I suspected he'd grabbed a quick Paulie cuddle while he was up there.

"I am. Is... everything okay upstairs?"

My husband spoke low in my ear. "He's fine. Doing his favorite activity right now."

"Eating or pooping?" I whispered, and he chuckled.

"Eating." He leaned back and brushed a strand of my hair behind my ear. I didn't have the lavender streak anymore. I'd dispensed of that years ago, and then I'd gotten rid of the nose ring after Paulie almost yanked it out when he was two months old.

We parted and turned, finding Kassie and Monty staring at us. The curve of a smile Kassie gave us was understanding, and I knew she could see our love. Monty frowned a bit, acting like the big brother he pretended to be when we were in high school, protective and wary of any boys who showed interest in me.

We walked a few blocks, and Monty led the way into a gorgeous building and waved at the concierge. "Is this where Auburn lives?" I asked, and he nodded, gripping the back of my neck and kissing the top of my head as we walked to the bank of elevators.

"It is. Kass, Sully, and I live in this building too. So do Cruz and his fiancée, Lehra. Auburn owns it. He and his family live in the penthouse."

"Why am I not shocked that Mr. Fancy Pants lives in the penthouse?" I teased, though my nerves were ramping up. Things were going okay so far, but now I was about to see my older brother and meet his wife for the first time. Then my dad would come. I had to swallow a lump at the thought of seeing him again. After that, I'd have to tell my story and pray they didn't hate me for my choices.

Dane, sensing my shifting emotions, gripped my hand in the elevator as we rose to the penthouse floor. It opened into a foyer, and we stepped out onto the ivory marble floor.

"I was thinking..." Monty said. "Maybe I should go inside first and warn him. I thought I was having an aneurysm when I first saw you, and Auburn is over forty now."

I nodded. "I wouldn't want to kill any of my family members with my presence," I said, only half joking because I was a bit worried about how my dad would take this. What if he had another heart attack from the shock of my return?

Kassie took my other hand and squeezed it as Monty let himself inside the apartment. Approximately thirty seconds later, the door swung open, and Auburn burst into the foyer and then screeched to a halt like a cartoon character. His eyes were wild and his normally perfect hair awry. I understood why a second later when he rammed both hands into the dark strands, his elbows winging out to the side.

"Evie. Holy fuck. You're... here. You're right fucking here. I thought Monty was fucking lying."

"Don't use that kind of language with your sister," I popped off, and his face cracked into a huge grin as he rushed me, wrapping his arms around my waist and lifting me off the ground.

"You're here, and you're still a smartass," he crowed, squeezing me so hard I could barely breathe.

"I just got here, and you're already trying to kill me," I croaked, and Auburn let out a boisterous laugh before loosening his grip and planting me back on my feet.

Cupping my cheeks with both hands, he stared down at me, his face transforming by the second from joy to sorrow and back to joy. "Do you have any idea how much I've missed you?" He swallowed hard and blinked, but he was unable to stop the tears from dripping down his handsome face.

"I missed you too," I cried, smashing my face against his chest and smearing makeup all over his pristine white shirt. With one hand on the small of my back and the other on the back of my head, my big brother rocked me from side to side, his nose buried in my hair.

"You still smell the same," he murmured, and I smiled up at him.

"You smell like expensive cologne and Icy Hot."

That made him grin. "Hell, I'm old, little sis." He studied my face for a long moment. "You look good, Evie. Are you..." The words stumbled a little before he started again. "Are you okay?"

My head bobbed up and down. "I'm really good, Auburn. Just glad to be home."

"Monty said you were kidnapped. Did they…" He lost his words again, and his face crumpled into abject misery. But I read his thoughts.

"No, they didn't hurt me like that. They weren't very nice to me, but it wasn't what you're thinking."

"Thank god," he said, pressing his lips to my forehead and leaving them there until a sweet voice called from behind him.

"Are we gonna stand out in the foyer and cry all day? Or could we do that inside where we have tissues and snacks?"

From the Texas drawl, I assumed that was his wife, Gianna. Stepping around Auburn, I was faced with a freaking goddess standing in the doorway with damp eyes and a wide smile. Her brunette hair was pulled into a full ponytail, and her rounded belly stretched against the sweatshirt she was wearing. I loved that she and Kassie were pregnant at the same time.

I walked to her. "Hi, you must be Gianna. I'm—"

She cut me off with a hug. "Oh, hush your mouth. I know who you are." She hugged me like I was her long-lost sister instead of someone she'd never met. Gianna's embrace oozed warmth, and I liked her already. "Come on inside, Evie. I'm sure it's been an emotional day, and I have pie."

With a sweep of her hand, she ushered me inside, and the rest of the group followed. The living room was spacious, with tall windows that afforded a stunning view of the city. Deep-cushioned furniture in a gorgeous blood-red color formed a square around a sleek wood coffee table. Even though I'd only met Gianna a few seconds ago, I could definitely see her influence in the room. It was both classy and warm.

I wandered to the black stone fireplace as Gianna directed Monty and Auburn to get to the kitchen for iced tea and food. She was funny, with a sweet Southern charm and a side of bossiness. I perused the photos on the mantel. A wedding photo of Auburn and Gianna. A ton of pics of their kids. And right on the end…

I picked up the silver-framed picture of me, Auburn, and Monty. I remembered this. It was taken the Christmas before I was kidnapped... before all our lives were irrevocably changed forever.

Hands settled on my waist, and I relaxed back against my husband. "I remember that girl," he said, peering over my shoulder. My hair was long and its natural caramel color in the picture. "You guys look good together. Happy."

"We were," I said, replacing the frame on the mantel before facing Dane. "What if they don't understand?"

"If they're the men you think they are, they'll understand. They may struggle at first, but they'll come around."

I stared up at the photo once again. I was sticking my tongue out at the camera, Auburn was cheezing like a chipmunk, and Monty was holding bunny ears with his fingers behind my head. We were all so young and carefree. I knew we couldn't reclaim our youth, but I craved that bond the three of us always had. The genuine affection behind all the teasing.

And I hoped like hell we could get that back.

CHAPTER 46

"CRUZ! TO WHAT DO I owe this pleasure?" I asked when I swung open the door of my apartment and found my youngest son standing there. He stepped forward and wrapped me in a hug that lasted a tad longer than our usual embraces.

"Hey, Dad. I needed to talk to you."

My chest warmed at the *needed* part. It had taken a while for Cruz to feel close to me once he'd found out I was his biological father, so I was thrilled whenever he sought me out for help or advice.

"Whatever you need, son. Come on in. You want something to dri—" My words froze when I saw who was standing in the hallway behind him. "Dr. Hart, what are you doing here?"

I realized it was apropos to have a cardiologist named Dr. Hart, but he was one of the best in the world, as well as being very relatable.

"Paul, good to see you. Cruz asked me to come by."

My eyes darted between them, and a bit of panic began to set in. My gaze stopped on Cruz. "Are you sick?" The words came out in a croak.

His big hand landed on my shoulder, and he crooked a half-smile at me. "No, Dad. I'm not sick, but we do need to talk. It's a good thing," he added at the end. "But it's going to be a bit of a shock, and I thought..."

"You wanted my doctor here in case I decided to keel over," I surmised, wondering what in the hell he could want to tell me that might upset me.

Then an idea popped into my head, and I smiled. "It's okay, Cruz. I'm not one of those dads."

"One of what dads?" he asked in confusion, guiding me toward my brown leather couch. We sat, and I flashed him a knowing look.

"If you and Lehra are expecting, I would be thrilled. I know you're not married yet, but like I said, I won't be one of those judgy parents."

He laughed, his mocha face flushing pink, and shook his head as Dr. Hart sat in the matching chair closest to me. "It's not that, Dad. I promise."

"Okay. Well, it's probably for the best because your mother would be pissed if you told me without her here." His mother, my beautiful Stella, was in Texas wrapping up some business so she could move here. With me. Cruz's fiancée, Lehra, had gone with her to help. "So, lay it on me, this shocking but good news."

My son inhaled a breath and swallowed hard before meeting my eyes with his matching ones. He was such a handsome lad, with his mother's Latino skin tone and my blue eyes.

"Dad, Evie is back." The words didn't register, and I stared at him blankly. "Did you hear what I said?"

It was as if he'd spoken into a long tunnel, like the sound waves were taking a while to reach my ears. But I had heard them. I just couldn't fathom them.

"My Evie?" I managed to say around my heart, which seemed to have risen up and lodged in my throat.

"Your Evie," he said kindly. "Your daughter is home."

My eyeballs hurt with the sudden flood of tears that inundated them. "She's..." I could barely get the next word out. It was a word I'd thought of for years, a word full of hope. "Alive?" I finished with my fists clenched in my lap. *Please, God. Don't let her have come home in a coffin.*

Cruz's arm wrapped around my shoulders. "She's alive and well, Dad. I don't know what all she's been through, but she seems very happy."

I. Crumpled. The Evie-sized hole inside me began to fill, and I folded over on myself with the effort to comprehend exactly what this meant. I was vaguely aware of someone doing something to my arm, but the only thing I could process in my one-track mind was the face of my daughter. As a beautiful, loud infant. As a pigtailed five-year-old. As an eye-rolling preteen. As a lovely teenager who loved to make others laugh. And as an almost-nineteen-year-old who had disappeared and left me a shell of a man.

The vague mumblings around me came into focus.

"Doc, what's going on?"

"Pulse is slightly elevated, but his blood pressure is actually good."

"Could he be in shock?"

I lifted my head and answered them in a voice hoarse with tears. "I'm not in shock. I'm just calm. Because for the first time in seventeen years, I feel... whole."

I wanted to sprint all the way to Auburn's apartment. I wanted to run and leap in the air and shout with joy through the streets of New York, but Cruz insisted on driving me. Dr. Hart concurred. The spoilsports. I felt like forty years had been lifted off my shoulders, like I was a young man again.

Dr. Hart had ridden with us and would stay downstairs in Cruz's apartment while my son and I went up to the penthouse. Where my daughter was. My baby girl. My Evie.

"Why is this elevator so goddamn slow?" I vented, and Cruz chuckled.

"Dad, we've only been in here for two seconds."

"Longest two seconds ever," I muttered, staring at the numbers over the door.

On Cruz's floor, I waited by the elevator with the utmost impatience as he let Dr. Hart into his home. *What the hell is taking him so long?* I peeked around the corner to see my son jogging down the corridor toward me.

"Can't you run any faster than that? I thought you were a Marine!" I called, causing him to break into a sprint the rest of the way.

"You'd make a good drill sergeant," he said, but I was already stepping into the elevator and sliding the card Auburn had given me into the penthouse slot. Approximately ten hours later—at least, that's what it felt like—the doors opened, and I saw my oldest son's door.

She's in there. Evie is actually in there.

All of a sudden, I felt nervous and placed a hand over my heart. The beat was hard—so hard it vibrated against my palm—but it was steady and sure.

"You okay, Dad? Do I need to call the doctor up here?"

I shook my head, still staring at that door, the only barrier between me and my daughter. And I was ready.

"No. I'm fine. Let's go."

The door swung open as if I'd willed it to happen. I think it was Auburn who pulled it open, but I couldn't be sure because... there she was. Standing beside the couch, twisting her fingers together at her waist.

My Evie.

It was her. On the car ride over, I'd convinced myself I would find an imposter, but this was definitely my daughter. She looked different, no longer the eighteen-year-old who I'd last seen. Her hair was darker and shorter, but my own blue eyes reflected back at me from her pretty face.

"Daddy," she said on a sob, and my goddamn feet began to move like I was an Olympic sprinter. And then she was in my arms.

All my broken pieces began to sew themselves back together as we held each other, my head on her shoulder and her face in my neck. We cried. A lot. And for a very long time.

Then I couldn't help it anymore. I had to look at her. Pulling back, I cradled her face, her precious, precious face, in my hands and memorized every inch of it. "I love you," I said, and I realized those were the first words I'd spoken to my daughter in seventeen years.

And they were the right ones because nothing was more important than love.

"I love you too, Dad." That filled in the rest of the Evie hole in my soul, and I kissed every inch of my daughter's face. Soft, gentle kisses of pain and longing and adoration. I'd dreamed of doing this for years. Showing my Evie how loved she was. How much I'd missed her spirit and her laugh in my life.

"Are you okay?"

"I am." Her hands slid down my arms and grasped my own. "Let's sit down so we can talk."

I almost stumbled on my way to Auburn and Gianna's red couch because I couldn't stop looking at my little girl. Well, she was all grown up, but she'd always be my little girl. I was aware of sniffles and sobs from around the room, from Kassie and Gianna, but also from my sons.

"First of all, Dad. This is my husband, Dane Osbourne." Cruz had informed me on the drive over that Evie was married, and I finally pulled my eyes away from her to look at the man who had come up beside her. He had dark hair with a splash of gray and a full, neatly trimmed beard. His eyes were dark brown and on my daughter, like he too wanted to make sure she was all right. I appreciated that about him.

"Dane, I'm Paul Bouvier." I stuck out my hand, and he returned the gesture with a firm handshake, which I also appreciated. Then I swiped at my face, finding it soaked with tears. "I'm not usually such a mess."

Our eyes met, and he nodded with a slight smile. "Completely understandable, sir."

Everyone settled onto the comfortable furniture with Evie between me and her husband. I was still processing the fact that she was married.

Gianna squeezed my shoulder. My first daughter-in-law was always such a comforting spirit. "Paul, do you need something to drink?"

"No, thank you, sweetheart. I'd just like to hear what happened to my daughter."

Evie leaned back against the couch cushions and blew a breath toward the ceiling. "It's a bit of a messy story. And long too, so if anyone needs to use the bathroom, I suggest you do it now. Otherwise, you'll mess up Auburn and Gianna's pretty, and no doubt expensive, furniture."

I couldn't help my smile. That was the trademark Evie wit I'd missed so much. She always had a way about her that put others at ease with smiles and laughter.

"We're fine," Auburn said, and Evie glanced at Dane.

They seemed to share some kind of secret conversation before my daughter nodded at him and then said to the room, "Okay. Here we go."

Chapter 47

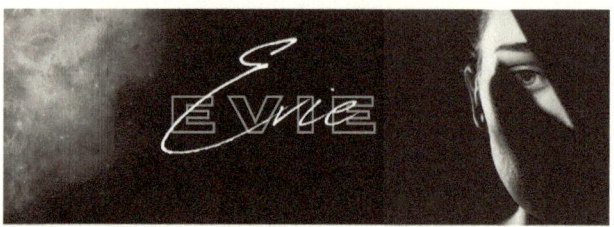

Whewww, this is going to be hard.

I shored up my resolve and began speaking to my family. "First of all, I want to tell you all that I love you, and I've missed you so much. I had to make a lot of choices." Inhaling a breath, I pushed my tears away so I could continue. "Choices that ripped my heart out to make, but please know that I had my reasons."

My father gripped my hand in his. I could see the effects of aging on his face and in the silver of his hair, but he was still so handsome. "It's okay, baby. We're here to listen, not to judge."

God, those simple words touched my heart and gave me strength.

My eyes darted around the room and saw the love reflected back at me. "As you know, I was in Cancún with my friends. There was a bonfire party on the beach, and we all had a really good time. When I got to my room, I realized that I'd lost my phone at some point in the evening." I shot a glance at my dad and decided not to bring up the fact that I'd gone back downstairs to find it so he wouldn't be mad at me. That would only serve to make him somehow blame himself.

"I wanted to go find it, so I retraced my steps to the beach. When I got down there, it was deserted. Except for one person," I continued, staring at the fireplace across the room because I wasn't sure I'd get through this if I looked at anyone. "I had danced with a guy named Felipe, and he seemed nice. When I told him I was looking for my phone, he pulled it out of his pocket."

"Do you think he pickpocketed it?" Monty asked from my right where he was sitting on a love seat with Kassie. Auburn and Gianna were on a matching sofa to my left, and Cruz was seated in a chair across from me.

"I'm not sure. It's possible. It was pretty dark down there. Anyway, we started walking back to the resort, and we passed a copse of palm trees." My mind took me back to the darkness and fear of what happened next, and I felt paralyzed for a moment. Dane, always able to sense my moods, laced his fingers with mine, and I flashed him a grateful half-smile, accepting the strength he was offering.

Just say it, Evie. This is the scariest part, so get it over with.

The words spilled like a waterfall from my lips in one run on sentence. "Someone was hiding in the trees and grabbed me from behind and put a rag over my face, and I thought Felipe would help me, but he was in on it."

I huffed out a long breath, and my shoulders sagged with the relief of finally saying it. Gianna broke up the iceberg of silence in the room with a hammer of levity.

"Well, I would like to kick Felipe in the damn nuts." I didn't think she was actually trying to be funny. The firm set of her lips told me that, but I laughed anyway, just a brief chuckle that soothed my nerves a little.

"I did. I kicked and scratched and punched, but there were two of them, and there was something on the rag that was making me sleepy."

"Fuck," I heard Monty mutter, and his wife leaned into his side as if to comfort him with her nearness.

"Yeah, I heard them say something about getting me to the boat, and then I don't remember anything until I woke up in a warehouse. I think I was still in Mexico, but I'm not sure. There were four other girls there too, and we were told we were being sold."

"Goddamn," Auburn grunted, swiping a hand down his face. "You were trafficked?"

I nodded. "Yes. They transported us to a house in New Orleans where our *owners* were to pick us up." I decided to skim over some of the details. "Then Dane showed up and rescued me and took me to a safe house. He was going to bring me home the next day."

"Safe house?" Cruz questioned and looked at my husband. "Are you a cop?"

"No, I'm a baker," he replied, throwing the occupants of the room into a state of confusion.

Moving on before anyone could ask anything else, I said, "He told me he was getting me away from the person who'd bought me. Luca Cappitani."

I could tell the name resonated by the shocked gasps from everyone around me. Then Monty's eyes met Cruz's, and they seemed to be communicating.

"What's that look about?" I asked, pointing a finger between the two.

Monty answered. "Cruz worked in a SWAT team capacity for a while. He was at that raid on the Cappitani estate."

"I'm the one who killed him," Cruz said quietly, and my brain almost fucking exploded.

Everyone except Monty seemed surprised, but none more than me. When I was finally able to find my voice, I pulled my hands away from the men holding them and pushed at the air with both palms.

"Wait, wait, wait. You're telling me that the brother I didn't even know I had killed the man who was going to buy me?"

"Seems so," he replied, and I shoved off the couch and rounded the coffee table. Cruz stood as I approached and accepted my overzealous hug.

"Thank you. I wouldn't have been able to come home if you hadn't done that. I know you didn't do it specifically for me, but thank you anyway."

When I looked up at him, his cheeks were flushed pink. "I was just doing my job," he said modestly, and I patted his face.

Returning to my seat was like wading through a swamp of disbelief. Everyone's eyes darted between me and the brother who had made this homecoming possible.

"Well, that was unexpected," I announced, and the tension broke as everyone chuckled. "Where the hell was I?"

"You were saying Dane rescued you from Luca," Monty said, his eyes suspicious.

"Yes. Right. Well, he was going to bring me home on a helicopter the next day, but then he found a bomb on it." Everyone gasped, and I shook my head. I was getting ahead of myself. "Sorry, let me go back for a second. Luca saw a press conference and recognized my picture as the person he was buying. He realized this was going to get very high profile, so he freaked out and decided to get rid of me."

My father made a little strangled noise beside me and I swiveled my head to take in the pain etching his features. "Are you okay, Dad?" I asked quietly. "Do I need to stop?"

With his thumb, he traced a soft stroke over my cheek. "No, baby. I need to know what you've been through." I stared into his blue eyes and read the resolve there.

"Okay, but if it's too much, we can save it for later." He shook his head, and I returned my gaze to the black stones making up the fireplace, my eyes tracing the grooves between the rocks to give me something to look at besides the pitying looks I knew were on the faces of my loved ones.

"From what I was told, if Luca Cappitani wanted you dead, he wouldn't stop until you were dead. So, Dane and I faked our deaths and went undercover."

"How did you fake your deaths?" Auburn asked. "We never heard anything about that."

"A friend took the helicopter up and then parachuted out before it blew up over the Gulf of Mexico. That made Luca think we had blown up too."

"Wow," Kassie breathed. "That was smart."

Monty chimed in. "How did you know all that about Luca? How did you know he planted the bomb on the helicopter?"

"I had... an inside source," I hedged and noticed the scowl of disbelief on my brother's face. "We changed our names and appearances and went into hiding."

Monty's attention went to my husband. "So your name isn't really Dane Osbourne?"

"It is now," he replied, and Monty's jaw tightened.

"What was it before?"

Fuck. I was hoping to avoid this topic of conversation, but my brother had been a detective for too long to let anything slip through the cracks.

Dane moistened his lips and announced. "My former name was Damiano Cappitani. I was Luca's son."

The room erupted in gasps and cries of shock, but the expression on Monty's face turned absolutely volcanic. He boosted himself off the sofa and was on Dane in a second, yanking him up by the front of his charcoal-gray T-shirt.

"You son of a bitch."

He cocked his fist, and with my heart pounding like a tightly tuned timpani drum, I jumped up and wedged myself between them. "Monty, stop!"

"Evie. Move," he bit out, and I shoved at his chest until I formed the slightest bit of wiggle room between the two men.

"No. You're acting crazy."

"Me? Crazy? Jesus fucking Christ, Evie. You show up here after seventeen years, three months, and eight days—yes, I keep count—and you tell us you're married to some piece of shit Mafia asshole. And you want us to just accept that?"

Dane's voice was low and dangerous behind me. "Yes, it's true. I was a piece of shit Mafia asshole, but you will not speak to my wife that way."

Fucking hell.

I reached behind me and gripped his thigh—hard—in warning as I faced Monty. His face was murderously red, and his eyes were narrowed on my husband. This was a damn nightmare.

"Did you plant the bomb that was going to kill my sister?" Monty asked.

Before Dane could piss him off more, I answered. "No, he didn't. His father directed someone else to do it. Luca was going to blow up his own fucking son, Monty. That's the kind of depravity I've been running from for the past seventeen years, three months, and eight days."

That took a bit of the wind out of his sails, and his body seemed to droop a little. "I feel like you're skimming over things, Evie. Leaving out details. Like what happened to the men who took you?"

Dane answered that with a curt, "They're gone."

Monty threw up his hands. "What the fuck does that mean? They're gone as in they disappeared on the streets of New Orleans? Moved to Zimbabwe? What?"

My husband's voice was scarily low. "Gone as in you never have to worry about them again."

Monty's mouth dropped open for a second, and then he closed it, his eyes fixed on Dane. "Ever?"

Dane's stare was wrapped in steel. "Ever." He'd just told my brother he'd killed them without saying the actual words.

Something passed between them, and Monty gave him a nod that felt a lot like grudging respect. His voice was slightly less confrontational when he asked his next question. "Okay then, why did you run instead of coming to us?"

"Because," I gritted out, "Luca Cappitani was a piece of shit criminal, but he was never convicted of a single crime. You want to know why?" I rammed my finger into Monty's chest. "Because he killed anyone who tried to testify against him. Or they disappeared like that." I snapped my fingers in his face.

Monty closed his eyes and gritted his teeth, but I wasn't done yet. "Or his other favorite tactic is killing or threatening to kill their families. Do you remember the case a few years back where the eyewitness changed her story once she got on the stand?"

"I heard about it," my brother admitted, "but we could have protected you."

"How?" I demanded. "Go look it up, Monty. Every person who went into the government's witness protection system ended up dead or coming out of hiding when Luca administered a warning by killing or maiming one of their family members. Every. Single. One."

My voice broke, but I mended it with all the strength I'd developed over the years. "How the hell do you think I could have lived with that? How could I have let him hurt you? Any of you." I turned in a circle and threw my arms wide to encompass all the people I loved as my voice rose. "I know it sucked not knowing what happened to me, but I'd rather have you all feel that internal pain than have to deal with the guilt of your deaths on my hands. Maybe that makes me selfish, but I did what I had to do to keep my family safe. I took the only control I could grasp on to, and believe me, it wasn't much. As for Dane, he's done nothing but protect me. He turned his life around because he loves me."

The muscles in Monty's chin relaxed, and I saw the slightest tremble of his lips before he pulled me into a crushing embrace. "Fuck, I'm sorry, Evie," he whispered. "So sorry. I just want to know what you've been through so I can put it behind me. The not knowing is agonizing. Every victim I came across while I was a police officer, I saw a little bit of you in them."

As Monty hugged me, Dane gripped my shoulders and spoke in a soft voice. "She's not a victim, Monty. She's a survivor. Evie is the strongest person I've ever met."

I couldn't see them because my face was pressed against Monty's chest, but I could sense the two men looking at each other over my head. Assessing each other. I loved them both so much, and I wanted them to get along. Or at least not to hate each other.

"You're right," my brother said. "She is so damn strong."

Dane spoke again. "You said earlier that you wanted details. If you'll have a seat, I'll give them to you. At least what I saw from my perspective."

My brother released me and kissed my forehead sweetly. "I'm sorry I lost my temper, Evie. I love you."

"I love you too," I croaked. He took a couple steps back and sat beside his wife, who had both her hands pressed over her mouth.

Dane positioned me between the couch and one of the love seats so I was facing the room. Though he was addressing everyone else, he remained facing me.

"The first time I saw Evie Bouvier, I didn't even know her name. It was a video the traffickers sent out to potential buyers." His tone was laced with disgust. "While the other women in the video looked scared as shit, the last one had bright blue eyes and two middle fingers held up to the camera. I think that's when I first started to fall in love with her. She was so goddamn strong and brave."

Dane's eyes held me spellbound. "I was ordered by my father to go pick her up, but I already knew I wasn't going to turn her over to him. There was no way I could. I wanted to save her, but this little wildcat turned it around and stole my heart. She's the one who saved me."

"I love you," I mouthed, and his face was the picture of serenity when he said it back.

"When I arrived to pick her up, she was giving the kidnappers shit, even though she was bound to a chair."

"Oh god," I heard my dad say, though I couldn't look away from my husband. I was as invested in his account as everyone else in the room.

"I made them uncuff her and leave the room. She had a bruise right here where Felipe had hit her." His thumb brushed over my right cheek before touching the barely there scar on my lower lip. "And her lip was split, courtesy of Ethan the fatass." We shared a small smile as he repeated the words I'd said to him that first night.

To my surprise, Dane sank to his knees in front of me and brushed his fingers over my chest, just below the hollow of my throat. "Her skin was raw here from where they'd taped *a goddamn number* to her chest."

Someone, Gianna, I think, let out a sob, but my husband wasn't done. He gently wrapped his hands around my upper arms. "There were finger-shaped bruises here where she'd been grabbed too roughly." His hands slid down to my wrists. "She had raw patches and bruises around her wrists and her ankles from the restraints."

As every eye in the room followed along, Dane detailed every single bump, bruise, and scrape he'd found on my body that night, his gentle fingers tracing over the ghosts of the brutality. When he was done, I cradled his face with my hands.

"And you took care of every wound I had."

He covered my hands with his palms and gazed up at me. "And I vowed that no one would ever hurt you again."

The room was silent for a long time before our family surrounded us. There were hugs and a whole lot of tears, but what touched me the most was when Monty reached for Dane's hand for a shake. I could see his mouth moving, but he was speaking too quietly for me to hear. They shared the tiniest of smiles though, and I prayed everything would be okay.

After the hug fest, everyone settled back into their seats, and we filled the family in on the rest of our life. The bakery. Our friends. My work at the Turtle Hospital.

"You always did love turtles," Auburn said, cracking a smile at me. "I kinda hated going to the zoo with you because you wanted to just stand there and stare at them."

"And you always said they were boring," I replied before letting my eyes drift around to the other faces.

Dane squeezed my hand and whispered, "It's time."

I nodded and took a deep breath. "And there's one more thing we have to share with you." All attention popped to me as I announced, "Dane and I had a baby last year."

CHAPTER 48

THE ROOM WAS SUDDENLY filled with a million questions from every direction, and I laughed and held up my hands. "We have a son named Paul Augustus, though we call him Paulie. He's nine months old."

My dad's hand covered his mouth. "Y-you named your son after me?"

"Kiss ass," Auburn muttered in my ear, and I elbowed him in the stomach, hearing his teasing chuckle.

Approaching my dad, I wrapped my arms around his waist, and he met my embrace. "You're the best man I know, and we hope our son turns out just like you."

His eyes turned watery. "Can I meet him?"

"Of course. He's at the hotel with my friend Charlisse."

Dad grabbed my hand and pulled me toward the door. "Let's go get him." Then he stopped and frowned. "Wait, I don't have my car."

"I'll drive you," Auburn said, grabbing his keys from the table near the door. "We already have a car seat in the SUV."

"I wanna come see the baby," Gianna complained.

Kassie chimed in, pushing herself off the couch. "If Gianna gets to go, I'm going too."

Auburn rolled his eyes and shook his head. "Everyone chill. We'll go pick up Paulie and bring him back here. There's no need for all of us to go." He leaned down and said in a low voice so only I could hear, "And I get to hold him before Monty and Cruz and cement my status as the favorite uncle."

That made me giggle. "Okay," I announced to everyone, "I hate to be *that mom*, but would everyone please wash their hands before we get back? Paulie was a preemie, and he ended up with RSV, so we don't want him to get sick again. That's why we had to wait so long after he was born before we could travel with him."

Everyone agreed with no fuss, and Dane and I followed Dad and Auburn from the apartment. Once we were in the car, I sent Charlisse a text to let her know we were on our way.

Dane and I were in the back seat, and I caught Auburn's eye in the rearview mirror. He smiled. "Gianna and I would really like it if you'd stay with us instead of at the hotel. We have plenty of room for all of you."

"Including Charlisse, Garfield, and Snoopy?" I asked.

"All of you. The kids are staying at Gianna's dad's tonight. Monty and Kass's son, Sully, is too. Tony and Tora were taking them to the zoo today, but they'll be back tomorrow so you can meet them."

I glanced at my husband, and he nodded. "Are you sure it's not too much trouble, Auburn? We're a lot to deal with."

Auburn chuckled. "My wife will have my head if I don't convince you guys to stay with us."

"Can't have that," I said, loving the relationship between Auburn and Gianna. There was an obvious age gap, but the power balance between them didn't reflect that. My bossy CEO brother considered his wife as his equal.

When we reached the hotel, Auburn left his car with the valet and told him we'd only be a few minutes. I snickered when the man practically bowed in the presence of my big brother. Though he wasn't in one of his custom suits, instead wearing a white shirt stained with my makeup from earlier, he still exuded power when we strolled through the lobby and to the elevators.

"I get to hold little Paulie first," my dad announced as we rode up to the twentieth floor. "I'm calling Grandpa privilege."

Auburn smirked with amusement. "Fine, but he's going to like me better."

"Blasphemy!" our dad exclaimed, and we all laughed.

God, it's good to be home.

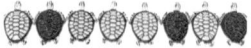

Watching my father hold my baby boy, his namesake, was better than I could have imagined. Tears of joy plopped from Dad's eyes onto Paulie's little blue onesie as he gazed down at him with awe.

"He is beautiful, Evie. Just incredible." He sifted his fingers through the inky silk of Paulie's hair. "All this hair. And those eyelashes!" My son did have amazing eyelashes.

Dad and I were sitting on the couch in Charlisse's suite while Dane was next door in ours, packing our stuff. Auburn was helping Charlisse with the animals and her bags. I probably should have been helping them, but I didn't want to miss a second of this special moment with my dad and my son.

"I'm washing my hands now," Auburn called on his way to the bathroom. "Be ready to hand over that baby, old man."

"I should have sold him on eBay when he was little," Dad muttered before snapping wide eyes to me. "Shit, I'm sorry, baby. That was insensitive of me to say. Because of... you know."

"It's okay, Dad," I assured him. "You can joke around in front of me."

He seemed to relax. "Okay, just let me know if I ever say anything to upset you. I'm sure some of the memories will never go away."

I tilted my head over onto his shoulder and stared down at my son, who was sleeping peacefully in Dad's arms. "I did have a lot of triggers at first, but Dane helped me with them."

"Tell me about that. About how he helped you," my father said, reluctantly handing over the baby when Auburn showed up and sat beside him.

So I laid it out for them. Told them a bit about the nightmares and how closed spaces and the dark bothered me. How Dane would sit on the veranda with me until the sun came up. How he went completely over the top in the lighting section at the hardware store. They got a laugh out of that. It was easier than I would have suspected to talk to them about what I'd been through.

"But I'm okay now. I haven't had a nightmare in years, and I don't have to sleep with the window open or a bunch of lights on. We still have one of the turtle nightlights, and I keep it on at night, but that's more out of nostalgia than anything else."

Dad kissed my forehead. "I know you and Dane didn't start out in a conventional way, but I like him. He kept my little girl alive and took care of her, so I'll always be grateful to him for that."

Dear lord, my heart was so full.

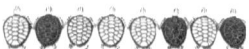

Paulie was a big hit with my family. He was pampered and cooed over, fed and bathed. We all had dinner together, and Dad announced that he wanted to stay over at Auburn and Gianna's too.

Cruz, Kassie, and Monty left about ten, and my dad and I stayed up talking till the wee hours. He told me a lot of things about my mother and why he'd stayed with her for so long. I was disgusted by some of the things she'd done, though I shouldn't have been surprised.

We finally called it a night, and Dad went to sleep in Jaxon's room while I crept into the guest room where my husband was sleeping. I checked on Paulie in the portable crib and found him sleeping like an angel, so I crawled into bed with Dane.

"Everything good?" he murmured, cuddling against my back and kissing the back of my head.

"All good," I sighed in contentment.

We were woken about dawn by our own personal alarm clock, and I groggily crawled from the bed. "I'll get a bottle."

"I'll get the baby," Dane said around a yawn.

When I returned with the warmed bottle, Dane was sitting up against the headboard with Paulie cradled against his bare chest. My breath caught at the intimate beauty of father and son together. The baby held a handful of his dad's hair in one hand. He never pulled; he simply grabbed a chunk of strands in his little fist like it comforted him.

"Well, my boys are certainly looking handsome this morning," I purred, curling up beside them on the bed.

"We are a couple of good-looking dudes," Dane teased, taking the bottle and popping it into Paulie's eager mouth. We watched his chubby cheeks move and listened to his sucking noises for a while before Dane asked, "Should we start looking for a place to live?"

"Is that what you want?"

"I want you to be happy."

"That's not what I asked," I pointed out. "Do you want to live in New York?"

He mulled it over before nodding. "I do. I think we belong here. Paulie will have a grandfather, aunts, uncles, and cousins." A sly grin slid over his lips. "And I've missed New York pizza."

Relief settled in my gut. "I was afraid Monty had scared you off yesterday."

"Nah, your brother is all right, and I don't blame him. I was a bit of an unsavory character in my past life."

"What did he say after he shook your hand yesterday?"

Dane's lips tipped up on one side. "He said he respected me but he wasn't sure he liked me. I told him I felt the same."

"Well, I guess that's better than nothing."

"I'll try to make an effort today when everyone comes over again."

"If he gives you too much trouble, let me know, and I'll deal with my brother."

Dane kissed the tip of my nose. "You're so protective of me."

I gave him a wink. "I'm a wildcat, remember?"

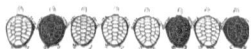

"Auburn and Gianna really know how to throw a party," Kassie said, stuffing the last bit of cupcake into her mouth and groaning. "And your husband is a damn baking genius."

"He definitely is." We were in the kitchen, and I peered around the corner into the living room. Dad was bouncing Paulie on his knees, making him laugh while the other kids looked on, enraptured with their new baby cousin. Gianna and Auburn's twins, Jaxon and Jane, were seven, and Kass and Monty's little boy, Sully, was six. I already adored all of them.

My eyes drifted to the balcony where my husband was standing beside the grill with Monty, both with beers in their hands. I returned to sit across from Kassie. "Our husbands are on the balcony together, and they don't seem to be attempting to throw each other over."

"I'm calling that a win," she said, eyeballing the platter of desserts Dane made earlier. "I had a talk with your brother last night and set him straight. I told him if he makes Dane feel uncomfortable with the family, you guys might decide to just move back to Florida."

Gianna walked into the kitchen and caught the tail end of the conversation. "Noooo, Evie. Please tell me you're staying. I'm already addicted to that little nugget you birthed." She waved a hand at me. "I mean, you and Dane are pretty cool too."

I laughed and reassured her. "We want to stay. We talked about it last night and decided to look for a place to live here in New York."

Her green eyes lit with excitement. "Oooh, goody. I think I can help." She tilted her head back and called, "Auuuuburn!"

Ten seconds later, he appeared beside her, hands going to her pregnant belly. "What? Are you okay?"

Her voice turned into a purr, and she walked her fingers up his forearm. "I was wondering if Evie and Dane could have that apartment that just opened up downstairs. Pretty please? I'd do anything if they could live in our building."

Oh, she's good.

My brother grasped her chin and kissed her hard on the mouth. "You don't have to bat those pretty eyelashes at me, baby girl. I was going to offer it to them anyway." Then he bent closer and whispered, "But I'll still take you up on that *anything* you were offering."

"Gag!" I whined. "We can hear you."

Kassie rolled her eyes at me in commiseration, letting me know their PDA wasn't an uncommon occurrence.

Auburn flashed me a look of chagrin. "You and Dane are welcome to the apartment. Consider it a gift."

"I'll talk to him about it, but we have money," I protested. We still had a chunk of the original seven million; plus, both our jobs paid well.

Auburn appeared to be deep in thought for a moment. "There's still your trust fund as well. I've been managing it for you, and it's grown substantially over the years."

I was a little stunned. I hadn't thought about that for a long time. "Thank you, Auburn. I guess I thought... I'm not exactly sure what I thought," I finished with a laugh.

"Do you plan on working? I'm sure there aren't as many turtle-related opportunities here as there are in Florida, but I know of an excellent fashion company where you could put your marketing degree to good use." He waggled his dark brows at me.

"Are you offering me a job, big bro?"

"If you want it. Monty and Cruz work at Bouvier too, so we might as well have the whole damn family involved."

"That sounds great," I said, fighting back the tears. "I'll talk to Dane about that too."

"Speaking of Dane," Gianna said, "have you tried these cupcakes?" She selected a yellow and pink one and held it up for her husband to taste.

His eyes rolled dramatically back in his head as he chewed. "Dear god, that's the best thing I've ever had in my mouth." Then he winked at Gianna. "Well, the second best."

"Again, Kassie and I are sitting right here," I griped, scrunching my nose up at them, though I wasn't really offended. They were pretty damn cute together, and I loved how happy my brother was with her. For years, all I'd seen were stoic photos of him online or ones where his smile was obviously forced. But that was all pre-Gianna. Now he just looked... happy.

"What kind of cupcake was that anyway?" he asked, ignoring my complaint.

"That was a Battenberg. The Neapolitan are good too," I told him, pointing at the black-and-white ones with pink frosting on top.

My brother snagged one of those, holding it up for inspection before eating half of it in one bite. "Mmmm. Maybe I'll open a bakery in the lobby of the Bouvier building and let Dane run it. Though I'd probably put on about forty pounds."

"Dad bods are all the rage," Kassie pointed out. "You should go for it, Auburn."

He poked his non-existent belly out. "I think I could pull it off."

"He just wants to look as sexy as us, Kass," Gianna claimed, resting a hand on the bump of her belly.

I propped my chin in my hand and watched as the three of them bantered back and forth. The family dynamic was beautiful to see, so accepting and filled with genuine love and affection.

Later that afternoon, Cruz's fiancée, Lehra, arrived, along with his mother, Estrella—who I learned everyone called Stella. She was also dating my father. They were seriously adorable together, and I was thrilled for Dad. He deserved a warm, lovely woman like her.

I found myself beside Kassie again, but this time on the couch with Paulie asleep in her arms. She bent to sniff his head. "God, I love how babies smell."

"Good, I'll bring him to your apartment when he dirties his diaper," I said dryly.

"I'll have plenty of diapers to change pretty soon," she said, indicating her swollen belly.

"I have something to talk to you about since you're an attorney," I told her, and she lifted her brows at me in question. "Once word gets out that I'm alive and back in New York, I'm assuming the police or FBI will want to talk to me."

"And you're worried about that?"

"Yes. I don't know the law, but I'm pretty sure having forged IDs and living under a false name isn't exactly legal. Plus, Dane, uh, took care of some things related to my kidnapping."

She nodded in understanding. "I'm sure he did what he had to do to protect you."

"He did," I agreed. "I just don't want him going to jail or anything."

Kassie reached over and rested her warm hand on top of mine. "I'll go with you to talk to them, Evie. We're family, and I've got your back. Always."

CHAPTER 49

THREE DAYS LATER, AUBURN showed Evie and I the apartment in his building, and we loved it. It was on the first floor and opened up to a private, fenced courtyard so our animals could run around and play while we were working. There were three spare bedrooms in case we decided to add to our family.

Yesterday, he'd introduced us to his realtor, who had shown us a couple commercial properties that would be great for a bakery. I'd chosen the one that was only a block from the Bouvier office building where Eden would be working. I loved that I'd have my wife within walking distance of my bakery.

I stood behind Eden and wrapped my arms around her in the apartment. Auburn had gone back up the penthouse to give us some privacy to discuss it.

"What do you think?" she asked, her eyes roaming over the hardwood floors and sage-green walls. "Does it feel like home?"

"You feel like home," I told her, kissing the side of her neck and inhaling her honey scent. The smell of my wife still intoxicated me, even after all these years. "But yes, this does feel like home."

"It's not too close to the rest of the family? I know they can be a bit overwhelming. Gianna has already warned me that she would be coming down to get Paulie snuggles every day."

Placing my fingers on her jaw to tilt her face toward me, I pressed my lips firmly to hers. "I want that. I want us to be immersed in family. You've missed out on so much, baby."

She turned and pressed her beautiful body against mine, arms wrapped around my neck. "Then I say we should take it. What do you think about Dad and Stella's offer?"

I chuckled. "You mean their *demand* that Paulie won't be going to daycare because he'll be getting spoiled by his grandparents every day?"

Eden nodded. "I like the idea, at least while he's so little. It would minimize his exposure to too many kids so he doesn't get sick again."

"Agreed. And maybe when he's a toddler, we can put him in that learning center Kassie mentioned. Maybe for a few days a week?"

"That sounds perfect. And you like the space for the bakery? The one close to where I'll be working?"

"I do. I think I'd like to make it like a chain of our bakery in the Keys, but perhaps with a new name?"

"So not Sweet Heaven?"

I ran my knuckles down the peachy skin of her cheek. "I was thinking *Sweet Eden*. Maybe have it like a Garden of Eden theme."

Tears filled her eyes but she nodded vigorously. "I love that. I'll get started on a logo design tonight. Oooh, we could have lots of foliage and 3-D apples hanging from the trees. What do you think about red and green for the colors? Not like Christmas green; something a little softer."

"I'll like anything you come up with. We can ask Auburn about interior decorators, and you can work with them." I could see her mind filling with ideas and feel the excitement thrumming through her. My wife loved a project.

"Have you talked to Fiero today?"

"This morning before breakfast. He said the house is fine." A smirk slipped across my lips. "He asked about Charlisse no less than three times while we talked."

Eden's eyebrows lifted in two perfect arches. "I thought they looked a little cozy at the Christmas party. She hasn't said anything about it though."

"Guess we'll see when she goes back to Marathon. I'm glad she agreed to help Maria and Barry run the bakery. I don't want to sell it because it belonged to Charles and Mimsy."

"And Maria is prepared to talk to the staff once news about the *return of Evie Bouvier* goes public?" she asked wryly.

"She is." We'd shared parts of our story with her so the staff at the bakery wouldn't be blindsided by the news. None of the gory details like my true identity, just the basics about Eden's kidnapping and our decision to go into hiding to ensure her safety. Maria had been very sympathetic and understanding. I only hoped everyone else would be as well.

"And she'll talk to Maz? I don't want everyone I worked with to think I was some kind of shady character."

I kissed the tip of her nose. "They won't. Everyone there adores you. They'll understand the concept of self-preservation. It's innate in humans."

"So, we're really doing this, huh?" she asked, gazing around at the apartment that would soon be our new home.

"As long as everything goes okay with the FBI this afternoon."

Because for all I know, I'll be in jail by the end of the day.

Evie and I walked into the FBI offices behind Kassie Bouvier, who marched like a goddamn boss when she was in lawyer mode. She was dressed in a black suit jacket, pale-green top, and sleek black pants. It looked like the outfit had been tailor-made for her pregnant frame, but considering she was married to a designer at one of the largest fashion companies in the world, that probably wasn't too far off the mark.

Evie wore a simple floral shift dress and sandals, while I was in a light-blue dress shirt and khaki pants. It was strange wearing dressy clothes after we'd been existing mostly in beach bum wear for seventeen years, but Kassie had selected our outfits for us. She said we looked demure and trustworthy.

We were shown into one of those interrogation rooms with the one-way glass along one wall, and Kassie sniffed her disapproval as we sat. "Well, this is fancy. I didn't realize this was an interrogation."

The older agent, dressed in a dark-brown suit, heaved himself into a chair across from us. "When one of the best criminal defense attorneys in the state calls and requests a meeting, we really like to roll out the red carpet."

Kassie's lips curved into something a little sweet and a lot sharp. "Why, thank you, Agent Saunders. I accept your compliment and your hospitality. This isn't actually a criminal matter though. It's more of a..." She tapped her chin in mock-thought. "Let's call it a courtesy call. I'm here to let you know that one of your cold cases has been resolved."

The other agent, a guy in his thirties with sandy hair and a goatee, leaned forward with his forearms on the table. "Which case?"

Kass looked down at her fingers, running a thumb back and forth over her smooth, pink nails in an oh-so-casual manner before raising her eyes back to the agents. "The disappearance of Evelyn Bouvier."

The younger man, Agent Peters, looked confused, but Saunders's posture instantly went ramrod straight. He'd apparently been around long enough to remember the case."

"And how exactly has it—" He froze when his eyes landed on Evie, who was sitting on a padded chair between me and Kassie. The man leaned forward so far, his stomach was practically flush with the table separating us. His mouth gaped open like a fish, and his sharp eyes narrowed and then widened as his composure slipped. "Holy shit. You're Evie Bouvier."

"I am," she agreed.

Saunders leaned back and rubbed a hand over his receding salt-and-pepper hairline, his eyes never leaving my wife. "Jesus, how long has it been? Fifteen, twenty years?"

"A little over seventeen," Evie specified.

The man had soulful brown eyes, but they held the edge of calculation, and I had no doubt he was good at his job. "Wow, okay. And who's your friend?" he asked, gesturing toward me. I did my best to appear unaffected, like Kassie had directed.

"This is my husband, Dane Osbourne."

He didn't appear to recognize me, and I sent a silent shout of thanks to Robert and Jamie Smith for their excellent disguise skills. "Can you tell me what happened to you?"

"I was taken by human traffickers," she replied calmly, and the man's lips turned down at the corners.

"I'm so sorry that happened to you," he said with genuine regret and sincerity in his tone. "We figured it was something like that. You didn't fit the profile for a runaway."

"Thank you, Agent Saunders."

"And where have you been all this time, Mrs., uh, Osbourne?"

"In the Florida Keys." She kept her answers direct and succinct, also courtesy of Kassie's coaching.

He lifted an eyebrow and nodded, scruffing his hand over the hint of a five-o-clock shadow on his jaw. "All right, I'll need to pull some files. Would you mind waiting for a few minutes? We'll also need to get fingerprints from Mrs. Osbourne for verification purposes."

"Certainly," Kassie said crisply. "Evie is thrilled to be here and help you put this case to rest." Okay, *thrilled* might be pushing it a bit, but speaking with law enforcement was an inevitable truth we had to deal with.

"Thank you," Saunders said, sounding a lot less combative now. "Peters, can you get our guests some refreshments?" *Ahhh, now we're guests worthy of snacks.*

Both men left the room, and Agent Peters came back a few minutes later with a tray laden with a variety of drinks and a basket full of snacks, including Chex-Mix, chips, and bags of cookies that I knew would taste like dirt. We declined food and each accepted a bottle of cool water before he retreated.

Evie fumbled with the lid of her water before I took it from her, cracked it open, and handed it back. "Sorry, I'm nervous," she whispered, which earned her a pointed look from Kassie. A look that told us there were probably cameras or at least someone monitoring behind that glass.

After a female worker came in and took Evie's fingerprints, we sat for almost an hour, not discussing anything more consequential than what we were having for dinner that night. Both agents returned, and Saunders had a laptop and a thick folder stuffed with papers.

They sat across from us, Peters lifting the lid of the laptop and Saunders knocking a knuckle against the worn manila file. "This is only the tip of the iceberg, but it's the most pertinent information. Would you like to tell us what happened to you, Eden? Sorry, Evie," he corrected, his 'mishap' letting us know he'd done a little research into our lives in Florida while he'd been gone. Yep, he was sharp.

"As you probably know, I was in Cancún with my friends on a Spring Break vacation. I think the resort was called Green Diamond." The older man nodded, and Evie launched into the story about going to look for her phone all the way to when she was fighting against the two men. "I heard them say they were taking me to a boat."

Peters took copious notes, his fingers clacking against the keys, while Saunders kept his eyes firmly on Evie. "What kind of boat?" he asked.

"I'm not sure. I'd lost consciousness by the time they carried me to it."

Saunders made a quiet grunting noise. "We became suspicious they were transporting kidnapped people by boat. The government is patrolling those waters more often now than they did back then."

"Happy to hear it," Evie replied.

"Can you tell me what happened next?"

My wife inhaled a breath and nodded. "I woke up in some kind of warehouse, in Mexico, I think, but I can't be sure. There were four other girls there too. Cara, Nesha, and two girls named Jennifer." Her eyes dropped to her lap. "I always wondered what happened to them. Have they been found?"

Saunders cast a look at Peters who began tapping on the screen of his computer before typing again. "There was a woman named Jennifer Anderson who went missing from the same area as you. Different resort though." His lips tightened. "Her body was found a few weeks later in Texas. I see missing persons reports for the other women, but nothing else." His eyes were shaded with sadness and apology.

A tear slipped down Evie's downcast face, and Kassie produced a tissue that seemed to appear from out of thin air and handed it over. Evie swiped her face and raised her head, firming her shoulders. "Thank you for telling me."

"Do you need a break?" Saunders asked kindly, and my wife shook her head. "Can you tell us what happened next?"

She told them what she could remember about the warehouse and then about being transported to the house in New Orleans. For almost an hour, she talked and they peppered her with questions about the descriptions and details.

"Just to clarify, there was a false wall in the back of the truck?" Saunders asked.

I reached for Evie's hand. This part was always the hardest for her to talk about, the tiny space she'd been trapped in, the lack of freedom that had given her monstrous nightmares.

"Yes. We were chained to the side wall, and then they closed the fake wall. There was barely room to breathe, and it smelled like urine and vomit. I felt like a caged animal."

Saunders winced and shook his head in disgust. "I know this is difficult, but these details do help us learn more about traffickers. We appreciate you sharing with us."

"That's what I'm here for. I don't like thinking of anyone else going through that," Evie said with a tremulous smile, but she didn't drop another tear. For the millionth time in my life, I was astounded by the strength and bravery of my extraordinary wife. "Anyway, like I said, we were taken to a house in New Orleans."

She told them what she could remember about the house. How many bedrooms she saw. The mattresses on the floor.

"I'm sorry I don't remember all the details. It's been a long time," she said.

Agent Saunders smiled. "You're doing fine. Better than I would be doing. What happened when you got to the house? Were you assaulted?"

Evie rolled her lips inward. "Not sexually. I overheard Ethan and Felipe saying that it was against the rules to have sex with us, but they did hit me. Dragged me by the hair. Chained me to a chair. I wasn't allowed to take a shower, even after sweating for at least ten hours in the back of that truck. And I remember being really hungry and thirsty."

I eyed the two agents who both had sour looks on their faces when she talked about the barbaric treatment.

"Do you remember seeing anyone else at the house?" Saunders asked.

"Um, I think maybe there was a guard outside, but it was dark and I was really tired, so I don't remember much about him. I could hear people coming and going, and then the house felt empty, so I assumed the other women had been picked up."

"Did someone come for you?"

And here we go. Kassie had counseled us to tell the truth as much as possible without incriminating ourselves.

Evie lifted her chin and skirted the truth. "I heard them say someone had bought me, but I escaped so I never saw him."

Good girl, I told her with a squeeze of her hand.

"Do you know the name of the person who bought you?"

She swallowed and announced, "Luca Cappitani."

You could have heard a pin drop in that room. Both agents stared at Evie like she'd grown a second head, and then Peters began typing furiously on his keyboard.

Saunders cleared his throat. "And was that name familiar to you, Evie?"

She nodded. "I knew he was some big Mafia asshole."

That drew a smile from the man. "Can you tell me how you escaped?"

Evie scrunched her face. "I don't remember everything. Like I said, I was hurting and sleep deprived. But when Felipe and Ethan were... distracted, I sneaked out." *If by distracted, you mean dead...*

"Through a window?" Saunder prompted.

"No, through one of the doors when the guard came into the house and went into another room. Once I was free, I saw a man on the street and asked him for help." She turned her head and smiled at me. "Dane saved me."

"You didn't think to call your family?"

Evie swiveled her head slowly back to the agent. "Funnily enough, the people who kidnapped me and planned to sell me didn't provide me with a cell phone. I found it quite discourteous of them."

Ahhh, there's my Wildcat.

Saunders cleared his throat to cover what I was sure was a chuckle. "Good point." He turned his attention to me. "Couldn't you have let Evie use your phone?"

"It was seventeen years ago. Not everyone had a phone glued to their hand back then." Again, sliding around the edges of the truth. I didn't actually say I *didn't* have a cell phone, but he seemed to accept the non-answer.

"What happened next?"

I picked up that question. "Once Evie told me her story and who was involved, we decided to run. I was aware that Luca Cappitani had a reputation for being ruthless, and I felt Evie's life was in danger."

Saunders propped his elbow on the table and rested the side of his index finger against his lips. "Just like that."

"Yes," replied.

"You just up and left your life to go on the run with a woman you didn't even know?"

Shrugging, I said, "I didn't have any family to speak of and I was between jobs." I met my wife's eyes. "We had an instant connection. It wasn't a hard decision."

He leaned over to look at the laptop and clicked on the screen a couple times. "Your marriage certificate says you were married in January, but you didn't even meet Evie until March when she went missing."

Fuck. I hadn't thought of that.

Kassie saved my ass with a dismissive hand wave. "Must have been a mistake at the county clerk's office. You know how busy those places can get. Someone must have keyed in the wrong month. Happens all the time." It was complete and utter bullshit, and we all knew it.

The agent looked unimpressed and shot back with an immediate question. "Who is Eden Osbourne?"

My wife lifted her chin. "That's the name I decided to go by."

Saunders was quiet for a long moment before asking, "Did you have your first name changed legally?"

"I did not."

"So, your driver's license and passport were forged?" *Shit shit shit.*

But Evie leaned forward a little and met the agent's eye with an unyielding stare. "Do you have a daughter, Agent Saunders?"

He seemed taken aback by the question, and it took him a second to answer. "I have two, actually."

"And if one of them found themselves in a... *situation*, what would you tell them to do so that one day they could find their way back to you?"

His face morphed into a grimace, and he reluctantly said, "Anything they had to do."

Evie nodded. "Good. Can we move on from this topic then?"

The two agents looked at each other incredulously before Saunders heaved out an exhausted breath and faced us again. "Why didn't you contact law enforcement?"

Again, I fielded the question. "The simple answer is Luca Cappitani. It was well known that anyone who tried to testify against him ended up missing or dead. There's a lot of stuff on the internet about it, as well as documentaries. You can look it up."

"But we could have protected you through the WITSEC program."

Kassie let out an indelicate snort. "And how well has that worked out for you in the past, Agent?"

His teeth clenched in anger at the program's abject failure when it came to witnesses against Luca. "Mrs. Osbourne, why did you bring a criminal defense attorney with you today?"

Kass reached for Evie's hand in a show of solidarity. "Evie brought her *sister-in-law* with her. As I'm sure you're aware, I'm married to her brother, Monty. However, if someone were to want to harass this poor woman about minor indiscretions *that hurt no one*, I'm certainly able to switch to my attorney hat at a moment's notice."

I could tell the man was completely exasperated, and I had to fight to keep my smile contained. But that urge quickly faded when he focused on me but spoke to Evie.

"Mrs. Osbourne, have you ever heard of Damiano Cappitani?"

To our credit, neither of us flinched.

"Is he related to Luca?" she asked.

He was still looking at me. "Yes, he's Luca's younger son."

She tilted her head in the picture of innocence. "Is he a criminal too?"

Jesus, I fucking love my wife.

Saunders floundered a bit. "Well, he... uhhh. We don't have any direct evidence that Damiano's a criminal, but he was on our radar because he's Luca's son." Then the agent built up a head of steam, his tone filled with more confidence. "Suddenly though, he disappeared. No one saw or heard from him. If I'm not mistaken, it was some time during the same year you went missing. Rumor had it he'd moved to Italy, but Peters checked that out, and there's no record of his passport leaving the United States."

Well. Fuck. He knows.

Kassie—the motherfucking queen of calm—stood and said, "Wow, Agent Saunders. That is a fascinating story. Really, it is, and I do appreciate a good tale, but I believe the Osbournes would like to get back home. They have a baby boy that's probably getting up from his nap about right now."

Saunders stood too. "It's my job to determine whether these two are involved in any illegal activity."

"Oh, good grief!" Kassie cried, throwing her arms up and letting them fall. "These are not the people you should be focusing on. I'm sure you can look on that little screen of yours and see that the Osbournes have had nothing more serious than a speeding ticket in seventeen years. In fact, they have been model citizens. Dane runs a bakery. Evie got a college degree and is the head of marketing at a hospital that rehabilitates sea turtles. She also goes into schools and talks to children about turtles and conservation. They rescued two pets and donate to charities supporting victims of human trafficking. Not to mention, seven months out of the year, they get up at the ass crack of dawn and patrol the beach to help preserve turtle nests. If you find any criminal activity in all that, then arrest them."

At some point during all that, she'd flattened her palms on the table and leaned over it. Peters and Saunders were both arching backward in their chairs with eyes as round as beach balls.

Kassie straightened and reached behind her, pulling Evie to her feet. "I have a good idea," she went on because the damn agents were rendered mute. Grasping Evie by the arms, she held her wrists out toward the agents, almost like an offering. "Why don't you put the cuffs on Evie really tight. So tight you leave bruises and make her have flashbacks to something no human being should ever go through."

Mother of God, no wonder she's considered the best defense attorney in New York.

Then Kass's voice turned softer, and she shifted Evie so the two women were facing each other, their hands clasped together. "Maybe you could treat this woman—this beautiful woman who has given up seventeen years of her life in order to survive one of the most brutal Mafia bosses of this century—perhaps you could treat her like her kidnappers did and mark her face, split her lip, make her bleed."

At that point, Kassie turned her glare on the agents again. "If so, make sure to take photos so I can share them with the press. I'm sure they would love to hear how a victim of human trafficking was treated by the FBI. But no matter what, I guarantee that Evie will not lose one ounce of her strength and resilience. She is the most amazing woman I've ever met, and she deserves nothing but our respect, not our scorn because she *maybe* fudged a little paperwork to stay alive."

Okay, I'll just be honest here. I'm really close to fucking crying.

Peters was staring somewhere in the vicinity of his feet, and Saunders's eyes were locked on the two women. He pressed his lips into a line, and I was pretty sure I saw his chin tremble. Then he stood and took a deep breath.

"You're right, Ms. Bouvier, and I apologize if I came across harshly. Mrs. Osbourne, you have my gratitude for volunteering to speak with us today."

His eyes flitted to me and held there, but they didn't hold any hatred, and I knew we were going to be okay. "You as well, Mr. Osbourne."

"Excellent!" Kassie chirped, switching to sweetness in an instant. "If you'd like to have a joint press conference to let the world know Evie has been found, we'd be happy to participate. I think the optics would be great for your office since the case went unsolved for almost two decades."

Ouch. Okay, maybe sweetness with a side of cyanide.

Then it was all handshakes and appreciation until Kassie led us out the way we came. Once we were down the hallway and out of earshot, Evie whispered, "Do you think they're going to let it drop?"

"Yep," Kassie said confidently, flashing us a smile. "Because I am goo-oood."

As we emerged from the building, we saw a familiar figure leaned against a lamppost. Monty was dressed stylishly in a patterned short-sleeved shirt and black pants that tapered to the bottom hem. He wore black loafers with no socks and looked like a dude that designed clothes for living while engaging in a little MMA fighting on his off days. Seriously, Evie's brother was brawny. Cruz was too, while Auburn was built more like me, taller and leaner but still muscular.

"Hey," Monty said, jogging up to us and kissing his wife's lips and then her belly. "How did it go?"

"Your wife kicks ass," I blurted, still jazzed up about the successful meeting.

"Yours does too," he said, smooching Evie's cheek. "But really, how did everything go? You all right, sis?"

"Really good, thanks to Kassie. I think everything is going to be okay now."

"Good," he sighed, shoulders lowering an inch in relief.

"I have one more favor to ask of you, Kassie," I said, and she swiveled her curious gaze to me.

"Sure. What's up?"

"Well, we have documents with our names on them and a certificate saying we're married, but they were forged. I would like us to have *legal* legal papers, not *illegal* legal papers, if that makes sense."

"It does. I have an expert in my office that can help you file the papers for a legal name change and all that. And a new marriage certificate, but you'd have to have a ceremony for that."

"Actually, that all sounds great, but I had something in mind in addition to that, and it would also affect Paulie." I had everyone's attention, and I laid it out for them.

When I was done, my wife threw herself at me and squealed. "You really want to do that?"

"I really do, Wildcat."

Monty looked at me with something akin to respect, which was all I wanted from him. He didn't have to think of me like a friend, but I did hope we could be mutually respectful for Evie's sake. And he had seemed to soften toward me a teeny bit the past few days.

He looked at his wife like she was the second coming of Christ and asked, "You hungry, Kasserole?"

"Are Pamela Anderson's boobs fake?" she asked with a raised brow.

"I refuse to answer any question regarding any other woman's boobs, on the grounds it may incriminate me."

Evie laughed her sweet laugh, and she looked so happy in the June New York sunlight. So happy and so free. "You're not as dumb as you look, Mon."

"Appreciate that. While we eat, we can discuss what you want for your wedding dress." He looked me up and down, appraising, and asked, "Can I design your tux too?"

"I, uh, of course."

Then he shocked the shit out of me by tossing a casual arm around my shoulders and grinning. "Cool, bro. Let's go feed our women."

And just like that, I felt the thrill of acceptance, the warmth of a family that was good and loving. And now I was a part of it.

EPILOGUE

SIX MONTHS LATER

"You look gorgeous," Juliette said, her eyes filling with tears as she adjusted my veil. My hair was longer now and back to its natural caramel color. Earlier today, Kassie and Lehra had set my locks in natural-looking curls that bounced around my shoulders while Gianna had done my makeup.

"Thank you for being here. It means the world to me."

She rolled her eyes. "Like I would be anywhere else when my bestie from the nestie gets married."

I laughed at the nickname from when we were kids at summer camp. "I know we've been married for years, but this feels special, having an actual wedding in front of all our family and friends."

"It's cool that you're doing it on New Year's Day since that was your original anniversary." Her big eyes sparkled as the door opened behind her.

Our other friends Holly and Arya entered the hotel room, followed by Madalynn and Emersyn, who were arguing. As usual.

"No way McDreamy's penis is bigger than McSteamy's," Mady was saying. "McSteamy is just so... hot."

"Hot doesn't translate to the size of the man's junk," her twin argued back.

"That's true," Holly threw in. "Some of the ugliest guys I've been with had huge cocks."

Arya shook her head and lowered her brows. "How does that even happen? Like, how do you end up in bed with an ugly guy?"

Holly shrugged and took a sip of her champagne. "Mostly dares but sometimes alcohol. Not every man looks like the men Juli writes in her books. Ugly guys deserve love too."

"But you married a handsome guy," Mady pointed out.

"Well, yeah," she said in a *duh* tone. "If I've got to look at him every day, might as well pick someone pretty."

We all laughed at Holly's feigned shallowness because she was so madly in love with her husband, Bubba. Who also happened to be Juliette's brother.

Juli also still lived in Texas and was, of course, a romance author. Arya had gone to medical school and was now an internist in California. Emersyn worked in their family business, and her eyebrows no longer resembled caterpillars.

And Madalynn Papadopoulos? Well, no one really knew what Mady did. She had graduated from college, but now she flitted around the world with a series of sugar daddies who all seemed to know about each other and were surprisingly okay with it. It was bizarre.

This wasn't the first time we'd seen each other since I'd come out of hiding. I'd made sure to call each of them the morning of the press conference so they wouldn't have to hear that I was alive on the news. Then we'd all gone on a retreat together—not to Mexico, thank you very much—in July. We'd spent the week together in our Florida home and reconnected.

"Time to get you dressed, Miss Bride," Juliette announced, handing me a tall flute of champagne. "Finish this off because you're not going to want to spill anything on your fabulous dress."

I drained the glass, letting the clear pink bubbles dance across my tongue before following Juli into the bedroom. Ten minutes and about eight-thousand buttons later, I emerged in the most gorgeous dress ever made. It was made of a lustrous ivory Baronet satin that seemed to flow in waves down the full princess skirt. The bodice was fitted with long lace sleeves that gave a peek of skin beneath.

"Damn," Emersyn said as she fanned her eyes to hold back tears. "If I ever get married again, I want your brother to design my dress. You look stunning."

Mady smiled and took my hand. "Makes me almost want to get married," she said and then emphasized, "*Almost.*"

"Let's all take a picture together," Arya suggested. "With Evie and our tattoos."

"Mine is on my ass," Holly pointed out.

"Then hike up your skirt, woman. Let's go. We've got a wedding to attend." Arya set up the camera and everyone gathered around me and bared their ink, mostly on arms or ankles, but yes, Holly's was indeed on her backside. The matching tattoos were of a lilac with a script E in the center. They'd all gotten them on the one year anniversary of my disappearance. My tears had flowed for a solid hour after they'd shown them to me back in July.

"Wow, look at that," Holly said, looking at the picture on Arya's phone, all of us smiling—and her mooning the camera. "I know all of you are going to want to get this blown up so you can have my butt plastered across your living rooms."

"Told you that you should have gotten it on your shoulder," Mady sang. "But nooooo, you insisted."

"Okay, cool it. Go sit down," I ordered, kissing all of them on their cheeks. Except for Juli. As my maid of honor, she was staying with me until my dad came to get me. I'd wanted to make all of them bridesmaids, as well as my sisters-in-law, Gianna, Kassie, and Lehra. And Charlisse. But nine bridesmaids would have been a bit much, so Dane and I had decided to just have one attendant each.

Though I did ask all of them to wear a lilac dress so they would stand out as special when they sat near the front of the ballroom.

Fiero would be standing up for Dane. He'd hidden out in Florida while the dust settled before moving back to New York. For about a month. And then he'd hightailed it back to the Keys with the excuse that he missed the beach, though we all knew it was a certain beautiful blonde that had drawn him back. I'd asked Charlisse what was going on with them once, and she claimed they were keeping it casual. But I saw how they looked at each other.

The girls left, but a second later, Mady popped her head back in the door and hissed, "Dear. God. The Bouvier men are coming this way down the corridor, and I'm pretty sure tuxedos were invented especially for them."

"I'm gonna run so you can have time with your family," Juliette said, pushing a small pack of tissues into my hand.

"Thank you for everything, Juli."

"Hey, it's the least I could do for my favorite ARC reader." She shook her head. "I still can't believe you were under my nose the whole time."

"I wish I could have told you. I wanted to support you every way I could, even if you didn't know."

"I'm not mad," she said, hugging me once more. "Love you, babe."

"Love you back." And then she skipped from the room. I seriously adored Juliette McNamara. She was like sunshine for the soul.

When my dad and brothers entered my suite a few seconds later, I saw exactly what Mady meant. They looked phenomenally handsome in black tuxedos and lilac bow ties.

I held the pack of tissues up and narrowed my eyes at them. "I do not want to have to use these, so don't you dare make me cry." Tossing them on the table, I pointed at my eyes. "Gianna did my makeup, and I don't want to mess it up, so don't be all sweet and shit."

Cruz reached me first, giving me a careful hug. "You look kind of okay, sis." That made me giggle.

"Agreed," Monty said, stepping in for his turn. "You look very okay. I totally kicked ass on this dress design, by the way."

"You did," I agreed with a grin.

Auburn reached me next and gave me a soft peck on the cheek. "As the best looking sibling, I have to say, you're a close second, Evie."

"Gosh, you're too kind," I told him, sarcasm heavy in my tone.

"You asked for it," he said, amused.

Dad looked on patiently, hands in the pockets of his well-tailored pants, until my brothers were finished. Then he stepped forward and handed over my bouquet. It was made of fresh white roses with tiny pearls and sprigs of lilac laced between the fragrant blooms.

"I had the florist nestle the flower you gave me in the middle." He pointed at the dried rose I had kept from our impromptu wedding in Treviso.

"It's perfect," I told him, hugging him hard and kissing his smooth cheek. He smelled like sandalwood and home.

"All joking aside, you're the most beautiful bride I've ever seen, Evie. I'm so happy for you."

Annnd cue the waterworks. Dad quickly pulled a handkerchief from his pocket and dabbed delicately at my tears.

"Way to go, Dad," Auburn teased. "You made her cry."

Our father smiled, his own eyes gentle and watery. "I couldn't help it. She's my baby girl." He pulled me close, and we swayed in place for a long moment.

In the distance, the music changed, and Cruz said, "I think it's time to go." Flanked by my brothers and holding my father's arm, we walked the short distance to the ballroom entrance. I felt surrounded and loved. Each of my brothers kissed the back of my hand before taking their seats inside beside their significant others and children.

A few months ago, Gianna had given birth to a little girl who they named Nancy after Gia's late mother. Kassie and Monty's daughter, Annabelle, was born a week later. Jaxon, Jane, and Sully were all thriving as the "big siblings." Lehra and Cruz would be marrying later this year, and I was pretty sure they both had baby fever, so it was only a matter of time till they had their own bundle of joy.

Our close-knit family was certainly growing, and if Dane had anything to do with it, we'd be adding one more member about nine months after our honeymoon in Treviso. I hoped so too. Paulie was an energetic and outgoing fifteen-month old, and we'd both love to give him a sibling who was pretty close in age.

The wedding planner opened the wide wooden door, and Dad and I stepped into the ballroom, which had been transformed into my dream wedding. I'd wanted real candles rather than the fairy lights that were so popular these days. I loved the traditional look of candles, and the planner had certainly come through. There were hundreds of votives, tapers, tea lights, and pillars, all made of beeswax, which gave the room a warm glow and a sweet aroma that was reminiscent of honey... Dane's favorite scent.

All eyes turned toward us, and I looked up at Dad. His chest was puffed to almost twice its normal size. "Ready to get more married?" he asked under his breath, and I grinned. Dane and I had considered ourselves married for years, but today we were making it truly legal in front of our friends and family.

"Let's do it," I said back, and we started walking down the aisle. Dane stood before me on the low, white-carpeted stage in a black tuxedo with velvet lapels. He looked damn edible with his dark hair skimming his broad shoulders. And that devastating smile of his was directed right at me.

Though my eyes were on my groom, from my peripheral vision, I saw the crew from Florida, including Robert and Jamie, the folks from the bakery, and my hospital coworkers. Rodrigo, the man who had been with Dane the night he rescued me, was smiling from the middle of the crowd, and Cooper was in the third row. He'd gotten a short leave from the Army and surprised us last night. My family and college friends took up the first two rows with our son sitting on Stella's lap. He blew me a kiss and yelled, "Hi, Mommy!"

Everyone laughed, and I leaned down for a quick kiss. "Hi, Paulie. Be a good boy for Yaya, okay?" He nodded and snuggled close to my father's wife. Dad and Stella had surprised everyone by eloping to Vegas one weekend, and all of us were ecstatic about it. They should have been together decades ago, but at least they'd found their way back together now.

We reached the front, and Dad kissed my cheek and shook Dane's hand before taking his seat beside Stella in the front row. My handsome groom and I faced Father Benedict, who was the priest who had "married" us in Treviso. Dane had managed to track him down and flew him to New York for our wedding.

With heavily accented English, the man performed our ceremony, and Dane and I exchanged vows. I didn't cry a bit. I was too busy smiling because this was a joyous occasion.

We both ended our vows with the words that were inscribed on the inside of my ring. As I said them to my husband, his fingers danced up my forearm, and I knew he was picturing the ink beneath my lace sleeve. It was my very first tattoo and was a peacock feather that matched the one on his arm. On the central vein of the feather, the tattoo artist had written in small scripty letters: *In the light and in the darkness... I choose you.*

"Did you know that female peacocks are called peahens?" I asked so only Dane could hear.

He chuckled and kissed the tip of my nose. "I love your brain."

I rested my hands on his cheeks. "I love your face."

With a wiggle of his eyebrows, he said, "Well, I love your—"

Pressing a finger to his lips, I giggled. "Save it for the honeymoon, Dracula."

When Father Benedict declared that Dane could kiss his bride, he dipped me for a long kiss, just like he had in Treviso, and all the women in the room let out a collective sigh. Yeah, my man was pretty damn swoonworthy.

Then he lifted me upright and held my waist, his pretty brown eyes fixed on mine. "I love you, wife."

"And I love you, husband."

Father Benedict gently turned us until we were facing the congregation, and with his Italian accent, announced, "I present to you, Mr. and Mrs. Dane and Evie Bouvier."

Yes, my husband took my family's last name. He knew how much it meant to me, and he wanted Paulie to grow up as a Bouvier. We had our son's name legally changed to Paul Augustus Bouvier last week. Someone from Kassie's office had handled that, as well as untangling all the legal complications related to Dane and I using aliases for almost eighteen years.

As we walked hand in hand up the plush white aisle, Dane stopped and scooped up Paulie in one arm. Everyone cheered, and our son looked delighted, waving with both hands like he was getting his own personal standing ovation. He was seriously the cutest dang kid ever.

We made our way up the aisle and past the rows of tall taper candles that glowed on either side of the door, and I knew, from this day forward, the light would always outweigh the dark.

Because we chose each other.

Because we chose *love*.

THE END

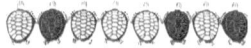

Thank you all for reading this book and the others in the Bouvier Family Saga. It has truly been my honor to write these characters, and I'm a little sad this series is done. If you are too and would like another little taste of the Bouviers, you're in luck. I'm so happy to announce that some of them will make cameo appearances in my standalone rom-com, which is Juliette McNamara's story.

If you want to read an excerpt, type this link into your browser:

https://BookHip.com/CAFXPGX. Here's a brief description to whet your appetite:

What happens when a romance author accidentally books herself a writing retreat... *at a swingers' resort?*

A whole lot of really funny shit, that's what.

Available now... Jade Dollston's new standalone rom-com:

The (Kinda) Secret Pineapple Island Swingers' Resort.

Juliette McNamara is a beautiful, intelligent (albeit a bit naive) small-town librarian who writes spicy romance books on the side. But she has a bit of writer's block, so she books herself a cottage on a Caribbean Island so she can concentrate.

Reno Swain, also known as *Reno Swoon* by puck bunnies everywhere, is a hockey player with his career up in the air. While he tries to figure out what to do, he goes on the trip his former fiancée booked for them.

When Juli and Reno run into each other at the Pineapple Island Resort and Spa, the chemistry is instantaneous. Juliette's writer's block seems to disappear as Reno's gorgeous green eyes and muscular forearms inspire some of the spiciest scenes she's ever written. They get together but agree it's only a vacation fling... nothing more.

The problem? Neither of them planned to develop feelings for the other.

When they meet again in the most unlikely of places, will their love thrive like a pineapple in the sun? Or will it wither on the vine?

Available now on Amazon, or you can order signed copies on my website: www.jadedollston.com

ALSO BY JADE

Bouvier Family Saga
Love Without Numbers Auburn and Gianna
Love Without Influence Monty and Kassie
Love Without Demands Cruz and Lehra
Love Without Control Evie and Damiano (Series Complete!)

The Fierce Protectors Series
Features six super-hot, possessive, growly former Navy SEALs who live to love and protect their women. They're all available on Amazon.
Dauntless Protector- Grumpy/Sunshine, Nanny Romance
Devoted Protector — Love After Loss
Deadly Protector — Second Chance Romance
Disgruntled Protector — Enemies to Lovers, Fake Marriage
Determined Protector — Single Parents
Damaged Protector — Age-Gap Forbidden Romance

You can also check out **Young Protector** — Deadly Protector Prequel
Novella

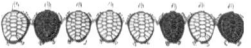

Standalones

The (Kinda) Secret Pineapple Island Swingers' Resort *If you love laugh-out-loud rom-coms, vacation flings gone rogue, and a hero who definitely knows how to handle his (hockey) stick, The "Kinda" Secret Pineapple Island Swingers' Resort is your next must-read.*

Rating the Book Boyfriend – Hilarious Holiday Rom-Com
Delay of Game – Angsty, funny sports romance
I Dream of Johnny – Genie Rom-Com

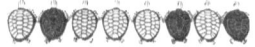

Highway to Hale Series
Coming in 2025

Follow the Hale Family, owners of Hale Cosmetics, in their amusing and dramatic search for love.

Book 1: Hale Yes
Book 2: Hale No
Book 3: Hale Damage
Book 4: All Hale the Queen

(Titles and order of books subject to change.)

Make sure to follow me on my social media accounts below or visit my semi-neglected website at www.jadedollston.com

facebook.com/profile.php?id=100081302873689

instagram.com/author.jade.dollston/

tiktok.com/@author.jade.dollston?lang=en

The best way you can help indie authors is to leave a review on Amazon, so if you'd be so kind, please hop on over there a drop me a review.

Playlist

Kiss From A Rose by Seal
You Don't Own Me by Lesley Gore
Hips Don't Lie by Shakira
Promiscuous by Nelly Furtado
SexyBack by Justin Timberlake
Round and Round by Ratt
Be Without You by Mary J. Blige
Grind With Me by Pretty Ricky
Livin' on a Prayer by Bon Jovi
Oh Pretty Woman by Roy Orbison
Smooth Criminal by Michael Jackson
You're Makin' Me High by Toni Braxton
Shut Up and Dance by Walk the Moon
Margaritaville by Jimmy Buffett
Stop and Stare by OneRepublic

ABOUT THE AUTHOR

JADE DOLLSTON IS A Texas author who loves reading, Doritos, and rum. She is married to her high school sweetheart, and they have one amazing daughter.

Her love of reading all things smutty has turned into a love of writing all things smutty. She enjoys a diverse selection of romance, and this is reflected in her writing style. Be prepared to laugh, cry, cringe, and fan your face, possibly all in a single chapter.

Jade is so excited to share her work with the world and hopes that you enjoy reading the words from her heart.

www.ingramcontent.com/pod-product-compliance
Lightning Source LLC
Chambersburg PA
CBHW020649110726
47901CB00001B/102